DARK
PLACES

ALSO BY LINDA LADD

Head to Head

DARK
PLACES

LINDA LADD

PINNACLE BOOKS
Kensington Publishing Corp.
www.kensingtonbooks.com

PINNACLE BOOKS are published by

Kensington Publishing Corp.
850 Third Avenue
New York, NY 10022

All Kensington titles, imprints, and distributed lines are available at special quantity discounts for bulk purchases for sales promotions, premiums, fund-raising, educational, or institutional use. Special book excerpts or customized printings can also be created to fit specific needs. For details, write or phone the office of the Kensington special sales manager: Kensington Publishing Corp., 850 Third Avenue, New York, NY 10022, attn: Special Sales Department; phone: 1-800-221-2647.

This book is a work of fiction. Names, characters, businesses, organizations, places, events, and incidents either are the product of the author's imagination, or are used fictitiously. Any resemblance to actual persons, living or dead, or events, or locales is entirely coincidental.

ISBN-13: 978-0-7860-1718-8
ISBN-10: 0-7860-1718-X

First printing: August 2007

10 9 8 7 6 5 4 3 2 1

Printed in the United States of America

PROLOGUE
The Angel Gabriel

The triple funeral took place in a spooky old church in Missouri, one that had been built many years ago. Its clapboards were peeling white paint, and someone had carved a big cross on the wooden door and then painted it blood red. A black bell hung from a pole in the yard, and the little orphan boy peeked around the worn front pew and watched through the open portal as a scarecrow-gaunt man in a black suit pulled down hard on the long rope. The slow, steady knell sounded scary and foreboding and made him shiver.

This place was far away from where the child had lived for the first ten years of his life. He had never even visited the remote, heavily wooded hills where his momma and daddy and baby sister were to be put into the ground. He'd never met the old woman sitting beside him and patting him on the hand and telling him she was his grandma. She smelled funny, musty and dusty like the dark attic in his Pittsburgh house where white sticky cobwebs clung to the rafters, and she used an old wheelchair that squeaked when the wheels went round. He would never get to go home to that redbrick house again. And he would never, ever see his momma, daddy, or baby Katie again.

His head still hurt something awful from the terrible accident that had taken his family's lives and left him alone. The deep cut wouldn't stop hurting, and he touched the white gauze bandage where it was wrapped around his forehead. Sharp jagged pains shot through his temple and made his ear ache. His head hurt so bad that he began to cry from all the suffering and anguish and grief and confusion and the strange, frightening dreams that plagued him since he had woken up in the hospital. Tears ran down his cheeks and tasted salty.

Grandma noticed his weeping and draped her arm around his shoulder, but he didn't like the strange old lady hugging him so close. He didn't like her, or the ugly church, or all the people dressed in black hovering around and staring at him. He loved bright colors and happy people, like his momma with her long, orangey-red ponytail that swung from side to side when she walked.

He was scared. He was alone. He wished he'd died, too, in the horrible car crash that killed his family, but he'd had on his seat belt and they hadn't. He had been in the back with Katie but her car seat had not protected her the way it was supposed to. A drunk man in a black pickup truck had crossed Interstate 579 on the bridge over the Allegheny River and hit his family head-on. He never saw any of them again.

Now, weeks later, the lids on the two long white coffins were shut tight, never to be reopened. They said his baby sister was in with his momma, and his grandma said Momma would hold Katie tight in her arms until the host of angels flew down and transported them off to heaven. Furtively, the little boy shifted his gaze upward to the ceiling rafters.

An old-fashioned fan rotated slowly, making the white lilies atop the caskets sway and dip in its breeze. A sweet, flowery scent wafted to him. The dark-blue hymnals in the shelf on the pew in front of him smelled old and moldy and the fan's blades wobbled a little and squeaked rhythmically, as if they might come down on the old preacher's head. He wondered if the blades would tear the angels' wings when they fetched his family, but throughout the somber service not one angel appeared.

Maybe his family had already gone off to heaven, flown away for good without him. He should've died, too. If he could drive, he'd crash a car straight into a tree and catch up with those angels flying high in the clouds.

The preacher had short gray hair and pale skin with lots of crisscrossed lines and wrinkles, especially around his eyes. After a while, he finally quit droning, and six men in dark suits picked up the two boxes and carried them outside. The day was sunny, late summer, the twenty-fifth day of August, but the air was heavy with humidity. Sweat trickled down the boy's tight collar, and he tugged at it, hating the clothes his grandma took from a battered green footlocker in his daddy's childhood bedroom.

His coat and pants were black and smelled like her and the round white mothballs covering the bottom of the trunk. He had never seen a mothball before, and his grandma's house looked like the one in Katie's book called *Little Red Riding Hood*. It was even deeper in the woods than the church and had kerosene lamps and a hand pump in the kitchen sink. His grandma told him that she didn't believe in new-fangled things, that God in heaven didn't cotton to people who were lazy. She lit candles at night and the oil lamp on his bedside table. It reminded him of the one his daddy used on camping trips. Everything in his grandma's house was sort of scary, even her, but she had been nice to him and rocked him by the fire that first night when the social worker had brought him there to live. She had wept for a long time, loud sobs that frightened him into silence.

Outside, everybody followed the coffins along a gravel path to where two rectangular holes gaped like hungry mouths. Furry green moss clung to cracked gravestones with burial dates that said 1809 and 1896 and 1937. He wondered how old his grandma was. She had deep furrows in her cheeks and blue eyes that weren't really as blue as his daddy's, but paler, as if the color had washed away.

He stood beside Grandma's wheelchair and didn't watch as they lowered the coffins, not liking to think of his family down there covered up with all that red dirt. Instead, he watched something crawling under his Grandma's thin white hair, a tiny little spider, or something. He wanted to pluck it out but was afraid to. He suddenly felt so sad that he wanted to bawl and bawl but was afraid he'd start crying and never stop. Nobody else was making a sound, just standing hushed and somber in their black clothes, like a bunch of watching crows.

"Come, child, it be over now," his grandma whispered, when the preacher finally closed his big black Bible. "The church ladies done fixed us up a feast celebratin' your folks goin' to heaven with the angels. Don't you worry none, they're in the most wondrous place, where there ain't no hurts or fears or tribulations."

He wondered what tribulations were as everyone filed out the gate under the big oak tree. Their shoes crunched on fallen acorns. People started to talk and laugh as if a spell had been broken. Other children ran and played tag and hide-and-seek while ladies set out food, but he wasn't hungry and didn't want to play. He wanted to be far away from them and the way they all stared at him.

Suddenly he missed his family terribly, especially Momma, and he wanted to say good-bye. He checked to see if his grandma was watching him. She was busy with the other women, so he sneaked back through the creaky metal gate. He wanted to be alone and cry where nobody could see.

The graves still lay open. Shovels were stuck in the mounds of dirt piled beside them. He stared down into the dark holes and wondered how his momma looked inside her coffin. She was real pretty, with lots of freckles and a big, beautiful smile. She must look awful now because nobody got to look at her after the wreck, but he was glad Katie was in his momma's arms. Katie was so little and sweet and would've been afraid to be alone in her own box until the angels came. He bet his daddy was lonely in his box and wished he was in there with him.

"Well, lookee here, boys! What ya doin' back out here, freak?"

Three boys were standing behind him. They were grinning but not with friendly, want-to-play-with-us? grins. They looked about his age but were all bigger than him. Afraid, he stepped away from them and stood between his parents' graves.

"I know, Freddy, let's push him in! Wanna get in there with your mommy?"

Frightened, the orphan looked down into the dark holes. "No, please don't, I don't want to."

"You a momma's boy, you a sissy, you scared?"

One of the boys lunged around and shoved him hard in the back. The orphan almost fell before he caught himself at the edge of the grave. The other boys pushed at him, laughing, and Freddy picked up a shovel and jabbed it at him until he lost his footing. Frantically, he flailed his arms but couldn't regain his balance. He fell into the gaping hole and landed hard on his back atop his momma's coffin. The breath knocked out of him, he stared up at the blue sky. The boys' faces appeared. They looked scared. Then Freddy laughed. "C'mon, let's bury him! Get a shovel!"

Clods of red clay rained down on his head, and he screamed and jumped as high as he could, trying to grab hold of something. The dirt walls crumbled under his scratching fingernails, and he knew the sides were too high to ever get out. Terrified, he dropped to his knees on the coffin and covered his head as his tormentors shoveled dirt in on him, faster and faster, more and more, until he was half covered in it. Then the avalanche of dirt stopped abruptly, and Freddy's voice rang out, muffled, frightened, yelling something about Angel Gabriel and running. Then all was quiet.

ONE

Well, let me tell you, there's nothing as exhilarating as being a two-dollar whore at Christmastime. You know, tra la la la la, and lookin' for a date, baby? Not that I'm really a hooker, mind you. I'm a Canton County detective at Lake of the Ozarks, Missouri, working an undercover prostitution sting, which means since dusk shadowed the world I've been meandering the perimeter of a giant truck stop just outside the town of Lebanon, wearing a teeny-weeny lime green halter top and denim short shorts. The current rash of battery assaults up and down Interstate 44 on truck-stop prostitutes, a.k.a. lot lizards, had initiated a six-county joint task force to catch the guys before they graduated up to murder, so here I am, freezing my buns off.

I do have on a floor-length faux-fur coat over my skimpy attire, one as white as freshly driven snow, which definitely rings of irony, if you ask me. It keeps me from hypothermia, however, and allows me to flaunt my feminine attributes to any interested onlookers. At the moment, I am doing the streetwalker strut up and down the side of the lot that edges a particularly seedy motel and honky-tonk bar full of bored truckers and true-blue lot lizards dressed like myself or even more so. I am also trying to keep my legs from turning blue under my elegant black fishnet stockings. No doubt about it, hookers above the Mason-Dixon Line must come from hardier stock than moi.

Until tonight I'd been stuck on sick leave, lots of sick leave, months, in fact, because my last case got me in big trouble, and when I say big trouble, I really mean, *big, hairy, Bad-ass* trouble. I have a six-inch meat-cleaver gash in my right shoulder to remind me of those good-ole, bygone days, but it's practically healed up now. And I got the cast off my broken shinbone two months ago, which was not soon enough, believe you me. All this happened last summer when I ran into a nightmare from my past who had sort of an unhealthy fixation on me.

But that's another story I don't like to think about, so instead I think about the man I met during that investigation and how much he likes me. I like him, too, not *love*, mind you, just *like,* but it's the kind of *LIKE* written in all capital letters. Actually I find it a bit incredible that my new beau, Nicholas Black, a.k.a. filthy-rich psychobabbler to the stars, finds a way to spend time with a regular, homegrown gal like me. After all, I'm not exactly his type. I have way too many scars and not enough highlighted blond hair to be a celebrity's trophy girlfriend. In fact, my hair's short and sun-streaked honey blond, and I'm fairly tall and lean with lots of muscles because I do yoga, kickbox, or run every day when I'm not recuperating from gunshot wounds, and whatnot.

Not that I'm complaining about Black's attentions. Actually he saved my life, too, from the aforementioned psychopath, but I saved his first, so I call that even. Truthfully, he's okay, I guess, except when he tries to run my life and psychoanalyze me about my childhood from hell, but he's getting better about that. Anyway.

A tinny male voice crackled inside my earpiece, "You sure look hot in those Daisy Dukes, Morgan, 'cept for all those giant goose bumps pokin' through those fishnets."

Budweiser D. Davis is my beloved partner, Bud for short,

the silver-tongued, immaculately dressed, auburn-haired, named after his father's favorite beer, Georgia-accented wise-ass. But he helped save my life, too. What can I say? I'm obligated to put up with these guys.

Into the microphone hidden in my plunging cleavage, I said, well, actually hissed, "You stomp around out here at night in spitting snow half-naked awhile and we'll see what pretty shade of blue you turn, Galahad."

I could hear the other deputies laughing in the background. They were my protective shadows lurking in the unmarked sheriff's surveillance van parked across the lot. I was being filmed, too, wow, a real movie star tonight. I guess that's what I get for being the only female deputy in our department. Well, there is one other woman, Connie O'Hara, but she's five-months pregnant and doesn't do bare midriffs particularly well at the moment. Therefore, I prance and freeze with ice on my eyelashes and a nose redder than Rudolph's, but all in my own special seductive way.

On the bright side, since early this evening, my trusty little band of men and I have busted twenty-eight truckers, six bored husbands, and one lesbian, all horny as billy goats. I guess that's worth turning blue over, but I'd sorta rather be back in Bermuda at Black's beach villa where he whisked me off to recover from my injuries. About an hour ago, though, I began to think another murder case would look good about now. Maybe somebody that got whacked in a steam room. Yeah, with a heated swimming pool and a bunch of hot tubs. Maybe I'll trot over to Black's digs later tonight and thaw out in his giant spa. Luckily he owns a luxury hotel on the lake, named Cedar Bend Lodge, where he keeps his gigantic penthouse apartment and lets me use its amenities whenever I like.

Bud was talking in my ear again. "Hey, guess what, Morgan? Somebody just called in a missin' person up north of the lake somewhere. Bet you're just dyin' to take it, right?"

My adrenaline went rat-a-tat-tat. Around here in rural mid-Missouri, missing-person cases were top of the line in the excitement arena. I controlled my glee as a pickup truck drove by, then slowed down when they saw me offering my wares. I put my hand over my mouth and whispered, "You know I am, but a couple of johns are nibbling on my line, as we speak. Hold off a minute and let me bust them."

Bud said, "Okey-dokey, but make it quick."

I hastily painted my come-hither-you-dumb-suckers look on my face, opened my thrift-store ermine faux fur and contorted into my ultra-sexy, provocative pose, remembering to display my grape-Popsicle legs to the very best advantage. Man, if I did attract another john, he'd probably turn to ice when he touched me, like Mr. Freeze in *Batman*. Then again he might have a heater in his car that I could press up against. Ah, ask and ye shall receive.

The two guys in the battered blue Dodge pickup decided just a little too late that I was a worthy conquest and had to swerve to the curb at the last second. I guess that's why they hit the lamppost with the Christmas star on top. Sometimes I'm just too alluring for my own good.

I looked up into the lightly spiraling white snowflakes and made sure the rocking glittery adornment wasn't going to fall on my head. That would be a catchy headline: POLICE-WOMAN/HOOKER SMASHED FLAT BY FALLING STAR. All business now that I had a couple of easy marks, I worked up some serious slither and sidled sexily toward my dynamic duo waiting under the streetlight.

"Hey, there, hotties, you looking for a date?" Sexy, breathy, freezing. Hey, I'd seen how the hookers do it on HBO.

The guy in the passenger seat said, "Hey, there, you sweet little piece of thang."

Huh?

My fellow deputies laughed heartily into my earpiece. Unprofessional, they are, yes. But I, being the only serious police officer in the group, ignored their glee, kept a straight face as I batted snow-crusted eyelashes at my twin Prince Charmings. I hoped all my old scars and bullet wounds were hidden under my skimpy attire. Sometimes my battle me-

mentos make the guys courting me get all nervous and jumpy. Except for Black. He just prescribes painkillers and tells me to duck and weave next time. He's got a couple of impressive scars himself from his Army Ranger days, I might add. Not that we're in competition, or anything.

Fortunately, Billy Joe Naughty Boy wasn't looking at my hatchet scar. He was looking at my Grapette legs with more than a little concern on his face. He had lots of dirty-blond hair everywhere except on top of his head, and a bushy beard with a little piece of Big Mac lettuce crusted in it. Wilted, maybe with a little Special Sauce, too. Dinner, I presumed. I resisted the urge to pluck it out as an act of goodwill and wondered if his gold nose ring made his nostril freeze in these cold climes. My kind of man, all right.

The driver leaned around and got into the act. My, he was so attractive, too. Mohawk haircut all spiked up with Dippity-do and tattooed race cars with flames coming out the back decorating his grimy hands. Also a suave charmer, he said with such self-confidence, "Wanna go party with us? We got lots of beer and Funyuns in back."

Jeez Louise, my dreams have surely come true—twin gourmands willing to share their stash of oniony snacks. Then I thought of the great party going on in the motel rooms just behind me, where more friendly deputies than you could shake a stick at were babysitting all my other eager suitors of the evening. I guess you can call that a party; half of them were having fun.

"You bet, I do, sweetie. What do you guys have in mind?"

Mr. Dreamboat at the passenger window chortled with lots of feeling, or maybe he was just embarrassed at my endearment. Or maybe he was a choking wildebeest in heat. I waited for him to regain his composure and draw breath and wondered if Nose Ring's burning, Christmasy leer could warm up my frozen kneecaps.

Mohawk behind the wheel had his visor down and was spitting on his palms and slicking up his mussed coiffure. I bring out that primping thing in the men I meet. Nose Ring probably would've primped, too, if he knew how. The latter finally figured out how to answer my question.

"Well, both of us are horny as hell, that tell you anything, darlin'?"

I didn't mention what that told me. But just think about bulls in heat, you know, barnyard creatures, scruffy coats, manure smell, and all that.

"Tell you what, sugar. I gotta nice warm room right back there in that motel." I tossed my head toward our makeshift incarceration units, chock-full of armed and gleeful cops humming "Getting To Know You."

NASCAR Hands backed up into a parking spot so fast he almost hit the trash receptacle on the corner. The boys were excited, I guess. Maybe I'm a regular Pamela Anderson with a Glock 9mm hidden in my gold lamé purse. Maybe I'm a woman who isn't unconscious, and that's the extent of their requirements. On second thought, consciousness in a woman probably didn't factor in their love life.

I strutted toward him as best I could. Truth is, I strut better in wool socks and hightop Nikes than in fishnets and black-patent stiletto heels. Nose Ring opened the door and stepped out under the streetlight to meet me, obviously an eager beaver. "Just how much's that nice warm room and hot little bod gonna cost us?"

Let me see, what am I gonna cost these two yokels? Donald Trump's entire wealth added to all Queen Elizabeth's palaces, with Prince Charles and Camilla Parker Bowles and his best polo pony thrown in. Not nearly enough. I observed them critically. They weren't exactly the aforementioned The Donald. Cash was not bulging from their pockets with nowhere else to go. They were hoarding Big Mac crumbs for minisnacks. Not wanting to scare them off, I said, "Twenty bucks each? How 'bout that?"

They both looked shocked, and the driver had not turned off the ignition. Uh-oh, maybe I had overrated my appeal. But I knew all was well when Billy Goat One beamed and squealed like Howard Dean at the Iowa caucus. "Hell, yeah! That's what I'm talkin' about!"

Hell, yeah, and get out your lawyer's telephone number. I presented my pearly whites in a sexy, sly smile and jutted my right hip out of my white fur, to clench the great deal they'd just made. Actually I was smiling because I was going to get to go inside and sit on the radiator where four happy-go-lucky, grinning deputies were gathered in the bathroom, guns drawn and all excited. It wasn't fair, they got all the fun of frisking and gloating and watching the looks of horror when they burst into the room. I just got to strut. I motioned at the motel. "You follow me, boys. Heaven's right next door, and I'm taking both of you with me."

The guy's doubled fist came so quick and hard against my cheekbone that it caught me off guard. My knees buckled and white stars exploded behind my eyes as he grabbed the front of my coat and heaved me headfirst into the front seat. He jumped in after me and slammed the door.

The driver yelled, "What the hell you doin', Leroy?"

Leroy said, "Shut up and floor it, Ethan!" He grabbed me by the hair and said, "You goin' with us, baby, and you ain't never gonna forget us."

That brought me to my senses real quick, and I began to fight and kick as Ethan stomped the gas pedal and screeched off, laying rubber on the pavement. Halfway down the block, Leroy got me by the throat and slapped my face, but I fought harder, desperately trying to get to the weapon in my purse. Ethan was swerving around and yelling, "Why you doin' this, Leroy? Don't hurt her too bad! She ain't done nothin'!"

I got Leroy a good one in the mouth with my fist. He cursed and tried to ram the top of my head against the dashboard, and that's when I saw the stiletto that had come off my foot in the fight. I grabbed it and drove the four-inch spiked heel down into the driver's crotch as hard as I could. Ethan's scream was as high pitched and girly as Beverly Sills in *Aida*. Then he lost control of the truck, screaming and writhing in pain until we slammed headfirst into a parked car. The impact threw me to the floor and Leroy against the windshield, bloodying his forehead. He fell back against the seat, and I had my weapon out and between his bleary eyes before he could blink.

"You aren't gonna forget me either, dirtbag," I gritted out, but then both doors flew open and about twelve of my fellow officers were there jerking my two assailants out and spread-eagling them on the ground.

Then Bud was beside me. "You okay, Claire? Man, that happened so fast."

I shoved my weapon back into my purse. "He sucker punched me in the side of the head, stunned me a little."

As I climbed down out of the cab, Bud examined the side of my face. "Yeah, your cheekbone's already startin' to bruise up. It's not bleedin' much, though. What happened?"

"I bought their Tweedle Dumb and Tweedle Dumber impersonation is what happened. Let down my guard a second, but that's all it took. Won't do that again."

I sat down on the curb and watched my friends flip the two hicks onto their stomachs, cuff them, and manhandle them across the street. The one with the stiletto wound was still crying and yelling that he was bleeding and something about fathering children. I touched my cheek and winced but found only a couple of drops of blood. "These spike heels come in pretty handy, Bud. Maybe I oughta wear them all the time."

Bud said, "Yeah. Maybe I'll get me a pair, too."

We grinned, and then he sobered. "Sure you're all right?"

I stood up. "I'm fine. He barely clipped me. Come on, this's been a barrel of laughs but let's get outta here and find our missing citizen, whoever it is."

TWO

"Hey, baby, bail me out and we can still get it on!"

I ignored that tempting invitation from Judy the Lesbian, who was sitting handcuffed in the back of our sheriff's van but I smiled politely so I wouldn't hurt her feelings. Dabbing at the small cut on my cheekbone with a Kleenex, I sat down in the passenger seat of Bud's white Bronco and clunked the door shut, glad to get in out of the cold. A minute later he slid in the driver's seat across from me.

"You gonna bail that Judy gal out, or would Black get jealous?"

That Bud. What a riot. "I think not. I'll put in a good word for you, though, if you wanna give it a whirl."

Bud grinned and fired up the engine. The car was so cold, our breaths plumed and hung around awhile for us to admire. It had to be down to twenty degrees and still dropping. "How about getting some heat on in here, man?"

Bud flipped the heater on high and the freezing blast hit me full in the face. I turned the vents toward him and pulled my fur collar up around my ears. The radio crackled with static, and Bud snatched the handset off the dashboard.

"Yeah. Davis here."

Jacqee, the sheriff's beloved airhead daughter, home for Christmas break from UCLA said, "You guys gonna take that missing-person report, or what?"

Bud let up on the button and turned his big, pleading gray eyes on me. "Claire, we've been out here working this whole freakin' night. You just got knocked up the side of the head. Let somebody else handle this one."

"I said I was okay. Now tell her we're on it."

"It'll make you late for your date with Nick."

I gave him a stare that bespoke hellfire.

Bud frowned and thumbed down the button. "Okay, Morgan and I are on our way. Let's hear it."

Miss Valley Girl crackled back, obviously put-upon. "Well, like, take forever to make up your minds. I'm right in the middle of my Pilates and I'm gonna go all stiff if I don't get back to it soon."

Bud and I rolled our eyes in tandem, a team in every way, but we made no clever retort. Jacqee was the sheriff's daughter, after all, and he did love her too much to fire her, stupid-speak and all.

"Well, see, this neighbor lady called in and said this guy named Simon something or other's front door's standing wide open, even with it snowing outside, and everything. Can you believe that we're supposed to have a foot of snow tonight? I sure wish I was back out in L.A. I could be down at Venice Beach everyday working on my tan and watching the guys play volleyball. Oh yeah, she said she thought she saw some blood, too."

"Have you notified patrol?" We always encouraged Jacqee with procedure. If we didn't, she would forget. She would forget her name, too, if she didn't have a driver's license with her picture on it and a bunch of Daddy's charge cards to look at.

"Well, duh? Daddy taught me how to do this police kinda stuff. There's a guy already out there, I forget his name, and he says it looks like there was a struggle."

"Roger. We got it," Bud said into the mike, then mumbled

something under his breath that sounded like idiot moron. "I'll be glad when Dude-ette's vacation's over and she goes back into twenty-four-hour-a-day tannin' mode."

I said, "Yeah, you and me both. And thanks."

"Yeah, and you're gonna get my ass canned. You know what Charlie said. You're supposed to be on light duty 'til the doctor gives you a clean bill."

"You call hooking outside for hours at night in this getup light duty? Not to mention getting slapped around and thrown into a truck by a couple of yahoos. Hey, I'll bite the bullet and take a missing-person case any day."

"Know why people say 'bite the bullet,' Morgan?"

Bud's birthday was the first day of December, and I had made the horrible, *horrible* mistake of getting him a book about the origins of popular sayings. I decided to play nice since he took the missing-person case against his will. "No, but I bet a pretty penny you do."

" 'Bet a pretty penny's' even more interestin'."

"Jeez, Bud. I'm taking that book back for a refund."

"The sayin' doesn't come from an American penny but an English penny coined way back in 1257, or sometime, by King Henry III, or one of those kings back then. It wasn't a good coin for regular day-to-day business in those days because it was gold, so they quit makin' it. So it got all rare and stuff, and then people thought it was shiny and pretty, and everybody wanted one for a good-luck piece."

"Fascinating. Oh boy, look out there, the snow's really starting to come down now." My valiant attempt to change the subject, uttered with great feeling, I might add.

"It's not stickin' yet." Bud switched on the windshield wipers and they made wet, sluicing, poor-me-I'm-trying-my-best sounds. " 'Bite the bullet' is from the Civil War. When they ran outta whiskey and painkillers, the army doctors would give the wounded guys a soft-lead bullet to put between their teeth while they were amputatin' their legs."

"Double fascinating. I bet you're a big hit nowadays at comedy clubs."

"All thanks to that cool book you gave me."

The snow had threatened all day but now it was really coming down with a vengeance, swirling and hitting the windshield in big, soppy splotches as we took Highway 54 and drove up toward the town of Eldon. The bridge spans were decorated in twinkling Christmas lights, red and blue and green and white, and the outlet mall near the lake was bustling with bundled-up people carrying most of their year's income in shopping bags. I wasn't much of a shopper, but I did have to buy gifts for a few people. Black was my major problem. Hell, what do you buy for a multimillionaire? The man's loaded and doesn't mind throwing it around, either.

"Bud, what'd you think Donald Trump's wife gives him for Christmas?"

Bud glanced at me. "Viagra?"

I laughed but that was one thing that Black definitely did *not* need. Donald probably didn't either. Thoughts came to mind of last night at Cedar Bend Lodge, in Black's penthouse living quarters with its palatial, black-marble bathroom. A certain little episode involving warm, soapy water and a great big bathtub made me shiver all over. Embarrassed, I blamed the cold chills on Bud's heater. "How long's it gonna take for this heater to warm up?"

Bud put his hand in front of the blasting air. "It feels hot to me." He tipped the vents back in my direction. "Why'd you ask about Trump? Havin' trouble buyin' for the guru?"

Bud persisted in calling Black that because of that renowned-psychiatrist thing. "How about a brand-spankin'-new couch? Maybe all those rich patients have worn the cushions threadbare."

"Right. Sorry I asked."

Bud braked at a stoplight and wiped some fog off the inside of the window. He punched the defrost button. "Give him that book you gave me. It's awesome."

I already had a book for Black. For some reason, I liked to give books to people. Not that I was that big of a reader myself, but I wasn't good at knowing their tastes and needs because I wasn't good at getting close to people. Bud and Black, and my good friend Harve were the only ones I had to buy for, except my Aunt Helen, who really wasn't my aunt but I thought of her that way. And I guess I'd have to get O'Hara something, too, since she was the only other woman in the department. Maybe something for the new baby.

"There's the turn, up ahead on the left."

After about ten minutes on a slick gravel road out in the middle of nowhere, we saw one of our dark brown sheriff's cruisers ahead, its lights still flashing in the darkness. It gave the falling snow an odd halo effect that was all golden and pulsating. And the snow was beginning to stick, frosting the roads and trees.

We pulled up behind the deputy's car and got out. The officer who'd secured the scene walked back to meet us. His name was Al Pennington, and he was fairly new to the department. He was dressed like Bud, in a brown department hooded parka, leather boots, and a black sock cap with a sheriff logo on the front. I coveted his outfit as I clicked toward him on my newly respected, slightly bloodstained stiletto heels. His military-cut blond hair was hidden under the cap, along with an impressive scar from a head wound he'd sustained while in the Air Force. His blue eyes that always seemed secretly amused gave me an up-and-down appraisal. This time they seemed amused by me.

He said, "Nice outfit. I hate to think what you're wearing under that coat."

"Yeah, I hate to think about it, too."

"Got one in the eye?"

"Yeah, not bad, though. What's up here?"

Pennington glanced up at the house. "Possible missing person. Name of Simon Classon. The neighbor down thataway called it in." I ran the name through my memory bank without much luck as I followed Pennington's pointed finger to a house about fifty yards down the road.

"Who's the neighbor?"

"Lady named Edith Talbott. She lives alone and has trouble walking 'cause of a bad back so she stays inside most of the time. Says that when she went out to get her mail, she noticed newspapers hadn't been picked up from Classon's box for a while, so she opened the mailbox and saw Classon hadn't been getting his mail, either, so she rode up here in her golf cart to see if anything was wrong. That's when she saw Classon's front door was open. She couldn't get up on the porch but she thought she saw some blood on the floor. That scared her, so she went home and called us."

"Is it blood?"

"Looks like it. I've called crime scene and put them on alert. They're ready when and if you need them."

"You go in?"

"Yeah, checked to make sure nobody was injured but didn't find anything out of the ordinary, other than what's in the front hall."

"Anybody else live here with him?"

"Neighbor said he lives alone."

"Okay, we'll take it from here. Good job, Pennington."

Bud pulled on his brown leather gloves and preceded me up the snowy sidewalk. We left footprints in the light powder. Mine looked like some kind of two-toed whooping crane scratching around. Bud's looked like Sasquatch. "Too bad snow wasn't already on the ground. Might've gotten some footprints."

"Yeah. Might anyway, if we're lucky."

The house was a two-story gray brick Colonial with lots of white latticework covering the banisters on the front porch. It looked like winter ivy was frozen solid but trying its best not to die before spring. Four steps led up to a long, wraparound front porch. We stopped at the bottom and switched on our flashlights. There was nothing visible on the treads of the stairs, but we edged up close to the banisters, just in case somebody had been nice enough to leave us a footprint.

The hall light was on, slanting a warm yellow glow across the porch. There was a clean welcome mat with a white angel blowing a long gold trumpet on a black background. It said "Merry Christmas" underneath the angel in flowing scarlet script. There was also a brass angel door knocker. I sidestepped the mat, took off my stilettos, put on the paper booties, and snapped on the rubber gloves that Bud handed to me.

Inside the house, it was warm as toast, despite the open front door. A small chandelier with lots of crystal prisms hung from the ceiling beside a flight of stairs leading up to the second floor. The crystals made little tinkling sounds from the cold gusts coming in the door. There was an oriental black table pushed against the stairs on top of which sat a red telephone with a built-in answering machine. A huge white statue of an angel with spread wings stood on a pedestal at the rear of the hall. The wall leading up the steps had about twenty portraits, all of male angels performing various good deeds.

Bud said, "Oops, we made a wrong turn and ended up in heaven."

"Nope, the streets outside aren't paved with gold."

"I'd say this Classon guy likes his angels."

"You think?" Sarcasm from me? Oh, yeah, my favorite pastime.

I looked down at the blood on the oak hardwood floor. It was in a spatter design. Sort of like a sunburst that burned out on one side. I squatted down and looked closer. The bloodstain was not fresh. At least two or three days old was my estimation. He'd been clubbed, it looked like, probably with the heavy angel doorstop lying on its side on the floor, the one with more dried bloodstains on it. See why I made detective? My powers of deduction are extraordinary.

Bud said, "Looks like we've got the murder weapon, if there is a murder." He's mighty intuitive himself.

There were no drag marks that I could see, not in the hallway, not going upstairs or out on to the front porch. Oh, yeah, the small round rug had bloodstains on it, too, all over the face of a blond-haired angel woven into the fabric. I lis-

tened for the sound of trumpets and harps but only heard the
faint sounds of a television filtering down from upstairs.

"We better check the place out, just in case Pennington
missed something."

For the second time today, I pulled the Glock out of my
shiny gold purse. "I'll go upstairs. You take down here."

I inched up the steps, still listening for twanging harps. At
the top of the steps, I realized the television was somewhere
down the hall to my right. Voices. Canned laughter. A TV sit-
com. It sounded like reruns of *Everybody Loves Raymond*. I
moved toward the sound. It turned out to be the master bedroom, and the door was standing ajar. The television was on
a shelf to the left of a tall cherrywood tester bed. A small
reading lamp was on the bedside table. Yes, it had an angel
on it, and the angel shade tilted slightly toward the bed as if
someone needed more light to read by. The blue-and-white
toile bedspread was thrown back, along with white sheets
and a thick blue quilt. Toile? For a guy? Something about
that just didn't seem right. A hardback book and a pair of
black half-glasses were lying on the coverlet, as if Simon
Classon had been reading in bed. A newspaper on the bed
was folded to the crossword puzzle. I checked the newspaper's
date. Three days ago. Pennington said his neighbor down the
road found some newspapers still in Classon's mailbox, which
might help us pinpoint the day he'd gone missing. My gut
told me this was more than a missing person and that Classon probably wasn't going to show up on his own. Maybe
someone rang the doorbell and he went downstairs to answer. Maybe somebody he knew. Maybe that's how the perp
got into the house. Made sense.

I leaned down and looked at the title of the book. *Angels
Above: The Complete Guide to Angelology.* Angelology?
This was beginning to look like somebody had quite an unhealthy obsession with the heavenly host. Maybe the guy
was a preacher. Or that Bosley guy from *Charlie's Angels* reruns that hung around when Charlie called up and gave the
angels their assignments. I looked around for a framed pic-

ture of three silly, giggling, skinny bimbos in skimpy outfits, but didn't see any.

I crossed the room to the closet, stood to one side with the Glock held ready against my shoulder, then quickly thrust open the door. The clothes inside mocked me and my big weapon. "Well, you never know what's going to jump out of a closet at you," I muttered in self-defense. I'd found monsters in closets before, I might add, among other things. I found lots of starched white dress shirts, tweed jackets with leather elbow patches, and argyle sweaters hanging inside. There were some ball caps on the shelf but not a single halo. No women's clothes in sight, either, so Classon obviously lived alone. I wondered if he had a girlfriend and where she was when the doorstop got itself all bloody and nasty.

There were two other bedrooms, smaller and less lived in, and a single tiny, old-fashioned bath. All neat and tidy, drawers mostly empty except for Classon's clothes stacked neatly here and there.

Angels decorated everything, and I mean everything, everywhere, from the dainty little angel figurines to angel books to angel wallpaper, angel towels, angel shower curtains, angel night-lights. Heaven on earth, for sure. Excuse me, Saint Peter, could you tell me how to get to the cherubs' dormitory? I was getting seriously eager to meet Mr. Classon and see if he played a harp or had wing bulges under his arms.

I was halfway down the stairs when I heard Bud give a short yelp. I bounded down the rest of the way and found him safe and secure in the kitchen. He was standing in front of the kitchen sink. The cabinet doors under it stood open. He appeared a bit sheepish.

"What happened?" I looked around at the yellow angel window shades and matching place mats and the red angel oven mittens hanging on the refrigerator door.

"Man, when I opened that cabinet, a bunch of spiders started running around. Shit." He shuddered.

It's a well-known fact around the station house that Bud

does not like spiders, or any other creepy crawlies for that matter. "Did you kill them?"

"Hell, no. They ran off too fast. God, I hate those freakin' things."

"What are you, Little Miss Muffet?"

He looked offended, so I said more kindly. "They're itty bitty, Bud. All you have to do is step on them with your great big size-thirteen shoe."

"I know, I know, but man, they're ugly as hell. Have you ever seen a close-up of one of 'em? They've got eyes that stick out on these kind of antenna-looking stalks, and stuff, and these fang things that they stick in you. And I'll tell you somethin' else. They're not all itty bitty, there's some back home in the Georgia woods as big as saucers. And they run real fast and jump at you. I've seen 'em."

"Well, if that happens, pull your weapon and shoot it. I'm not going to worry much until I see one the size of a cat. Now that'd be scary."

Bud shuddered at that image.

I said, "You already checked under there, I take it."

This time he appeared slightly ashamed. "Not yet. I was gonna look for some Raid first."

"For God's sake, Bud."

I knelt and shined my flashlight into the dark corners. "Well, well, it looks like Mr. Classon forgot to clean his house. There are spiderwebs everywhere under here."

"Yeah? Told ya."

I angled the beam and held it steady on a foil-wrapped package wedged up into the pipes. "Whoa, now, lookee here what I found."

I knocked away some webs with the flashlight and pulled out the stash. "I bet this'll weigh out at half a kilo of cocaine, all parceled out in little plastic Ziploc bags, too. Looks like Classon's not so angelic, after all."

"Think he's dealing?"

"Oh, yeah. Or he's saving up for a rainy day."

"Pennington should've found this."

"Maybe he's scared of spiders, too."

I stood up, and Bud slammed the cabinet door with his toe. "Everything clean upstairs?"

"Yeah. I think he might've been reading when somebody knocked at the front door. Looks like he went downstairs to see who it was, and they jumped him in the foyer. Maybe one of his baser clients."

Bud said, "Yeah. Maybe somebody thought his prices were too high. I'll run his name and see if we get any hits."

"Right. I'll see if I can find an address book with names of his friends and relatives. We need to apprise next of kin that he might be missing, then we'll have to get a statement from the neighbor lady before we leave here. My gut's telling me it's drug related, and wherever Classon is, he's in big trouble."

"Yeah, likewise. Unless he fell, gashed his head on the doorstop, and drove himself to the hospital. I guess that could've happened. Or maybe his angel friends flew him there."

"Call the hospitals while you're at it so we can rule that out."

"Right. I'm on it."

THREE

When the emergency rooms came up blank for Simon Classon, we branded the case a bona fide missing person/assault, secured and documented our evidence bag to take downtown, then called for our nutty but expert criminalist, Johnny Becker, a.k.a. Shaggy, to sweep the Classon crime scene. By the time we skidded down the ice-slick road, trudged up onto the neighbor's front porch, and I stomped the snow off my stilettos, it was getting close to ten o'clock.

Bud said, "Better not let this lady see what you've got on underneath that coat, or she might brand you a hussy and bar the doors."

"If you'd grabbed the duffel bag with my sweats and Nikes and thermal socks like you were supposed to, I could've changed a long time ago and wouldn't be freezing my toes off in these stupid shoes."

"So I got in a hurry and forgot. Sorry. You want my coat?"

"Keep it. It doesn't go with my fishnets."

The house was an old forties-style bungalow with yellow stucco walls and an open-air balcony just above the front porch. A gaily patterned swing set at one end, dusted with snow and longing for July nights and lightning bugs. There was no storm door, only an old wooden one that looked original to the house. It had a rectangular window with frosted glass, and after a few minutes, the door opened a crack that was, just maybe, wide enough to squeeze a piece of typing paper through.

"Yes?" A teeny-weeny grandma voice, not at all sure she wanted to let anybody in her house without a signed warrant.

"Mrs. Talbott? Edith Talbott?"

"Yes?" A little less concerned, but not much. The door widened enough for an anorexic inchworm to wriggle through.

"I'm Detective Claire Morgan from the Canton County Sheriff's Department. This is my partner, Detective Bud Davis."

"Have you found Mr. Classon yet?"

"No, ma'am." I smiled at the faded blue eye now peering out through the crack. "We thought maybe you could help us find him."

"I don't know where he is. I didn't do anything to him. I mind my own business and expect him to do the same."

Bud said, "Yes, ma'am. We just need to talk to you for a minute or two."

"Go ahead then, talk to me."

"It sure is cold out here, ma'am." To prove it, Bud energetically beat his gloved hands together and exhaled a smoky breath.

"You blaming me for that, too, are you? I'd say weather like this is to be expected this time of year. Winter's like that, you know. Cold, sometimes snowy."

Bud slanted me a we've-got-a-real-wiseass-here look, then we both eyed the eye in the door. It blinked. Twice.

"Well, let me see your badges. I watch TV. I know how killers get in people's houses pretending to be cops. And I know what badges that come from Toys "R" Us look like, too."

We got out our legitimate badges and let Cyclops eyeball them.

"Well, okay, I guess, but I'm gonna call the sheriff first

and make sure you're for real. It's a little late in the evening to come knocking on a person's door without calling first, don't you think? You stay right where you are and don't try anything." The door shut in our faces. The lock clicked, then two more.

"Hell, it'd be easier gettin' into the Oval Office with a hand grenade." Bud shuffled his feet some more to keep warm. I shivered patiently and blew into my gloved hands to warm my frozen nose. My bruised cheekbone was beginning to ache.

Finally, the door opened all the way and revealed to us the inhospitable Mrs. Talbott. She was leaning on a cane, a big aluminum one with a curved handle, but it was painted red, white, and blue like the American flag. She was little and wrinkled and prim, and looked exactly like Granny in the Tweety Bird cartoons, all the way down to her white-haired bun. I looked around for a birdcage. There was a brown wicker one on a table by the front window but it was empty. Maybe Sylvester finally got lucky.

"Well, I'm sorry if you became chilled waiting out there, but a lady my age can't be too careful. I am eighty-seven, you know. And I watch *America's Most Wanted* and *Cops* and *NYPD Blue*. *Law and Order*'s pretty good, too, and the Court TV channel is nothing less than a public-service network, in my opinion. I see how criminals like to treat us senior citizens. That's why I had bars put on my windows and the Brink's alarm system put in. I don't got a lot but what I got is gonna stay mine." She glared at us, and we smiled graciously, also fans of those programs.

"Yes, ma'am, we appreciate your caution." When she finally let us step inside, her home was a relief after the angel grotto down the street. Not a cherub or seraph in sight. Lots of books, stacked newspapers, and a giant big-screen television muted on a rerun of *Sex and the City*. Hmmm. Looked like Mrs. Talbott had a feisty streak.

"Go ahead then, sit down, and I'll fix you some tea. I am not going to even offer you coffee because it's not good for

you. Green tea is all I drink and all I fix for myself or anybody else." She glowered at me, then Bud, as if we were
going to pull our weapons and shoot her dead if she didn't
produce some Folgers in a hurry.

"I do love a spot of green tea," said Bud, suddenly the
British lord with a southern accent. Next he'd be asking for
crumpets and yelling tallyho.

The fireplace was crackling and popping, all excited
about its real, live hickory logs. I backed up to it, my frozen
feet grateful for the heat. Sometimes winter sucked. Most of
the time winter sucked. I perused a bookshelf full of old silver-
framed family pictures circa 1912 while my backside began
a slow spring thaw. Bud settled into watching Sarah Jessica
Parker do the dirty on television. She didn't have on much,
but she did have on a pair of stilettos like mine, so she was
safe from attack. Hers were red and definitely not from
Goodwill Industries.

It didn't take Granny long to return, pushing an old-
fashioned, mahogany tea cart with a tarnished silver tray on
top. She leaned heavily on her patriotic cane and seemed relieved when she got to sit down in a big easy chair covered
with blue and pink floral chintz. With all the grace of Princess
Diana's dowager aunt, if she'd had one, the old lady began
what amounted to a British high tea ceremony. She had ar-
ranged six cucumber sandwiches and six little square cup-
cakes on a white plate covered with red roses. The pattern
was called Old English Roses. I knew that because my Aunt
Helen had a whole set of similar dishes, including the prized
cake stand.

Sweet old Granny latched her keen blue eyes on my face.
"Tell me, Detective Morgan, or Claire, if I may, why are you
dressed like a whore? Have you been involved in one of
those prostitution stings that I like to watch on *Cops*? And is
that where you got that bruise on your face? Truth be told, I
think it's just good enough for those johns, to get caught and
embarrassed that way. My late husband was known to frequent a house of ill repute before we spoke our marriage

vows, but he never did so afterward, not once. I wasn't the kind of woman who'd put up with a roué."

Bud said, "A rue what?"

I said, "A roué, Bud."

Bud looked perplexed. "What's a rue a?"

I said, "You know, a roué, a rake."

Bud said, "What do you mean a rake? Like for leaves?"

Mrs. Talbott showed her impatience. She pursed her lips and addressed Bud directly. "It's a rogue, a womanizer, a ne'er-do-well, a profligate, a Bill Clinton. No sir, I will not abide hanky-panky."

Bud brightened considerably. "You know where the phrase 'hanky-panky' comes from, Mrs. Talbott?"

Oh, brother. I made plans to sneak that book out of Bud's house and burn it to ashes.

However, Mrs. Talbott was over her miff and perked up. "No, my dear boy, I do not."

"Well, back in the old days, magicians used to wave handkerchiefs around so the audience would watch that hand and not notice what he was really doin' with the other hand. Thus, 'hanky-panky.' "

"So where'd the panky part come from then?" the old lady demanded, apparently not pleased at all with his explanation.

Bud shrugged. "I guess they just sort of added that on, you know, like hocus-pocus. Just for the sound of it, I guess. You know, a rhyme."

Mrs. Talbott smiled, revealing her impressively white, Tom Cruise dentures. "Detective Davis, I must say I find that intriguing. How did you know that?"

"I have this really cool book. It's got just about every popular sayin' there is in it."

"Indeed. How very interesting. I must say I've learned something today. I still like to learn new things, even though I'm an octogenarian."

Okay, enough of the small talk already. "Mrs. Talbott, what

can you tell us about Simon Classon? Do you know him well?"

Mrs. Talbott presented me with a dainty, rose-covered teacup. She handed a matching cup to Bud and dropped in two cubes of sugar with tiny ornate silver tongs. I hadn't seen a sugar cube since I was a little girl; I didn't know they still made them. Maybe I'd get a box of them for my next fancy tea party.

"No, I don't know him well. The only time I ever saw him was at the mailbox. He was very good about fetching his mail every day. Sometimes he would walk down and bring mine up onto the porch, you know, if it was raining or snowing, although I am perfectly capable of getting my own mail. You see, I have to walk with the cane but I manage quite well. I used to have to use a wheelchair but not so much anymore."

"Did you ever see anyone visiting Mr. Classon? Does he have family that you know of? A girlfriend or wife?"

"Yes, of course, I saw various cars stop in front of his place from time to time. I never paid much mind to it, though. I suspect he might be more apt to have a boyfriend."

Bud said, "He's gay?"

"Well, I've seen him prancing around and acting rather like a fop. Conclude what you may, young man."

Bud said, "Does that mean gay?"

I said, "A fop is an effeminate man, Bud. Mrs. Talbott, did you ever see men or women going in and out of Mr. Classon's house?"

"They call that a fop, really? You're kiddin' me," Bud said. He laughed.

Mrs. Talbott shook her head. "No, none that I could identify, if that's what you mean. But I do know, and for a fact, that he thinks he's an angel come to earth to help others."

My hand froze the teacup at my mouth in the middle of a sip. I swallowed the warm, fragrant tea then said, "I'm sorry?"

"You heard me right. He thinks he's a real angel—the

Bible's full of male angels, you know. Most of them, actually, I think, are male."

Bud said, "So he came right out and told you he was an angel?"

Mrs. Talbott sipped daintily and dabbed the corner of her mouth with a lace-edged white linen napkin. "No, but I saw as much on his website."

"He's got a website?"

"That's what I just said, isn't it? Mercy, you young folks. I was the Camdenton librarian hereabouts for almost thirty-five years. I'm retired now, of course, but I am completely computer literate. I Googled him once, just out of curiosity, you understand. He's got his own website called callupanangel. com. Which is quite corny, if you ask me. Silly, even. Really." She gave a little offended sniff.

"He has a few angels around his house, too." Sometimes I am prone to understatement.

"It's truly a rip-off, my dear. You see, he purports to be able to converse with angels on his clients' behalf. He calls them angel readings, and he has a chatroom, and everything."

Bud laughed, then realized by Mrs. Talbott's glower that she wasn't joking around. He said, "You're kiddin'."

"No, young man, I assure you that I am not. If I remember correctly, he said online that he does not speak directly with his client's angels, but that he has his own personal guardian angels who speak to other people's angels for him, then he relays the message to the gullible nincompoops who fall for his nonsense."

Bud said, "And he's paid a hefty fee for these angelgrams, I take it?"

"Of course. I believe he quoted a price of $80 for a full reading. He'll take cash or any of the major credit cards, and he says he speaks to Uriel, Michael, and Gabriel. They're all archangels in the Bible, in case you've forgotten your Sunday school lessons. I taught Sunday school to little ones for near forty years."

Very few of my foster parents had taken me to Sunday school, so I said, "Is this website still up and running?"

"I suspect so. It was linked to that school where he works."

Bud and I exchanged a significant look. We do that sometimes. "What school is that, ma'am?"

"The Dome of the Cave Academy for the Gifted. Have you heard of it?"

I had heard of it, vaguely. "It's nondenominational, if I remember correctly? A boarding school for troubled young teens, right?"

"Yeah, bright kids, supposedly. It's northwest of here, way out in the woods," Bud said. "I was up there once on a call."

"Really?" That surprised me.

"Yeah. A kid ran away, but it didn't amount to nothin'. It turned out he'd caught a bus home to Paducah, Kentucky, and his parents called and informed the school he'd made it home safely. It's a pretty cool campus, almost like a prep school."

"Yes, that's where you need to go to find out all about Simon Classon, I suspect. The people out there will know him much better than I. Actually, I always considered him sort of a lunatic. Imagine anybody giving him eighty hard-earned dollars to contact angels. Silliest thing I ever heard of."

I said, "What does he look like? I guess you wouldn't have a picture of him, by any chance?"

"No, I don't. But they've got one up on the first page of his website. He's fairly handsome, I suppose. Stocky man, who doesn't take care of himself the way he should. I saw him smoking out at the mailbox on several occasions. Held his cigarette in one of those long white cigarette holders my mother used back in the 1920s. I suppose he's probably in his thirties, maybe even forties, with that dishwater shade of blond hair. Sometimes he dyes it red or black. It's red right now, I think. He fixes it in sort of a pageboy style, I guess you'd call it. Talks all the time, mile a minute, at least he did with me. Never let a person get a word in edgewise. I wouldn't be surprised if he was one of those junkie types you see on *CSI*."

"Did you ever see him take drugs or sell them to anyone?"

"No, but I doubt he'd do such a thing out in the street for everyone to see, now would he? No, but he's a big phony, going on with all that angel cockamamie stuff. I bet deep down he's a devil in disguise. He probably has 666 tattooed on his scalp."

Bud said, "Like Damian did, huh?"

Edith was really warming up to Bud now. "Do you like those *Omen* films, young man?"

"Yeah. I like the part where Lee Remick crashes over the banister. She played the mom, right?"

Mrs. Talbott nodded. "I liked that part, too. And when the priest got impaled on the iron cross in the churchyard, that was quite remarkable."

I interrupted the Ebert and Roeper review and got us back on track. "Do you have any reason to suspect that he's a bad person, ma'am? Maybe into drugs himself?" I thought comparing Classon to Lucifer was a bit out of the mainstream, as far as casual remarks go.

"I saw him throw rocks at my cat once. Snuffles was just sitting on my wheelbarrow watching him. She's dead now, poor kitty, but I had the dear little thing for years and years. I don't trust anybody who mistreats animals. And I can assure you that the archangels wouldn't frequent a chatroom with somebody who throws rocks at cats."

Well, there you go. I thanked her kindly, and we finished our green tea before we headed back to Angel Land to see if Shaggy the Great had uncovered any evidence for us. Tonight I'd go calling on the angels via Classon's website, and tomorrow we'd visit the ones holed up at the Dome of the Cave Academy for the Gifted, whatever the hell that turned out to be.

The Angel Gabriel

The little boy trapped inside the grave stopped crying as his tormenters ran away. Eyes wide and frightened, he squinted up into the sun until a figure blocked out the bright glare, dropping a cool, dark shadow across his face. He could see the person above him had golden hair the sun turned into a shining halo. The angels had finally come for his family, and he was terrified. Then he saw an arm reach down to him and a deep voice said, "Grab hold, and I'll pull you outta there."

Grasping the proffered hand with both his own, he held on tightly as his savior lifted him upward as if he weighed nothing. When he was out in the sun again, he scrambled to his knees and stared up at the most beautiful creature he'd ever seen. The angel's hair was pure gold, silky, and long enough to brush his shoulders. He wore all white, and his eyes were blue and clear and smiling. It *was* an angel, he thought, thunderstruck, come to earth to escort his family to heaven. Maybe if he begged, the angel would take him, too.

"Are you really the Angel Gabriel, the one from my Sunday school lessons?" he asked, too scared to speak above a whisper.

Then the Angel Gabriel laughed like a regular person. He

knelt down on one knee and wiped the dirt off the boy's cheeks with his white tunic. "Hell, no, those brats just call me that 'cause I'm the preacher's son and have all this blond hair. You can call me Gabriel, though, if you want to."

"But you're wearing all white like the angels do, and you look just like the pictures of angels."

"Thanks, kid, but I'm no angel, believe me. And these ain't angel robes, either. You're that orphan kid, aren't you? I just got back from my karate class in town or I would've been here for your mom and dad's funeral. I saw what those guys did to you. Now don't you worry about them no more, you hear? They're a bunch of punks."

He hadn't thought about being an orphan, but that's what he was. He wondered if the angel thought he was ugly. "You don't think I'm ugly, not even with this?" He pointed to his head injury.

"Nope. You think I am?"

"No. You look like an angel."

"Don't worry about those kids anymore. I'm gonna be your best friend from now on. And if you stick close to me, we'll show those jerks what they get if they mess with us. Deal?"

The boy stared up at his bright savior and wondered how old he was. Fifteen, sixteen, maybe, about the same age as Betsy, his babysitter back in Pittsburgh. "You sure do look like the angels in my Bible. You sure you're not the one coming to get daddy and momma and Katie?"

"Nah, they already came for them anyways. Probably when they were out on the highway when they got killed. Whisked them up to heaven in the blink of an eye. That's what the Bible says happens. And I heard the angels always snatch their souls out of their bodies right before the crash so they don't have to suffer much pain."

"Really? I don't remember much about the crash. I remember waking up in the hospital, though."

"Yeah, well, you don't need to be worrying about it no more. The Bible's a cool book to read. My dad made me study it since I was littler than you. I'll teach you lots of things, now that you're my special friend. Want to come out in the woods and see my secret hideout? Nobody else's ever been out there but me, but I'll show it to you, if you promise to God you'll never, ever tell another soul about it. I bet your grandma'll let me show you around and take you back home later, before it gets dark. Yeah, let's do that. But you gotta promise you'll be my friend and never tell my secrets, not even to my dad or your grandma. You promise?"

"I promise. I'll never tell anybody anything about you. You'll be my special friend, too."

"Good deal. C'mon, let's tell your grandma where we're going, then I'll show you some really cool things."

Looking up at the beautiful, blond-haired boy, he felt certain this being was divine, really the Angel Gabriel who just wasn't allowed to tell anyone who he was. He'd saved him from the bullies, and from being buried in the grave, hadn't he? He had to be the Angel Gabriel, and the angel wanted him as his special friend. For the first time since his family had died, he smiled and felt hope.

FOUR

It was well after eleven before I got back to the sheriff's office where I'd left my black Ford Explorer. That made me more than a couple of hours late for my date with Black, but he probably wouldn't mind. He was a busy man himself, and he'd gotten used to my irregular hours and understood that my job took precedence over our hanky-panky. Maybe if I got out a big red handkerchief and waved it back and forth, I could distract Black from my late arrival. We'd agreed to meet at my place at nine, and he didn't have a key so he was probably standing outside, freezing and mad as a hornet. I wondered where Bud would say "mad as a hornet" came from? Oh, great, now I was doing it.

The snow was floating straight down in huge white flakes in the smoky beams of my headlights. So beautiful and clean, cloaking the world in peace and quiet like the Christmas card I got the other day from my car insurance agent. But that was only an illusion. Crimes were happening all around Lake of the Ozarks, even now on this cold, snowy night. Silent and stealthy, violence in the purple shadows, and in one of those terrible, dark places Simon Classon was probably in some very big trouble.

Shaggy and the rest of the forensics team hadn't turned up much yet in the way of evidence but they were taking samples of blood and hair back to the lab and would let me know as soon as they had some results. I'd already contacted the Dome of the Cave Academy for the Gifted, a.k.a. the dumbest name I'd ever heard of in my life, and it was closed, of course. But I finally got the custodian on my cell, some guy named Willie Vines, who gave me the phone number of the school's director, a Dr. G. Richard Johnstone. Mr. Director was at home in his house on campus and seemed genuinely surprised to hear about Classon's disappearance. He said Classon had been on vacation for the last week so no one had thought much about his absence. Said he was the resident angelologist on staff and taught classes on the hierarchy of angels, seraphim, and cherubim. Bud said it sounded like a class about sea urchins to him.

In any case, Johnstone appeared suitably concerned, promised they'd search the school thoroughly, and called back twenty minutes later with word there was no trace of their chief angelologist anywhere on campus. At that point, we decided there was little more we could do until tomorrow, not with a heavy snowfall settling in over the lake.

So it was closing in on the midnight hour when I turned into the gravel road that led down to my tiny A-frame house. My friend Harve Lester has let me live there rent free for the last few years because we'd been partners in the LAPD back in the good old days before he got hit with a bullet and paralyzed from the waist down. Something I try not to think about too much because it was my fault. He lives in an old house he inherited from his grandmother about a quarter of a mile up the road from me, and as I passed it, I saw him sitting in the window. Sometimes he watched for me like that, just to make sure I made it home safely. He waved his arm, and I flashed my lights in answer. If I wasn't so late meeting Black, I'd stop and have a Heineken with him.

A couple of minutes later, I rounded the last curve on the road and caught sight of my house. I stomped the brakes so hard my Explorer did a sideways skid off the snow-slick road and knocked snow off a whole row of bushes. I blinked and stared through the wet snow plopping against my windshield. I wiped the inside of the glass with my hand and looked some more. Wait a minute, whoa, and what the hell? Then I saw Black come out of the huge, glassed-in front porch on my house and start striding down the road toward me. Only thing is, I don't have a huge, glassed-in front porch on my house. At least I didn't that morning when I left.

Black was wearing Levi's and a black cashmere sweater under a brown suede coat and heavy black leather snow boots that he'd picked up the last time he went skiing in Gstaad. That's in Switzerland. I know because I asked him. He's usually wearing expensive suits hand-tailored in Hong Kong and made out of rare yak hair or something, but it was snowing tonight so he dressed down for our date. He motioned for me to drive into the attached garage beside the huge, glassed-in front porch. I hadn't had the garage this morning, either.

I pulled my SUV inside, killed the engine, and then Black was there, opening the door for me. Did I mention that, despite all his wealth and fancy clothes, he was gentlemanly that way?

"Merry Christmas, Morgan." He had started calling me that because he disliked the habit I had of calling him Black. Sometimes he called me Claire, usually when we were in bed and pretty breathless.

"Who said you could do all this to my house?" Ungracious, true, but I was pretty damned shocked.

"Harve did. Said you'd love it but he wasn't sure you'd appreciate the surprise part."

"Well, I hate surprises."

"I like them. Come on, let me show you what I've done." Then he saw the puffy bruise on my cheek. "What the hell happened to your face?"

"Nothing. Just ran into a criminal type."

"Good God, Claire, it's your first day back."

"Yeah, bad things happen."

"How did it happen? Has a doctor looked at it?"

"Forget it. It's nothing, just a little bump." Then I climbed out of the car, looked around the garage, and cleverly changed the subject, "You're awfully smug about remodeling my entire house without my permission."

Black merely smiled and took my hand. "You're going to love it, trust me."

He led me to a white door that I suspected led into the new huge, glassed-in front room. When he hit a button beside the door, the garage door slid down behind us with a low, efficient purr. Hey, this meant no more scraping ice off windows in subzero weather, hallelujah and praise the Lord. I was suddenly a heck of a lot more gracious. I smiled, too, and to my embarrassment, felt a bit giddy.

"How in the world did you get all this done so fast? Jeez, I left here at seven this morning."

"Yes, it's amazing, all right, what you can accomplish with twenty carpenters, five electricians, and four plumbers, and a significant cash bonus to get the job done. Besides, you've been promising to get me a key to the front door and you haven't done it. So I got a front door I already have a key to."

"Okay, I admit it. This is pretty cool."

Black smiled. I smiled. We were a smiley couple tonight. My smile faded a little. The book I got him was going to look pretty damn lame, even if I put a big red bow on it. I could hear it now: What'd Black get you for Christmas, Claire? He remodeled my house and gave me a big glassed-in room with a garage and everything. What'd you get him? A book. My stomach dropped a bit. Black, on the other hand, was in his element.

"Close your eyes."

"C'mon, Black, give me a break here. You know I don't like playing games."

"Humor me."

I shut my eyes and let him lead me into his megasurprise. The filthy rich and their games, what's a poor girl to do?

"Okay, open your eyes and behold paradise."

I opened them and beheld paradise. "Good grief, Black."

The room was bigger than it looked from outside. Completely furnished, completely decorated down to the appropriate law enforcement and NRA gun magazines that I liked to read, and burning vanilla candles, and all in a single day, too. Beige carpet, brown suede sectional, a crackling fireplace, and oh, happy days, a hot tub, partitioned off with French doors, the kind that had little miniblinds inside the glass. Oh, man, did I ever love those doors with the miniblinds inside the glass. Dozens of candles were lit all around and the ones on the ledge behind the hot tub framed a view of my private cove through a curtain of gently falling snowflakes.

"Like it?"

"Are you frickin' kidding me?"

"Then take off your coat and let me see you." He unbuttoned my less-than-luxurious, weasely fur and gave my body a slow once-over. "My, you do look lovely in that outfit."

"You ought to like it. You bought it."

Black nodded. "Ah, yes, I remember that day well. Last summer, I believe it was, when I took you sightseeing in my favorite Louisiana swamp and you beat up this guy and then later we found our first corpse together? No wonder I'm so turned on." He grinned and carved all those damn dimples in his cheeks. His gaze dipped to my hooking togs again. "And the fishnet stockings and skunk fur are definitely eye-catching."

He slipped his arms around my waist and pulled me tightly against him. He was as warm as I was cold. "You're earlier than usual, only two hours late tonight."

"Sorry, couldn't be helped. A missing person came in."

"You're ice cold. Go change into something warm. I brought in dinner, and it's still warm."

"Chef Pierre from the hotel, huh?"

"I don't cook except on special occasions."

"This seems pretty special to me."

"You bet it is. It's been almost five months since you

frisked and handcuffed me the first time. Tonight can be our first-time-you-arrested-me anniversary."

"It's still a bit extravagant, even for such a momentous occasion." So what if I've grown to using bigger words since I met Black.

"There's more." Black handed me a long silver remote. "This controls everything. The hot tub, the TV, garage door, alarm system, computer, Internet access, fireplace."

"You got me an alarm system?"

"Yeah."

"I'm an armed officer of the law."

"With lots of enemies."

True, a plethora of them. See, what I mean about the big words. I looked around. "What? No unfolding bed and dimmed lights like Doris Day did for Rock Hudson in *Pillow Talk*?" Black and I had watched that old movie late the other night on the 13-inch TV in my bedroom loft. He'd asked me if I had any binoculars so he could see the screen.

"That's where I got the idea to put a new bed upstairs. I'll unfold it myself. Ditto with the lights."

"You got me a new bed?

"I got *us* a new bed, yes."

"King-size, right?"

"California king-size. I can't sleep in that barracks cot you call a bed. Not without a killer backache in the morning. Where'd you get that thing anyway? A garage sale at a monastery?"

"Black, I really appreciate this, I really do, but you've gotta quit getting me expensive gifts. It's making me feel funny."

"This is the only big thing I've ever given you, and it's an early Christmas present, but okay, fine. If it makes you uncomfortable, this'll be it. No more gifts."

That's Black for you. Using all his fancy degrees in psychology, never arguing with me, just killing me with kindness.

Black said, "Let's eat, I'm starving. And tell me about

your day. You know, how many men you enticed into sin with that hot body of yours and then threw into jail, stuff like that."

"Let me get changed, then I'll tell you about all my new boyfriends now languishing behind bars."

Upstairs, I found a huge bed that took up most of the loft. It was covered with a luxurious gold satin comforter that looked soft enough to sink to the floor in. I suspected there were black silk sheets underneath. Black liked gold-and-black decor, almost to the point of absurdity, but he had those silk sheets on the bed at his place and they felt like heaven so I wasn't going to argue that point.

I took a quick shower, washed my hair, dressed in Levi's and a black sweater, not cashmere but Wal-Mart chenille, just so we'd be the Olsen twins, then I actually combed my short blond hair and brushed my teeth with orange-flavored Crest. Black's influence, I guess, but I drew the line at lipstick. I am not a makeup kind of woman. I stood at the top of the stairs looking down at my new huge, glassed-in front room and couldn't believe it was mine. When I reached the bottom of the steps, Black handed me a glass of white wine. I wished it was a bottle of Coors as I followed him to a new teak dining table with four matching swivel chairs upholstered in brick-red Ultrasuede. I do love swivel chairs. I do love brick-red Ultrasuede.

"You gotta stop doing this kind of stuff for me. I'm serious now, Black. This isn't your way of putting a brand on me, is it?"

"I'm not the type to brand things." He sounded miffed.

"What about all your monogrammed shirts and cufflinks? And what about the big brass *B* on the gates outside all your houses?"

"Well, that's different."

"We've talked about this before, you know. Let's just take things slow, get to know each other, don't redecorate each other's homes, et cetera."

"You don't like it?"

"Of course, I like it. Who wouldn't? But it seems sort of much for the length of time we've been dating. Sort of extravagant, I guess." Sort of?

"I've been spending more time waiting around here for you than I have at home, so I added a few amenities. What's the harm in that? It's a Christmas present, nothing more, nothing less. Tell me about your missing-person case."

He was good at changing the subject on purpose, too, but I didn't mind. The truth was, I was delighted with the improvements on my shabby little A-frame, which now resembled Elizabeth Taylor's Swiss chalet. Maybe it's in Gstaad, too. Maybe she and Black are neighbors and borrow cups of sugar and stuff like that. But the book I bought for him still seems plenty crappy, even if it was a full-price hardback. I was going to have to find something else to put with it. Maybe some stocking stuffers. Maybe a deodorizer pine tree to hang on the rearview mirror of one of his Mercedes.

Black said, "Who's your missing person?"

"His name is Simon Classon, and he works out at the Dome of the Cave Academy for the Gifted. Ever heard of it?"

"Yes. I'm on the advisory board there."

That captured my attention. "No way."

Black rocked back in his chair. "Yeah, for about four years. I know Rich Johnstone a little. He's the director. It's a charitable tax deduction."

I watched him retrieve two dinners in white carryout boxes from the new microwave oven that I hadn't noticed until then. But Black didn't do carryout from McDonald's or Wendy's, like us regular folk. His came from his very own four-star restaurant, Five Cedars. "Caesar salad and coconut shrimp, and caramel cheesecake for dessert. Sound good?"

Suddenly my stomach remembered that I hadn't fed it all day. It complained with a good rendition of a runaway freight train. "Coconut shrimp's my favorite. And I kill for cheesecake." I picked up my fork with not a little relish and watering of the mouth. "You know this Simon guy, by any chance?"

"Nope. What's he do at the academy?"

"He's the chief angelologist and suspected resident dealer of campus drugs."

He stopped eating and stared at me. He has the bluest eyes this side of Sweden. Not just blue, but rich and deep and azure. They looked real warm and cuddly right now, but I've also seen them when they looked icy enough to freeze me to my chair. That was back last summer when I was accusing him of murdering people, but I haven't been accusing him of anything much lately. No, lately we've been pretty much hitting the hot-and-heavy-affair description. Told you that I LIKE him.

Black tore me off a hunk of crusty French bread and dropped it on my plate. My manners were beginning to rub off on him, I guess. "Angelologist?"

"That's right. He teaches classes about angels and seraphim. And he's got a website, too, where he sells angelgrams to the unwary among us."

"Yeah, who doesn't nowadays?"

"Sell angelgrams or have a website?" Black ignored my wit and forked up a bite of shrimp. I followed his lead and found it fantastic. I dug into my gourmet food without further ado. I preferred fast food, but gourmet wasn't so bad in a pinch.

Black was enjoying his fare, too. He always waited to dine with me, no matter how late I showed up. Secretly, I thought that was pretty cool of him. Most men I knew put their stomachs first. Bud and Harve, for instance.

"Yeah, and guess what else we found? A stash of coke under his kitchen cabinet hidden in a bunch of cobwebs."

"If he's a dealer, I guess you suspect foul play?"

I nodded. "There was blood spatter in his foyer, and it looks like an angel doorstop was the assault weapon. Shaggy's got it now. We'll know more tomorrow. He's comparing a hair he found on the doorstop to some in Classon's hairbrush."

Black said, "How about calling up the website and checking it out?"

"I'd love to. I was planning to go over to your place later and use your computer."

"See. I knew you could use this stuff. It'll help you with your cases and keep me from getting bored while I wait for you to drag in hours late every night."

"Alas, the penalty one pays for dating a cop."

"Ah, but the positives far outweigh the negatives. I'll show you all the benefits of a California king-size bed later."

"Looking forward to it, but again I say, you've overdone it this time."

Black ignored me. He pretty much ignored anything we disagree on. If we didn't argue about it, it didn't exist. He is a famous forensic psychiatrist, did I mention that? Writes books, and everything. He helped me on my last case, once I finally proved to myself he wasn't the serial killer I was after. Truth is, he can be pretty helpful sometimes. Like now.

At the touch of a button, the television came on. It was one of those flat kinds that hang on the wall, I forget what you call them. Plasma, maybe? Never checked them out because I never expected to be dating a moneybags. He had placed it over my new fieldstone fireplace. I guess it looked better there than a moose head. He showed me how to connect to the Internet provider and asked me the name of Classon's website.

"callupanangel.com."

"Cute." A minute later Classon's picture bloomed up on the opening page surrounded by a border of flying angels hoisting flaming swords. He was an attractive man but his features were a little too effeminate for him to be called handsome. It was hard for me to guess how old he was; he looked anywhere between thirty and fifty. He definitely had on eyeliner and lipstick and his hair was dyed Ronald McDonald red and cut in a shoulder-length bob. He had on the black half-glasses I'd found on his bed. He had a nice

smile. I didn't detect any wings or glowing halos or di-
aphanous white robes about his person.

"You sure this guy's a man?"

I knew he was thinking about last summer, but I didn't
want to think about that case right now, not so close to bedtime, a.k.a. nightmareville.

"His neighbor intimated that he might be a girly man."

"I'd say she's right on."

"Yeah. This is stacking up to be a weird case."

Black said, "Want to order an angelgram? It's a steal at
eighty bucks. I'll put it in your stocking."

"I would if he was around to call up his angel buddies.
What does it say about his background?"

Black moved the cursor and clicked on a small box that
said "Bio." The screen flashed, and he read aloud. "Simon
Classon was born in South Africa, the only child of a hus-
band/wife missionary team. Came back and grew up here in
Missouri." We skimmed the screen together and found that
both of his parents were dead. No siblings. No other family.
Classon was alone in this world. "Went to school at the University of Missouri–Columbia. Got a master's degree there
in comparative religions."

"Wonder where he learned to talk to the angels? He's got
archangels on speed dial, you know."

"I'm in the mood to talk to some angels myself," Black
said, switching off the set and giving me a look I've come to
know rather well. "What do you want to try out first? Our
new hot tub or our new bed? You choose. Either one's okay
by me."

"Hot tub," I said. "It'll relax us, and all that."

"Yeah, and all that." Black smiled and jerked his sweater
off over his head. I took a moment and admired his six-foot-
three-inch physique of hard-packed muscles and tanned
skin. I smiled and pulled my sweater off over my head. He
grinned and admired my big ugly meat-cleaver scar. A sort
of tit-for-tat kind of thing.

The hot tub turned out to be hot and bubbly and romantic with the smell of vanilla and the feel of warm, slick skin. The California king-size bed turned out to be big and soft and comfortable, and after some very slow and pleasurable lovemaking, I fell asleep snuggled in Black's arms, wrapped in those silky black sheets he insists upon. What can I say, the guy's not too bad to hang around with.

FIVE

I was pretty much dead to the world when the phone chirped at five a.m. the next morning. I rolled out of Black's arms and onto my side, slightly disoriented by the sheer magnitude of the bed. I rolled some more and reached the opposite shore. I snatched up my cell phone and said a groggy hello but the phone kept up with the parakeet tweets.

"That's mine," Black mumbled, reaching for one of the three private cell phones he toted around, black, gold, and red, no less. Indeed, the two of us had an abundance of phones and phone numbers. I'd come to learn, however, that a call like this on Black's red cellular usually meant an emergency. It's the number he'd given to me, and to his family in Louisiana, who, I had learned the hard way, had a few Mafia connections, but, hey, some godfathers have okay brothers, too. I sat up on my side of the bed, and then rose, shivered, and pulled on my old red fleece robe, and walked to the wrought-iron wall edging my bedroom loft.

Like Oprah over Lake Michigan, I gazed down upon my new and huge front room with its wall of decorative, arched windows and beheld a world cloaked in pristine white, everything in the world outside frosty and glazed, and covered by a good foot or more of snow. The lake looked inky and frigid and deep, and somehow sinister in the stark black-and-white tableau.

Then again, it was a beautiful sight to behold the first thing in the morning, the proverbial winter wonderland, and my initial irk at Black's remodeling efforts was fading fast. In fact, I felt a certain amount of glee welling inside me. I picked up the upstairs all-purpose remote—yes, Black had provided two of the state-of-the-art clickers, so I'd never have to run downstairs to change the plasma's channel, I guess. I pushed the button for the fireplace and below, gas logs burst into roaring flames. I smiled and felt like Paris Hilton. All I needed was a little dog that looked like a rat and wore Versace.

Black was still listening to the person at the other end. I knew the matter was ultraserious when he said, in that slight, incriminating tone of annoyance he did so well, "And you are telling me that nobody there is capable of dealing with this?"

I'd heard that tone a couple of times myself, even though we were still in the honeymoon stage of our relationship and he knew better than to condescend to me too openly. I suspected the employee at the other end was doing some fairly fast dancing to soften Black's aforementioned show of ire. Then Black said, resigned but still overtly peeved, "All right. Order the Lear fueled and I'll be there as soon as I can."

I watched him flip the cell phone shut. He turned and faced me. His hair was mussed, a small strand actually sticking up in front, which I can tell you didn't happen often, not with Black's wont for celebrity barbers. I found it endearing and wished I had a Polaroid camera to prove he had an imperfect moment now and again. Like everybody else, he had human hair that got messed up when he slept on it. I had begun to wonder. Like Bud, he looked perfect most of the time. I resisted the urge to smooth it down. I also resisted the urge to dive back into bed with him for some more lively amorous gymnastics. Guess mussed hair turns me on.

Instead, I returned his serious expression and said, "Good morning. Or is it?"

"It's not." He stood up, splayed his fingers, and ran them back through all that thick black hair, thus fixing the mussed problem, so I admired his great physique some more while he pulled on an expensive black flannel robe. He'd brought me one like it, too, but I preferred trusty Old Red. "I've got to go to Paris. An emergency with a patient."

"Paris? You mean, like in France?" I wasn't expecting that. Who gets a call to go off to Paris at five o'clock in the morning? Name one person, other than Colin Powell or Condoleezza Rice, maybe.

"Yeah. Paris, the one in France." Black walked around the giant bed, which took some time, sat down, and pulled me onto his lap. He squeezed me close, and I put my arms around his neck with my cheek against his hair. "Come with me, Claire. We'll spend Christmas together in Paris. I'd love to show you the city." When I didn't snatch that bait right off the hook, he got more creative with the incentive package. "How about midnight mass at Notre Dame Cathedral, and then Christmas brunch at the Jules Verne on the Eiffel Tower?"

That Black. He gives new meaning to jet-setting, champagne wishes, and caviar dreams. I, on the other hand, went Ford Explorer–setting and had five-percent-beer dreams, or just plain nightmares. I attempted to explain my reluctance. "I can't just take off on the spur of the moment, Black. You know that. This new missing-person case just came up, and besides, it doesn't sound like much fun spending Christmas alone in some ritzy French hotel doing nothing while you take care of patients."

"I've got an apartment off the Champs Elysées that you'd find very comfortable."

But of course he did, silly me. "Oh, yeah. I guess you've got apartments all over the world just in case, don't you?" The remark sounded sarcastic, yes, and I wondered why it had come out that way. Black donned his benign look of an-

noyed indulgence, as he tended to do when I nixed his plans
or needled him a bit, but he remained steadfastly patient.
Not many in the world of Nicholas Black ever even attempted to thwart his wishes, but he was getting used to my
backbone, I guess.

He said, "No, I don't keep apartments everywhere, only
in cities where I have private clinics." He scrutinized me momentarily, but I refused to squirm. "Didn't you tell me Charlie ordered you to ease back into work? I understood yesterday's
sting was supposed to be it for a couple of weeks."

Uh-oh, here came the single biggest bone of contention
between us since we became an item last summer, but it was
quite a big bone, T.-rex femur, as a matter of fact. Black had
this ridiculous notion that I should up and fly off with him on
his deluxe private jet whenever he snapped his fingers. I'd
done it a few times when I was out on medical leave and had
a bunch of casts on, but now I was healed up and back on the
job and he knew that.

"I wish I could." I was equally diplomatic, and sort of
slightly meant it, because he *was* offering Christmas in Paris,
after all, and Black did know how to show a girl a good time.
He looked encouraged, so I skillfully changed the subject as
I'd learned to do in such instances. "How long's this trip
going to take? You'll be back by Christmas, right?" After all,
I did have a book and some as-of-yet-undisclosed stocking
stuffer to wow him with, come December 25.

"I don't know. It's just a week 'til Christmas Eve. I'll try
to make it back before that, if you're absolutely determined
not to go with me." Yes, absolutely was pretty much the right
word. We stared at each other, both realizing Christmas by
oneself could get lonely. Black was nothing if not valiant.
"Can't Bud handle this case by himself for a week or two?
Maybe the guy will show up on his own. I could throw in a
couple of tickets to *Swan Lake* at the Bastille."

Swan Lake at the Bastille? Jeez, that really tempted me
not to go. But how would he know that I'd rather have a couple of root canals than sit through a ballet with dancers

dressed up like big, tiptoeing white birds? Also, I was not used to somebody making demands on my time, even polite ones, but Black wasn't really being overly pushy and demanding. I'd been single too long, I guess. Fiercely independent. In control of my destiny. I didn't want to hurt his feelings. I wanted to go with him, kind of. I felt uncomfortable, pulled in two directions, and the old suffocation dropped down on me, the way it had when my late ex-husband tried to control my every move. I'd vowed a long time ago never to let that happen again. Not even with Nicholas Black, who had definitely wormed his way deep into my LIKE.

Black, being a shrink and therefore, a master of perception, read my hesitation in right-on fashion. "Okay, so be it. I know how much you've been looking forward to getting back to work. I'll go alone, but I'm going to miss you."

See? Sometimes this guy just makes me melt into mush. I considered reneging on my decision, because truth be told, Bud *could* probably handle the Simon Classon case just fine. And who knows? The angelologist just might've already turned up and at this very moment could be snuggled and snoring in his little angel bed in his little angel house. Or, not. Then I remembered again Black was a crack psychiatrist and could very well be playing the old reverse-psychology trick on me.

My cell phone picked that moment to chime in with the *Mexican Hat Dance*, no sissy bird chirps for me, and I grabbed it before the second stanza. Two calls before 5:15 A.M.; we're a real popular duo today.

Bud's voice. Gruff, sleepy, excited. "We got a body that might be Classon's."

Adrenaline punched through me, blood sang through my veins, happy as a Disney tune. I left Black's lap in a hurry and paced while I talked. "It's a homicide, then?"

"Don't know yet."

"Where'd they find him?"

I watched Black shake his head. He did not look thrilled.

He said, nope, muttered, "Well, that kisses Paris good-bye." He got up and headed for the bathroom. A minute later the shower came on.

Bud said, "Somewhere out around that school he works at. One of the instructors slid off in a ditch last night, and when the wrecker showed up this mornin', they found a corpse in the woods. How long's it gonna take you to get ready?"

"Five, ten minutes tops."

"Put on somethin' warm. It's freakin' freezin' out there."

I was out of my robe and into jeans and a black turtleneck before the line went dead. I pulled on a clean gray sweatshirt with SHERIFF DEPARTMENT on the front in glow-in-the-dark yellow, pumped with excitement at getting back to work in earnest. I do love my job, even in snow and ice and frigid weather and Christmas traffic. As I sat down and pulled on thermal socks and worn black-leather combat boots, I heard Black brushing his teeth. Now I had a legitimate excuse not to go to Gay Paree and mingle with all the French America-phobes. Besides that, my book for him would look even more paltry on top of the Eiffel Tower with all those sparkling Christmas lights and panoramic views of the Seine River. The pirouetting swans would have to live without me, too.

Black was back, hair combed, wearing a cream-colored sweater and denim jeans, smelling like Irish Spring soap, alert and ready to jet. "I take it they found that guy you're looking for?"

"They found a body they think might be Classon. Bud'll be here any minute."

"Was he murdered?" Black was into murders, too. Big-time. Gave him fodder for the forensic psychiatry cases he dealt with when he wasn't busy playing shrink to Hollywood stars and abused political wives. Nick Black, Man of Many Talents. Plus some.

"Not sure yet, but it looks like it."

"Guess that means I'm headed to Paris solo."

I picked up my badge and dropped the chain around my

neck, then retrieved my well-worn leather shoulder holster from the bedside table. "Yep, sorry, maybe I can tag along with you next time."

"I'll hold you to that, Morgan."

While he finished dressing, I threw some cold water on my face and brushed my teeth, then retrieved my 9mm Glock from underneath my pillow. Since my last case, the hair-raising, *Hellraiser*-ish one, I prefer to sleep with my weapon. Black doesn't mind because he was there last summer, so he sleeps with a loaded gun nearby, too. Legal, of course, since Missouri enacted its new concealed-weapons law. He carried one before that, too, but I chose to overlook it. Black watched me strap on my shoulder holster and slide the Glock snugly into its bed. I secured the snap, and no longer felt naked.

"Man, what is it that's so damn sexy about a woman wearing a shoulder holster?"

"Maybe if you're a good boy, I'll wear it to bed when you get back."

"Good God, Claire, give me a break. It's hard enough to take off without that image dancing in my head."

We laughed together but waited to say our good-byes downstairs in my huge, glassed-in front porch, which looked even more huge and glassed-in in the light of day. We had two or three minutes tops before Bud arrived, so we took full advantage of it with lots of rubbing around and kissing and touching and heavy breathing. When Bud's white Bronco nosed around the bend, Black stepped back. "Okay, I'm out of here. Be safe. Duck and weave, and all that."

That was Black's way of telling me to be careful, sort of an inside joke. He grabbed an aluminum travel mug with the Cedar Bend Lodge logo, filled it with coffee, pulled on his heavy black parka, and headed for his slick Cobalt 360 cabin cruiser docked in all its magnificence at the end of my teensy-weensy dock. He just loved to speed across the lake in the Cobalt when he came to call because it cut off about twenty minutes' driving time around the jagged, hilly shoreline. I downed some coffee myself and watched him wave one arm at Bud before he climbed into the cabin cruiser, fired it up, and eased it expertly away from the dock. He was going to have one helluva cold trip back to his heliport at Cedar Bend Lodge.

About a minute later, Bud was outside leaning on the horn, and I slipped on my department-issue brown parka, checked to make sure my gloves were still in the pockets, poured out a couple more aluminum travel mugs of hot black coffee, and headed outside. It was daylight now but overcast with an angry, gunmetal sky threatening even more snow. The wintry air hit me as I stepped out onto the front porch, bracing and invigorating, but not as cold as I'd expected. My breath smoked out in front of me and snow, unblemished but for Black's boot tracks, squeaked underfoot as I negotiated the front steps. I suddenly realized that I felt great, on top of the world, but maybe that's because I had on warm clothes, my Glock was loaded and back under my left arm where it belonged, and I was on the job full-time. Smiling, I slid into the passenger seat and presented Bud with his java.

He took it gratefully, looked askance at me, and said, "Don't tell me. Those crazy TV people from *While You Were Out* came calling on you last night and left you a big room with lots of fancy windows on the front of your cabin?"

I sipped my coffee. Nonchalant. "Nope. Black's Christmas present. Gave it to me early."

"I hope to hell he's got me down on his list somewhere."

"He'll probably just give you a big boat or a Jaguar or something. He doesn't know you that well yet."

"Maybe I'll invite him out for beer and wings." Bud had the Bronco in four-wheel drive and backed up over my icy driveway and maneuvered a U-turn without a single skid. He was better at winter driving now than he'd been when he'd first moved up north from Atlanta. He pulled the gearshift down into drive. "Yep, wish the doc had a rich sister I could date. I've been wantin' a new house, too."

"Have they positively identified Classon yet?"

"Nope. Said the body's hanging from a tree limb."

That got my attention. "Suicide?"

"Dunno. Uniforms're waiting for us to show before they cut him down. Said we need to get the victim out of the tree before kids start comin' out of the dorms across the road and buildin' snowmen. Apparently, the body was left in sight of the school."

"Great, that's all we need. A bunch of hysterical teenagers converging on the crime scene and staring up at their favorite dead teacher. The media would love a few pics like that. C'mon, let's get going. We shouldn't hit any major traffic this early and with these road conditions."

"Snowplows are out clearin' the roads. Man, I bet there's thirteen, fourteen inches on the ground."

"Yeah, Buckeye and his crime scene guys aren't going to like getting out in this stuff."

"Maybe the perp left footprints that we can follow straight to his house, we nail him, then we go to IHOP for breakfast."

"Sure, and maybe aliens will take us to Venus, too."

Bud concentrated on driving, certainly a tricky affair for a homegrown Georgian, and when we rolled past Harve's place, gray smoke already drifted lazily from his chimney. I had a fireplace now, too. Jeez. I never thought I'd have a fireplace of my very own. Or a plasma TV. Or a hot tub. Or a man like Black wanting me to go to Paris with him. Miracles do happen, I guess, and they were hitting me like manna from heaven.

The Angel Gabriel

In the deep woods where the orphan boy walked behind the Angel Gabriel, it was shady and cool and quiet with lush green ferns and lots of underbrush and baby trees, all dappled and dancing with sunshine. Spiderwebs hung suspended between tree branches everywhere, and looked pretty and sparkled like great nets of silver silk. He avoided them as he trailed his new friend, their feet crackling through layers of dead, brown leaves. When they reached a wide, rushing stream, its clear water gurgling and splashing over flat brown rocks, they sat down together to rest on the bank and dipped up water in their open palms.

"There's some great big fish in this little river, kid, smallmouth bass and catfish, too. I'll teach you how to catch them if you want me to. I like to catch things, you know, trap them alive. I've gotten lots of frogs and lizards, chipmunks, too, and other stuff like that, right along here. I get 'em for my experiments."

"What do you mean, experiments, Angel Gabriel?"

Gabriel turned to him, then he smiled and shook his head. His yellow curls shivered around his face. "Now you gotta quit calling me that, okay? I told you I ain't no angel."

"Okay, but you sure do look like one."

"I wish. Archangels are pretty cool, you know. Especially the one named Uriel. He's an archangel, like Gabriel. It's just that more people know about Gabriel, is all. You know there's seven archangels, but some Bible scholars think there's even more than that?"

"What's an archangel anyways?"

"They're the angels that do God's good work for him. Dad says only four of 'em are really in the Bible. Gabriel's the messenger that came down and talked to the Virgin Mary and the shepherds in the field, and all that. Michael's sort of an avenger kind of angel that cast Satan out of heaven, and let me tell you, we don't never, ever want to ever mess with the Archangel Michael or he'll smite us dead right where we stand. He's the most powerful of all of 'em and the boss over all the other archangels. He's got special people he blesses, too, and we aren't gonna ever mess with them either, you hear?"

The orphan nodded but the idea of Archangel Michael coming down and smiting him with a sword was about the scariest thing he'd ever heard. He looked up at the sky but didn't see anything on fire and headed at him, just the pretty green leaves tossing in the wind.

The Angel Gabriel said, "Uriel's my favorite angel, though, 'cause Dad says he's the "Fire of God." He stands at the Gates of Eden and holds a fiery sword so nobody can get to the Tree of Knowledge, and he warned Noah about the Flood, and things like that. And he's in command of thunder and terror, and stuff. Best of all, he watches over hell."

"Wow. Wish I was like Uriel."

"Well, I can call you Uriel if you want. We can have some secret names that only we know about. You can be Uriel and I'll be Gabriel, okay?" The orphan smiled with pleasure and decided he liked having secrets. He'd never had any before, and it was fun!

Gabriel smiled. "C'mon, now, I've got some traps set

down in my special fishing hole. Let's go see if I caught anything. Take off your shoes and socks, and we'll wade."

Uriel followed obediently, and the cold water felt wonderful against his hot feet. The bottom was sandy and felt soft, and minnows darted this way and that in little silver streaks. A few yards upstream, a fallen log had dammed up the water in a big, deep pool with a little waterfall trickling over the top.

"This here's my favorite place. I keep most my traps here. I dammed it up all by myself." Gabriel squatted down, reached up under the logs, and pulled out a glass cage. A thick brown snake coiled up on the bottom.

"Look here, kid, I caught myself a great big water moccasin. You ain't afraid of snakes, are you?"

Uriel hadn't seen a snake up close before, but he shook his head and tried not to look petrified.

"Well, they ain't gonna hurt you, if you don't hurt them first. I like snakes a lot. I got a whole collection of them in my secret hideout. I like all the creatures out here in the woods. They're my friends. They'll be your friends, too, as long as you stick by me."

"I'll stick by you forever, Gabriel. I like snakes and other animals, too."

Smiling, Gabriel reached down and ruffled Uriel's hair. Uriel grinned, pleased, hoping Gabriel could be like his older brother.

"He's still alive, Uriel. Let's take him home, and I'll show you some more snakes."

They waded in the rippling water until they reached the top of the hill. Gabriel stopped and pointed down to the hollow below. Overgrown with vines and bushes, and hidden in the trees, Uriel could just make out an old, dilapidated building.

"Know what that used to be, kid?"

"Uh-uh."

"An old hunting and fishing lodge, you know, sorta like a

motel. It's been rotting out here for years. Hunters and fishermen used to drive down here outta St. Louis and Kansas City until they closed the place up. Nobody ever comes round here anymore." Gabriel looked down at Uriel. "But me and you. It's all ours, and nobody's gonna ever know what we do back here."

"Kind of like a secret clubhouse?"

"You're a smart kid, ain't ya? Nobody knows about this place but me. Your grandma owns it, I think, but since your daddy left home, nobody even remembers about this old lodge."

Most of the doors in the lodge hung askew on the hinges. Rusted metal bedsprings were in rooms with broken windows and sweet-smelling honeysuckle vines twining up to the open rafters. One room had a big gray nest buzzing with hornets.

Uriel smiled, pleased to have his awesome new friend. He'd learn to find his way through the woods from his grandma's house and hang out in Gabriel's secret hideout. The bullies from the church wouldn't bother him out here in the woods, not with Gabriel around to protect him.

SIX

Once we reached State Highway W, we headed north and found the entire county buried under enormous mounds of snow. It looked to me like pictures of the Sahara Desert after a giant sandstorm. But the snowplows were out in force, scraping the roads so people could get back to maniacal Christmas shopping. But with such a heavy snowfall, public schools would probably get out for the day. Bud made good time, considering the adverse conditions, but it didn't really matter. We were too late to save Simon Classon. His killer was long gone, but that didn't mean we wouldn't get him.

The snowdrifts were awesome. Great, hulking mountains alongside the roads, mounded up tree trunks and banked against some homes nearly to the eaves. Only the lake remained uncovered and black. No boats buzzing about. Black had the water to himself today.

The Dome of the Cave Academy for the Gifted was north of Buck Creek near a little place called Rocky Mount, so we took rural gravel roads down through dense woods for about twenty minutes before we came to the school's entrance gate. It was pretty hard to miss with a great log archway branded with the academy's wordy name in scorched black letters. Through the snowy woods, we could see some school buildings off to the right, rough-hewn log buildings with dark-green metal roofs, all very rustic but with a modern twist. They formed a quadrangle, in the middle of which sat a little white church with a steeple. It didn't look to me like anyone was up and stirring, at least not outside on the grounds.

About sixty yards ahead we spotted a couple of brown sheriff patrol cars, and a big neon green wrecker emblazoned with RUSHIN'S TOWING SERVICE painted in white on the side. We pulled up behind the truck and were met by two deputies. I was glad to see it wasn't Connie O'Hara on call today. Traipsing around on slick ice did not go well with pregnancy. Instead, Pete Hancock and David Obion, two of our new recruits, had taken the dawn call. Both were in their early twenties, and sometimes made me feel old. They had strung yellow crime-scene tape among the trees edging the road. It stretched out into the woods a good distance from their vehicles.

I asked Hancock. "What you got so far?"

He was bundled up, a big, muscular guy who lifted weights fanatically and looked like a hulking linebacker in his bulky parka. He had intelligent dark eyes and skin, clean-shaven but for a bushy Tom Selleck/Magnum mustache. His cheeks were flushed red from exposure to the cold air, and he kept licking winter-cracked lips.

Obion was stamping his feet and rubbing his gloved hands together. He was taller and leaner and was an all-around serious kind of guy. He constantly asked questions about police procedure, by the book and all that. He carried a sheriff's department manual with him at all times. All I could see was his face and brown eyes, the same exact color of Kraft caramels, looking out from inside the tight drawstring of his black fur hood. That reminded me to pull up my own hood. Our breaths steamed in and out with each word uttered and hurt our lungs if we inhaled too deeply.

It seemed unnaturally quiet, but somewhere in that snow-muffled, silent woods, an angelologist was hanging cold and dead from a tree limb. Obion pointed a gloved finger out through the trees and said, "The body's straight through there, in that big oak tree yonder."

I said, "Anybody else been inside the perimeter?"

"No ma'am, I taped it off myself. The scene's intact."

Bud said, "The wrecker guy go in to see if the vic was alive?"

Hancock shook his head. "They knew he was dead the minute the headlights lit him up. Look; see for yourself."

We followed the two officers down a slight incline, where a vehicle had slid off the road and landed on its side in the snowbank. Three of us negotiated the icy terrain successfully, but Bud immediately slipped and slid down the hill on his back. But what do you expect? He's Atlanta-born. While he cursed rather impressively and brushed himself off, I examined the wrecked vehicle. It was a brand-new, Sonic-blue Ford mustang convertible that no doubt wished it lived in Miami with other models that went topless. I made a mental note to check out who was in the car and when the accident had been called in. Could have been the perp trying to get away in a big hurry; stranger things had happened. I said as much to Hancock.

"Could be right. Belongs to some guy who works over at the academy. The guys in the tow truck said he walked back to the school and stayed the night after his car turned over on his way home. He called them this morning to pull him out. We told them to hold off until crime scene finishes with the car."

"Good job. Tell you what, Hancock. Contact the school and request that any staff still on the premises be ready for interviews sometime this morning. We'll go over there after we secure the body and finish with the crime scene."

"Right."

Hancock and Obion turned and trudged with great, deep footsteps back toward their vehicles.

"There's Classon. Man alive, look at him." Bud was

pointing up into the tree limbs, and I followed his gaze to a five-foot-diameter oak tree, standing stark and black against the gray sky, its massive branches coated with about six inches of snow.

Thirty feet up, suspended from the fork of two big limbs, hung a large black trash bag. Although it was crusted with snow, we could see a human head protruding from the top, the trash bag's bright yellow drawstring handles tied around the victim's neck in a big, droopy bow. From our vantage point the face looked bluish and frozen, like a face trapped under a sheet of ice. If it was Simon Classon, he wasn't smiling like in the picture Black had pulled up on his website. It looked like the killer had tied a red ski rope around his neck to hang him and secure him to the limb. A square of silver duct tape covered his mouth.

The shiver that shot over my flesh had nothing to do with the freezing temperature. Visions of my last case stabbed my mind, lots of silver duct tape on lots of nude women, and worst of all, the deep, visceral fear I felt when a screech of duct tape was torn off to bind me to a bed. A swift, internal shake sent those ghosts back into the dark. All that was over and done with; the killer locked up tight in a hospital for the criminally insane. More comforting was the fact that Black checked with the doctor every week, just to make sure we didn't have to watch our backs. Still, we both kept guns under our pillows and awoke sweating and trembling from nightmares. No sir, this was somebody else entirely. Another monster slithering up from the dark places to wreak havoc on the innocent and unsuspecting.

"There aren't any footprints leading in, Bud. He got him up there before the snow started."

"Yeah. Good God, look at the blood frozen to his head. He was alive and still bleedin' when the perp hung him. I reckon he was assaulted in his front hall, then transported alive out here for some sick reason."

Simon Classon's head tilted to one side, and blood had

run down from his head wound and frozen into an eight-inch blood icicle that protruded off his temple. Snow had formed a cap atop the red hair on the other side of his head and looked as if he wore a jaunty white beret.

I said, "What'd you make of the perp putting the body in a trash bag?"

"Hell if I know. So the bears don't eat him?" Bud, at his most amusing. But he wasn't smiling. Neither was I.

"Why would the perp care if the body was scattered? You think he wanted us to find Classon intact?"

Bud shrugged. He was chewing Juicy Fruit. "Maybe we'll find out when we see what's he's done to the vic inside that bag."

"Right." Another involuntary shudder. Not sure I wanted to know what the black plastic hid, I said, "Okay, now we've got to figure out how to get the body down without corrupting the scene. Buckeye'll be here soon with his team. You think we can get him down with the wrecker's winch?"

Bud shook his head. "Won't reach. Maybe we oughta call a fire truck out here with a rescue basket. If the perp left anything behind, it'll be under the snow cover, anyway. Let's get some pictures around the base of the tree, then the truck can back in close enough to reach him. Buckeye'll have to go up first and get his photos of the body before we bring him down."

"Get Buck on the phone, Bud. See what his ETA is and then call the fire department. I want Classon down ASAP and out of sight of the school."

It took us a while to search the perimeter for footprints or other evidence, of which we found nada, of course, then Bud and I huddled in his Bronco with the heater on full blast until the coroner showed up. Bud found a doughnut on the floor that had fallen out of the box a few days ago, brushed it off, and polished it off for breakfast. He was fastidious as hell in his attire and personal grooming, but when he was hungry, he overlooked things like dirt and contamination. However, it did happen to be a cake Krispy Kreme with pecans on top, so I took the petrified chunk he offered me and dunked it in my coffee to soften it up.

About twenty minutes later, Buckeye's crime-scene van pulled up, followed closely by a rumbling Canton County fire truck. When I got out into the cold to meet them, the sky was roiling and boiling with more mottled gray clouds, raring to dump another foot or two of snow on the lake.

Buckeye Boyd was our medical examiner and coroner, and pretty much looked like Captain Kangaroo on that old kiddie show, but without his buddy, Mr. Greenjeans, hanging around the house grinning. Buck liked to fish; in other words, he had fanatical bass-fishing tendencies. He had an entire room in his house devoted to tall, shiny bass-fishing trophies, and about 600 rods and reels and multicolor plastic worms. He also gave one awesome fish fry for the sheriff's department on the last day of August. He was excellent at his job and hadn't made a mistake that lost a case in the ten years he'd been in charge.

"Hell, I thought we were in for some peace and quiet after all that shit last summer," he said. He drank some coffee out of the Minit Stop Styrofoam cup he was holding. The luscious smell of vanilla cappuccino drifted to me.

My good friend, twenty-something John Becker, a.k.a. Shaggy, Shag, or Shag Man, brought up the rear. He was hatless, gloveless, and drinking from a forty-six-ounce cup of Mello Yello in ice, which pretty much sums him up. But a criminalist extraordinaire he truly is. If there was one shred of evidence left behind at a crime scene, he'd sniff it out. He grinned.

"'S'up, Claire? This case oughta be just what you need to get yourself all warmed up and back in the saddle."

"I'm pretty much up to speed already. Was the star of a prostitution sting last night."

"Crap! You mean I missed you wearin' those Daisy Dukes and fishnets? Damn, why didn't Bud call me like usual? That where you got that bruise?"

I nodded, but Buckeye ignored Shaggy's levity and squinted from snow glare as he examined the snow-laden branches above them. "Well, this one should throw you headfirst back into the fray. Hell, look at that, he's got the vic hanging out here like a fresh deer carcass."

I said, "Buckeye, I'm going up in the basket with you and Shag."

"You got it, but it'll be a tight fit."

It took a few hours past forever to position the truck far enough away not to disturb the ground directly underneath the tree but close enough to retrieve the victim. We climbed inside the basket and said nothing as the levered arm raised us slowly into the treetops. The basket hit a snow-covered branch and showered Bud, who yelled a few Dixie-type obscenities down below. The closer we got, the worse the victim looked. It was definitely Simon Classon. I recognized him right off, despite the blue-tinged skin and the blood-red icicle the size and shape of a unicorn's horn growing out the side of his head. Shag took pictures from every angle, and I distinctly hoped Mr. Classon really didn't have close relatives who'd have to see how the killer had left him.

I looked at Buckeye. "Got a guess on cause of death?"

"I'll know more when we get him out of that bag. Could be loss of blood, if the blow to the head didn't kill him. But my guess is he probably froze to death out here."

"When do you plan to do him?"

"Today, I hope. This afternoon, probably."

"Bud and I need to be there. We'll be done out here mid-afternoon at the latest, but give us a call before you start the autopsy."

While Shaggy filmed retrieval, Buckeye examined what he could see of the body. "By the shape of the bag, I'd say his legs are bent up under him, probably in a fetal position, but it's anybody's guess what else the killer did to him. Question is, why put him in a bag and how the hell did he get him up this high? We need a goddamn truck to get him down. He'd have to've gotten him up here in daylight. No way could he have done this in the dark. Hell, somebody should've seen the perp in the act. The school's right there, for God's sake."

I leaned around and tried to see how the perp had secured the body to the limb. "He must've somehow thrown the rope over the tree limb and hoisted him up."

"So how'd he tie it off?"

"The rope doesn't go down to the ground. He had to have tied it off while he was up here with Classon."

Shaggy chimed in, video camera whirring while he carefully filmed everything we said and did. "What gets me is, why would he put the body here so close to the school where somebody might see it?"

"That's the question of the day." I turned in the basket and found a clear view of the main buildings, as well as the old white clapboard church. "If Classon ever regained consciousness, he could've seen people moving around at the school."

Buckeye said, "Could be that's what the perp wanted all along. Maybe that was part of the torture, for him to see people over there and not be able to call out to them."

"Pretty morbid shit," Shaggy said.

"That's the least of it," I said.

While Shaggy videotaped, Buckeye strapped the body to the side of the basket, then used his pocketknife to cut the rope around the victim's neck. I leaned down and examined the deep gash on the man's left temple. The thick blood icicle was frozen hard to the skull. He had to have been alive when he was hung up in the tree, his heart still pumping out enough blood to form a chunk of ice of that size.

Once we reached the ground and got the body unstrapped, Bud gazed down at the plastic-wrapped corpse lying on its side. "Man, we gotta get this guy."

I snapped on my latex gloves and knelt beside the body. I examined the tape over the victim's mouth, and then pushed aside the top of the bag to see if he had been garroted or strangled with a noose.

"He wasn't hanged. Looks like the perp tied the rope off underneath the armpits to support his weight so he wouldn't strangle. Whoever killed him wanted Classon suspended up there, alive and suffering."

Buckeye said, "Let's take the body in as it is. I don't want to open the trash bag out here in the snow, not at this temperature. If he's been out here very long, we'll have to thaw the body before I can perform the autopsy anyway. Help me get him on the stretcher."

As Bud and Shaggy readied the stretcher, I stared down at Simon Classon's face and wondered who could have hated him so much that he'd go to this much trouble to make sure he died slowly and painfully and in sight of his friends and colleagues. I thought about the angels plastered all over Classon's house and wondered if he was with them now. So when he opened his eyes and looked at me, my heart stopped.

"Oh, my God, Bud, he's still alive!"

SEVEN

We got Simon Classon loaded in the crime-scene van and en route to the hospital in nothing flat. I rode in the back while Buckeye Boyd swerved and slid around slick curves on icy roads with the skill of Tony Stewart at the Talladega NASCAR track. Bud was right behind us in his Bronco, and he was keeping up with us, inferior southern driver or not. I covered Simon Classon's body with a couple of morgue blankets, but there wasn't a heater in the back because they'd never had occasion to transfer a live murder victim before. Buckeye advised me to leave the trash bag on Classon for added warmth until we got to the emergency room. I leaned over and held the covers down atop him, trying to lend my warmth to his half-frozen body.

Truth be told I was shocked at this bizarre turn of events and trying to get over it, but, man, the fact that he was alive might mean he could tell us who did this terrible thing to him. Simon Classon wasn't moving at all, not breathing, either, as far as I could tell, but once in a while his ice-crusted eyelids would flutter a little. I had to try.

"Simon, can you hear me?" I still wore my latex gloves, so I pulled the tape off his mouth, deposited it into an evidence bag, and then leaned very close, watching his blue lips, hoping they'd move, that he'd say something, anything, that would help us find his attacker. "Who did this to you, Simon? Please, try to talk, try to tell me. Who did this?"

Simon Classon didn't move, didn't utter a word, not even a groan, and I gave up and tried to hold his head steady as Buckeye careened down snow-covered roads, obviously as shook up as I was. We made it to the Canton County Medical Center in under twenty minutes, and I jumped out of the way as the trauma team met the van at a run and pulled the collapsible gurney out and rushed Classon inside. Buckeye and I both raced after them, flashing badges to hospital security as Classon was wheeled through swinging doors into a green-draped trauma room.

"What happened?" The doctor in charge was as young and baby-faced as Noah Wyle, but very calm and collected as his team hoisted the victim onto the examination table. His nameplate said Dr. Bingham.

"Attempted homicide. We thought he was dead until he opened his eyes."

"Okay, get him out of that bag, stat."

About that time, Bud rushed in and we stood out of the way to one side as the nurses took scissors to the black plastic encasing the victim. I knew one of them from my stay in the hospital last summer. Her name was Chris Dale, and she was probably one of the best registered nurses in the county. I was glad she was on shift. When the plastic bag finally came away and was tossed on the floor, Buckeye immediately snatched it up and stuffed it into a large evidence bag, obviously not expecting the man to survive. Inside the garbage bag, Simon Classon was zipped to his neck in a brown, military-issue down sleeping bag.

Bud said, "So that's how he survived all night in this weather."

I moved closer as Dr. Bingham unzipped the front of the bag, and the nurses peeled back the flaps to reveal the body. I froze when they screamed in horror and backed away from the table. Then I realized that Simon Classon's nude body was partially wrapped in some kind of white, gauzy substance that looked like angel hair, the kind of stuff people used around Christmas trees.

"What the hell—?" the doctor began, then jumped back himself as five or six huge spiders skittered out from inside the sleeping bag. Chris Dale screamed as a large brown recluse tried to run up her arm, hysterically batting it off and onto the floor. The doctor stomped on it, and I realized in one sickening moment that it wasn't angel hair wrapped around Simon Classon's body but arachnid silk, as soft and white as gauze, a fuzzy cocoon spun by the spiders trapped inside the sleeping bag with their victim.

The emergency room collapsed into pandemonium as more spiders escaped and fell off the table onto the floor. The doctors and nurses tried to kill as many as they could. Bud was behind me, watching in mute revulsion, until a big spider darted at him. He smashed it under his boot, but my skin crawled with abject horror at what Simon Classon must have suffered, bound alive in a sleeping bag with dozens of poisonous spiders.

When all the spiders were dead, the shaken medical team returned to the patient. Shaggy had arrived with his camera and was filming the terrible sight. He moved around Simon Classon's body, documenting the white stuff clinging to his skin. A couple of nurses were crying, but others were quickly cutting through the sticky webs with trembling hands, working desperately to save the horribly tortured man.

As the webs were cut away and scrubbed off with alcohol, the gaping wounds in Classon's legs became visible. I knew instantly what they were. Brown recluse bites injected a kind of poison that rotted the skin away, like flesh-eating viruses, and left gaping deep holes in skin and muscle tissue. I counted six open, oozing wounds on his legs, a horribly deep one on his belly, and several more on his chest. I shut my eyes and forced myself not to run away. When I looked at Bud, his face was so white and bloodless I thought he might pass out.

Dr. Bingham had gotten over the initial shock, however, and had Classon connected to a heart monitor. I watched the slow, barely visible blip run across the screen. The nurses were still attempting to scrub the web off Simon's bare skin.

Unable to watch any longer, I moved across the room to where Buckeye was examining the down sleeping bag where it had been tossed onto the floor, along with its deadly inhabitants. Even with my extensive homicide experience, I couldn't believe my eyes, couldn't believe anybody could savagely torture another human being in such a way.

Buckeye looked at me. "This is the most horrible way to die I can ever imagine. For his wounds to be this deep and infected, he had to be trapped in that bag with those spiders for a long, long time."

Bud groaned. "Oh my God, this is gonna give me nightmares forever." He still wore that sick look on his face.

Buckeye said, "The perp's got battery-heated socks inside the sleeping bag. Just enough warmth to keep the spiders alive and biting. Jesus Christ, they must've been crawling all over him for days."

I said, "Three days. We think he was assaulted at his house three days ago."

I looked back at the table where the trauma team was cutting off the silver duct tape binding Classon's wrists together. I could see the imprint where the tape I'd removed from his mouth had kept his screams of terror and agony silent.

I said, "Whoever did this to him cannot be human."

Nobody answered because Simon Classon's abused body chose that moment to give up the fight. He flatlined, and the shrill, insistent buzz of the machine sent the trauma team into frenzied action. They got out the heart paddles, called clear, and shocked his chest. The pulse line remained flat. They did it again, then twice more, before the doctor stopped. He looked at us. "It's no use. He's gone."

Nobody said a word for a few seconds, then a young

nurse sobbed. When she ran from the room, Bud said, "God-damn it to hell."

I looked down at Buckeye, where he still knelt by the sleeping bag and realized my hands were trembling. I was shaking, too, just like everyone else in the ER. I knew one thing then. The man or woman who'd committed this was not the run-of-the-mill murderer. He was a monster, some-one without heart or soul or conscience. And he was out there somewhere, probably still in our own vicinity, with more spiders and more sleeping bags, and other victims or-dained to die unimaginably horrific deaths.

The Angel Gabriel

"Okay, Uriel, now for the secret part. Follow me, but watch where you step, in case any of my snakes got loose."

Gabriel led him to the far end of the old hunting lodge, into a small room that had a beat-up, rusted water heater. Gabriel pushed away a bunch of bottles and trash, then shoved the water heater to one side. There was a trapdoor underneath.

"Watch this, Uriel." Gabriel pulled up on a metal ring and when the door was up, he sat down and dangled his legs over the edge. He jumped down and disappeared, and when Uriel looked down into the dark hole, he saw Gabriel standing about ten feet below.

"Sit on the edge, Uriel, and I'll lift you down."

When they stood together in the dark tunnel, Gabriel picked up an old oil lantern and lit the wick with a match. He started off down the slanted dirt passage holding the lamp out in front to illuminate their way. "There's a natural cave under the hunting lodge. I found it one day when I caught a mouse under the water heater. I think they used it to keep the rooms cool in the summer, 'cause I found vents in each room that lead down here. There's even a hot spring out in the center that they used for hot water, I bet."

The fairly steep descent ended up in a large, domed cavern. It smelled funny, unpleasant like match sulfur and old, moldy leaves, maybe. A faint ribbon of sunlight poured through a narrow fissure in the rock high above their heads and made the cave dim and smoky. There were metal cages and glass aquarium tanks sitting around everywhere.

Gabriel said, "I got all these old fish tanks at this big flea market downtown to keep my animals in. Some of them are cracked and don't hold water but that don't matter for my spiders and stuff." He put the caged snake on the ground and hunkered down beside a large glass aquarium. "Hey, Uriel, look here. You know what this is?"

Uriel knelt beside him and peered through the dirty glass. Clumps of dried grass and creek pebbles lay thick on the bottom, and a big tree branch was wedged between the sides with some cardboard covering the top. Spiderwebs clung to everything, and Uriel noticed a big lump about the size of a tennis ball lying on the bottom, all wrapped in the grayish-white webs. A big, shiny black spider was sitting in the middle of the web. It looked about an inch long.

"Don't ever put your hand down in there, Uriel," Gabriel warned. "You remember that, okay?" He waited for Uriel to nod, then he said, "That there's a black widow spider, and she's got venom in 'er that's about fifteen times deadlier than a prairie rattlesnake. That's how they kill their prey."

Uriel stared at the awful, ugly spider, instinctively leaning back a little.

"That's right, don't you get too close. They're our friends and stuff, because I raise them down here and everything, but you gotta be real careful. See that red thing on its belly that looks like an hourglass? That's how you tell if she's a widow. She has lots of babies, but she eats them so I have a bunch of little cages to put them in. You can't put spiders together in the same cage or the big ones will usually eat the little ones. I like poisonous things, don't you? But I mean it, you gotta know what you can and can't do with 'em. I got a bunch of books I stole outta the library about all kinds of bugs and spiders."

Gabriel gestured around the cave. "Oh, yeah, I got wolf spiders and some big hairy tarantulas that live around here in the woods and lots and lots of brown recluse spiders, too. Some people calls 'em fiddleback spiders cause they got this thing that looks like a violin on their backs. Talk about something that makes ugly bites. People's flesh just rots away where the recluses bite them, did you know that? I mean, it makes huge open holes in arms or legs, or anywhere on the body, really, some sores get as big as a grapefruit and raise up like volcanoes around the bite. I've seen it myself in pictures I found at the library."

Uriel felt a little sick. "How come it makes holes in people?"

"'Cause of it's real deadly poison. They call it necrosis when the skin rots away, I think. It just rots out tissue around the bite and keeps getting bigger and bigger. Every bite doesn't do that, but lots of times it does. This black widow here has another kind of venom called a neurotoxin that sort of paralyzes stuff, then the poison liquefies the flesh of its prey so it can eat it easier. See, how it works, Uriel, is this: the widow catches prey in its web, like flies and mosquitoes, stuff like that, then she pokes little holes in 'em and sucks out the body fluids. And the female one always eats the male, too, after they mate. You know how girls are." He laughed.

"What's mate?" Uriel asked, not sure he'd ever want to mate, whatever it was.

"Oh, c'mon, you know, mate, so they can have baby spiders. They call them spiderlings, bet you didn't know that, either, did ya? I'm breeding spiders. See all those cages over there? They're full of spiderlings. You can help me keep them in food and water."

Uriel shivered at that idea but pretended he was just cold. "Why do you want so many around?"

"I just like them, is all. And sometimes I use them to scare people. "

"You do?"

"Yeah. At the last church picnic, I sneaked one on top of your grandma's mashed potatoes when she was talking to one of the ladies, and you should've seen her throw that plate. She fell out of her wheelchair trying to get it off her and scraped up her knees real bad." Gabriel laughed at the memory and ruffled Uriel's hair. "I told you I ain't no angel. Hey, man, I gotta idea. How about scaring Freddy with some of my spiders? He deserves it after what he did to you."

Uriel wasn't so sure what to think about Gabriel making his grandma fall out of her wheelchair, she was so old and all. She seemed so frail and breakable. "I don't know. All that sounds sort of mean to me."

Gabriel frowned. "Well, Freddy scared you just about to death, didn't he?"

"Yeah, I guess so."

"Didn't you think they was burying you alive? I heard you screaming like you was scared as hell."

"Yeah. I was real afraid 'til you came and got me out."

"Then we need to pay him back. We'll use a snake, if you don't like the spider idea. You know what, though? Most people is more afraid of little bitty spiders than of great big snakes. I just don't understand it. Spiders are so little and really beautiful with all those long legs, and the way they spin those beautiful webs. Webs are made out of silk, you know, and the designs look almost like your grandma's lace curtains."

"It's sort of pretty, all right," Uriel admitted, looking at the webs tangled around inside the aquariums. "But what's that big lumpy thing on the bottom?"

"That's a chipmunk. I put it in there with the widow to see what would happen. The widow killed it and wrapped it all up in those webs. It took her a long time but I guess she wants to keep it fresh to snack on later." Gabriel grinned. "Ain't that something? They eat lots of different kinds of insects and even some small animals like frogs and lizards, too. They can't kill a human being, but they might be able to kill a little baby, I bet. Especially if lots of them bit it."

Uriel nodded and tried to see the chipmunk through the fuzzy white cocoon. As far as he could tell, there wasn't much left of the poor little thing.

That night after dinner, Uriel listened to a strange old radio almost as big as a television set. Grandma called it a Motorola console and said she liked to listen to gospel music and St. Louis Cardinal games. He said he liked Pittsburgh Pirates the best, and she said that he'd get to hear Pirate games when they came to play at Busch stadium.

Just before bedtime, she gave him a glass of milk and some homemade oatmeal cookies with raisins. They were good, and he liked the supper she made, too—ham and sweet potatoes and green beans from the big garden she tended in her backyard. She said he could help her pull weeds, and they'd can tomatoes and corn to eat in the winter. She kissed him good night and turned down the wick until the room went dark and he was afraid.

Hiding his head under the quilts, he started to cry because he missed his momma and daddy and Katie. He thought about Gabriel and his hidden cave under the hunting lodge and wondered if Gabriel had gone back there after they'd sat on the porch with his grandma and eaten slices of her cinnamon apple pie. His grandma told him that Gabriel was a good, Christian boy and would be a good influence on Uriel.

Uriel stiffened when he heard soft scratching sounds. He thought of the creepy spiders and stuff down in Gabriel's cave. Goose bumps rose on his arms and made him shiver, but when the scratching didn't stop, he finally peeked out. Somebody was outside his window. Then he saw it was Gabriel, shining a flashlight up on his face. Uriel scrambled out of bed and tiptoed across the floor and tugged open the old sash window.

"Hurry, get dressed, Uriel, we're gonna have some fun!"

"But what about grandma? What if she finds out?"

"She ain't gonna find out nothin'. I heard her telling some church ladies at prayer meeting that she takes some medicine every night to make her sleep good. Hurry up now, we don't got all night!"

Hurrying as fast as he could, Uriel pulled on some cutoff jeans, his old Reeboks, and a black Pirates T-shirt. He peeked out into the hall but the house was quiet and dark, and his grandma was snoring down in her room. Getting pretty excited now, he climbed out the window. Gabriel was holding a burlap bag. Something inside was buzzing loudly and moving around.

"What's in there, Gabriel?"

"A hornet's nest. We're gonna do a little payback on Freddy for what he did to you. Let's go."

In the woods it was dark as pitch, with frogs croaking, locusts screeching, and other things rustling in the bushes. Uriel was scared, so he kept close behind Gabriel until they came out on a blacktop road. Gabriel's motor scooter was there, and he hung the bag on the handlebars then helped Uriel climb on back.

Uriel was elated when they took off, the cool night wind blowing his hair over the top of his bandage. He held on tightly around Gabriel's waist. He'd never ridden on a motor scooter, but he wasn't afraid, not with Gabriel around. After about ten minutes, Gabriel found the right mailbox and pulled up under a bunch of walnut trees. They climbed off, and Gabriel whispered close to Uriel's ear, "You gotta be real quiet, got it? They don't got a dog that I know of, but his dad's a big duck hunter so he's got a shotgun that he might shoot if they see us sneaking around."

That sounded pretty scary to Uriel, too, but he said okay.

Gabriel took the bag full of hornets and headed through some woods that edged the long graveled road up to the house. Freddy's house was a one-story farmhouse a lot like Uriel's grandma's, and a light or two shone from the front windows. They crept through some lilac bushes hugging the side of the house. Somewhere inside, they heard a late-night television show and a man laughing.

"That's his daddy," Gabriel whispered. "Freddy's room's in the back, and look what a baby he is. He's got a night-light on."

When they were underneath Freddy's bedroom window, Gabriel lifted Uriel so he could see the Superman night-light on top of the dresser. Freddy was asleep on a bed right under the window. The window was open so the cool air could get in, and Gabriel lowered Uriel back down, then smiled and put a forefinger to his lips. He took out a pocketknife and cut some slits in the screen, then wedged the top of the bag through the hole. Hornets flew in an angry brown wave out into Freddy's room. Gabriel dumped the nest on the ground under the window and dragged Uriel a safe distance away, where they hunkered down and listened. He smiled when Freddy screamed louder than anything Uriel had ever heard before. His terrified shrieks echoed out into the quiet night until Freddy's mom ran into the room and flipped on the overhead light. When she screamed, too, Gabriel grabbed Uriel's hand and they ran like deer through the darkness, laughing and breathless when they reached the motor scooter.

EIGHT

By the time we got Classon's tortured body bagged and on the way to Buckeye's office, the young students at the academy were up and outside their dorms building snowmen and throwing snowballs at each other. Fun in the snow, not exactly mourning central. Inside, however, where instructors roamed the halls, there was lots of whispering and watching us. We stopped somebody and asked where we could find the director and were led down to the far end of a wide corridor where we met the director's young, built private secretary, Christie, who kindly offered to bring us breakfast trays from the school cafeteria. Bud and I weren't particularly hungry after what we'd just let out of that black plastic bag in the ER but did accept an offer of hot coffee.

Yes, indeedy, Christie Foxworthy was the absolute epitome of the kind of woman wives did not want their husbands hiring to take dictation, to fetch coffee, or do anything else within one hundred feet of their husbands. Her name was worthy of her looks, a fox she was, you betcha, and she couldn't be much past the obligatory eighteen as she clicked hither and fro on spike heels quite similar to the ones I wore while pretending to be the town slut. Christie's were lime green, however, her version of Christmas cheer, I suppose. All I knew for sure was that Bud liked the looks of her. I could tell by his round, bulging eyeballs as she left us waiting in her office to summon the big man.

"Whoa, didn't know they made 'em like that anymore. Johnstone's got excellent taste in Girl Fridays."

"Yeah, Bud, Bond girls with transcription skills are hard to find around here."

Then Christie was back from her foray into boss territory with sad news from the director. She even frowned with pouty, glistening, cinnamony lips as she gave it to us.

"I'm so sorry but Dr. Johnstone's involved in an important overseas call. It's taking longer than he expected. Would you mind too much waiting across the hall in our conference room?"

Her accent was as Brooklyn as Bud's was Atlantan.

Bud said, "Not at all, Miss Foxworthy. Or is it Mrs.?"

"It's Miss." She gave him a sultry look and swung shoulder-length, sun-streaked blond hair with a headtoss worthy of Christina Aguilera. I hoped Bud could put the brakes on his drool long enough to interview the woman.

I said, "Actually, Miss Foxworthy, we'd like to ask you a couple of questions, too, if you have a few minutes."

Christie stopped in the doorway and turned her comely gaze on me. I'm not sure she had noticed me before because I'm not Bud. Bud was pretty good looking, hot, actually, charming even, and did that testosterone thing for some women, especially young ones turned on by a slow southern accent and the big gun bulge under his arm. He probably bulged elsewhere, too, at the moment.

"Me? Why do you want to speak to me?"

"Are you acquainted with the victim, Simon Classon?"

"Yes, of course. I know everyone affiliated with the academy."

I waited for it to dawn on her that she'd now answered her very own question. She continued to look at me inquisitively. Okay, better that I pound it manually into her head. If only I had a wooden mallet.

"Since you know the victim, you might be able to help us in the investigation."

She still stared without blinking as if my words were incomprehensible, or maybe I was invisible and didn't know it. I looked at Bud for help and was slightly embarrassed by his goofy, toothy grin. His Crest Whitestrips were doing their job.

After a while, she said okay.

Now we were getting somewhere. We trailed her into the conference room. I glanced down the hall to my right at a group of people who stood murmuring in low tones and watching us surreptitiously. Bud kept his eyes on Christie's little bottom twisting back and forth in her short tight black skirt as if trying to escape its restrictions.

The conference room was really a teachers' lounge with several large tables with folding chairs, but we headed for two large black rocking chairs.

"Would you like your coffee while you wait?"

"That would be very nice."

"Here, let me take your coats."

We shrugged out of our matching department-issue brown parkas and stuffed our gloves in the pockets. She hung them both on a brass coatrack in the corner and busied herself at the counter pouring our brews into small white Styrofoam cups.

Outside a big plate-glass window I could see tree-spiked, snowy hills and, in a distant clearing, some kids were using big cardboard boxes as sleds. They were having lots of fun; obviously, they hadn't been in Classon's angelology course. Maybe somewhere on campus someone was sniffling and taking on about Simon Classon's untimely death. I just hadn't seen him or her yet. In fact, nobody seemed the least bit upset by the murder. But wait until they heard the gory arachnid details. Serious upset would soon follow.

Christie was back. She handed me my coffee and then Bud took his and held it cupped in his palms as if it were frankincense and myrrh and she was Balthasar. She dragged a third rocker close, crossed one long leg over the other for Bud to look at, and waited for him to get all excited. She didn't have long to wait.

I said, "We appreciate your cooperation, Miss Foxworthy."

"I really can't be away from my desk very long. The phone's been ringing off the hook all day."

I decided to find out what a New Yorker was doing down here in the Ozark Mountains of Missouri. "Sounds like you're a long way from home."

She looked mightily surprised. Maybe nobody else had ever noticed that she said *kawfee* instead of coffee.

I decided to wow her some more. "Brooklyn, right?"

"Why, yes." She was warming up to me. I guess she thought I was a genius, or maybe a New Yorker, too.

Bud said, "I love New York. I was up there last summer."

"Really?" Even more interest in Bud now. She recrossed her deadly legs. Man, Bud was on the edge of his rocker now. So was his tongue. She said, "Were you on vacation there, or what?"

"I was on a case, but I took in a Broadway show or two. I guess it seems kinda quiet down here to you after all those taxis honkin' and jets goin' over."

"Yeah. This is the most boring place I've ever been in my life. I miss the city like crazy, but I had to get outta town fast."

Aha. "Why was that, Miss Foxworthy?"

"Oh, I had this boyfriend threatening to kill me if I didn't marry him, but he was hooked up with some pretty bad guys, if you know what I mean." She winked at me.

I stared at her, trying to figure out if I knew what she meant.

"You mean like Tony Soprano, badda boom, badda bing, and all that?" Bud laughed, just in case.

Christie said, "Yeah, badda boom, badda bing. But Tony Soprano's fictional."

Right. Thanks for clearing that up, Christie. "How long have you worked here at the academy, Miss Foxworthy?"

"Almost a year now, but it seems like ten years." She lowered her voice. "I hate this place, I mean, really, really hate it. I get to take night classes, because I work here, and I hate those, too. But I've got to finish my certificate in astrophysics."

Yeah, and I'm Frosty the Snowman with a degree in biochemistry. "That's very impressive."

"Yes, it is, isn't it? Everybody thought I'd end up being a hairstylist, or nail technician, or something, but look what I got going now." She beamed like a 100-watt lightbulb. Bud beamed back. 200 watt. Jeez. They could make a movie out of this interview. *Brooklyn Molls Gone Wild.* All Christie had to do was pull up her shirt and flash her implants.

"I didn't know they taught astrophysics hereabouts. Actually I don't know a lot about the curriculum here at the academy, other than the course in angelology."

"Oh, that angel course is an elective. This isn't a religious institution. But they have lots of electives for the kids, you know, that's where you can choose what you want to take but it doesn't count toward any of our certificates."

Do I look stupid and uneducated? Is that it? Does Bud look like a dunce? Well, that might be pretty much on target at the moment, especially when Christie keeps crossing and recrossing her silky, naked, tanning-salon legs. Not even fishnets for the Brooklynite, not even in December subzero weather.

"So, tell us about Simon Classon. Did you know him well?"

She nodded. We waited. She nodded again, in case we didn't hear it.

"So you *did* know him?"

She nodded. Okay, she was great with yes or no answers but let's see if she could speak out loud in basic sentences. I thought up a question she had to answer with real nouns and verbs.

"Where was Mr. Classon from?"

Eyes on mine, thinking, thinking, almost there, come on, Christie, you can do it, grab that thought, hold on tight.

She said, "Missouri?"

"You're not sure?"

"Why do you say that?"

"Well, your answer sounded like a question."

"Did it really? I didn't know that."

I started to ask her if she ever attended UCLA with Jacqee but decided snide would be over her head, anyway.

"What kind of person was Mr. Classon?"

"He was pretty much a bastard. I took that angel class but I hated his guts, actually."

Okay, now tell us what you really think, Christie.

Bud grinned, impressed by her honesty, I guess. He said, "You didn't care for him, huh?"

"No, sir, I did not."

"Why not?" The girl was straightforward, once you got her focused.

"He was just really hateful and mean to everybody. Nobody likes him, you'll find that out. Everybody's afraid of him."

"Afraid? Why is that?"

Bud and I were leaning forward now, ready to hang on her every word but probably for different reasons.

Christie looked at the door, obviously fearing eavesdropping directors. "He has a lot of power around here, you know, under-the-table sort of stuff."

"I guess I don't know exactly what you mean by under the table."

She gave me a "how-stupid-are-you?" look. "Well, you know," she dropped into whisper mode, "he's got pull with members on the advisory board. He gets people he doesn't like fired, and stuff."

"Thus making him extremely unpopular with the staff," said Bud.

"Except for the ones who kiss his ass. They get whatever

they want. You know, big raises and good offices, stuff like that."

"I see." Sounded to me like any thriving business with more than one employee. Even down at the sheriff's office, I could name a couple of people with brown noses and sore knees.

"Did Mr. Classon have any special friends that he liked to hang out with?"

"Not really, even his secretary secretly despises him. Talks about him terrible when he's not around." Christie glanced at the door again. "This is confidential, isn't it? You won't tell Dr. Johnstone what I'm saying, will you?"

I thought it was a little late to be asking that. "We'll keep your statement quiet. Did you ever have a run-in with Simon Classon yourself, Ms. Foxworthy?"

"Not really, well, okay, maybe once or twice. I really can't stand him. Truth is, he scared the hell out of me." Whisper mode was creeping back in. "Remember, you can't tell my boss all this stuff. He'd throw a fit and probably fire me, but it's God's truth, I promise."

Well, now, if we had Christie's promise, what more could we ask for? "Tell us about the times you had trouble with Simon Classon. What happened?"

"Well, he liked to call me up and bawl me out over the phone. He did that to lots of people so I got to where I'd just hold it out from my ear and let him rant on without listening. Sometimes I'd even put the phone down and go back to my typing. I mean, sometimes he acted, well, almost, you know, almost insane. His face'd get all red and splotchy and he'd stalk around and throw things on the floor. I mean, he just went berserk sometimes."

"What caused these outbursts?"

Christie gave a shrug and shook her flowing hair around like those girls in Herbal Essence commercials. "He's a nut-case. What else can I say?"

Bud glanced at me, then said, "And you believe everyone feels this way about him?"

"Everybody I know hates him, even some of his students. I think he acted better in the classroom, though, after all, he was talking about angels. He should have taught the class on devil worship, if you ask me."

Bud and I exchanged another look. I said, "You have a class on devil worship here?"

"Oh, yes, it's one of our most popular. It's an elective, too. But it's not called that. It's called Paganism—Its Influence on Modern Religion. But they have discussions about Satan and evil, and how some people like to worship the devil, you know, stuff like that. The kids all love it. I liked it a lot when I took it. Mr. Rowland's a really good teacher."

Holy crap. What kind of school was this? I wondered if Black knew what was being taught at this little conclave in the woods. "Would it be possible for us to have a catalog of classes and maybe even a roster of the students taking each class? I'd also like to have information on each instructor's educational background."

"I can get all that for you. Uh-oh, I hear my phone ringing. Can I go now?"

Bud said, "Sure. And thanks for everything, Christie."

"You're welcome, Detective Davis."

We gave her time to twist herself out of the room, then Bud said, "Devil worshipping 101, huh?"

"Sounds like a class we might ought to audit, huh?"

"Yeah. Wonder if they teach grave robbing, too?"

"Actually, we do have a class called Basic Forensic Science, which isn't much different from grave robbing, if you think about it."

A tall man now stood in the doorway, a certain Dr. G. Richard Johnstone, if my hunch turned out. He was dressed in a pure white, expertly tailored wool suit, starched white shirt, and white tie. Forget about not wearing white after Labor Day; each to his own. I checked for white bucks like Elvis Presley used to wear and found bare feet in leather sandals instead. Jerusalem Cruisers? I momentarily felt sorry for his toes, but hey, if the boss man didn't mind snow in his sandals, who was I to object?

On the other hand, his tan rivaled that of Ernest Hemingway after a yearlong stint at Key West, and his eyes were a strange color, very pale gray, almost white. He had a real lion's mane of bushy blond hair that might've looked better pulled back with a snow-white scrunchy. There was a faint white scar that ran into his hairline, and just below, his right earlobe glinted with a showy diamond stud. Clean shaven and handsome in an angular, hard sort of way, he had crow's-feet at the corners of his eyes and lots of muscles that made me think he partook of lots of sports. Free weights, too, maybe.

I stood up, slightly embarrassed that he'd heard Bud's sarcastic remark, but not overly much. Name me a reputable school that taught Satanesque subject material. I never took that course at LSU.

"Hello. I'm Detective Claire Morgan from the Canton County Sheriff's Department and this is my partner, Detective Bud Davis."

He walked forward with right hand extended. "How do you do. I'm Dr. Johnstone, director here at the academy."

I shook his big, brown hand, a firm, dry handshake, then Bud took it. "Hope I didn't offend you, Dr. Johnstone. Just jokin' around a little."

"No offense taken, detective. We do have some rather unorthodox classes taught here at the academy, but most are subjects requested by the students. Our students are young but they're extraordinarily bright. Nearly all of them have IQs close to the genius level. It's one of our requirements."

Bud grinned. "And I thought the University of Georgia had a tough admission policy."

I said, "Where do your recruiters find these geniuses, Dr. Johnstone?"

Dr. Johnstone turned those pale-as-crystal eyes upon me. I didn't blink under his stare because I knew he was trying to cow me. I don't cow easily, ask Black.

"The truth is that most of our students have been in trouble with the law but are so gifted intellectually or artistically that the juvenile authorities think they should be given a second chance. Thus, they end up here with us."

Bud said, "So in essence you're running a school for evil geniuses."

I thought that was pretty damn clever, so I smiled. Dr. Johnstone did not see the mirth. In fact, he bristled, and said, "That's not the least bit funny. These poor children are at risk and we are helping them become productive citizens."

Obviously irked, Bud said, "Oh, yeah, I forgot. They can learn all that, plus how to devil worship in ten easy steps?"

I felt a certain degree of miff myself. Who did this guy think he was? "You suppose any of your troubled geniuses are capable of murdering your angelology professor?"

Again, those pale eyes found me and tacitly said: "You're quite the bitch, aren't you?" My scornful gaze replied in the affirmative.

"Perhaps you'd like to come in to my office and finish your interview there. I'm sure we'd all be much more comfortable."

Right. And if I had to hazard a guess, we'd all be recorded there, too.

Dr. Johnstone led us across the hall, through Christie's office and into his own large domain. Christie pretended to type as we went by, as if she hadn't already spilled her guts about the detestable and dead Mr. Classon.

Johnstone had a large desk, a really large desk, all white, including the blotter, and about the size of Kansas City. He took the long way around. He also had a sitting area at the other end of the room with a long white couch facing two white wing chairs. The walls were stylishly all white, too, except the wall behind his desk, which was adorned with strange red masks that looked suspiciously like Beelzebub. Maybe he was the one who taught everybody about hell. I looked around at the white carpet and drapes, and white tables and chairs and white lilies in a white vase, and for a moment I was blinded and thought I was outside in a snowstorm.

"Please sit down," he said, gesturing at the two white leather wingback chairs facing his meticulous desk. We obeyed, but a glance at Bud's deep scowl told me he was not as enamored with Jesus Johnstone as he was with the little Foxworthy pretending to type in yonder antechamber.

"I'm sorry to have kept you waiting. I was speaking to someone on our advisory board. He was in Paris so I really couldn't cut it short."

Damn. That meant Black was butting in. "Had he heard about the murder?"

"It is deemed a murder, then?"

Bud said, "Oh, yeah, deemed a murder's putting it mildly."

"I was told that he hanged himself."

Bud said, "Not unless he zipped himself up in a sleeping bag with a bunch of brown recluse spiders first."

I watched Johnstone closely, and he did look initially shocked, then revolted. But who wouldn't?

"Are you joking again, Detective, or is that true?"

That annoyed Bud, and he's as easygoing a guy as I ever worked with. "I don't joke about murder victims, sir. This man was tortured to death and that's not funny."

"Did I understand you to say he was in a sleeping bag full of spiders? My God, that's . . ."

Words escaped him, so I provided some.

". . . something a devil worshipper might do, maybe even a disciple of Satan. Maybe even somebody who liked to wear those red masks you've got up there on your wall. I guess none of your brilliant students requested a class on how to murder a teacher, did they?"

Johnstone studied me as if I were a nasty little roach that he wished to smash under his chilly bohemian sandals. "You know what, detectives? I believe we might have gotten off on the wrong foot here."

Yeah. About a size-eighteen wrong foot. "Could be."

"I'm sorry if I offended you. Truthfully I was a little insulted to hear the two of you making fun of my students."

"We weren't making fun of your students. But it does interest me as to why you'd offer a class that discusses evil with troubled teenagers. Looks like that's just asking for more trouble, don't you think?"

"You misunderstand the purpose of the class, I think, Detective Morgan. It's not a class about the devil or evil. In fact, that subject is rarely discussed. It teaches about pagan religions and the evil influences within them, as well as the Inquisition and other periods where the church committed heinous acts in the name of God. It acts to balance our other classes in that area, angelology and comparative religions. We have independent studies on all the major religions of the world, as well, including Wicca."

"Oh, yeah, Wicca. Ain't that a coincidence, my grandma was a practicing witch, too." Bud, the laugh riot. The still pissed-off detective. Actually I was surprised he knew what Wicca was. I doubted if it was prevalent in Georgia.

I did not like this guy. Bud did not like this guy. And we both have good instincts. I tried to remember if Black had said he liked him, or not. Then again, Black was an important man, and Johnstone would be on his best groveling behavior around him. And Black was rich and made giant donations. I resumed my staring contest with Chief Pale Eyes. I noticed how a recessed spotlight in the ceiling beamed down on his leonine head and made a circular reflection around his chair. Yep, he was definitely going for the halo effect. He seemed less good-looking as the seconds ticked by.

Okay, Morgan, get hold of yourself. Time to be civil and ignore all those internal red warning lights blinking like a berserk railroad-crossing sign. The man did apologize. You catch more flies with honey than vinegar, et cetera, et cetera. Pleasantries were called for.

"Tell me about those masks you've got hanging on the

wall, Dr. Johnstone. They're very interesting. Where did they come from?"

Johnstone turned and admired his collection. He warmed up to the topic, even smiled at us. Honey did work. "I picked them up when I was last in Hong Kong. Actually, they're Indonesian devil masks, but that's not why I bought them. I thought the craftsmanship was extraordinary. Did you notice the one in Christie's office? It's a depiction of a female demon. I brought it back to her. She took it to her paganism class and showed it around to the other students."

I nodded as if impressed and wondered what Christie thought of that kind of gift. Demon Secretary. Not exactly a subliminal message. But time to get back to it. "What other subjects are taught here at the academy, Dr. Johnstone?"

"Just about everything. We have art and music, lots of fine arts, because most of our students are very artistic in nature. We have a core curriculum, of course, English, literature, biology, algebra, social studies. It's the electives that are unorthodox, but we cater to our students' interests. They're interested in lots of things, Detective, and not just macrame and cake decorating." His tone dripped with a degree of condescension that made me stiffen, and I knew right off where I'd like to stick a cake on his person. Or jerk up some serious macrame knots. He smiled, as if reading my thoughts. I smiled, as if vowing to put him on death row if he dared to jaywalk.

Bud must've sensed a certain degree of sizzling hatred between us because he took over in his tactful way.

"Where were you last night when the body was found, Dr. Johnstone? As far as that goes, I hope you can account for yourself during the time since Mr. Classon disappeared."

"Oh, I assure you that I can. Actually, I haven't stepped foot off the campus for at least a week. Just been too busy with the holiday break coming up, not to mention the big New Year's Eve gala. That's our biggest fund-raiser of the year. My quarters are here on the grounds at Director House, actually, so I suspect lots of people can verify my whereabouts any time of day you ask about."

"Maybe you'd be good enough to allow us to tour the campus and interview the employees, sir? Do you have any objection to that?"

"None whatsoever. Please feel free to go anywhere and speak to anyone you think might be helpful. We all thought the world of Simon and certainly want his killer apprehended as soon as possible."

Bud and I stared at him. Mr. Friendly, all of a sudden, gushing niceties about the so-called angelologist from hell. I didn't believe a word he said.

NINE

"Did you get a load of that guy? The son of a bitch thinks he's God."

Bud was right on target with that evaluation. "Yeah. Or Jesus, if you consider his footwear."

We were standing right outside the aforementioned Jesus's office, and then there she was, the academy's public information officer summoned by His Greatness to escort us around the place. Her nameplate read June Green, and she had to be the dowdiest woman I'd ever laid eyes on. Auburn hair, lots of it, past-the-shoulders long and coarse and fly-away but held back in a black barrette, a pretty face but the same kind of flowery, 1950s dress that Mamie Eisenhower might've worn to Ike's inauguration.

Her first words: "Poor old Simon. He's been a legend here at the academy for many, many years, you know."

Not the kind of legend he was going to be in the future, I thought. I noticed that she didn't mention she was sorry the guy was dead. I wondered if Simon had used up some cell phone minutes yelling at her, too. I'd interview her last.

"Dr. Johnstone said I was to take you over to Simon's office. It's in Blue Building, I'm afraid."

"Blue Building?"

"Yes. All our buildings are known by the color the interior corridors are painted. It helps the students identify them."

Bud said, "That's a little elementary for the geniuses that go here, isn't it?"

"Oh, believe me, they're very bright."

I looked at the white walls and white tile floors. The nearest office had white walls, too, not to mention Jesus's arctic office. "So this is White Building, huh?" I catch on quick, you see. Yep, sharp as a tack I am.

Bud said, "Hey, Morgan, maybe we oughta paint our cells down at the station. Thieves go in yellow. Murderers go in blue, rapists in red, get my drift?"

I laughed. June didn't. She glared at Bud. He stared back. Man, something about this place was bringing out the worst in Bud and me. But, hey, maybe that's what we needed. Maybe that's why Simon had been such a bastard. The school poisoned people's psyches.

June finally pried herself out of her scathing eye lock with Bud. "Dr. Johnstone ordered all interviews done in the Blue boardroom. That's in Blue Building, too."

Made sense. A lot more than June Green did.

Bud said, "Hmmm. Interesting. I guess they make you work in Green Building, huh? Considerin' your name's Green, and all."

"There is no Green Building, Detective."

"Well, that explains that," said Bud.

I said, "Actually, I'd like to interview the staff members in their own offices, if that's all right."

June's mouth fell slightly open. She looked like I'd jerked a rug out from under her. Her olive-colored eyes grew round and troubled and for one mere instant I thought she would throw herself bodily to the floor and weep inconsolably. "Oh my, Detective, I just don't know about that. Dr. Johnstone specifically said I was to take you to the Blue boardroom. . . ."

"Don't worry about Dr. Johnstone, Ms. Green. We'll explain to him that we insisted."

"I don't know, you see, I'm really not at a level yet where I can arbitrarily make these kind of decisions."

Bud said, "What's he gonna do? Fire you?"

June looked like she wanted to say "Yes, you big smarty pants, that's exactly what he's gonna do," but instead she said, "Who would you like to interview first?"

I glanced down at the rosters and faculty list that Christie Foxworthy had printed out for us, but I already knew who I wanted to get my hands on first.

"I'd like to speak with Mr. Classon's secretary."

"Actually, we call them personal assistants here. I'll call down to her, but I warn you, she's awfully distraught."

Or, if Christie was correct about Classon's secretary's secret feelings about her boss, she was off throwing a keg party for all her friends at the nearest Holiday Inn.

Bud said, "We'll be gentle."

June and Bud now exchanged their best "nuh-uh, I hate you the most" looks. I don't think they like each other. Maybe I think that because of the slight snurl of June's little bow mouth. And the slight growling coming from deep inside Bud's throat. Oh, well. That's why we have partners.

"You know what, Ms. Green? I think we can find our way there on our own. I know you're very busy." Yeah, crawling around on your hands and knees worshipping your superiors. I was getting major bad vibes from this place, yessiree. I decided I better shake that off, and now.

"Oh, no. Dr. Johnstone asked me to take you there personally so I really must."

"Don't want to spend time in the village stocks, huh?" said Bud.

Stare down, big time. Dueling eye sockets. I burned a couple of warning holes in Bud's face. He wasn't helping things here. We were off to a bad start, to say the least. It wasn't often during an investigation that we hated everybody we interviewed. Maybe the nice people were employed at the lower-level positions, like in most big companies.

"Oh, yes, I almost forgot. Dr. Johnstone asked me to present you with his book. He always provides complimentary copies to visitors of the academy."

Even irksome detectives investigating him? But I took a book. Hey, it was free. Maybe I could add it to Black's other stocking stuffer. Bud and I took the books and thumbed through them.

Bud said, "There's nothin' but pictures in here."

June said, "That's right. It's a photographic history of the academy."

Bud said, "Wow, now I'm really impressed."

June bristled up for a couple of seconds then finally came out verbally with what her expression had been saying all along. "You're really quite rude, aren't you, Detective Davis?"

"Who, me?" Bud threw her his most disarming grin. June's eyes grabbed him by the throat and squeezed with all her might.

"Thank you for the books. I'm sure we'll enjoy them. I do like the cover," I added, trying to make up. It was a great big picture of the director in his white suit, his chest swelled out with pride, fluffy lion's mane groomed to perfection and sprayed with a gallon of Pantene for fine hair. I looked to see if he was wearing Jesus sandals but the picture was cropped just below his knees.

"You're welcome," June said, admirably refraining from calling us jerks, or worse.

Yep, this investigation was getting off to an ultrarocky start. Bud and I were going to have to cool it down a bit, yeah, become the more pleasant, sweet-natured detectives we usually were, or Charlie would ream us out and jerk us off the case. I wondered if our replacements would fall prey to the same negative energy inundating these hallowed, color-coordinated halls.

"Please follow me," said June. Clipped. Cold. June hated our collective guts. Oh yeah, big-time.

We followed her at a fast pace down a long white hall, then down an equally white stairwell that led to the snowy, pristine basement. We left the building at a door where a student was shoveling enough snow to fill a dump truck. Bud and I slung on our coats in tandem. Coatless, June wrapped her arms around herself and trudged angrily across a concrete sidewalk that led to the next building.

Halfway there, Bud politely offered June his jacket. He was trying to make up, too. June responded with a snippy, "No thank you, detective."

Bud raised his brows at me, as if he considered her a challenge.

A right turn in the sidewalk led us into Blue Building. It was nice inside, but blue, really blue, cobalt maybe, and the blue emotion was reflected in the faces of most of the employees we met. Happy was not a good word to describe the Dome of the Cave Academy for the Gifted. I wondered what the suicide rate was among the faculty and staff.

We walked down a long hallway to the far end where we discovered an equally blue office that said SIMON CLASSON, ANGELOLOGY on a brass plate the size of a computer screen. Inside we found his secretary, a.k.a. personal assistant. She was dry eyed until she saw the badges hanging around our necks. Suspicious behavior? Hell, yes.

The instant waterworks were impressive, however, and continued when June Green introduced us and fled back to Jerusalem and her white-clad savior. I sniffed the air for raw onions stashed in the Kleenex Simon's secretary was swabbing her eyes with but smelled nothing except the faint scent of the roses sitting on the table beside the door. Uh-oh, they were red. And in the Blue Building, too. Should've been violets. Somebody was in deep doo-doo.

The sobbing lady's name was Maxine Knight. She had very short black hair, almost G.I. Jane, with a couple of white streaks around the face that could be natural gray. Fortyish, G.I. Jane–gaunt, too. She wore a velour running outfit, magenta with a yellow stripe down the leg. Not exactly mourning black. I guess people in Blue Building didn't have to wear blue, after all. She wound down her deluge of false tears with lots of snuffling, then ended it abruptly by blowing her nose in a bunch of tissues and dropping the whole wad into a wastebasket under her desk. Nonetheless, we were impressed with the quantity of water she produced in the three minutes we'd been in her office. Be nice, be professional, I told myself and looked pointedly at Bud to reinforce my new motto. He knows the look from our previous investigations.

"I realize this is awfully soon to have to talk about Mr. Classon, Ms. Knight, but we really need to ask you a few questions."

"I understand. Christie called down and warned me you were coming. I guess you'd like to look around his office."

"Yes, ma'am. That would be helpful."

"Could I get you something to drink? Coffee, hot chocolate, maybe? There's a faculty lounge with vending machines right down the hall."

"Sure. Hot chocolate sounds great."

Maxine asked Bud if he wanted some, too, and he said yes, ma'am. He was in civil mode. He followed me into Classon's adjoining office.

I said, "Well, this's intensely blue, isn't it?"

"Yep. The academy is good at color schemes. Other kind of schemes, too, if my guess's correct."

"You getting a bad vibe around here?"

"Uh-huh. I keep looking behind me to see if I got a knife in my back."

"You and everybody else who works here, I bet. Okay, let's take a look-see."

The office was very nice, nicer, in fact, than the arctic wasteland of Directorville. The furniture was black, desk, too, oriental in design but looked more like a knockoff from Pier One than the real kind Black would have sitting around in his mansions. There were lots of angels, of course, everywhere, even more so than in his house, some hanging from the ceiling on fishing line. They bobbed around every time the heat kicked on. I wondered where he hid his drugs.

Bud said, "I'll check out his computer and see what he was up to."

"Here you go. It's still really hot."

Maxine was back, carrying blue ceramic mugs, certainly in better spirits, with a bright smile and everything. Tears had their uses, I guess.

"Thank you, Ms. Knight."

"Call me Maxine, please."

"Okay." I took the mug. There were a measly three miniature marshmallows floating on top. Price must've gone up when it started snowing. "Do you know Simon's password so we can get into his computer? Otherwise, we'll have to confiscate the whole system and cart it downtown."

"I know the password. Actually, it's easy to remember. It's archangel. His user name is sclass.domecave.org."

Bud was already pecking on the keyboard. "Archangel's got an *h*, right?"

"Yes, sir." Maxine was polite.

I said, "Maxine, could we sit down somewhere and have a little chat?"

"Sure. We've got a private conference room down the hall that we could use."

"How about us sitting down in your office?"

"Okay."

We left Bud to his hacking fun, and I sat down in a comfortable blue-and-yellow flame-stitched armchair positioned across the desk from her. I dug my pad and pencil out of my leather bag and flipped open the cover. Armed and ready.

"How long have you worked for Simon Classon, Maxine?"

Maxine sat behind her desk with her hands folded on top of her calendar blotter. I noticed her fingers were squeezing so hard that her knuckles turned white. Her fingernails were unpolished and bitten to the quick. Maxine was the jittery sort. I made a suggestion.

"No need to be nervous. This is just procedure. We'll be interviewing everybody who had contact with the victim. You spent the most time with Mr. Classon, so we chose to interview you first."

"I know, really, I do. But I've never been shaken down by

the police before. I'm a law-abiding citizen. No rap sheet at all. Isn't that what you call them? That's what they call them on *CSI*."

"We're not shaking you down, ma'am. Now, how long have you worked with Simon Classon?"

"About three years now. Will be on June first."

"How long was Simon Classon employed here at the academy?"

"He's worked here for years and years, sixteen, maybe? He attended classes here before that, too, I think."

"Really. How did you happen to become his secretary? Did you apply for the job?"

Maxine nodded, and her long, dangling Christmas earrings, three silver jingle bells on each ear, swung against her neck and made sleigh-ride sounds. "Yes, you know, he had lots of trouble keeping personal assistants. He is, I mean, was, hard on the people working for him."

"Hard? How do you mean?"

"Oh, he's real demanding. Shrill. Moody. Hateful. Nasty."

I met her gaze steadfastly. "Doesn't sound like you liked him much, Maxine."

"Well, I guess I could put up with him better than most people. I'm a pretty easygoing person and he needed me, so he treated me better than other people."

"How do you mean?"

"Just to be his friend. Everybody needs at least one friend."

"Yeah." I didn't have many more than that, but that was beside the point. "So you consider yourself his only friend here at the academy?"

"Uh-huh. He probably thought he had some friends but most of them were nothing but suck-ups who really loathed him behind his back."

Loathed him, huh? "Does that describe you, too, Maxine?"

Maxine's face looked startled, then she glanced around as if Classon's ghost might walk in and go off on her. She lowered her voice. "Okay, listen, truth is, I hated him, too. Nobody knows that, though, and I don't want it to get around."

Uh-uh, Christie knows it. Probably everybody else, too. "You ever have words with Simon Classon? An argument or serious falling-out?"

"Not really. Everything depended on his mood when he came in the morning. He could be nice at times, of course, but it never lasted long, believe me. And usually that was to get something he wanted out of people."

"So you're saying you never had a serious disagreement with the victim?"

She shook her head and her earlobes gave me a rendition of "Sleigh bells ring, are you listenin'?" "I just never said anything back to him. That's the trick. Just listen to his rants and keep working, that was my motto. Sometimes when I did that, he'd feel guilty afterward and try to play nice, but I had to avoid eye contact and act the victim."

"Doesn't sound like much fun to work under conditions like that."

"Oh, God, no, it sure wasn't fun. Not even pleasant. But like I said, he wasn't half as hard on me as he was on the others."

"What others?"

"Well, the other professors really got on his nerves. He called them morons and stupid idiots. They hated him back and avoided him like the plague. Nobody came down to his end of the hall unless it's absolutely necessary. I've known people who'd walk outside in the pouring rain to avoid his office."

"And who might they be?"

"Well, one was Stuart Rowland. He's a professor here, too. He teaches paganism, but he's really a pretty nice guy. He and Simon really, really hated each other's guts."

"Why?"

"Well, I can't say for sure. One thing was, Stuart didn't like the way Simon threw things at him."

"He threw things at him?"

"That's right. Whatever was nearby. Staplers, books, anything. I hate to say it, but I think Simon had some underlying psychological problems. Maybe a personality disorder, too, you know, something that made him act despicable."

"Despicable?"

"Yes, I'm sorry, but that's the best way to describe it."

"Have you ever known Mr. Rowland to get into it physically with Simon? You know, shove him or make some kind of threat against him?"

"Oh no, Stuart Rowland's pretty mealymouthed, I'd say. He'd trash Simon behind his back, but when he was up against Simon, face-to-face, Stuart pretty much wilted and went away. But everybody did. Simon was a real hard-ass. He could say the cruelest things, you just wouldn't believe how awful and demeaning he could be."

"Is Mr. Rowland on campus today? I need to talk to him, too."

"I doubt it. He ran his car in the ditch across the road last night on his way home. He slept in his office last night, so I bet he went home this morning after they got his Mustang pulled out."

Suddenly I was more than anxious to check on the whereabouts of Professor Devil Worshipper for the last few days. "Do you expect he'll be here tomorrow?"

"Should be. The director announced not long ago that regular classes will resume tomorrow."

"I see. Do you know of anyone else who made threats against Mr. Classon?"

Maxine nodded. "Just about everyone did, but always behind his back. Joking, kinda, making up scenarios of what we'd do to him if we got a chance. Just for fun, you know, being silly."

I stared at the docile little woman. She was describing her boss as Hitler, for Pete's sake. Had Classon really been that bad?

"If you had to guess who perpetrated this crime, who would you say?"

She actually laughed. "Again, it could be anybody, anybody at all. Especially after he ran off Wilma."

"Who is Wilma?"

"Wilma Harte's her name. She was a girl who worked as a part-time custodian here while she took some of our classes. Actually I remember that she took his class, too, and the course on paganism, if I recall. Simon got to picking on her in class, embarrassing her in front of the other students, stuff like that." Maxine shook her head and played me another sleigh song. "Poor kid. Wilma was a bit eccentric, you know, into slasher movies like *Halloween* and *Hellraiser* with lots of killing and blood and gore. She painted her fingernails black and stuff, wore lots of black clothes. Sorta into Goth, I guess you'd say, but she was likeable enough. She had this long red hair that she always wore in pigtails. Sometimes she seemed a little simpleminded but harmless. I do know she had lots of trouble making passing grades, but she didn't cause anybody trouble that I know of. She certainly wasn't evil like Simon."

So we'd graduated now from mean and cruel to just plain evil. Maybe I should take Maxine's opinions with a grain of salt. Nobody could've been that bad, except maybe Adolf Hitler or Satan's spawn.

"You speak of Wilma in the past tense. Is she deceased?"

"Nobody knows. She just up and disappeared one night. Some think she was depressed and might've gone off to commit suicide, that's how upset she was. No one knows for sure what happened to her."

"When did this happen?"

"I guess it's been a week or so now. Simon really liked to single her out for his abuse. I mean, he found fault with every single thing she did, right or wrong, until I guess the poor kid just couldn't take it anymore. She wasn't a very strong person. Psychologically, I mean. You might ask Christie Foxworthy about her. They were sort of friends for a while, I think. I used to see them eating lunch together once in a while. They took Stuart Rowland's class at the same time, too, I think. The one about pagans. But then I heard they had a falling-out and couldn't stand each other. So I guess you can't really take all this as gospel." She shrugged.

"Anyone else here a friend of hers?"

"She worked with another custodian named Willie Vines. And Stuart seemed fairly chummy with her after she took his class."

I made a note to check out Wilma Harte's friends about her disappearance. It seemed a bit coincidental that she took off right before Simon's murder, the man who'd been harassing her. There hadn't been a missing-person or a suicide report on her in our county or I would have heard about it. Maybe we could track her down. It sounded like she might have more than a few interesting things to tell us about Simon Classon.

"You said that Wilma Harte was a custodian here, right?"

"Yes." Maxine shook her head. "I guess she knew how Simon felt about her. She gave him a Christmas card right before she left, and he ripped it up into little pieces right in front of her."

"Why? Did they have some kind of run-in? Exchange angry words?"

"Not that I know of. He just didn't like her, and confrontation wasn't Simon's style. He did his nasty stuff behind the scenes. He had a knack for manipulating board members. The director, too."

"How did he manage that?"

"Nobody could ever figure out how he got away with the things he said and did. I heard once that somebody in his family donated some land to the academy way back when. I don't know if that's true, but he sure gets away with murder around here." Maxine realized her faux pas and colored with embarrassment. "Sorry, Detective Morgan, I didn't mean that the way it came out. But really, why, I've seen him go into somebody's office and swipe everything off the desk, then stalk out and slam the door like a little baby. The director never did a thing about it. I'm surprised somebody didn't punch Simon in the nose a long time ago."

Now somebody had done much worse than punching Classon in the nose. Somebody who, I now believed, could be just about anybody who knew him. The man was not thought well of, to put it mildly.

"Did anything unusual happen around here in the last few weeks or months? Anything that particularly upset Mr. Classon?"

"Well, except for Wilma taking off so unexpectedly, I can't think of anything. But Simon was glad she left. He couldn't stand her for some reason. Oh, one thing, Simon had a fit last month when they gave a personal assistant in Building Red a surprise baby shower."

"Why?"

"He said people shouldn't have to buy baby presents for every little bitch who got herself knocked up."

I couldn't think of anything to say to that for a moment but Maxine added, "But it wasn't even required that anybody had to buy her a gift, just if you wanted to you could. It was her first baby, and she and her husband didn't have much, so most of us gave her something."

"Okay. Anything else you can remember that might be pertinent to our investigation?"

"No, not that I can think of."

"Anybody around here you think might be capable of murdering somebody, Maxine? Anyone with a terrible temper, for instance? Anybody who stood up to Mr. Classon's rages or tried to strike back, either openly or secretly?"

"Actually, the director held up pretty well against him, but then he'd give in to whatever Simon wanted. Know what you ought to do? Check into the salaries around here. See how the ones who sucked up to Simon got big raises under the table."

"Did you get a big raise under the table, Maxine?"

She hesitated, even looked guilty. "Yeah. Every year. That's the real reason why I kept working for him."

"Where were you last Wednesday?"

Maxine looked scared in a big hurry. "You think I did this? Me? Oh God, I'm innocent, I swear."

"No. It's just a question I have to ask everyone I interview."

"I was at a Christmas party at my daughter's house. Actually I took off a few days when Simon was on vacation and helped Amy cook and clean up after the party. Amy had everyone on her staff from the medical clinic out to their house. She's a doctor in Osage Beach. So's her husband."

"And there are people who can verify you were at that party?"

"Oh yes, all of them. We played charades and bingo."

I closed my notebook and stood up. "Good, then it sounds like you don't have anything to worry about. Okay, I won't take up any more of your time. Thank you for your cooperation."

Maxine rose from behind the desk. "Detective? How did he die? I heard that he was found hanging from a tree limb."

"Yes, he was." I waited, not ready to release further details. The director knew so it was probably traveling like wildfire through the school's grapevine.

"I never would've believed he was the type to commit suicide. That surprises me, it really does. He had things too good around here. You sure he killed himself?"

"We don't know exactly what happened at this time, Ms. Knight, but I can tell you that it was definitely a homicide. That's why my partner and I are here."

"Wow. I guess a person just can't be as mean as Simon and not have something horrible come down on him sooner or later. You've heard that old saying, haven't you, detective, about what goes around comes around?"

I'd heard it, all right, but throwing staplers wasn't in quite the same league as the horrific torture somebody put Simon Classon through. Nobody deserved to die in that sleeping bag. And Bud and I were going to have to sort through a whole slew of suspects this time, all of whom had it in for the victim. It might be easier to find somebody who *did* like the man. So far he was almost as popular as Saddam Hussein at the White House.

The Angel Gabriel

Uriel caught the big yellow bus the next morning and rode into a town called Osage Beach with a bunch of kids he didn't know for his first school day in his new life. All he thought about, though, was going back to the secret cave and tending to all of Gabriel's creatures. His grandma would let him because she liked Gabriel so much. She said a bunch of times that Gabriel would teach him godly ways and to listen to him.

At school Uriel was shocked to see teachers weeping as they walked down the halls. A bunch of little girls were carrying on, too. Then, in the corridor outside the principal's office, he heard an older girl say that Freddy was dead. Uriel stopped and stared at the girl when she said Freddy died from an allergic reaction to hornet stings, then she looked down at him and said, "What are you staring at?"

Uriel forced down a sick feeling, then ran down the hall to the elementary rooms. Gabriel was there, waiting for him at the water fountain. He took Uriel aside and squatted down so their eyes met. "Look, kid, don't you dare go all crazy on me. Wipe those tears off before somebody sees you and gets suspicious." He glanced around to see if the kids at the nearby lockers were listening. They were pushing each other and laughing. "Now, listen up, Uriel, I made a bad mistake last night. But hell, I didn't know Freddy was allergic. He went into this bad thing called anaphylactic shock, I think that's how they pronounced it. Things like this's gonna happen to bullies like Freddy. They always get theirs. We didn't mean it but it had to be God's will, see? Anyways, no need to get racked up over it, he's up in heaven now, and that's a helluva better place than down here. That's for sure."

Uriel felt funny inside, kind of like he was going to throw up. He swallowed hard. He'd never live that down on his first day at school. Now Gabriel was smiling, nodding, and ruffling his hair, like nothing was the least bit wrong. Surely Gabriel knew what he was talking about. And Gabriel didn't mean for Freddy to die, anyway. God must've thought Freddy deserved to die.

"You ain't gonna tell on me, right, Uriel? Remember how you promised you wouldn't ever tell my secrets? You're still my special friend, ain't ya?"

Uriel nodded then looked down the hall to where Gabriel's basketball buddies were yelling for Gabriel to get a move on.

"Gotta go, Uriel. Bell's gonna ring any sec. We'll talk later, okay? Just keep your mouth shut and keep thinkin' about what he did to you at the funeral. It's definitely God's will, just like everything else is. Some people are just on God's books to die young. They act up and they get taken to heaven early for it. Or down to hell, if they're really bad."

Gabriel hurried off toward his friends, and Uriel walked into his classroom and sat down. The kids around him were whispering about Freddy, and pointing to his empty desk in the front row. Later that morning when they were having mathematics, Freddy's big brother came to clean the stuff out of Freddy's desk. He was tall, even taller than Gabriel, with short blond hair, and his eyes were red and puffy like he'd been crying all night. He wore a sweatshirt that said USM. Uriel wondered what the letters stood for.

A few days later, Uriel went to another funeral at the white clapboard church and stared down into the gaping grave. This time everybody that showed up moaned or wept, especially Freddy's family. His momma cried the most and kept crying out, "No, no, no, this can't be, he can't be gone! I won't let you take him! Oh God, why? How did the hornets get in? Why didn't I check that screen?"

Uriel knew exactly how she felt and wondered if he should go up and tell her about how angels came early and took Freddy so he wouldn't suffer much. Uriel was afraid to. Instead, he sat in back, close between his grandma and Gabriel and listened to the preacher say good things about Freddy's family.

The casket was open, and Uriel filed past like everyone else and stared, horrified, at the boy inside. Freddy's face was grotesquely swollen from the hornets. He couldn't even tell it was Freddy. They closed up the small casket and carried it out to the grave. As they lowered Freddy into the ground, Gabriel whispered to Uriel, "Now look who's goin' into a grave. Not you, Uriel, but him. He deserved it, too, don't you forget that. Freddy got what was coming to him. From now on, anybody messes with us, they get it where it hurts. We're gonna be God's own avenging angels, Uriel and Gabriel, and we're gonna make bad people pay. You got that, Uriel? You with me all the way?"

A thrill shot through Uriel, sorta like he felt when his daddy let him put the match to bottle rockets on the Fourth of July. He realized he could do something about people who hurt him now. What he felt was powerful, now that Gabriel and God were on his side. Uriel smiled and whispered in Gabriel's ear. "He sure did deserve to die. Nobody better mess with me, not ever again."

"Attaboy." Gabriel looked pleased. He ruffled Uriel's hair then they went to the heavily laden tables under the trees and filled their plates with sliced roast beef and scalloped potatoes and green beans and cherry pie. The church ladies were all really good cooks, and the boys ate until they couldn't eat another bite.

TEN

It turned out Bud had to confiscate Classon's computer anyway, and after a lengthy phone conversation with the director, we got permission to take it with us. We interviewed every instructor but never found one who cared for Simon Classon, not even a wee little bit. It was slightly disconcerting. Even Osama bin Laden had his cohorts. Classon didn't deserve to die such a horrific death, but apparently Bud and I were the only ones who held that opinion.

We had lunch in the academy's cafeteria, which was more like a food court in a mall, except with no franchises, just pizza or spaghetti or cheeseburgers. We ate thick-crust pizza with pepperoni and black olives and watched the dark geniuses dip their french fries in catsup and play the computer games set up in each corner.

"Gee, Morgan, I can't even detect that these kids have Bill Gates IQs. You'd think they'd have enlarged cerebrums like aliens or something unique to set them apart."

"Maybe they're not all that gifted. Maybe Wonder Director embellishes things a bit to attract donors like Black."

Bud slurped his slurpee through the straw. "Hell, we can't believe a word anybody says around here. Know what? This

all might be some new reality show, and they're all in it together, playing us. Let's look for hidden cameras."

"I've never heard of a school where everyone is dysfunc-
tional. Dr. Phil would have a heyday with these people."

"Wait a sec, Black knows Dr. Phil, right? Maybe we
oughta have Black give him a call and clue him in."

"Maybe Dr. Phil went here, too."

We dumped our trays into the trash bin and headed outside into snow glare and lung-burning cold air. We'd already
informed Christie the Fox that we'd be back tomorrow for
more interviews. She asked us in pure Brooklynese who we
wanted to *tawk* to.

We headed down to Buckeye Boyd's office to witness the
autopsy of our unlikable, unmourned-as-of-yet victim. I was
not exactly relishing the coming hour, even less so when I
found my boss, Sheriff Charlie Ramsay, there, all riled up
and unruly and red faced.

"It's about time you got here, I've been sitting around
here waiting for ten fucking minutes."

Wow, ten whole minutes. One-sixth of an hour. Whew, he
must be exhausted. However, I didn't display my sarcasm or
my wit for fear of being sacked royally, cursed out, or both.
Actually, Charlie's a great guy, a good friend, he just likes to
cuss if you're not punctual. Truth is, he likes to cuss if you're
punctual, too.

"I heard about what happened to this vic, and I want this
psycho pervert caught and put away for good. Dadburn freak."

Oh, yeah, I forgot, Charlie never uses the Lord's name in
vain, but dadburn and dadgumit and goldangit were quite
acceptable. He was a practicing Southern Baptist, after all,
and I wondered what he'd think of our new friend Savior Director in White.

"Hey, Sheriff, you know this guy, G. Richard Johnstone,
the director out at the Dome of the Cave Academy for the
Gifted?"

I received a horrid scowl from my superior. I cringed inside but took it standing up.

"Yeah, yeah, I met him a coupla times. Hell, that's the stupidest fucking name of a school I've ever heard. What's it supposed to mean, anyway?"

Bud entered our conversation unaddressed. He does that sometimes. He's a gutsy sort. "It means all the kids out there are geniuses in training."

"Yeah, right, Davis, but would you know one if you saw one?"

Bud shrugged off Charlie's question, recognizing a bad sheriff mood when he saw one.

"Okay, let's get this thing started." Buckeye said happily. The victim was stretched out on the steel table in front of us under glaring lights.

Man, I hate autopsies but guess it'd make me pretty much a sicko if I enjoyed them. Then again, Buckeye and his staff enjoyed their work and they weren't sickos, not all of them, anyway.

Grumbling profanely about having to put on protective robe, gloves, and mask, Charlie stepped up to the table. His voice sounded mechanical through the ventilator apparatus. "Good grief, can a spider really make that deep a wound?"

I said, "Yes, sir. Brown recluses can. And there were at least a dozen of them inside the sleeping bag with the victim."

Charlie turned his gaze on me, and he did not look happy. Not that he ever did. But now somebody got killed at Lake of the Ozarks, which was his territory and should be murder free, dadgumit. Actually, our homicide rate was pretty low, except for a couple of really bizarre cases of late.

"Today is December 17, 2:00 P.M. Present at the Canton County Coroner's Office are Sheriff Charlie Ramsay, Detectives Bud Davis and Claire Morgan, Criminalist John Becker, and myself."

Shaggy was already in place, video camera on and rolling. He was dressed in long, baggy nylon shorts and a sweatshirt with the sleeves cut off, despite heavy drifts of snow on the ground. He'd decided early in life that he was a California beach bum but never quite made it out to sunny L.A. So he was pretty much just a bum. But a lovable one who was damn good at his job, in fact one of the best in the state.

"The victim is a Caucasian male, age thirty-four, weight 180 pounds, height five foot ten. Cause of death has been determined to be multiple poisonous spider bites exacerbated by hypothermia."

I took a place at the foot of the table. Charlie and Bud stood on either side of me. I stared at the open holes of purple rotting flesh on Simon Classon's body, some as big as six inches across. A sense of renewed horror assailed me as Buckeye described the wounds. I winced when he started probing inside them with a scalpel. I frowned when he plucked a dead spider out of Classon's hair and placed the shriveled arachnid on a piece of paper. Charlie said something I won't repeat.

Buck said, "There's a deep wound on the side of his head made by blunt force trauma. I estimate the necrosis from the spider venom took at least 24 to 36 hours to reach this kind of depth and level of tissue deterioration." He turned to us. "God, I've never seen anything like this in my life."

I felt sick when I thought of Classon taped up inside that sleeping bag with all those spiders for two or three days. He was tortured to death, and I wanted the guy who did it. I wanted to get him so bad I could taste it. I said, "Have you ever seen a fatal spider bite around here before, Buckeye?"

"Occasionally, if the victim can't get himself to the hospital for some reason. But it's rare. Get more deaths from snakebites, but they're rare, too."

"Are brown recluse spiders prevalent at the lake?"

"You bet. Probably got some in every house in Missouri. They like to stay out of sight, hidden in dark places, thus their name. Most people get bit putting on clothes that've been packed away in a closet or attic. Shoes, too. They like to hide in old shoes. I remember one case where a three-month-old little girl died when the mother got the stroller out of the basement. A brown recluse nest was under the seat but she couldn't see it. Just a couple of bites, but that was enough to kill the baby."

"Damn." Bud shook his head and looked at me. I didn't know about him, but I was sure as hell going to shake out my boots from now on.

Buckeye made a Y incision, but I'd seen autopsies too many times to get queasy. One thing I knew for sure, I'd never forget how Simon Classon had opened his eyes and looked at me, his face stiff and blue and partially frozen. I wonder if he had really seen me, if he had known who I was, if he had tried to move his lips and tell me who had done it. He was a man who liked to push people around but this time he'd pushed somebody a little too hard, somebody who had a screw loose, anyway. Chances were we'd solve this case. After all, we had about a hundred suspects to choose from.

After the autopsy was finished, I wisely accepted Charlie's invitation to join him for the short trip back to the station. I also wisely listened to his profane harangue about me catching the murderer quickly before he struck again. Though my ears went numb from my ride with Charlie, I survived and helped Bud set up Simon's computer, then got down to typing my written reports, which Charlie also happened to mention in his gentle way. I wished now I had my Explorer, but when the snow started in earnest again, we both packed up some work and Bud took me home.

I'd promised to drop by and have dinner with Harve, so I made Bud stop at a big Kroger's in Camdenton and help me pick out a Christmas tree. Harve loved Christmas, and it had become sort of a tradition in the last few years that I get him a tree about a week before Christmas. At Harve's front gate, Bud helped me wrestle the tree out of the back of his Bronco and then I told him to take off, I'd walk the rest of the way home later. I liked walking in deep snow, I told him, which was a big lie, but I knew he was eager to get home.

Harve was waiting at the open front door. Just over fifty

now, he had iron-gray eyes with hair to match, worn in a buzz cut that gave him a military look. He sat in his fancy motorized wheelchair, and I leaned down and gave him a quick hug. He was a good guy, my best friend in the whole world, and he was paralyzed from the waist down. Strong as an ox, he lifted weights daily and could bench-press as much as any man in my department. We'd been partners once upon a time in L.A., and I blamed myself for what had happened to him. As I dragged the big tree inside, I tried not to think about that. It was Christmas. Time for happy thoughts, happy, happy, happy. Forget spiders and sleeping bags and necrosis. Ho ho ho.

"Nick coming over, too?"

"Nope. Black's in Paris with all those French maids in little white lace aprons and short black skirts. I'll probably never see him again."

"Yeah, right. Looks to me like he's got it for you pretty bad." He grinned as I dragged the six-foot Scotch pine into the window alcove where we always set up his tree. He already had the tree stand in place. "So, Claire, how'd you like the home improvement surprise?"

"What do you think?" I fought with the tree until it stood up, then got it in a half nelson and shoved it down into the red tree stand. "It's pretty cool. But Black's getting a little too possessive for my liking."

"He gets a kick outta that kinda stuff. Thought you might give me hell for letting him have his way with your house."

"Black has his way with just about anything he has a mind to."

"True, true. You gotta admit it's pretty awesome that he went to so much trouble. Besides, the house is yours now. I got a lawyer out here last week and deeded it over."

I turned around, truly shocked. "You did what?"

"That's right. The cabin's yours. Free and clear."

"Harve, I'm not taking the cabin. It's been in your family over fifty years."

"You're my family now. I want you to have it. An early Christmas present. Be gracious for once."

Jeez. I was starring in a Cinderella story for the last few days. Imagine what Santa Claus was going to stuff down my new chimney.

Harve's grin was as cheesy as George Hamilton's in *Dancing with the Stars*.

"I don't feel right about this, Harve."

"I can't let Black make a big gesture and make me look bad. Let me do something for you for a change."

"Well, okay. Thanks. Wish I had something as big as a house to give you."

"You give me a lot."

We usually weren't so serious and we both got so embarrassed that we looked away until Harve said, "How about some homemade beef stew and Mexican cornbread? It's steaming hot on the stove."

My stomach clapped with glee. "You got yourself a deal, Harve."

The food was great, and over the meal we delved into the facts of the Classon case. I trusted Harve with my life, and he had one of the most brilliant investigative minds I'd ever encountered.

He said, "It's interesting that he used spiders to kill his victim. You don't hear something like that very often."

"Yeah, it's creepy as hell."

"He's got to have some way to capture them and handle them without getting bitten."

"Buck says brown recluse spiders are indigenous to Missouri. You seen many around here?"

"Oh, yeah. My aunt was bitten by one when I was a kid. It still makes me sick to think about the hole it made in her leg. God, I'll never forget it."

"Did she die?"

"No, but she had a horrible place in her calf where the tissues were destroyed. It took four skin-graft surgeries to get it done." He sipped some coffee and shook his head. I could identify with his memories of his aunt. I'd seen Classon's body. "Want me to do some research on indigenous spiders and see what I can find out?"

Harve ran a web-designing business and also did some research work. He was a whiz at digging up facts, and I jumped at the offer. "You kidding? Thanks. I have some state-of-the-art stuff at home, thanks to Black, but not much time. We're still interviewing out at that damn academy."

"By the way, I've seen lots of recluses and black widows down around your cabin through the years. So watch where you step."

"Great. Now, that's gonna help me sleep better."

"Maybe you'll get a visit from the Orkin man for Christmas."

Harve smiled, but I couldn't work one up. Nothing about this case was the least bit funny, especially the way Simon Classon died. I'd never been afraid of creepy crawlers before, I'd left that to Bud, but I'd never seen up close and personal the flesh wounds they left behind, either. I shivered involuntarily, and realized with some alarm that I was spooked. Big-time. And I better get over it fast.

My purse started a muffled "Mexican Hat Dance," and I grabbed my cell with more enthusiasm than I liked to display. Black was slated to give me a call tonight, and I knew it was him before I heard the familiar, deep voice.

"Miss me, Morgan?"

My heart did a little quickstep jig, which I instantly berated as silly sentiment. "You mean you've been gone?"

"Thanks a lot."

"Just kidding. Sure, I do. Nobody's around to build additions on my house and fetch me gourmet grub."

Harve laughed, and then made wriggling spider motions with his fingers and pointed to his computer out in the attached sunroom. Always the gentleman, Harve was giving me some privacy.

Black said, "Everything okay with you?"

"Yeah. I'm at Harve's house. We're having dinner, then we're putting up his Christmas tree."

"Wish I was there to help."

"Yeah, that'd be nice." For the first time, I really, and I mean *really*, missed him, but I couldn't say that without feeling ultravulnerable and thus, stupid, so I said, "I hear music in the background. Where are you?"

"I'm having dinner at the Crazy Horse Saloon."

"Really? Must be a late one. Isn't that the place you told me had all the nude dancers?"

Black gave a low laugh. "They're not completely nude. The guy who owns this place is an old friend. I treated one of his dancers once, so it's sort of a tradition to have dinner with him my first night in town."

"Uh-huh. Sounds like you're having a good time." And it sounded like I didn't like it, which made me sound like a real sap.

"Well, I've been at the clinic until now. The patient's begun to have flashbacks that make everybody a little nervous."

"What kind of flashbacks?"

"Scenes of bloody murder, actually."

"No joke?"

"No joke. The trick is determining if they're dreams or the real thing."

"Sounds interesting."

"It is. What about you? The director called me today about Classon's death. He called everyone on the advisory board."

"Yeah, I know. He kept us waiting while you talked. I hope you didn't happen to mention that I discussed the case with you."

"You know better than that. He said Classon hanged himself."

"Not exactly. Get this. We found Classon hanging from a tree limb bound up in a sleeping bag full of poisonous spiders."

There was a momentary silence at the other end. I listened to the snappy music in the background and wondered what the dancers had on, probably not much more than a few colored spotlights. Maybe that's what I should do for a living instead of attending autopsies and cutting half-dead bodies down from limbs.

"You're not joking, are you?"

"Nope. It's pretty brutal."

"Any leads?"

"Everybody I've met so far hated the man's guts, so we have our work cut out for us."

"The director told me they're going to include a special memorial service for Simon at their fund-raising gala on New Year's Eve. He'd called to see if I would be attending."

"Okay."

"I miss you."

I looked to see if Harve could hear me. He was hunched over his computer. I lowered my voice, just in case. "I miss you, too." Actually I hadn't had much time to miss him yet but I figured that would kick in once I got in the big, king-size bed he got for me and started worrying about spiders hiding out under the black satin sheets.

"That's good to hear."

"When are you coming back?"

"I'm aiming for the 23rd but I can't pinpoint it." He paused. "Have any plans for Christmas Eve?"

"I'll probably be working."

"Just so you're home before midnight. I want us to spend Christmas Day together."

"That sounds good." Actually, it did sound good to me. The background music was getting raunchier, with lots of male laughter and applause, and I tried not to envision who was doing what up on that stage.

"Had brunch on the Eiffel Tower yet?"

"Wouldn't be any fun without you to wow."

"Well, figure out if your patient's Jack the Ripper, then jet back home. We could use your thoughts on this one. Some-

body really, and I mean *really*, hated Classon's guts to subject him to torture like this."

"Are there other victims?"

"Not yet. This looks very personal to me. I mean, Black,
the perp made sure Classon suffered in a big way. The vic
was in that bag with the spiders at least two days, probably
longer, considering the size and degree of the wounds."

"My God. That's vicious. I've never heard anything like it
before."

"Yes, sir. It's bizarre, all right."

"Any gut instincts?"

"Not yet. I think it's probably somebody from that weird
school of yours. By the way, I think the director is a real jerk.
Am I wrong?"

"I don't know him that well. Our relationship's strictly
professional. I don't attend the meetings but I've been to their
major fund-raiser a couple of times. He's eccentric, I guess,
or he wouldn't be running that kind of school. I understand
they do some good work with the kids out there."

"Do you know they teach paganism to their little charges?
With discussions on devil worshipping, and other evil do-
ings?"

"What?"

"That's right. Bud and I thought it sounded a bit off center, too."

"First I've heard of that. I guess you're checking that roster."

"Oh yeah, tomorrow, first thing."

"Hold on." Black muffled the phone and I heard him talking to somebody in rapid French. Flawless, too, I might add.
The only thing I understood was *merci*.

"They're serving dinner now. Guess I need to go." He
hesitated. "Keep my side of the bed warm."

"Sure. Same back to you, Black."

He laughed, and then he hesitated again, longer this time.
I listened to the snappy music until he finally came out with
it. "Listen, Claire, if you have one of those bad dreams, re-

member how we do it, just take deep breaths and keep the light on."

I hadn't had the nightmare in a while but maybe that was because Black was usually in bed with me, and we both had loaded guns under our pillows. He had moved into therapist mode, however, so I played along. "Quit worrying about me. I slept alone most of my life. It's not going to kill me."

"That's right, but it's killing me."

I had to smile. He had definitely said the right thing. "You'll live until we meet again. Watch those naked dancers and think of me."

"I don't have to watch anybody to think of you, and they're not completely naked. Look, I'll call you tomorrow and see what you find out about the devil worshippers. Maybe there's a chapter in my new book about this. Remember, duck and weave and check your bed for spiders."

We said our good-byes, but his last remark lingered. I wasn't particularly looking forward to slipping between those soft satin sheets by my lonesome, but I'd definitely heed his advice about unwanted eight-legged bed partners. Okay, so I was definitely spooked. But who could blame me?

ELEVEN

By eight thirty the next morning Bud and I were back at the academy ready to wrap up our interviews. The snow had dwindled down to mere spitting during the night, an evening I spent enjoying the new toys Black had given me, but alone, and thankfully without a single brown recluse in sight. They were all probably frozen for the winter, if spiders freeze, which made me wonder where the hell the perp had gotten so many lively, venomous spiders to kill with. I do hope Harve comes up with some good background stuff on the life and times of arachnids.

We avoided White Building and its resident Jesus imper-sonator and made our way down to Red Building, which I suppose would be the appropriate place to study Lucifer and other hellish subjects. The sun was out, the sky a brilliant blue that tempered the windchill some but still brought out the blush in my cheeks. In Bud's, too. Lots of kids were out building snowmen and pelting snowballs at each other, like regular teens with regular intelligence instead of mad ge-niuses.

Inside Red Building a skinny black-haired girl wearing faded jeans and a red Santa Claus sweatshirt was sitting in the stairwell sketching the distant forested hills. She looked about thirteen. Bud asked her where we could find Stuart Rowland, Devil Instructor. She laughed and pointed down the hall. "He's at the far end. The office with the crossed pitchforks and flames coming out the door."

So now the kids were comedic geniuses. We walked down the tomato-red hall, looking for fire. Instead, we found Rowland sitting behind a black desk in an office that looked a lot like Classon's except it was a cheerful shade of scarlet. He was a small man, probably late thirties, dressed in a gray cardigan sweater with an open-necked green shirt and blue jeans. He had on snow boots and wore round tortoiseshell glasses that made him look scholarly. He had shaggy dark hair and looked like the kind of teacher female students would flirt with.

"Stuart Rowland?"

He glanced up from the Dell laptop computer he was typing on. He immediately looked wary, slapped down the lid of his laptop, and jumped to his feet. "You're from the sheriff's office, aren't you?"

He probably guessed that by the big yellow letters spelling out SHERIFF on the back of our parkas and the badges hanging around our necks. "That's right. I'm Detective Morgan and this is Detective Davis."

"Oh yes, I've heard all about you. Both of you."

I guess he didn't want Bud to feel left out. "Is that right?"

"Oh, yes. You wouldn't believe the rumors flying around campus. I guess you've deduced I killed Simon because of this class I teach, right? Well, you're barking up the wrong tree, I can tell you that."

Bud looked at me. "Well, Morgan, I guess that answers all of our questions. Guess we can shut down the case and blow this place."

Bud and his razor wit. "We're not accusing you of anything, Mr. Rowland. We're just interviewing Mr. Classon's colleagues here at the academy."

"I understand that, of course. I just want you to know right off the cuff that I'm not involved in any way, form, or fashion in what happened to *that man*."

That man. With a definite disgusted ring. "Might we sit down, sir? Have a little chat?"

Rowland looked around, nervous as the proverbial feline, maybe more so, then he put one finger to his lips and gave us some interesting hand signals. Clearly, he thought his office was bugged. Uh-oh. Shades of paranoia, maybe with a little schizophrenia thrown in. Bud and I watched Rowland quickly bundle his small frame into a tan James Bond belted overcoat and a sissy pink-and-orange-paisley fringed scarf. Academia cool. He motioned us to follow, and we did, outside the nearest exit to a small patio with round wrought-iron tables covered by a good foot of snow. Nobody else in sight. Wonder why?

"Is there a reason you wanted us to interview you out here, Mr. Rowland?"

"Because, detective, my office is bugged by the director. He'll deny it, of course, but hidden cameras are everywhere. Hidden microphones, too. This place is not what it appears on the surface."

Boy, tell me about it. "Why do you say that, Mr. Rowland?"

"Because I've worked here long enough to know that if you don't play the director's game, and, yes, Classon's, too, you get canned. They rule this place like two kings and they squash people that stand up to them like ants under their thumbs."

"How long have you worked here?"

Rowland gave a snort. "Too long. I've got my résumé out everywhere. I want to leave. Anybody with an ounce of integrity has already gotten out of here."

"I see. What can you tell us about Simon Classon?"

To our surprise he began to hum the Wicked Witch song from *The Wizard of Oz*. Rowland said, "Know what that is?

Classon's theme song. Everybody hums it under their breath when they see him coming. Perfect, isn't it, for a bastard like him? Prissy little shit."

He shook a cigarette out of a pack of Camels and kept glancing around. Paranoia Man.

Bud said, "So you didn't much care for the victim?"

"I'm telling you that Simon Classon was the worst human being who ever set foot on this earth. He demeaned everybody he ever met, that's all he did, all day long, demean other people, tear them down, and you know why? So he could build himself up. Talk about insecure, that man was threatened by anybody nice or good-looking or happy, yeah, especially happy. He couldn't stand anybody to be happy. If he couldn't be happy, nobody better be. Forget the smiles, the good mornings, forget anything but kissing his ass."

So there you go.

A big fan of Butch Cassidy, Bud said, "Quit sugarcoating it, Rowland. Tell us like it is."

"Sorry, but I get so pissed off just thinking about Classon. Yeah, I'll say it, sure I will. I'm glad that bastard is dead. I wish I could have hung him up in that tree and watched him strangle in that noose. It would've made my day, hell, it would've made my year, my life, for God's sake."

Bud glanced at me, then said, "Okay sir, let's try to take it down a notch. I mean, all this is making you sound guilty."

"I know that, detective." Sarcasm. "I'm just being honest. I was honest with Simon. He knew I hated his guts. That's why he saddled me with that asinine paganism class."

"He suggested the class?"

"Suggested?" Rowland laughed, as contemptuous a sound as I've ever heard. "He didn't suggest shit. He ran this place. Johnstone's nothing but a figurehead here, a pawn, not smart enough to know he's Classon's puppet. Simon used Johnstone's vanity and played him like a freakin' fiddle."

Well, now, a man who likes his similes can't be all bad. "You believe that Mr. Classon ran this school?"

"Oh, yeah. Ask around, but everybody here's so damned

scared, they probably think he'll come back from the dead and get them fired."

Bud said, "Mr. Rowland, man, you gotta chill before you have a stroke or somethin'."

"What do you mean? This's the happiest I've been in the six years I've worked at this hellhole."

"Okay. Really, we've got to calm down now. There's no need to get your back up so hard." The words were hardly out when I cringed, expecting Bud to explain the derivation. I was not disappointed. Maybe he was only trying to get Rowland's mind off Classon and onto something else.

He said, "Rowland, you know where they got that saying about getting your back up?"

"What?"

"It goes way back to the Dark Ages and refers to the way cats arch up their backs and strut around on their toes."

Rowland scowled, blew out smoke. "So?"

"Just thought it was interesting."

Rowland looked at me, obviously confused. I shrugged. "Bud's got this book I gave him on phrase origins. It annoys me, too."

Rowland did not look remotely impressed, but he'd stopped spewing hatred, too. We remained silent as he pulled out a red Bic lighter, to match his office, I guess. He lit up and puffed like a crazed adder for several seconds.

"All right, all right. Sorry I went off on you guys. I just have all this anger built up inside, rage, really, at what goes on around here. The only redeeming element in this school are the students, and hell, they'd be better off somewhere else, anywhere else. This place sucks all the positive energy out of people, makes them bitter and angry and frustrated."

"We're beginning to notice that," I said.

"Good." More puffing, interrupted at one point by a fit of congested hacking. Smoking sucks. People ought to wise up.

I stepped out of the shade hugging the wall and into the blinding sun where the temperature wasn't ten below zero.

"It's good you've calmed down, sir, because we need to ask some questions. Don't freak out, please, but where were you on the night of December 16?"

"That was Wednesday night, right? I usually have dinner alone at home. Sometimes my neighbors see me getting my newspaper at the curb, though. Sometimes they don't. I'm not a social man. I can't help that. I've never been."

Bud looked at me, and I said, "And that's what happened on Wednesday? No one saw you or spoke to you?"

"Wait, that was the night I slid my Mustang into the ditch." He acted relieved. I could understand why. "I stayed here at my office on the futon. It's rare for me to work late. I sure as hell don't owe any loyalty to this hellhole." He drew in on the Camel and the tip glowed red. "You know what that bastard Classon called me once over the phone, detective? A brat. Can you believe that? A grown man! I have a master's degree, for God's sake. I'm retired military and served my country honorably, and that asshole called me a brat. But hell, that's his MO, he calls people terrible things, and everybody has to put up with it because he controls that idiot, Johnstone, in his stupid white suit and sandals."

I could see now why Rowland wanted to talk to us outside. The insults he was spitting out were pretty provocative.

"He really call you a brat, no kiddin'?" Bud said. "I wouldn't've liked that kinda crap, either."

"Yeah, and that's mild to what he usually called me."

Bud's brow was all furrowed and sympathetic and seemed to soothe Rowland's ruffled feathers. "Tell you what, detectives, I'm sorry if I'm coming off like a jerk, but you know how it is, sometimes the truth's got to come out. People around the lake need to know what goes on out here. Man, the morons that run the place need to be exposed for what they are, and then fired."

Right, and maybe Rowland was just the one to do it, starting with Simon Classon. I said, "Yes, sir. I understand how you must feel. Tell me, did you kill Simon Classon, Mr. Rowland?"

.

Rowland gazed at me, apparently shocked. He blinked once and came out with a long, put-upon sigh. "Oh yeah, I'm glad you asked that. Yep, you got me cold. I did it. Couldn't stand him being around me any more so I hung him out in the woods, then slid my car in the ditch so I'd be a prime suspect."

"Is that a confession, sir?"

He stared hard at Bud then shook his head. "Are you kidding me? No, of course, I didn't kill Classon. I was being sarcastic, ever heard of that?"

Oh yeah, we've heard of it. And to think I thought *we* were good at it. "I wouldn't be quite so cavalier with your police statements, Mr. Rowland. Somebody, like us, maybe, might believe you and take you in for murder one."

He sobered instantly. My threat was empty at this point, but Rowland didn't know that. "Now, if I were you, Rowland, I'd find somebody to verify your whereabouts for the last few nights. Especially the night of December 16. Okay?"

He frowned, stared across the quadrangle at Building White for a moment. "Okay. I just remembered that on the night I stayed here on campus, a custodian stuck his head in and asked me what I was doing."

"And this custodian's name?"

"Willie Vines. Yeah, you better check him out, too. He's a weird duck, if I ever saw one. And that girl he hung with, too. Wilma. She took my class and was into all kind of weird shit, showed me this devil holding a pitchfork tattoo on her ankle. I liked her, though, but Classon didn't. He didn't like any custodians. In fact, rumor had it he accused Willie Vines of dealing dope to the students. Just FYI, you know."

Bud perked up. "You got any firsthand proof of that, Mr. Rowland?"

"I don't use, if that's what you're asking."

"That's what I'm askin', all right."

"I'm not into that shit, but lots of people around here are. Have to be, to keep showing up for work."

"Want to name a few of them for us?"

"No."

We waited a few seconds for him to change his mind. He didn't.

I said, "All right. I guess that's it for now, Mr. Rowland. But a word of advice. Get a grip on your temper. It doesn't look good for you to lose control like you did today. It could even make us consider that you might lose control if you get angry enough, you know, and hurt somebody, even kill them."

"I didn't kill Classon or anybody else. But I hated Simon, and I mean *loathed* him. You would've, too, if you'd known him when he was alive."

"Thank you for your time, sir." Bud paused at the door. "And you know, don't you, that there are people you can hire to debug your office? Might think about it."

"This place is so full of psychos, we're trippin' over them," Bud said as we took leave of our newest and bestest suspect.

"Tell me something I don't know. Let's go find this Willie Vines guy and see if Rowland's right about him dealing drugs. Simon had a stash at his house, so maybe they were in cahoots and had a falling-out. Or maybe a rival supplier took Classon out as a warning."

"Drug dealers don't give warnings with spiders."

"What about the old Colombian necktie?"

"Slitting throats is quick and easy. This took a lot of time and effort."

"So the killer's a sadist."

"You bet he is."

We found the custodian mopping the cafeteria. He looked a lot younger than I expected, more like the students laughing and talking in the serving line. Bud had the angelology roster, compliments of Christie the Fox. Cross-referencing had the same students taking paganism, too. We'd have to interview them all but first of interest was Willie Vines.

"Mr. Vines?"

Vines jerked around, startled. Then he grinned. "Don't many people call me mister, not around here."

He was a cute kid, bushy hair, blond, so unruly it kinked up in tight ringlets. He'd look like Shirley Temple at ten if it was longer. He had blue eyes, bloodshot but watchful. He watched me introduce myself and Bud. His smile was white as the weather outside. Did everyone use Crest Whitestrips now?

Willie said, "It's about Mr. Classon, right?"

"Yes. We're interviewing all faculty and staff."

"Somebody finally got him, huh?"

"That's right. And we're here to find out who."

"Do you think I did it?"

"We don't know who did it at this point, Mr. Vines. We're trying to understand who does what around here."

"I thought he was a mean man but I wouldn't never hurt him or nothin'."

"Why don't we sit down somewhere? Over there in the corner, maybe? Do you have a few minutes to talk to us?"

He propped his mop against the wall. "I guess so. But I'll get in big trouble if the director catches me goofing off."

Bud said, "Hell, I'll vouch for you. Everybody's supposed to cooperate with us. How about a soda and cheeseburger while we talk? On me."

"Sure thing. Thanks."

"Make it three, Bud."

Willie Vines followed me to a table in the far corner. He looked uncomfortable, scared, even, but somehow pleased, too. "Ain't really allowed to sit down in here. I can't even go in some buildings to the water fountain. Even in the summertime when it's burning hot."

"Sounds like you work for a bunch of jerks."

Willie rubbed his fingers across his thin blond mustache. His gaze darted around, and I noticed he had a habit of rubbing a discolored spot on his forehead, a birthmark, maybe? "Yeah, they're jerks. Especially Dr. Johnstone."

"By the way, Willie, it's okay if I call you Willie, isn't it?"

He nodded. Watchful, lots going on underneath that calm expression.

"We talked to Mr. Rowland over in Red. He said you check the buildings every night. That true?"

"Yes, ma'am."

"Did he sleep in his office night before last?"

Willie nodded. "Yeah. I check the exit by his office a coupla times a night, usually. I saw the light on and stuck my head in to see why he was there so late."

"Do you check all the exits around campus every night?"

"Most days I don't come on until dinnertime, around four-thirty or so, then I clean up in here and check doors after everybody's in bed."

"I guess you didn't see anybody lurking around on the night of the murder?"

"What night was that?"

"Did you notice anything unusual any night this last week? Anything you found suspicious?"

"No, ma'am. Everybody was just glad Mr. Classon was gone on vacation."

"Doesn't sound like you liked him much."

Willie fiddled with a black onyx initial ring on his right hand. It was that old-fashioned kind teenage boys used to give to girls, one with a fancy gold *W*. Willie was uncomfortable now. "No, ma'am. He weren't very nice to people."

Bud showed up with a heaping tray of fast food. "Man, this place is dirt cheap. All this just cost me five bucks."

Bud sat down and handed out our fare. Willie unwrapped a cheeseburger, looking around at the other kids, amazed he was eating in the cafeteria, just like anybody else.

"Guess what, Bud? Willie said he can't sit down in here. Said the director won't permit it."

"Bummer, Willie. Bet you'd like to tell the director where to stick it, huh?"

Willie chewed his burger, chased it with a swig of Vanilla Pepsi. "Yeah. He's . . ." he glanced around, acting guilty as hell. "I shouldn't be saying stuff like this. They fire people here all the time."

Bud said, "You aren't gonna get fired for talkin' to us. Tell us more about Dr. Johnstone. He give you lots of trouble?"

"Yeah. He's a weird man. I got treated better at the hospital where I used to mop floors. They pay me better here, though."

"What'd you mean 'weird'?"

"You know, just likes to mess with people's minds. Like last summer, he comes up to me and says, 'You aren't doing your job, son. I saw some weeds this morning on campus, at least fifteen inches tall, and I want them cut down.' So I says, 'Yes sir, where is those weeds and I'll get right on it.' Then he says, 'That's your problem. Find them and take care of it by the end of the day, or you're fired.'"

I sipped my Pepsi. "Somebody needs to talk to that guy. Tell him he's not God Almighty, just a crackpot in summer shoes."

Bud said, "Yeah. Somebody oughta give him a lesson in nice."

Willie grinned, looked a little less cautious. He liked us. I wondered if he had any friends. He struck me as a serious loner. "You live here on campus, Willie?"

"I got a little place that I can stay at when I want, just down the hall over there." He pointed past the kitchen. "I got a little house, too, a ways down the road from here. Got it left to me."

It occurred to me that Maxine Knight had mentioned Willie's name. "Mr. Classon's secretary said Classon disliked another custodian here and picked on her. You know anything about that?"

For the first time, Willie forgot calm and caution. He stiffened up and looked angry. "Yeah, she's my friend. Her name's Wilma Harte. She's real nice, too, real nice."

"How do you mean?"

"You know, she just did stuff for people, stuff nobody paid her for. She left here and didn't tell nobody why, but everybody thinks it's 'cause of Mr. Classon. I'd come down to the boiler room where we got our desks and she'd be cryin' her eyes out."

"What kind of things did he do to her?"

"He called her stupid or made fun of her work shoes being cheap and ugly, stuff like that. She liked horror movies, and he said she was the horror and oughta star in them."

Tears actually welled in his eyes.

I said, "I'm sorry, Willie. You miss her a lot, don't you?"

"Yeah. She was a real good friend to me, but that didn't stop her from going off and not saying good-bye. She'd get real down, you know, depressed, I think you call it, especially when Mr. Classon got to pickin' on her. I really hate to say this, I sure do, but maybe Mr. Classon got just what he deserved. Maybe it's a good thing he's dead and won't hurt nobody no more."

I watched him stuff some fries in his mouth and decided that yessir, that certainly seemed to be the general consensus.

I said, "Oh yeah, Willie, one more thing. We've been told you might be dealing some drugs around here. That true?"

Bud and I watched his face go about three shades whiter. When he answered, he stuttered, "N . . . n . . . no, no, ma'am. Not me, it ain't me. It was Mr. Classon who got drugs for the kids who wanted them around here. I swear to God it was him. Who told you that about me? I bet it was Mr. Rowland. I heard that he said that about me sometimes. Well, he's a lying dog, if he said that."

"Then you won't mind us taking a quick look around your office, right?"

Of course, we couldn't do that without a warrant, but Willie didn't know that. He was innocent of dealing, too, if his next statement was any indication.

"Sure, come on. You can do it now. It's right down that hall over there. You can look through anything of mine you want to."

We got up and followed him, but he was too eager to

show it to us for me to get too excited about finding anything incriminating.

His office was down the hall beside the food line. He strode off ahead of us, and Bud and I followed him in to a room holding two desks, one on opposite ends of the room. Both had bulletin boards above them. Bud took Willie's side, and I walked over to the one Wilma Harte had used. Her bulletin board had two movie posters pinned up, along with a schedule for last year's St. Louis Cardinals' games and a color photograph stuck in one corner. The bigger poster depicted the movie *Hellraiser* with a picture of its star, that cutie Pinhead, with all the nails protruding from his head. I prefer men without nails in their head, but to each his own. I'd met up with a few guys I'd like to use a hammer on, though.

The other poster was for the horror spoof *Scream*. I had actually seen that film once at Bud's house, but it paled in comparison to my own personal nightmares, so I wasn't particularly impressed. I took off the photo and looked at it. Willie and a girl smiling at the camera and leaning on mops together in the cafeteria. The official custodian pose, no doubt.

"Is this Wilma with you?"

Willie was standing over in the corner, shoulder against the wall, calmly watching the detectives snoop. Mr. Look-Wherever-You-Want-To-But-You-Won't-Find-A-Damn-Thing. He said, "Yeah, that was taken at the first of the school year. I wish she was still here. I sure do miss her."

I examined Wilma Harte's face. She looked pretty much dead-on to Maxine Knight's description. She was kinda stocky and muscular and strong-looking. She had on a hot-pink polo shirt, and her dark-red hair was plaited into pigtails tied with yellow ribbons. She had lots of freckles and was cute in a Pippi Longstocking holding-a-baby-nanny-goat sort of way. Didn't look particularly Goth-like to me. No black lipstick or devil tattoos in sight. Maybe her Goth look was a seasonal thing.

I rifled through Wilma's desk and found the usual paper-clips, rubber bands, and empty ink pens and yellow Post-it notes. Bud found pretty much the same in Willie's desk. Nary a stash of coke or meth or deadly brown recluse in sight. It looked like Willie was going to pass muster, at least until we found reason to serve a search warrant. Then we might pull out the air vents and check behind the ceiling tiles and under the carpet. Willie Vines's furnace-room office appeared clean, and he bore no track marks on his arms, which he offered up with more innocent enthusiasm, so we thanked him politely and left him to fetch his mop. At least he'd gotten a free cheeseburger out of the ordeal.

The Angel Gabriel

For a long time after Freddy was in the ground, Gabriel and Uriel never mentioned him. Uriel's grandma would bless Freddy and his mother when she had Uriel pray on his knees with her each night, right after she mentioned Uriel's own family. She always asked the Lord to let Uriel's momma and daddy take care of Freddy up in heaven. Uriel didn't like that prayer. He didn't like a mean kid like Freddy being with his own nice family. He said his private prayers later and told them not to speak to Freddy in heaven because he'd knocked Uriel into their grave. They'd listen to him; he knew they would.

One time they went to Freddy's house with his grandma's famous fudge-swirl cake and sat around and listened to Freddy's mother cry and say how it was her fault about the hornets and how strange it was. Freddy's big brother was there, too, and he looked tough and angry and said he'd heard a motorcycle that night. That scared Uriel and he covered his face and pretended to cry so everybody would feel sorry for him and his grandma would take him home.

That afternoon he met Gabriel in the secret cave and told

him what Freddy's brother said. "Don't worry about him. He can't prove nothing. Nobody saw us."

After that, they spent a lot of time together in the cave, and Uriel learned more and more about bugs, especially the spiders. He liked to spend every waking minute with Gabriel and was jealous when Gabriel went to basketball and choir practice without him.

Then one day when Gabriel was off with his other friends, Uriel shuffled through piles of leaves. It was late autumn and most of the red and gold leaves had turned brown and covered the ground. He was on his way to the old lodge when he saw a stray mongrel puppy caught in one of Gabriel's animal traps. Its little paw was all smashed and bloody inside the steel teeth, and Uriel stared at the little thing twisting and biting at its own foot. It was trying to get free.

Something moved deep inside Uriel, a kind of thrill that sent goose bumps rippling up and down his arms and legs. He shivered all over like a wet animal, then he knelt down a few yards away and watched the puppy struggle. Blood was spattered all over the dead leaves and the trap and puppy's snout. It looked real pretty, all scarlet and bright red like a cardinal's feathers. The dog kept making sad little yelps and whines of pain, and Uriel was fascinated with the way it wriggled and looked so scared and frantic. He could take a big rock and bash it in the head, and it would die and go to heaven. He could send living things up to heaven any time he wanted, like they'd done with Freddy. More shivers shook through him, and he liked the way that felt, liked it a lot, liked it more than anything else he'd ever felt, even Christmas morning when he'd come downstairs and found the presents Santa Claus had left.

The woods were quiet, except for the puppy's howls of pain and panic. Gabriel would like it if Uriel killed something for them to dissect. He'd smile and mess up Uriel's hair and tell him he was a good kid. Uriel stood up and looked around for a big rock. It was so big and heavy that he could barely lift it, but he got it in his hands and carried it over to the frightened little dog. The puppy growled and clawed the ground and tried to get away.

Uriel decided that he couldn't hit it with the rock without getting bitten, so he picked up a big stick instead, long enough to keep him safe. He raised it up high over his head and brought it down on the dog's back. The dog screamed with agony and fought weakly, but Uriel hit it again and again, harder and harder, until it lay still and lifeless. Then he picked up the big rock again and smashed in its head. He felt blood spatter on his hands and face, and it felt warm, almost hot. He liked the way it felt.

Uriel smiled. The puppy had probably already flown up to heaven. Gabriel said the animals they killed went to heaven, too, and were pets for Uriel's family.

"Now, you're happy, little sweet puppy, now you don't have to cry and hurt any more. I fixed that for you, and I'm glad I did." He said a little prayer, then he got the dog out of the trap and carried it back to the cave. Gabriel was still at choir practice, so Uriel dumped its body into a long glass tank where a couple of big brown recluses had their webs.

When Gabriel came in later with a Pizza Hut sausage-and-extra-cheese pizza, he nodded approvingly and told Uriel that he'd done a good job. He said Uriel was an avenging angel and soon he'd be as good as Gabriel at sending things to heaven. Uriel smiled, very proud.

TWELVE

After we marked Willie down as super cooperative, we managed to locate and interview most of the students in Classon's classes and found them a tiny bit more complimentary to Classon than his esteemed colleagues had been. In fact, the words bastard, devil, horrible, or Lucifer never came up at all. Charlie gave me a call, politely requesting my presence in his office, so I headed downtown and left Bud to wow all the teenage girls with his big white grin and Georgia drawl and good looks. When I got there, I was sorry I'd come.

Charlie said, "Sit down, Claire, run the case for me."

I sat. I told. "Everybody hated his guts. Everybody wanted him dead. Everybody's a suspect. Ever heard of *Murder on the Orient Express* by Agatha Christie?"

Charlie actually smiled. He must've seen the movie where everybody on the train takes turns stabbing the victim. Pleased that Charlie appeared to be in a fairly good mood, I waited while he took some time filling his black pipe. He never remembered the building's rigid no-smoking rules. None of us reminded him, either.

"Got your paperwork done yet?"

I shifted in my chair. "I just got here, Sheriff."

"Let me have them the minute you do. I'm not rushing you, though."

Yeah, like hell. "I'll try to get the reports in today."

"How's Nick?"

I frowned. "Okay, I guess. He's in Paris on business."

"So you're still with him."

That was rather personal but everybody seemed to consider our relationship their very own *Days of Our Lives*, so I decided not to take umbrage.

"We see each other when he's in town."

"He's a good guy."

Part of his recommendation was due to the fact that Black was his biggest campaign contributor and they'd known each other for years. Then again, Black *was* a good guy, so I said nothing, just gave my best perfunctory nod.

"I've got a new assignment for you, Claire, and I don't want any argument about it."

Uh-oh. That cut any objections right off at the knees. How could I argue with that? I said nothing again.

He swiveled in his chair and pulled a file out of his desk drawer. I found my tongue. "I'm right in the middle of the Classon case, sir. It's a big one that's going to take a lot of my time."

"I know that, detective. This is part of that case. Don't get so dadgummed wadded up."

Okay. Told you he had dumb sayings. I went on saying nothing. I was getting good at saying it, too, but it paid when dealing with your boss and superior who was devolving rapidly into a foul mood.

"I don't like this business with fuckin' spiders and garbage bags. Don't like it one fuckin' bit."

Charlie was fond of the *F* bomb, used it often, enjoyed himself with it, did it awfully well, actually.

"I want that fuckin' lunatic locked up."

I finally thought of something pertinent to say. "Me too, sir."

Charlie stuck his pipe in his mouth and held it with his

teeth as he flipped open the file. He gazed at me. Was it, could it be, sheepishly? I tensed. Charlie was not your run-of-the-mill, sheepish kinda guy.

"Okay, thing is, I got this letter." He held up a sheet of paper torn from a yellow legal pad. I nodded as if it meant something to me. "It's from this guy named Joe McKay. Says he's helped out the police before. I checked him out and found out he's on the up-and-up."

"What do you mean helped out the police?"

"Helped them solve cases they weren't getting anywhere with."

"How'd he do that, sir?" I was deathly afraid of where this was going, and my instincts were right on target.

"He's an honest-to-God psychic, that's how."

My stare could be described as dumbfounded. I tried for calm, didn't make it. "Sheriff, please, you don't believe in that crap, do you?"

Charlie puffed on his pipe. The smell was barely bearable. "Hell, no, but a couple of my old friends in the Corps do. They verified what he said, said he knew what he was talking about, had helped them."

I waited, all sick to my stomach and wary, like he was going to sucker punch me in the gut. He did.

"Like I said, I got this letter from this guy and he says right here that a man was going to get killed in our jurisdiction. He said he saw a black trash bag and spiderwebs."

"Lucky guess," I suggested.

Charlie ignored my black humor, but he never had found me very amusing. "The postmark on this envelope dates back to last summer, Detective. I kept it because he mentioned some references, and as I said, they're people I know and respect."

"And how does this affect my investigation?"

Charlie didn't mince words, didn't ask my opinion. "I want you to let this guy work with you and Bud. Show him the crime scene, let him read your reports, do whatever you need to do to get this fuckin' perp behind bars."

"Oh, Charlie, no, don't make me do this."

Sometimes when under stress or wigged out by particularly horrible commands, I revert to his given name. That was a mistake today.

He took his pipe out of his mouth so he could glower at me better. "That's an order, Detective. Give the guy a chance. You might be surprised at what he can do."

Hocus-pocus suddenly came to mind, that, and charlatan, quack, phony, nut, and crackpot.

"Yes, sir."

"I want you to meet him, talk to him, see if he gets any of his vibes or visions or whatever the fuckin' hell he calls them."

"Yes, sir. I should have some time next week to get together with him."

"That's good because he'll be here any minute."

Shit, to put it in a nutshell. "Now?"

"That's right. Surprisingly enough, he lives around here. I'm amazed you've never heard of him before."

Me, too. I had a vision of my own, and it involved driving around town with the Amazing Kreskin, afraid to think thoughts for fear of being eavesdropped on.

"Good, here he is now. You ready to meet him?" Charlie was looking over my head and through the glass door of his office. He motioned for his tiny secretary, Madge, to usher the man in. I turned to see if he had a pink aura or something ephemeral around his head.

He had an aura, all right. He was about the best-looking guy I'd ever laid eyes on, except for Black, maybe. Tall, buff, long dark-blond hair that almost reached his shoulders. A couple of days unshaven, probably going for the bad-boy look. He was wearing tight jeans and brown leather hiking boots, a black sweatshirt that said USC, and an unzipped black parka with brown fur around the hood. Oops, he forgot to wear the obligatory black leather jacket. No self-respecting bad boy would be caught dead in a parka, but hey, maybe psychic bad boys got cold riding around on motorcycles in subzero weather. But funniest thing, I disliked him at once, didn't trust him, either. Why, I do not know. He smiled at me and I wondered if he could read my thoughts. Just in case, I thought, *You don't fool me, you clown.*

"Hello. I'm Joe McKay." He nodded at us. "Sheriff. Miss."

Miss? Who the hell did he think he was, calling me miss? "I'm no miss, McKay. I'm the lead detective on this case."

McKay stretched out his hand, a real friendly, smiling psychic. "Glad to meet you, Lead Detective."

I decided to be up-front. "If I shake your hand, you gonna read my mind?"

Charlie said, "That's enough, Detective. Shake the man's hand and quit being a fuckin' smart-ass."

I shook his hand.

McKay put his forefinger to his forehead and said, "Oooh, she doesn't like me. She doesn't want me helping her with this case. She thinks I'm a con man."

I looked at Charlie. "You're right. He can read minds."

To my surprise, both men laughed. Problem was, I wasn't trying for levity.

Charlie reached out and clasped McKay's hand. "Welcome aboard. Don't mind the detective here, she'll warm up to you if you help her get her man."

Well, that made me sound like either a Las Vegas gold digger or a Royal Canadian Mountie.

McKay said, "That's okay. Most police officers resent me at first."

"Have a seat, Mr. McKay."

I sat down, too. I looked at him again. He was sexy, I decided. I wondered about his background, where he'd come from, why he'd turned up all of a sudden and saddled me with his mumbo-jumbo crap.

"Tell us about yourself, Mr. McKay," I invited.

"Not a lot to tell. I'm from around here originally but have spent the last fifteen years in the Marine Corps. Demolitions."

Now I'd have to worry about him blowing up things. And

uh-oh, Charlie was a Marine. Now they'd have that Semper Fi bonding stuff going on all over the place. I didn't have a chance.

"Semper Fi," said Charlie

"Semper Fi," said McKay.

"Vietnam. What about you?"

"Iraq."

See what I mean? They discussed their respective military careers for a few minutes, and I wondered if the Amazing Kreskin knew so many details because he committed the murder himself. Made a lot more sense to me.

"So you live around here? Where?"

"North of the lake. I inherited a house up there. It's pretty remote, but that's what I like about it."

Charlie said, "We appreciate your contacting us. I was pretty shocked when your prediction panned out."

"Yeah. I thought I should apprise you when I first sensed what was going to happen. I hoped it wouldn't, of course."

I said, "Well, don't keep us in suspense, Master Yoda. Who did it?"

McKay laughed again, but Charlie removed his pipe and glared at me.

"If you can't act professionally, Detective Morgan, then I'll have to put Bud in charge of the Classon case."

Well, ouch. Point taken. "Yes, sir. I'm sorry, Mr. McKay. I'm just not used to deferring to psychics during my investigations. I'm sure I'll get used to it, given time." Yeah, two or three decades.

"Like I said, nobody's glad to see me until after I prove myself. Believe me, it's you who'll be solving this case, Detective, not me. I'll just try to help when I can."

"Thank you so much. I'm really so thrilled."

"Detective, I'm warning you." Charlie, at his most restrained. But his face was the color of a ripe raspberry. Very close to bursting.

"Yes, sir."

"Well, there it is. I'm going to let you two go get acquainted. Introduce him to Bud, too. Mr. McKay will fill you in on what he needs from you, and I expect you to listen to him and quit being so damned uncooperative. Hell, if he can help us, we'd be stupid not to use him."

McKay said, "Thank you, Sheriff Ramsay."

Thank you, Sheriff Ramsay. I parroted in a screw-you internal growl.

"Take him out to Classon's house, then show him where the victim was found. See if anything comes of it. Keep me posted."

And that was that. Charlie was done, washed the psychic out of his hair and into mine. Well, okay. I'd handled worse things in my life. I almost died a couple of times, actually. I could handle a so-called police psychic.

Outside the office I tried to exchange amenities in the best way I could and without gritting my teeth.

"If I've got to take you along, come on, but don't think I'm going to babysit you or listen to a bunch of John Edward crap."

"Yes, ma'am. Lead the way."

Okay, so his amenities were better than mine. I've never been known for amenities, and I wasn't starting with him.

"Meet me outside, McKay. I have to get the key to Classon's house. I guess you want to go there, right?"

'Yes, ma'am. I need to handle some of his personal possessions. See if I feel anything."

"But of course."

McKay smiled and sauntered off down the hall like a reincarnated James Dean. I realized my teeth were making strange gnashing noises, so I strode off to the evidence locker. When I exited at the front entrance, my new psychic friend was sitting atop one huge Harley-Davidson motorcycle. He saluted me with two fingers and gave me a sassy grin. I nodded, then got into my Explorer, wondering if I could lose him in traffic. But oh yeah, I forgot, he could zero in on me with his mind.

I backed out, wondering why Charlie hadn't shoved this

guy off on Bud. They were more of a pair, both cute and benignly arrogant. In the rearview mirror, I watched him put on his helmet, fire up his cycle, then swerve smoothly in behind me. We traveled like that until we hit the open highway that led north to Classon's house. I drove carefully, just under the speed limit, in order to annoy him. It didn't take long. After five minutes he swerved out and sped up until he was alongside my driver's window. I glanced at him, and he saluted again, did a really impressive wheel stand, then shot off ahead of me.

"You just got yourself a ticket, pal," I said, no, grumbled. I reached for my flashing light then returned to my senses. It would be childish to arrest him. More importantly, Charlie would jerk me off the case. Calm and confident again, I proceeded at speed limit. About two miles up the road, he was sitting just off the road, waiting. He waved as I passed by. I ground my teeth. The psychic was a smart-ass, too. Great.

By the time I reached Classon's road, the day had clouded over, and I remembered that snow was forecast again, not as heavy but just as much trouble. I stopped the car in front of the house and got out, wondering if Granny Talbott down the road was eyeballing us during *Sex and the City* commercials. I waited politely as he killed his engine and hopped off his bike. He took off his helmet and hung it on the handlebars.

"You drive like my grandma," he said.

I had a great comeback, of course, but why waste it on him? "Please follow me, Mr. McKay."

"Yes, ma'am."

"You can stop any time with the ma'am business. Detective Morgan will suffice for now, since I plan to pass you off to my partner ASAP."

"Yes, ma'am, Detective Morgan."

Oh boy, it was going to be a helluva long day. It was already a long day. "This is where we believe Simon Classon was initially assaulted and then abducted by the perp. A neighbor down the road reported him missing, and a couple of deputies secured the scene until Bud and I got here. We later determined that he'd been missing going on thirty-six hours."

We reached the front steps and I ducked under the crime scene tape and climbed to the porch. McKay clomped up after me and stood looking around while I took out my penknife and slit through the tape securing the door.

I handed him latex gloves and paper booties, snapped on my own, and said, "Got anything yet?"

He was his usual good-humored self. "Might take a minute or two."

"Right. Just tug on my sleeve when the visions start."

"You'll probably know without me having to touch you."

"God is good."

I unlocked the door and walked inside. He followed but, alas, he was frowning at me now.

"Look, Detective Morgan, I know you don't like anything about me but there's no need for us to keep knifing each other. It won't help matters. I'll be glad to work with this Bud guy, if you're opposed to my being a part of your investigation."

I looked at him and felt a little bit like a jerk, but only a little. "Sorry. It's not just you. I'm this way with everybody. You'll see."

"Whew, that's a relief."

I smiled woodenly to prove I didn't hate him. His smile was the same easy one he'd worn since he'd walked into Charlie's office.

"Well okay, McKay, now we're best buddies. What do you want to do here?"

"Just look around."

"You got it. I'll just hide and watch."

"I might need to take off these gloves when I pick up things."

"Okay. We've impounded the assault weapon and the scene's been swept. Go ahead, I'll watch in awe."

McKay ignored that. I had a feeling he planned to ignore me from now on. He'd made the overture. He was done. I leaned up against the wall and watched. Actually, I was interested in how a so-called police psychic went about his so-called business. Must be spooky to get visions of murder and mayhem and God knows what else. Like my dreams of late.

He walked to the staircase and placed his right hand on the newel post. Then he moved up a few steps and looked upstairs. He put his hand on the banister and closed his eyes.

"I see him upstairs in bed, reading. He came down here to answer the door."

Not exactly genius. Bud and I figured that out in five minutes. I waited for him to identify the killer. Now that would impress me.

"He knew him. He let him in. That's how the killer got him."

I wondered if it was correct etiquette to interrupt visions or if that was a no-no. So I waited until he opened his eyes and looked at me.

"Very good. Now who did you say it was?"

"I didn't get that, not yet."

"Oh, darn. Now we'll have to keep investigating. But we really do appreciate your help."

McKay laughed. "You're something else."

"I'm sure you are, too." I glanced around. I could smell the dried blood in the carpet, strong and vile in the closed-up house. "What's next?"

"I'd like to look around some more. That okay?"

"Sure."

He started upstairs with me on his heels. He walked straight down the hall to Simon's bedroom. He stood in the threshold for a few seconds, then moved to the bed. It was just as I'd seen it on that first night.

"Okay if I lie down on the bed?"

"You're not getting kinky on me, are you, McKay?"

"Not yet." The look he gave me was, well, smoldering, I guess you'd call it. He did smoldering pretty well, too. Too bad I wasn't remotely interested in him.

"Not ever, actually."

"You married, then?" He was a straightforward psychic.

"Your visions didn't tell you?"

"I have to touch you to get that kind of vibe." He didn't give me time to think up a proper put-down. "You aren't wearing a wedding ring."

"I like to keep my private life private."

"Got it, loud and clear."

So, back to business he went. He lay down on the bed where the covers were thrown back. He didn't touch anything for a few moments, then he picked up Classon's book and his reading glasses. He closed his eyes and just lay there. Okay, ho-hum, boring, I stifled a yawn. Maybe he was just taking a nap. Poor guy, probably couldn't sleep because of constant disturbing visions. Boy, was I ever having fun in my head today. I shrugged off my keen wit and waited, wondering if he really could help me. But if he gave even an indication of a snore, I was out of there.

Then he jumped up, and I don't mean he sat up, then got to his feet. He jumped to his feet off the bed. Man, that had to be hard to do. He looked strange, upset, not so easygoing anymore.

"What's the matter?"

"He was really unhappy, angry, mean-spirited, full of hatred and bitterness."

"You got all that from lying on his bed."

"Yeah, and I'll tell you what, I'm pretty unnerved right now."

I could tell that. He paced around some, looked out the window. "I feel what they feel sometimes. Physical pain, too. But I'm getting real bad vibes about this guy. He enjoyed hurting people, like it was some kind of hobby."

"You're right. Simon Classon was not Mr. Congeniality."

"No, he was despicable."

There was that word again. "Okay, but he still didn't deserve to die the way he did."

"Didn't he?"

Now there's a shocker. "You think he did? Maybe I ought to show you the body and see what you think then."

"Yeah, maybe you should."

"Are you serious?"

"Yeah. Is he still at the morgue?"

I nodded. "Do you mean right now?"

He walked up close and before I could object, he grabbed my hand and held it between both of his. Shocked, I stared at him but his eyes were closed. When I tried to pull away, he let me go and opened his eyes.

"You're in danger, Detective. I see you in the hospital, I see a broken bone in your leg, I see you in dark places, close dark places with spiders and other little creepy things all around you, and I see a head injury on your victim. Here," he pointed to where Classon's blood icicle had been.

I was surprised by his accuracy, but then I realized his problem. "Sorry, pal, but you're about five months too late on the hospital and that leg prediction. Been there, done that. And we already know about the spiders. How about moving your time-travel dial ahead a few months?"

"You need to take me seriously. Never know, maybe it'd save your life."

"What makes you think I don't?"

He grinned, and then he looked at his watch as if he'd forgotten something. No Rolex like Black's solid-gold timepiece purchased in Geneva. McKay wore a beat-up old Timex, still ticking I presumed. "I gotta be somewhere now. Can we finish this some other time?"

Now he was making a prediction I could go for. "I guess so. But Charlie wanted me to show you the spot where we found the body. And I was going to show you around the school where Classon worked and see if you get any tingles. I can tell you I did. All of them dark and yucky."

"No need. I know my way around the academy."

"Is that right? How?"

"I attended a couple of classes there before I joined the

Corps. You're right, you can count the normal folks out there on one hand."

"You must have less fingers than I do."

He smiled and headed downstairs.

I followed. "Wait a minute, McKay. When were you there?"

But McKay had his helmet in place and was revving up the chopper. Purposely drowning me out, I had a feeling. "I said, when, McKay?"

He took off, wheeling around in the middle of the road and heading off north as if he couldn't wait to get away from me.

Well, hey, pal, the feeling's mutual.

THIRTEEN

By the time I pulled up and parked at the academy, all was quiet and day had turned to night. The clock on the old church said 5:15. Maybe all the Mensa kiddies were at dinner in the reasonably priced food court. I suspected I'd find Bud there, too, since that was where they kept the food. I braved frigid air and slippery surfaces as I tramped down curving, partially cleared sidewalks toward Blue Building. But there were so many footsteps from the students playing, I guess, that I could use them to escape the slick spots. I was right, of course. Bud was there, having something to eat. A woman sat next to him. A fairly young woman, maybe close to forty, dressed informally in a tight black sweater, and even tighter black jeans tucked into tall black boots with four-inch spike heels. She had five gold necklaces of different lengths hanging around her neck.

Bud finally noticed me. "Hey, Morgan, have a seat."

I sat down beside Bud, curious who he was making time with now. "Am I interrupting anything?"

"Nah, this is Beulah Asholt. She's vice-director here. Ms. Asholt, my partner, Detective Claire Morgan. "

Asholt stuck out her hand. Long cranberry-colored nails

that looked impressively lethal. Obviously she never had to type her own memos. She squeezed my hand like we were a possible item and gave me one big, fake grin. "Pleasure to meet you, ma'am. Bud's been tellin' me all about ya'll's investigation."

I hoped to hell not. "You're from the south, too, I gather."

"Gee, how'd ya know?"

Her accent was much more severe than Bud's and more embarrassing to listen to, I might add. Problem was she didn't know it.

"Where are you from, Ms. Asholt? Georgia, too? Like Bud?"

"Oh, no. I hail from the great state of Alabama. But I tell ya, it's good to run into a brother from the land of Dixie, like Detective Davis, here."

I waited a second or two for them to bust out in "I wish I was in the land of cotton" and sway together under crossed Confederate flags. It didn't happen. No flags available, I guess.

"How long have you worked here, Ms. Asholt?"

"Since last summer. August first, to be exact."

She pronounced it summuh. She pronounced all her *r*-ending words that way. I didn't like her much already. But hey, I didn't like anybody lately. I was becoming antisocial. I was in a real bad mood, too. I didn't like professors getting eaten up by spiders, I guess. Or psychics telling me my days were numbered. Or assholes who ran pseudo prep schools. After admitting my problems, however, I tried to lighten up. I smiled, a grim caricature that resembled an annoyed skeleton. Time to get to know Ms. Southern Belle a little better.

"How do you like it here at the academy?"

"I just luv it. I luv playin' at office politics. And I'm damn good at it, too." She laughed and winked as if Bud and I should find that admirable.

I said, "And office politics reign supreme around here, I bet."

"Oh, yeah, is that ever true. I learned right off what I had to do to survive around here. Kiss Simon Classon's butt and you'll get whatever ya want."

"Really?"

"Yes'm."

Yes'm? Bo Peep was truly grating on my nerves now. I liked southern accents but Bud's southern charm was just about the only deep-south drawl I was going to put up with. Maybe because Bud's was for real. This lady was as phony as a three-dolluh bill.

"So you're sayin' you're a brownnoser." Bud was frowning, seemed slightly put off himself now, as if Asholt was no longer such a welcome member of his southern charm school.

"Sure, that's the only way ya get ahead in places like this. Not just me, pretty much everybody around here. Classon told people what to do, and trust me, they did it, or else he'd get 'em. I fired ten people right aftuh I got here just 'cause he called down and told me to. I'm no fool. I know which way the wind's blowin' and so I use it to my personal advantage."

I said, "Gee, you sound like a real jerk." Sometimes I'm downright forthright.

Asholt seemed stunned for a moment, as if I'd slapped her across the face with a glove and challenged her to a duel in the back lot of Tara Plantation. Too bad I couldn't. It would be serious fun. Maybe I should. I thought about it. She was gathering her wits now, no doubt thinking, uh-oh, gotta brownnose, gotta brownnose, do it, do it, quick, quick, think up something good to say to soothe the ruffled-up detective missus.

"Now, Miss Claire . . ."

She pronounced that Miz Clayruh, and that did it for me. "Look, ma'am, don't call me Miz anything. You got that? I'm not Scarlett O'Hara and neither are you. This is a homicide investigation, and I'm the detective in charge. I prefer you to call me Detective Morgan and just park that whining southern accent because it doesn't cut it with me. Do you understand me or do I have to put it in Alabaman?"

Shocked, yes, she was. Her practiced phony charm wasn't working on that mean ole Yankee gal, gee whillikers, yee haw, and let's go make some praline candies. But she got her nose back in joint real quick. "I am truly sorry, Detective Morgan, if I offended you. It was unintentional, I promise you."

Yeah, I'm sure. Her southern accent had balanced itself to a normal rendition of Birmingham environs, if I was any judge of southern climes. Just as long as she never, ever called me Miz Clayruh again. I felt hostile, bristling even, and I blamed it primarily on how much I loathed and detested brownnosers, especially proud, self-admitted ones. One type you didn't meet a whole helluva lot. Only a very self-confident, well-practiced suck-up would openly admit it, I'd say. I controlled my bone-deep aversion to the woman. "No problem, ma'am. Now, I need access to your student records starting today and going back to the first day the academy opened its doors. Will that be a problem?"

"Of course not. In fact, you can get that information in my office. I'll need to check with Director Johnstone first, you understand."

"Okay. Why don't you scurry up there and see what you can do?"

Bud looked askance at me as I watched Ms. South of the Mason-Dixon leave in a real hurry. "Wow, Claire. That went well. What'd you have for lunch? Three-inch nails?"

"C'mon, Bud, you can't like her."

"What's like got to do with it? Hell, I don't like anybody around here. But I'm tryin' to be civil. And she was a big fan of Bear Bryant. Said she actually met him once at a U. of A. publicity day. Now that's something."

"Oh, well, now I've changed my opinion. She must be Mother Teresa."

"You're in one helluva foul mood."

Right. And I knew I was, tried half-heartedly to analyze my funk for a second but Bud beat me to the punch.

"You miss Black, don't you? Sleepin' alone at night is makin' you all grouchy, huh?"

"Shut up. And that's not it." I glanced around the cafeteria. "I don't like being on this campus. I don't like the people who work here. It gives me bad vibes that I can't shake. You know, like I should do the world a favor, throw all these people in jail, and swallow the key."

"God, Claire, what's wrong with you? Shake it off already. We've got a job to do."

I glared at him, but he was right. I was being unprofessional. Time to get it together and put some serious brakes on my personal opinions. "Sorry. You're right. The way Classon died has made me edgy. I'll get myself up to snuff."

Bud brightened. "Up to snuff. Know where that comes from?"

"Oh God, please make him stop."

"Yes'm, Ms. Clayruh, way back in the 1600s everybody used snuff. That's finely powdered tobacco, if you don't know, and lots of professional baseball players use it nowadays, but they're changing to Dubble Bubble now because Skoal causes cancer. Anyway, back then people could sniff it to see if it was good quality. So, if something's good, it's up to snuff."

I leaned back in my chair. "I am so glad to know all that, Bud. It's going to help in this investigation, I can feel it."

Bud shook his head, then he said, "You hungry? Maybe if you ate something, you'd feel better. Act better, even. How about a cappuccino? Here, let me go get you one. And by the way, Merry Christmas and all that good cheer and peace on earth stuff."

I watched him stroll over to the cappuccino machine. He turned, waved, and blew me a kiss. I couldn't stifle my smile. I shifted my attention to the kids eating at the surrounding tables. They all were having a great time, laughing and talking, acting like regular goofy teenagers. I probably acted like that once a long time ago before people I loved started dying off one by one. I ended that train of thought in its tracks, and refocused on the chattering students. I wondered if they knew about all the ugly stuff going on at the highest levels up in Director Jesus's office. I thought not, but they probably wouldn't care. Probably didn't even know who the director was, probably thought he was some Bahamian sandal salesman floating around campus.

Bud was back. "Here you go. Drink this and turn back into the real Claire Morgan. Then you can tell me what put ya in such an insult-slinging mood. Hell, I bet our friend Beulah has puncture wounds in her forehead."

"Sorry. I just want the guy who did this, and we're not exactly getting anywhere fast." I picked up the hot coffee that Bud set down in front of me. I took a careful sip, and it tasted good, sweet. "He's going to do it again, Bud. I know it. Even the psychic knows it."

"What psychic?"

"That's right, I haven't told you the good news." I filled him in on Joe McKay, and Charlie's decree on letting him horn in on our investigation. Bud stared at me, eyes all round and disbelieving, as if I was one of George Lucas's Cantina creatures.

"You are kidding me, right? Not funny."

"That's what I told Charlie. He disagreed."

"Man, this doesn't sound like Charlie. He always pooh-poohed all those medium shows and talkin'-to-ghosts stuff."

I'd never in my life heard Bud say pooh-poohed, not in any context, but I let it pass. I was back to my usual agreeable self.

"Unfortunately, not this time. He ordered me to take the so-called psychic to Classon's house and give him a look-see. That's where I've been so long."

"No shit? Did he come up with anything?"

"Oh, yeah. Get this. He saw spiders, head injuries, you're in danger, detective, you know, the usual ESP crap."

"He said you're in danger?"

"Yeah, but don't fall for that vision-quest stuff. He's not for real."

"Hey, I'm not going to laugh in his face. Sometimes they get it right. You ever see *Psychic Detectives* on Court TV?"

"The only thing I'm in danger of is losing control and punching Beulah in the nose. But I'm almost over that."

"And to think meeting Bear Bryant was wasted on her."

"Gotta raise your standards for lunch companions. Come on, let's go find Scarlett and snoop around in her files."

We trekked over to Asholt's office. Darkness cloaked the buildings in shadows, and inside the quadrangle, the church clock bonged six times. Mrs. Harper, Asholt's secretary, a heavyset lady with gray hair pulled back in a tight bun and held in place with an unlikely pair of black-lacquered Chinese chopsticks, was efficiency personified. She was finishing up her work for the day, but she showed us with precise, no-nonsense instructions where the student files were and how to access them correctly. She said Birmingham Belle was in conference with Jesus, and my ears instantly started burning. I waited for an irate call to come in from Charlie any second now, because truth be told, I was out of line with the woman. Getting angry and personal with her was unprofessional. I wouldn't do it again, uh-uh. I glanced around Asholt's office, looking for Confederate flags hanging on the walls or old movie posters from *Gone with the Wind*. She'd probably superimposed her face over Vivien Leigh's. Instead, there were lots of framed graduation certificates hanging around, most of them from Podunk junior colleges in rural nowhereland. Figured.

Half an hour later, it was Bud that got the call from Charlie. A command performance, no less. His turn to meet Psychic Joe and show him the murder scene. I told him not to let the guy touch him, and he said I didn't have to worry. He took off, and I sat down behind Mrs. Harper's computer and typed in Joe McKay. He'd told me he'd been a student here at some point in time, and I needed to check that our. I minimized the screen when Ms. Beulah waltzed in, said a pleasant, drawl-less "Hello, Detective, anything I can do to help?" I politely declined, and she looked relieved, snatched her red coat with a sequined Christmas wreath on the lapel, flipped her green muffler around her neck in a fashionable drape, then slunk like a kicked dog the hell out of there. I often have that effect on people, southern phonies, or otherwise.

Then the closing-time exodus began in earnest, and the staff disappeared with all the urgency of Cinderella at the stroke of midnight, only earlier. Just the way I liked it. Jesus stuck his head in Beulah's office door and told me I should make myself at home but he was quitting for the day because of the dinner he was hosting at his house at 7:30. He didn't invite me. Bud, either. Luckily he didn't chastise me for jumping onto Asholt with both my hobnailed boots, either. A pleasant surprise.

The building grew silent and dark to match the waning day's journey into night. I could snoop to my heart's content. Joseph McKay's name bounced up on the screen. I read his statistics, found that he'd been enrolled at the academy almost fifteen years ago. Everything was pretty much fill-in-the-blank personal statistics, six foot one, 185 pounds, blond hair, blue eyes, et cetera, et cetera. There was no box to check for ESP or psychic whiz. Then I hit pay dirt. The "other comments" line. Hey, hey, hey.

I clicked it in a hurry, and there it was in all its ugly details. McKay had been expelled from school, kicked out, sent up the river, and why? For putting a live garter snake in Simon Classon's roll book. Anybody heard the term personal vendetta? I read on, almost drooling on the keyboard, and found that he was quite the troublemaker, had been sanctioned four times by his instructors, three of them by Classon, who wrote a lengthy, overly nasty account of McKay's tasteless prank and how much mental suffering it had cost him, angst, even. I guess his angels were off duty that day, too. I read on. Psychic Phenomenon Boy was a real mess. Caused all kinds of consternation, problems, nearly drove Classon and Jesus nuts. I liked him better all the time.

Then I delved some more into his past but hit a brick wall when I tried to find out who recommended McKay for admission and funded his scholarship. Beside the green blinking cursor it said confidential. Aha. Highly suspicious and something to look into. I printed all the screens containing Joe McKay's data. Maybe Charlie'd like to take a peek at his guy's penchant for juvenile delinquency. Maybe then he'd take him off the case and thereby improve my hideous mood.

I checked out the rest of the files for incorrigible students, printed the screens, then shut down the computer, bundled into my parka and gloves, and headed out to my car, suddenly eager to talk to my boss. Across the quadrangle, the library building was aglow with yellow, beckoning lights in every window. I headed there, craving more incriminating ammunition against McKay and wondering if they had any microfiche of the local newspaper articles about campus deaths from spiders or snakes in roll books. Inside, it was warm and cozy with expensive tan leather couches and chairs grouped around for students to study on. Must be Building Tan. Only one kid in sight. Sound asleep and snoring with odd, puffing sounds. Probably allergic to ecru. I walked up to the checkout desk.

A man immediately got up from behind the counter. He'd been working on a laptop. He left the lid up. Typical man.

"May I help you?" He smiled, a tall black guy with black-rimmed square glasses, thick hair parted on the left, quiet voice, nice manners, good teeth, polite. The run-of-the-mill librarian, to be sure.

"I'm Detective Morgan from Canton County Sheriff's Department. I'd like to use your microfiche machine, if that's okay?"

"Sure thing. No problem. Have you used microfiche before?"

"Oh, yeah. I'm a detective, remember?"

He laughed. "Then I'm sure you have. I'm Morton DeClive, the head librarian here. Nice to meet you."

"Same here. And may I say, Mr. DeClive, you're the only normal person I believe I've met since I stepped foot on this campus."

"Tell me about it."

Good vibes at last. A man I could talk to without wanting to double my fist and deck him.

He said, "That was terrible. You know, what happened to Simon."

I nodded. "Yes, it was. He a friend of yours?"

"No."

"Did you like him?"

"Hell, no."

Like I said, he had a nice smile. He displayed it now. "Did you have any specific run-ins with Mr. Classon?"

"He called to bawl me out regularly, usually on Wednesdays."

"Wednesdays?"

"Yeah, go figure."

"He died on a Wednesday."

"That's right, he did. You think that's significant?"

I shrugged. This case was already so weird, nothing would surprise me. "Who knows? Maybe."

"Nobody liked him, at least nobody I know of, but not enough to kill him. Most people just ignored him and reamed him out behind his back. I've seen grown men stick out their tongues or give him the finger after he walked by."

"Really? That seems a bit childish."

"Yeah, but it sure felt good."

We laughed together. I liked him. I can't believe it. I actually liked someone on the staff of the Dome of the Cave Academy for the Gifted. He took me to the rear corner of the main room and showed me the microfiche setup. Then he told me he had a list of all articles about the academy printed in the local newspapers. I asked Morton if he'd print them out for me to read through at my leisure, leisure which I really didn't have, but I sure didn't have the time or inclination to sit in the library until the ten o'clock closing time, even with Morton DeClive for company.

I perused briefly and gathered up a handful of brochures advertising the academy and its dubious perks while he printed out an inch-high stack of news articles. He offered to loan me a file of the academy's own news releases, which he kept in his desk for personal reference. I jumped at that and invited him to please include anything else he thought might be of interest to the investigation. Told you we were both polite. On the other hand, I was building up a volume of homework that didn't look inviting, but what else did I have to do? Black was gone, and I'd already done my Christmas shopping.

It turned out I didn't have to worry about what to do with my time. My cell phone burst into song just as I reached my Explorer. I dug in my handbag for it as I slid into the driver's seat.

"Yeah. Morgan."

Bud said, "Joe's had a vision. Says he saw the second murder victim. Charlie said for us to check it out."

"No way."

"Uh-huh. You're to meet us there ASAP."

"Who'd he say it was?"

"Stuart Rowland of Satan fame."

"Yeah, right. We just saw him this morning. Where's he live?"

"Lake Road 565. Know it?"

"Yes. Gotta box number?"

"390. His turnoff's close to the SP Quick Stop. We'll meet you there."

My adrenaline pumped up to car-lifting levels, and I pulled out and called for backup as I gunned my way out of the parking lot and fishtailed onto the gravel road. Lake Road 565 was about fifteen minutes away, on a road lined with outlying subdivisions. I made the quickstop in ten, eager beaver. Ahead of me, I saw Bud's Bronco turn off the highway and head toward Rowland's place. I sped up, caught them, and then jumped out in front of Rowland's driveway almost before my engine died.

Rowland's house was a fifties ranch, tan brick, large picture window beside a burnt-orange front door, very neat and well-kept. The window was draped. No lights on except for an outdoor coach light at the end of his front walk. The garage door was open, and the blue Mustang we'd last seen outside the Classon crime scene was parked inside.

"Stay here, McKay. We'll check this out."

"Okay, but he's already dead. Inside some kind of trunk or chest of some sort. The killer's gone."

Bud said, "You sure?"

I said, "Let's go. Bud, take the back. I'll go through the garage. McKay, yell if anybody comes out the front door."

I unzipped my parka and pulled out my Glock and settled it in my hand as Bud melted into the night around one end of the house. I moved to the front of the Mustang and put my palm on the hood. It was cold. I snapped on my Maglite and checked around the car so I wouldn't get jumped. All was in place, no spiders, no snakes, no sicko serial killers.

I pressed my back against the wall by the door and tried the knob. It turned easily. I nudged it open and felt for a light switch. I found it and light flared. I darted a quick look. The kitchen was empty so I stepped inside, leading with my gun. No sound. White cabinets, red-tiled floor, gleaming stainless-steel appliances. Nothing out of place, no sign of a struggle. I caught motion out of the corner of my eye and swiveled my weapon. It was Bud at the undraped slider, gesturing for me to let him in. I backed my way there, pushed up the lock with my flashlight.

"See anything?"

"Not yet."

Bud took one side of the kitchen. I took the other. A swinging door led somewhere, and I motioned Bud to go through first. He took it low and I covered him, then hit the light switch. One lamp in the corner came on and illuminated the living room, decorated Christmas tree and all. The tree lights weren't plugged in and some ornaments lay broken on the floor. Nothing else was disturbed. We checked out the three bedrooms and two baths. I sheathed my weapon and looked around. Then I saw it, a flat-topped antique red steamer trunk that Rowland used as a coffee table. A Christmas gift tag was stuck on the top.

"There it is, Bud."

Bud said, "What's that tag say?"

I looked at it, then at him. "It says, 'Don't open until Christmas.'"

"Goddamn. Something's moving around in there. Listen."

Soft, scratching sounds were coming from inside.

"You hear it?"

"Yeah, something's in there, all right. Cover me, Bud, I'm going to open it."

A graphic vision of Simon Classon's body flashed across my mind, and I knew Stuart Rowland was in there, just like McKay had predicted. I braced myself for something horrible. Bud trained his gun down at the trunk, and I pulled the padlock free and jerked up the lid. I shined my flashlight inside.

"Oh my God, what are those black things?"

Bud's face looked revolted.

"Scorpions," he said in a low voice. "Jesus, look at all of 'em."

And Stuart Rowland was in there with them. He had on blue sweats. His wrists were taped together, his face covered by an Indonesian red devil's mask like the ones the director liked to display on the wall behind his desk. Dozens of small black scorpions, tails up and poised, were teeming all over his body.

I shivered uncontrollably, then nearly jumped out of my skin when somebody pounded on the front door. Bud and I both turned and set our weapons on the door. A male voice yelled, "Police, open up!"

Bud sheathed his gun and opened the door, and a man wearing an Osage Beach police uniform trained his weapon on Bud's chest.

"Get your hands up now. Now!"

"Whoa, man. I'm Canton County Sheriff's." He held up the badge hanging around his neck. "Thanks for backing us up so fast."

"What backup? I just got off duty when the owner of this place flagged me down. Said somebody's breaking into his house."

"No way. The owner's dead."

That's when Stuart Rowland stepped into sight. He said, "What the hell are you talking about? I'm not dead. And what are you doing in my house?"

Bud and I stared at him a moment, then I said, "Keep him outside, officer."

Warily, we moved back to the trunk. Five or six scorpions had scuttled out of the trunk and were crawling around on the floor, but most of them were still crawling all over the body. I smashed the ones on the floor under my boot, then used my fingertips to lift off the mask. I gasped and backed away in aversion. Bud stepped closer and stared down at Christie Foxworthy's bulging eyes and taped mouth with complete and utter horror.

Avenging Angels

One night about a year after Uriel arrived at his grandma's house, Gabriel picked up Uriel and they went riding around on his motorcycle He liked to drive the fifteen miles to a town where railroad tracks ran under an Interstate bridge. Hoboes liked to congregate and drink whiskey there.

Gabriel and Uriel hid in the bushes and listened to them talking together about how they'd been in prison and gotten beat up, and stuff like that. Gabriel said they were evil, sinful men, and should probably be sent on off to heaven, but there were too many to deal with, so they just watched and listened. Sometimes they'd wait until the tramps passed out and then sneak to the fire and steal their duffel bags and booze.

Tonight they stole a bottle of vodka. Gabriel wiped off the top of it and took a big swig. He handed it to Uriel, and Uriel took a drink, too, then coughed and choked because it tasted horrible and burned his throat.

"You big sissy," Gabriel said. "You gotta learn to drink like a man. I started drinking beer when I was just nine. C'mon now, drink some more, it'll put hair on your chest. That's what those old farts under the bridge say, I heard 'em."

Uriel didn't like it and didn't want to, but he did, just a sip at first, so Gabriel wouldn't get mad. Then they took turns passing the bottle, and Gabriel took out a pack of Camels.

"Well, you might as well start smoking, too. It makes you feel good, once you get used to it. Daddy'd skin my hide if he found out I was doing this stuff, but hell, he smokes a pipe, and that's okay. He's a hypocrite, ain't he?"

Uriel nodded as Gabriel lit up and passed the cigarette to him. He puffed it and choked some more, but he thought it looked cool, and he wanted to be like Gabriel, just exactly like him, in every way.

They sat there awhile, drinking and smoking. Sometimes Uriel only pretended to take a drag on the cigarette. The smoke was caustic and burned his mouth, and he didn't like it. And the vodka was making him feel dizzy.

"Let's go, Uriel, we better hightail it home. Got school tomorrow."

Gabriel let him off at the edge of the woods like always, and Uriel ran down the dark path through the woods that he knew so well by now. A full moon was shining, guiding his way but he skidded to a stop when he saw his grandma was awake and waiting on the back steps.

She stood up and held onto the banister. "Where have you been, young man?" Her voice was harsh. Angry. He'd never heard her use that tone before. She grabbed his arm, her gnarled fingers biting into his skin. "What's that stink on you? Is it cigarettes? Lord help us, child, what have you been up to?"

In the distance, far out on the highway, the buzz of Gabriel's motor scooter echoed in the quiet darkness. His grandma squeezed his arm tighter. "Was that the preacher's son you went sneaking off with? Was it?"

"No, ma'am, I just couldn't go to sleep so I went out for a walk 'cause the moon's so bright."

"You little liar, you sinner, you are not to be with that boy anymore, you hear me? I forbid it! Freddy's brother thinks he had something to do with that poor child's death, and now I wonder if it's true. You get in the house, and don't you dare ever step foot out at night again. And don't you be hanging around with that boy anymore, either."

Scared, Uriel ran into the house and slammed his bedroom door. He pushed a chair up under the doorknob so she couldn't get to him. She did come and rattled the door and said a bunch of bad things about Gabriel. He covered his ears and didn't listen, and then he got angry that she was telling him what to do. He'd already sent people to heaven, hadn't he? He was an avenging angel, wasn't he? He wasn't going to stop being Gabriel's friend, no matter what she said. Gabriel was his best friend, his secret friend who loved him and took good care of him.

The next day at school, Uriel told Gabriel what happened, and Gabriel said they couldn't let Uriel's grandma tell Gabriel's dad about the smoking and drinking. He said that maybe it was time for her to go to heaven and be with the rest of Uriel's family. Uriel didn't know what to think about that. It didn't seem right, because she had taken him in and made him chocolate chip cookies and pineapple upside-down cake. She was okay most of the time.

"I dunno, Gabriel. Who'd take care of me then? Who'd I live with?"

Gabriel frowned. "Yeah, you're right, we don't want you goin' into some kind of foster home. I guess we don't have to send her up to heaven, but we got to fix her where she won't tell my daddy or keep you from hangin' around with me. Tell you what, I know this older guy, a real weirdo, who gets me drugs sometimes. I'll get some that makes her sleep all the time. Old folks sleep a lot anyways. Nobody'd ever know. You can tell people she ain't feeling well, and I can say I'll be glad to go over and check on her every day and we'll say we'll go to the grocery store for her, run all her errands, and all that. And that'll make us look good, too."

"Yeah, Gabriel, I like that idea a lot better. She ain't that bad, to send on to heaven, I mean. That's the first time she ever yelled at me, or got on to me, or nothin'."

So that night Uriel ground up a bunch of the small white

pills Gabriel gave him and stirred them into his grandma's cup of green tea when they were watching the Cardinals play baseball on television. It didn't take long for her to fall asleep in her chair, either. She was so still that Uriel poked her with his finger to wake her up. She didn't stir, and he put his hand over her mouth to see if she was breathing. She was.

Gabriel said the pills would knock her out all night and probably most of the next day, too. He was right. He was always right. Uriel left her sitting in her rocker, her head lolling onto her frail chest, and ran through the woods to the old lodge. They were going to try smoking pot tonight, down in the cave where nobody would ever know. Uriel couldn't wait, was really looking forward to it. Gabriel said it would make him feel like a real live angel, soaring high in the sky, maybe all the way up to heaven.

FOURTEEN

At first I felt only disbelief as I stared down at Christie Foxworthy's contorted face. I was so sure it had been Stuart Rowland locked in that trunk. Unable to speak, Bud turned from the trunk and staggered a few steps away.

"Okay," I said. "Okay, Bud. Let's get a grip now."

I slammed the lid, afraid more scorpions would scuttle out. Bud was leaning against the wall now, staring at me. His face was white; he looked sick.

"Okay," I repeated, more than a little shook up myself. I walked to the front door where the police officer was standing. I said, "This is now officially a homicide crime scene. Let's mark it off with tape and if you can, keep anybody else out there the hell away from the house. Bud, you call Buckeye and animal control and tell them to get out here ASAP."

Bud stared at me, ashen and silent.

"C'mon, Bud, snap out of it. You all right?"

He nodded, but didn't look so hot. He said, "Man, she was just so young to die. Not like this. Who could've done that to somebody like her? What kind of person?"

I shook away my own sense of horror. "The kind that did it to Classon, I guess. And we've got to get him. Black and

McKay both told me he'd probably kill again. We can't let that happen."

Bud needed something to do, something else to think about. I said, "Make those calls, Bud. And get hold of Charlie, too. Tell him who she was and how she died. See if he wants to come out here and take a look at the scene."

I tried to ramrod my thoughts into order. But all I could think about were the clicking and scratching still going on inside the trunk.

Bud said, "I want her out of that trunk. Now."

"Me too, but we can't, and you know it. Come on, man, do your job. We need Buckeye here before we remove the body. He needs to do the scene because the killer left clues this time, count on it."

"What do you think Christie was doing here? At Rowland's place?"

"Let's go find out."

Bud followed me outside. I sucked in some fresh air, but what I saw in that trunk wasn't going to leave me for a long, long time. Unlike Classon, I knew this victim personally, had talked to her. That made it different, more personal. Stuart Rowland had a lot of questions to answer.

We ignored Joe McKay. He hadn't gotten the victim right but he'd led us straight to the crime scene. He sure as hell wasn't off the hook yet. His information was pretty damn dead-on, even for a psychic. I'd seen a couple of those shows on TV. The psychics came up with random numbers and sketchy details, something like the victim was left in a cornfield near a red silo. They sure as hell didn't get the address down pat. McKay well could've done it himself so he could magically describe it to us. But the main question was why? And why Christie Foxworthy? How did she fit in to all of this?

Outside, I found Stuart Rowland sitting in the passenger seat of a red Ford Taurus. A woman sat in the driver's seat.

"Who's the lady?" I asked the officer.

"Mr. Rowland said she was his estranged wife. That's his word, estranged. Name's Nancy."

Bud was still briefing Charlie on his cell phone, having to repeat himself before Charlie would believe him, I guess, so I walked over and rapped a knuckle on Rowland's window. It slid down, and he said, "What in God's name is going on? Nobody's telling me anything."

"Come with me, Mr. Rowland, and we'll have that talk."

"Right now?"

"Right now."

"Okay."

"My partner will need to talk to your wife."

"Why? She just gave me a lift home. She doesn't know anything about this."

"It's procedure."

"I don't know anything," the woman said, leaning over to peer out at me. She was a faded kind of pretty, blond turning to gray, early forties, maybe, a little bit heavy, stylish red rectangular glasses, perfectly groomed. She looked more than a little concerned.

"Yes, ma'am. Detective Davis will explain everything to you. Mr. Rowland, please step out of the vehicle."

Rowland followed me to my SUV, and I let him in the passenger's side. I climbed in behind the wheel, twisted the ignition key, and waited for the heater to warm up. He was breathing heavily. I could see his breath pluming in the cold air.

He said, "Are you going to tell me what's going on?"

"I was hoping you could tell me."

"Tell you what? Good God, give me a break here! Who broke into my house and what did they take?"

I stared at him, considering. I decided to be forthright. "We found a dead woman in your house, Mr. Rowland."

"What?" Drawn out, long, breathy, shocked. Genuinely, it looked like. "No, no, that can't be, that's impossible."

"It's possible, trust me. And she hasn't been dead very

long. My guess is maybe two or three hours. Where have you been the last few hours?"

"Me? Why, why, I've been with Nancy. We've been separated for a couple of months, so I took her out tonight and tried to patch things up. You know, we had dinner at the Five Cedars restaurant out at Cedar Bend Lodge, and I surprised her with champagne and roses and all that. But you gotta tell me. Who got killed? Why was she in my house? Nobody should've been there."

"Good questions, Mr. Rowland. Anybody have a key besides you?"

"My wife does, of course. . . ."

"How about Christie Foxworthy? Does she?"

Rowland's face lost all color. I could almost see it draining away inch by inch. He stared at me, apparently stunned into silence. Then he said in a stricken voice, "Christie's not dead. She can't be."

"I'm afraid she can be."

"I don't believe you. I just talked to her this morning on the telephone."

"Well, she's dead now. Did you kill her, Stuart?"

Stuart startled me by bursting into tears. He wept unabashedly for several minutes, his face cupped in his open palms. He kept saying, "No, no, no, she's not, she can't be, I don't believe it."

I would've offered him a tissue if I had one. If he was faking those tears, he was a regular Sir Anthony Hopkins.

"I take it you had a close relationship with the victim."

Rowland tried to stop crying but couldn't. His words were muttered hoarsely, between broken sobs. "Oh, God, God, I loved her, I did. I tried not to, tried to break it off. That's what happened with my wife. She found out about Christie and me."

"Do you know why Christie was at your place?"

"No. She knew I was trying to get back with Nancy. She knew. I told her again today. I told her I was going to be gone tonight. Why would she come over here?"

"We'll find out. Do you know anybody who might want to do her harm? Anybody making threats against her?"

"No, of course not. The women at school didn't like her much. She was so young, so beautiful. . . ." He raised a teary face. "You sure it's her? Maybe you're wrong? You could be wrong, couldn't you?"

"No, sir. It's definitely her. I interviewed her myself the day Classon died."

Charlie's blue Jeep Cherokee skidded to a stop across the street, and I watched him get out, slam the door, and stalk angrily toward the house. He ducked under the crime-scene tape and spoke animatedly to the off-duty Osage Beach police officer, who listened for a few seconds, then pointed in my direction. When Charlie looked at me, I raised my hand in acknowledgment, then turned back to Rowland.

"Tell me about you and Christie. Exactly what kind of relationship did you have with her?"

Rowland was sniffling, wiping wet eyes. He couldn't stop crying. His words came out in sobs, voice all choked up. "We were having an affair."

"Did anyone else know about it?"

"No. She would've gotten fired. Me too, I guess."

"And when your wife found out, she left you?"

He nodded. "Christie called once and Nancy picked up the phone in the kitchen. I didn't know she was there; she'd gotten home from work early. Oh, God, God, God . . . Why was Christie out here? She shouldn't have been here."

"Anybody else see you at Cedar Bend Lodge with your wife?"

"Sure. We ate in the main dining room. Some of Nancy's coworkers came in and we chatted with them for a little while. After dinner, we sat at the lobby bar and listened to music and drank champagne. People saw us there, too, I guess. I paid with my credit card, so you could check that."

"What about you? Anybody been threatening you? One of Classon's friends, maybe?"

"No, no. Remember, I told you, Classon didn't have any

friends." Comprehension dawned, and he said, "Oh my God, you think they came after me and got her instead?"

"Maybe. Maybe she came over for some reason, to pick up something, get some possessions she'd left here if you'd broken it off, something like that, and surprised the killer waiting inside for you to come home. Could've happened that way."

"Oh my God. I can't believe this, any of it. This cannot be happening."

I watched Buckeye pull up in the white crime scene van. He'd made good time. He and Shag got out and carried their aluminum cases inside the house. Charlie followed on their heels. Bud was still in the car with Nancy Rowland.

"Mr. Rowland, are you aware of any kind of connection between Christie and Mr. Classon?"

"She hated him, I know. Why'd you ask that?" He stared hard at me. "Did the killer hang her like he did Classon? Is that it?"

"I can't divulge the details, Mr. Rowland. Will you be available to come in tomorrow and finish this interview?"

He nodded, stifling more sobs. "What about my house?"

"Get a hotel room or go home with your wife. It'll take a couple of days to process the scene. Where does Nancy live?"

"She's leased a place in Camdenton."

"What's that address?" I wrote down what he told me, then said, "Don't leave town, Rowland. We'll want to talk to you again."

Rowland wiped his face with his sleeve and composed himself enough to face his wife. I didn't envy him the ride home with her. The poor woman's humiliation had just begun.

About the time I finished up, the animal control officer had arrived and was getting out of his truck. Brett Walker was a guy I knew pretty well from two nasty Rottweiler attacks I'd handled last year. He probably still had scars on his hand from capturing those vicious dogs.

"Hey, Claire. Did I understand Bud right? You really got scorpions in there?"

"Yeah. Lots of them. Not a word to anybody, though. I don't want the media getting hold of this."

"Right."

"Just a heads-up, Brett, it's pretty brutal in there."

"Right. Thanks."

Charlie was standing just inside the front door. He looked solemn, mad as hell, and ready to jump on somebody with both boots.

He said, "Where's Bud?"

"Interviewing Rowland's wife."

"She gonna be able to alibi him?"

"Maybe. Bud'll know soon."

Charlie gestured at the red trunk. "The vic still inside?"

"Yes, sir."

"With a scorpion."

"Yes, sir. But not just one. Dozens of them."

"This is crazy. What the fuck is going on around here?"

Good question, I thought. "We ought to get some trace this time, sir. He did her here, we're pretty sure. Percentages say he had to leave something of himself behind."

Brett Walker was removing the scorpions one at a time, picking them up with some large tweezers and dropping them into a lidded metal box with breathing holes in the top. There was a lot of blood in the bottom of the trunk from where she'd been hit in the back of the head. Nobody said anything. I could safely say everybody in that room was rattled to the core. I was. And that sure as heck didn't happen often.

It took us all night to process the crime scene. Buck had summoned his people on call, and they were still working when I left around dawn. Bud left when I did, and he felt better now that Christie's body was out of that awful trunk and on its way to the ME's office.

I walked into my house, exhausted, and fell onto the bed with my clothes on. I lay awake, though, opening that trunk in my mind, over and over, and dreading to meet up with my old enemy, sleep. The nightmares started the minute I slept.

FIFTEEN

After four hours of back-to-back dreams that were more like horror flicks, I dragged myself out of bed, showered, dressed, and avoided looking at the footlocker at the end of my bed. My first stop was Charlie's office. I had a bone to pick with him. Mr. Psy-Fi had to go. And now, at least, I had the right kind of ammunition to shoot him right out of the investigation.

When I arrived, Charlie was yelling into the telephone, so I paced the corridor outside. I was anxious. Two victims meant a possible third, a probable third. I wasn't going to let that happen. Bud had been ordered back to the academy, re-interviewing staff and students about Christie Foxworthy. Better him than me. I felt fatigued, in the mood to kill anybody who messed with me. I hadn't heard from Black, either, which ticked me off considerably, but I'd be damned if I'd waste my hard-earned money on a transatlantic call. He was probably suffering a porn hangover from watching nude dancers all night.

"Okay, he's all yours." That was Madge, Charlie's wee secretary, who'd run the station for the last seventeen years. She was a little birdlike munchkin who barely reached my chin, even with the stilettos she always wore to bring her up to five feet.

"Morning, Sheriff." I tried to indulge in pleasantries right off the bat because he wasn't going to like what I had to say. Besides, I didn't feel flippant or glib. Not after seeing Christie's horror-frozen face. I felt like finding a psychopathic killer and watching his execution.

Charlie snorted. "Buck said that girl had over fifty stings on her body."

"Brett Walker said she would've died pretty quick."

"Thank God for tender mercies."

I thought it wasn't too tender, or too merciful, either. It was a damn horrible way to die.

"Well, what's your take on this so far?"

"I think it's personal. Both victims. He wanted them to suffer. To experience stark fear. Another thing, he struck so fast the second time. Could be he wanted to shut her up, or Rowland. Could be a warning. And Bud and I think drugs might be involved. We found a stash of coke in Classon's house, and Bud's following up on a possible drug connection between Classon and Christie Foxworthy right now. Maybe he was her dealer."

Charlie dropped down into his leather chair, making the springs squeal for their life. He swiveled back and forth and my tense nerves endured the racket, but barely.

"Sit down, Claire."

I obeyed. He fondled his pipe like an old, adored lover. His wife hated his smoking, didn't allow it at home, so he made a point to enjoy it freely at work. The smell didn't gag anybody so nobody said anything, not that anybody had the guts to. Especially now, since two murders had occurred on Charlie's turf.

He said, "Tell me what you've found out."

"We've already interviewed most of the staff about Classon. Bud's out there now working on Christie Foxworthy's friends."

"Tell me about that school."

"You ever been out there, sir?"

"I've met Johnstone. He seemed okay, if I recall."

"He wears a white suit, sir. With Jesus sandals. He collects devil masks from Asia."

"So, he's a crackpot?"

"Worse, he's a pompous crackpot."

"You suspect him?"

"It's not out of the realm of possibility."

"Find anybody else suspicious? With motive?"

"Everyone described Classon as a monster, devil, bastard, and it goes down from there. The librarian's cool, I think."

"Really got it pinned down, huh? What about alibis? Everybody accounted for at the times of the murders?"

"Most are. Still have some to check out. More now than before."

"Anybody you think is capable of this kind of cruelty?"

"Who knows? Nobody ought to be able to commit these acts. Whoever it is, he's a sociopath and has probably learned to hide his dark side from people around him."

Charlie sighed. "At least the media morons haven't gotten word of it yet. Make sure they don't."

"Yes, sir. It's probably too cold for prima donnas. All those pretty commentators might get chapped lips."

Charlie grinned. Great. Just the moment I was looking for. Time to wipe that happy expression off his face and make him mad. I hesitated, afraid for my life, I guess.

"One more thing, sheriff. I really need to talk to you about that guy, McKay."

Charlie's eyes pinned me to my chair, daring me to complain. "Yeah, what about him? I heard he put you on to the location of the second victim."

I took the dare. I'm reckless like that. "True, which I think ought to put him first on my suspect list."

Charlie didn't explode, just waited for me to go on. Good sign.

Now was the time for some fast, persuasive talking. "I had an opportunity to delve into the enrollment records at the academy. He attended classes there about fifteen years ago. And just take a guess what he was expelled for."

Charlie leaned back in his chair. He stuck his pipe back in his mouth. "He put a snake in Simon Classon's roll book."

Flabbergasted, yes, I was. "Good guess, sir."

"I know all about Joe's past, Claire. So tell me exactly, why do you suspect him?"

Was Charlie nuts, or what? "He put a snake in the first victim's personal property and Classon got him expelled. That sounds like they weren't exactly Starsky and Hutch. Sounds to me like he might have resented Classon, hated him, even. Then he suddenly alerted Bud and me to the second vic's crime scene. Gave us precise directions. And nobody's shown me proof positive that he even has ESP abilities. Sorry, sir, his word just doesn't cut it for me." There, it was out in the open in plain English. Good for me. I think.

"How did you know he'd gone to the academy?"

"He told me, so I looked him up on the school's computer system."

"Doesn't sound much to me like he's trying to hide anything."

"It could've slipped out."

"Maybe."

"Sir, with all due respect, you've got to let me check him out some more. My gut tells me he's involved, and I trust my instincts."

"What else did you get on him?"

"I found out his tuition was funded by an anonymous source. Tell me that's not just a little bit suspect. Think about it, sir, don't you think it's kinda funny that he showed up here all of a sudden, immediately wormed his way into my investigation, and led us straight to the second victim? Maybe so he'd know what we're doing? Perps are known to do that, to keep themselves a step ahead of the police investigation."

Charlie glared at me. I braced against the hard look and held to my guns. "I want permission to keep him at arm's length. I don't want to have to apprise him of my movements.

I don't trust him, sir. I don't like babysitting him and having him tag along everywhere I go. Neither does Bud. And I want to interrogate him about his knowledge of the Christie Foxworthy crime scene. I don't believe he's psychic, and I want a chance to prove it."

Charlie commenced with another heavy sigh, put upon and not liking it. He struck a match and puffed his pipe. He said nothing. I said nothing. This was procedure, actually. This is how Charlie relaxed and thought the deep thoughts. A minute later, he stood and walked to the windows. Outside, I could see snow spiraling down against a heavy sky full of gray cotton. I could see a lighted star swinging on its lamppost like a square dancer doing a do-si-do. We were going to have one helluva white Christmas.

"It's snowing," he said.

"Yes, sir."

His gaze remained on the street below. I heard the sounds of tires spinning on ice. Probably Bud arriving. "You're good, Claire, very good. I should've told you the truth from the beginning."

Double uh-ohs. I didn't like the sound of that. I didn't like the sound of what he said next, either.

"That confidential donor for Joe McKay?" He turned around. "That was me, Detective. I funded him, and I handled the problem with the snake in Classon's roll book."

"You're kidding." Please, please be kidding me.

"No. And you're right, it happened about fifteen years ago. I felt sorry for the kid. He had family problems and got into trouble for vandalizing an old building out in the woods. Tried to burn it down. He was pretty messed up back then. I saw something in him, I guess. His lawyer sent him to a child psychologist, who said he was really bright. Suggested the academy was a place he could lay low, get himself an education or skill to support himself until he reached eighteen. My Sunday school class at Trinity Baptist paid his tuition, you know, adopted him. One of his teachers told us she thought he really did have ESP."

I sat there, staring stupidly at him. "I don't know what to say, sir."

"He did all right a couple of years, then started pulling asinine pranks. He liked to scare people, pull practical jokes. He just went too far with the snake."

Yeah, I'd say. "Why'd he do it to Classon?"

"He never did say. He told me Classon deserved it. Classon insisted on pressing criminal charges if Joe wasn't kicked out of school. So Johnstone expelled him. That's when I gave Joe a choice, jail time or join the military. So he joined the Marines, and that's where he's been until his discharge. I wanted to give him a chance to prove himself, especially after he warned me with his prediction last summer. That's why I brought him into this case. And I believe he's got some kind of psychic gift that I don't even try to understand."

"Don't you think it's a bit of a coincidence that Classon suddenly shows up dead now, right after McKay comes back into the picture? Why should he care who offed Simon Classon if he hated his guts?"

"He said others were going to get hurt. And now he's been proven right again. He said he wanted to prevent that."

I took a deep breath then another one, but I'd be damned if I'd let McKay in on my case. "I don't want him tagging along with me, Sheriff. I'm asking you to give me a pass on that, please. Bud and I can get this done on our own. You know that. And he's a primary suspect now, whether you like it or not."

"I don't think Joe's capable of the kind of torture the perp's using on his victims."

"Sir, all I'm asking is permission not to rule him out until I'm sure I can."

Silence. One beat. Two beats. Three beats. "Okay, you got it."

Pleased at Charlie's capitulation, I pressed him, but very gently. "Can you tell me what he did in the military?"

"Special Ops, secret missions, that kind of stuff. Highly decorated. Specialized in demolitions."

"Top secret, huh?" Impressive, I had to admit.

"Yes. He turned himself around completely. It was the discipline, I suspect, and being a part of something. He had a tough life, lost some family members, had a mom who suffered severe depression. She finally committed suicide."

"How'd he lose his family members?"

"I'm not sure. Maybe it was a car crash. I really don't know."

"We got a file on him somewhere?"

"I'll have Madge look it up for you. Now get the hell out of here and get back to work. I'll notify McKay that he's out."

I scuttled out of there pronto, pleased as punch.

Dark Angels

Uriel's grandma never bothered them again. She was always groggy, couldn't remember a thing, and Gabriel's dad
began to think she might be suffering from Alzheimer's dis-
ease. They had plenty of white pills because Gabriel had
begun to sell dope to other kids at school. So Uriel and Gabriel
were free. They could do whatever they wanted, whenever
they wanted. They experimented on animals they caught,
and Gabriel even found a black-market kind of place where
he could order exotic spiders and bees and scorpions and
even poison frogs, from mail-order houses in Australia and
the Amazon and Asia. The UPS trucks brought the ship-
ments to Uriel's grandma's address, and Gabriel pretended
he lived there.

It was fun to get new creatures, and sometimes they
would keep his grandma unconscious for days at a time, and
she would be confused and wet the bed. She cried a lot and
said she just couldn't remember anything anymore, and sometimes Uriel would feel sort of sorry for her, then he would remember that she was going to take Gabriel away from him if
she was ever herself again. So he kept putting white sleeping

powder in her tea, and she never caused them any more trouble.

Gabriel had gotten a job in town at the hospital as an orderly. So after a while he bought himself an old white van without any windows. He got it cheap because it was an old dry cleaners' delivery truck that had lots of miles on it. It still had racks in the back to hang clothes on, and there were boxes of plastic bags left over that they'd used to cover dry-cleaned clothes with.

That's when Gabriel decided it was time to take somebody back to the cave and send him to heaven. They cruised the road every night, looking for anyone out alone, and Gabriel decided the first victim probably should be a young girl or old person who wouldn't be strong enough to put up much of a fight. They drove around in nearby counties, looking for a likely candidate, but nobody was ever hitchhiking alone or riding a bike home or anything, so they ended up checking out the hoboes under the Interstate bridge.

One night they got real lucky and found just one old tramp lying drunk beside a campfire that had almost burned out. It was strange. They tiptoed up, afraid they'd wake him, but then realized that his skin was hot to the touch and he was mumbling stuff they couldn't understand. He was real sick with pneumonia or something, and Gabriel said he was a perfect candidate to send to heaven and put out of his misery.

They backed the van up to the fire, and together they dragged him and finally got him up into the back compartment. He wasn't too heavy, and he kept saying, "Baby, baby, that you? I missed you, baby. . . ."

Uriel wondered who he was talking about, but the old man never really opened his eyes. They stopped the van on an old logging road where there was a well-hidden back entrance into their cave, and Gabriel slung him over his shoulder and carried him the rest of the way. Inside the cave, Gabriel laid him on the ground.

"What're we going to do with him now, Gabriel?"

"Well, let me think. We gotta get him off to heaven pretty quick. He sure ain't gonna feel nothing. I bet his temperature's way over 100. Let's just see what it is."

He pulled a thermometer out of his pocket, the one he'd stolen from the hospital ER when he was cleaning up late one night. He stuck the end of it in the old man's ear, and the digital screen read 103.

"Yeah, he's probably dying, all right. Let's just sit here and see how long it takes him to die. Or we could help him along like you did with that puppy over there."

He pointed at the cage where Uriel had put the puppy a long time ago. The carcass was covered in lots of webs now. It'd smelled awful for a long time, but the sulphur of the springs helped mask the odor of dead things, so it wasn't so bad any more.

"We could dump him in with those new scorpions we got and see what they do."

"Yeah, or we could just slit his wrists and see how long it takes him to bleed out. I heard a doctor at the hospital sayin' how a girl committed suicide in a plugged-up bathtub, and the blood was almost three inches deep. He said she left a note sayin' she didn't want to make a mess for her mom to find. That's pretty thoughtful of her, isn't it?"

"Yeah. Let's do that. He needs to go on up to heaven and be with his baby again. He's got nobody to take care of him but us. Let's just cut him and see what happens."

They each took hold of one of the man's arms and drug him to the big galvanized washtub where Gabriel kept captured animals until they could kill them with spiders or snakes. The last one was a baby raccoon they'd put in with a big black scorpion from Egypt that they'd ordered from an exotic pet store in Scottsdale, Arizona. Gabriel lifted the man and sat him upright in the tub with his back leaning against the taller edge.

"What're we gonna cut him with?" Uriel looked around, searching their cutting tools in the wooden shelves against the wall.

Gabriel smiled. "Look here, Uriel, I brought you a present from the hospital. It's called a scalpel. That's what the surgeons cut people open with. I stole it out of the OR. It's sharper than a razor."

Uriel took the scalpel and smiled. "Gee, Gabriel, that's real nice of you. Man, I bet it'll slice through about anything."

"Hey, Uriel, you wanna do the cuttin' this time? You like to see blood spurt. You wanna send him to heaven all by yourself?"

Uriel looked at the man's flushed, gray-whiskered face and the way he was drooling. There was dried vomit on his shirt and snot rolling out his nose. He was dying anyway. They were angels of mercy who could put him out of his misery and pain. And Uriel would get to see his blood, all of it.

"Okay. Show me where I gotta cut him."

"I've been studying up for this stuff in some of the medical books I found at the clinic. And I made an A in biology last semester, too. There's this artery in the neck, you know. Right here." Gabriel pushed the man's head to one side with his forefinger and pointed at the side of his neck. "See. But it spurts out really far, if you slice that one open, because it's close to the heart and it keeps on pumping until he's dead. So it'll be real messy. Why don't we save that for some other time, when we're outside and won't get a big mess in the cave? We'd just have to clean it up."

"Okay."

"Let's just slit his wrists like that girl who killed herself did. I got a stopwatch. Let's see how long it takes him to stop breathin'."

Uriel took the scalpel and tested it on his fingers. It was sharper than any of their knives. Gabriel took the old man's right wrist and laid it on top of his stomach. "Look how his veins stick out. That's the way it is with old folks. So cut them. Go pretty deep, too. I got choir practice at church at eight o'clock, and Dad'll be mad if I show up late again."

"Shouldn't we say a prayer, or something first, Gabriel? So the angels will know to come down and get him and God can be waiting for him."

"Yeah, good idea. Here, let's hold hands."

They clasped hands and Gabriel prayed for the man's soul and for God to please have mercy on him. They, the angels of mercy, were sending him home to be with the Lord, where he wouldn't suffer anymore.

"Amen," said Uriel. Then he took the razor-sharp scalpel and made a deep, vertical cut on the inside of the exposed wrist. The old man jerked and groaned a little. Uriel moved the hand down on the bottom of the tub and then picked up the other one. He cut it the same way, but this one took two swipes with the sharp blade. Then he and Gabriel sat down in folding chairs they'd stolen from the church and ate Backer's barbeque potato chips and drank Dr Peppers and watched blood drain into the tub.

SIXTEEN

Bud and I spent the afternoon out at the school, getting nowhere fast. Everyone was just as shocked about Christie Foxworthy as we were and more of them showed it. She wasn't universally hated. We knocked off around five, and I spent some time typing reports at my office desk and trying to figure out the connection between Classon and Christie Foxworthy that got them both killed.

At six-thirty I headed home. Snow was still spitting at me, making the roads a little slick, but not bad, passable anyway. I stopped at Harve's long enough to take him the milk and eggs he'd asked me to drop off. He was busy on one of his headhunting assignments so I took off for my place. No lights on, of course. A pitch-black, uninviting home. I hit the button for the garage door and it slowly slid up.

I pulled in, got out, unlocked the door, flipped on the light, and gazed around my new place. It was really nice, and really empty. I checked my phone answering machine. There was no message from Black, but he would've called on my cell phone, anyway. I slung my parka on a chair and picked up the giant remote. I flipped on the fireplace. I considered the hot tub but decided it wouldn't be much fun, not with gruesome visions of scorpions dancing through my head. I looked at the big TV. Maybe I could do some research. There were some things I wanted to know about spiders and scorpions.

I pulled up my Internet provider and Googled poisonous spiders. I got about a million hits. I clicked the first one and got a nice close-up of a spider that I really could've done without. Bud was right about eyes on stalks. Yuck. I read all about necrosis and scrolled through stomach-turning pictures of oozing brown recluse flesh-eating wounds, much like Simon Classon's. I read enough to keep me awake all night and feel imaginary things that made my skin crawl. I was so creeped out, it was pitiful.

I thought for a moment about Simon, as hated as he was, alone out in the dark woods in that sleeping bag. He must've felt those spiders crawling over him, up his legs and arms, over his chest, but he couldn't yell, couldn't move his hands to kill them. He must have struggled desperately inside, squirming around frantically and making them bite him even more. I actually shuddered, a long one that went down the length of my spine.

And Christie. The look in those wide-open, staring eyes haunted me. Pure horror. I wondered if the killer had dropped the scorpions in on her one at a time. Brett Walker said most of the scorpions weren't deadly individually, except for one, which was an especially lethal species called the Egyptian fat-tailed scorpion. I typed that name in and brought up its picture. It was one ugly son of a bitch. Had two large pinchers and a long tail with a stinging spine. Said it was one of the deadliest scorpions in the world. But its range was Northern Africa.

Where did the killer get so many spiders and scorpions? I entered "habitat" with my original search words. It was the dead of winter, below-zero weather. They couldn't survive outside, could they? What did they do, anyway? Freeze and revive? Hibernate underground? I read several articles and found some mail-order places where you could purchase them, exotic snakes and nasty-looking, poisonous insects from Australia, Africa, Asia, and South America. And I bet there were black-market outlets, too. That's probably how he got them to Missouri, but he had to have some kind of lair, a dark place, warm and sheltered, where he kept his cages, or whatever he used to contain them. He sure as hell couldn't let them run free around his house. I searched more about scorpion and spider habits and got creeped out some more. It said they ate each other. I shivered again, then jumped out of my skin when my home phone rang. I definitely had to get my nerves under control.

I walked to the kitchen counter and picked up. It was the long-lost Black.

"Hey."

"Hey."

"Where have you been? I've been trying to get hold of you on your cell all day."

"I've had the phone with me."

"Check the batteries. You've got to stop letting them run down or you're going to get yourself in trouble some day. I've been worried about you."

"I figured you were still at the Crazy Horse, you know, enjoying the food."

He was quiet momentarily, then he said, "Well, well, I do believe you're jealous. Wonders never cease."

"No, I'm not. Where are you?"

"Still at the clinic. I'm leaving tomorrow for London. Jacques and his wife are spending Christmas there, so I'm going to drop by and say hello. Exchange presents, and all that."

That would be his Cajun-Mafia godfather brother and sister-in-law from New Orleans that I met last summer, but I didn't dredge up his familial criminal connections. "I guess that means your patient's head is functioning properly."

"He's out of the straitjacket."

I smiled a little, then realized he probably meant it. "I'm glad you're coming back. It's getting lonely around here."

"You miss me? That's a good sign, Claire. Especially since you actually said it out loud. How's your case coming along?"

"He's a serial."

Silence. Then, "How do you know?"

"I found a girl named Christie Foxworthy with fifty-seven scorpion bites all over her body."

"Oh, my God."

"She worked at the school, too."

"Was she hanging in a tree? Black plastic bag?"

"No, she was locked in a trunk in the Satan professor's house. Who, incidentally, turned out to be her lover."

"What about suspects?"

"I have a gut feeling."

"Tell me."

"Charlie saw fit to saddle me with this psychic wunderkind who pointed Bud and me right to the second vic's crime scene, address and all."

"A real psychic?"

"As if there are real psychics?"

"Some are legitimate."

"Wow. That's surprising, you being such a famous, respected shrink, and all that. I thought you guys scoffed at psychic phenomena."

"I take it you do."

"I believe in facts, concrete facts, and what I see with my own two eyes."

"You sounded like Jack Webb just then. You know, the guy on *Dragnet*?"

"Hey, he was one helluva detective. I've seen the reruns, and he always solves his crimes. In a polite police voice, too."

"Any results yet?"

"No. So many good reasons for killing Classon have turned up that I don't know who to arrest first. Christie was better liked but is just as dead."

"And Classon seemed so angelic."

I tried to laugh but couldn't quite dredge it up. And Black could always make me laugh, even when I was depressed by memories of horrible, grotesque corpses, like right now. Maybe that's why I liked him, that and his big, expensive gifts. And lots of other things. He was helping me deal with my past and all the pain I'd kept inside since I was little, that was worth a big something, I guess.

"Tell me about this so-called psychic. What's his name?"

"Joe McKay, and actually he's my primary suspect at the moment, believe you me. I don't trust him. And get this, he had an altercation with Classon years ago that got him expelled from the school and forced into the military. Now he shows up here and, bingo, this place becomes murder central."

"Sounds like a legitimate motive to me, if he holds grudges. How long ago?"

"Fifteen years."

"That's a long time to hold on to some boyhood grudge. It's unlikely he'd work up as much rage as it took to kill Simon Classon the way he did."

"He's also Charlie's protégé, did I mention that? But I'm not backing off, trust me."

"Why am I not surprised?" Black paused, and I heard a voice murmuring in the background.

"Who's that?"

"Room service. I worked late and skipped dinner, so I ordered something sent up." He paused. "I miss you, even more than I thought I would."

"Maybe nude dancers aren't all they're cracked up to be."

He laughed. Maybe that's why he liked me, too. I made him laugh.

"You gonna make it home for Christmas?"

"By hook or by crook."

I thought of Bud's book and was glad he wasn't there to talk about where hooks and crooks came from. I sat up straight when I heard the roar of a four-wheeler filtering through the silent darkness outside my house. A minute later somebody stomped across my porch and banged on my front door.

"Wait a sec. Somebody's here."

"You never have company. What time is it there?"

"Going on eight."

I peered out the window and found Joe McKay standing on my porch. He smiled and waved at me like I was his long-lost sister, then pointed to the door.

Black's voice came from the phone. "Who is it?"

"Remember that psychic fraud I told you about?"

"Yeah. What's he want?"

"I'm about to find out."

"Maybe you shouldn't let him in your house so late at night. You said you suspected him."

"I'm an armed officer of the law. You think he's going to abduct me?"

"He could make a move on you. I did when I was your primary suspect."

I smiled. He sure did. And I rebuffed him for as long as my roaring hormones let me. I sure as hell wasn't rebuffing him anymore. "You better hurry home. I might find myself a new boyfriend, a.k.a. suspect. One who psychically anticipates my wanton desires."

"Don't open the door."

"Eat your dinner. Call me later."

I hung up, unsnapped my shoulder holster, and opened the door.

"Well, well, look who's here. If you'd called first, I would've been gone."

"Is this a bad time?"

"Think about it and maybe it will come to you."

"May I come in? It's snowing out here."

"Oooh, more psychic predictions."

I stepped back. He came in, all frosty and flushed and male. He pulled off his leather gloves and rubbed his hands together. "Mind if I warm up by the fire?"

"Be my guest. What do you want, McKay? And how did you know where I live?"

I stood back and watched him hunker down by the fire and warm his hands. He unzipped his parka and held it out to catch the heat. He didn't look at me when he answered. "I remember from last summer when all the media were televising aerial shots of your house."

"Thanks for reminding me."

He stood up and turned around. He grinned. "That was some case. You were quite a hero."

I did not want to talk about last summer. "So are you, according to Charlie. He said you're a decorated vet."

"Nah, just doing my duty. The guys that don't make it back are the real heroes." He glanced around. "Nice place. I like hot tubs."

I stared at him, wondering if that could possibly be the clumsiest come-on I'd ever heard. It wasn't.

"Charlie said you didn't want me helping on the case anymore. If I said or did something to offend you, I'm sorry."

"Nope. It's just that you're my prime suspect. So, I don't particularly want to share confidential information with you."

"Me?" He looked truly surprised. Some psychic.

"That's right. Think back, use your powers. Simon Classon, a certain snake in a roll book, expulsion from school, mutual hatred. And now you suddenly have knowledge of a murder victim's whereabouts. You add it up."

"That thing with Simon was nothing but a harmless prank. He liked to embarrass the kids in my class. I gave them a treat. Shouldn't have done it, though. I know better now."

"And Christie Foxworthy's body?"

"I saw the house in a vision. I knew it was Stuart's place and made the assumption that he was in the trunk. I'm wrong sometimes. If you don't believe I have the gift, how can I convince you?"

"You can't."

"But you've got to believe me."

"Wrong. What do you want, McKay? I'm busy trying to pin these crimes on you."

"How about a truce?"

"Look. We don't need a truce. You do your thing, and I'll do mine. We don't need to be involved or in communication at all. Thanks for coming by and all, but time to go away and leave me alone. Sorry, but you're out of my investigation, and you're staying out."

"Listen, detective, you're in danger. I've seen you in the hospital, clear as day, and it wasn't in the past. It's coming. Soon. That's the only thing I've seen so far. You're going to end up hurt, or dead, if you're not very, very careful."

"I'm a police officer, McKay. Danger comes with the territory. And don't think I'm not careful. I carry a gun and everything. And I don't scare easily, if that's why you're here."

"The guy who killed Simon is not normal."

"No kidding, Sherlock."

"He's focusing in on you. I know it. I can feel it. I can see it."

"Yeah? Maybe he's figured out where my house is."

"I didn't do it. I'm trying to help you." He glanced around, as if some bogeyman was going to jump out of the closet and throw a bucket of spiders on me.

"Okay. I get it. There's a serial murderer on the loose and I should be careful. Got any more specifics for me? Something I could actually use?"

"Goddamn it, lady, you're going to get yourself killed. Just like Classon and that poor girl. You've got to listen to me!"

I thought of deep, oozing spider bites and the scraping sounds the scorpions made, the look on Christie's face. An internal shudder started up and just wouldn't stop.

"When and where, McKay? Tell me that. That would be useful."

"I see a dark place, and it's hot and humid there, with a funny odor, and you feel trapped and want to get out but can't. That's the sensation I keep getting. Not very pleasant, right?"

"Sounds like a grave."

I don't know why I said that, but the expression on his face shook me some. He looked ghastly ill for a second, and I thought he was going to faint. Then he stared at me as if I were an apparition.

I said, "Are you okay?"

He seemed to come back to himself then, and he headed for the door. He turned back after he'd opened it, his face as white as the curtain of snowflakes falling behind him. "Remember what I said. Be careful. You're next."

Then he was gone with a blast of cold wind off the lake. I shut the door and slid the bolt. Now that was a threat if I ever heard one.

SEVENTEEN

Unfortunately the Dome of the Cave Academy for the Gifted closed down from Christmas Eve through January 22. Even more unfortunately, Bud and I couldn't prevent the kiddies and faculty from going home for the holidays. On the good side, Bud and I had spent the last week questioning the students and staff about Christie Foxworthy so were able to finish up our interviews just about the time the exodus began. Everybody was leaving, and some for good, no doubt, once their parents heard that somebody had a penchant for murdering people affiliated with the school in the most horrific ways possible. Rumor had it Jesus might even close the academy down indefinitely until the crimes were solved. I was afraid our perp might be heading out of town, too.

Cars were lined up in front of the dormitory and happy laughter floated in the frosty air, along with waves, good-byes, and Merry Christmases. The monthlong shutdown was putting a crimp in our investigation but police officers have families, too, albeit neglected ones. Charlie gave nearly everybody the afternoon off, as well as Christmas Day. For the past few years, I'd volunteered to man the front desk so everybody else could have downtime, but this year I actually had a guy to spend the holidays with. Me. Imagine. I didn't have to feel too guilty, though, because a new and gung-ho kinda guy named Carl Marston could take my place. He was young and unmarried, and his family lived in Missoula, Montana, so he couldn't make the trip. Secretly I was glad. Okay, I admit it. The last few Christmases I'd been lonely, nothing to do, nobody to be with, unless I crashed somebody else's family and watched them exchange gifts. Not fun.

Hey, and it was looking more and more like it might be the same thing this year. Black hadn't called and probably wouldn't make it home in time, anyway, which truly did suck. But worse things had happened, so there you go. I'd live. The book I'm giving him was all wrapped and ready. It would wait. And I had two undeniably grotesque homicide cases to keep me warm and fuzzy.

As Bud and I walked out to our SUVs parked near the old church, I looked up at the sky. It was bright and sunny for a change. Clear blue skies, but the air was absolutely arctic. The ground was covered with snow over a foot deep, and the temperature was predicted to dip below zero after nightfall. We stopped between our vehicles, and I leaned back against my fender. Bud had been assigned the background check on Christie Foxworthy.

"You have time to check out Christie's family yet, Bud?"

"Oh, yeah, Dad sounded pretty shook up. He's in the merchant marines somewhere in the South China Sea. Mom sounds like she could care less. She's a real piece of work."

"Any word on the boyfriend and Mafia connection she mentioned to us?"

"No, can't say death by scorpions sounds like a Mafia hit, either. But I'm on it. Charlie said we can go to New York if we have to."

"It doesn't wash with me. The perp's from around here. Homegrown. I can feel it."

"Yeah. Me, too."

"I'm interested to hear what Brett can tell us about that big species of scorpion he thinks killed her."

"We'll get him, Claire."

"I know."

I tried to lighten things up, tried to smile, but these kind of cases had a tendency to take the cheer and goodwill right out of the holidays. I was having trouble thinking about anything else.

"Your mom and stepdad make it in yet, Bud?"

"Yeah, they pulled in last night around seven. Mom's in my tiny kitchen as we speak, slaving over homemade cranberry sauce, cornbread dressing, and roast turkey."

"Mmm, sounds good."

Bud grinned. "You bet it does. My stomach's been growling since Thanksgiving. Hey, wanna come over and eat with us tonight? Mom likes you. Thinks you're the right kind of girl for me. Told me I should've beat Black to the punch."

"I'm way too sloppy for you."

"True."

Across the quadrangle a boy and girl hugged and kissed with enough enthusiasm to warrant a lewdness charge. They finally let go of each other at her parents' embarrassed urging. She got into the backseat, and they drove away quickly, no doubt afraid the boyfriend would chase the car like a dog in heat. We watched the boy hang his head and shuffle off down the hill toward Red Building, as if facing the gallows.

Bud said, "Ah, young love. It's a bitch, if I recall."

"Wouldn't know. I didn't have any boyfriends at that age."

He looked at me. "Why not?"

I realized that I'd never mentioned my tortured youth to him, had it buried too deep, I guess. Black's therapy sessions must be working. I'd actually come out to Bud with a scrap of personal information.

"Never was in one school long enough." I felt uncomfortable and wanted to change the subject. Probably not a good therapeutic sign. I opened the door of my backseat. "Here, I got you a little present. You know, for Christmas."

"I got you something, too."

I pulled out a gift bag. "I guarantee it's not a book you can quote out of."

"Damn. I'm already disappointed."

We grinned, both feeling sappy. Partners are a funny business. You loved them almost like a husband sans the sex, if you were smart, and spent most of your waking hours with them. A life-and-death friendship where one of you could die any minute. A narrow tightrope to negotiate at times, especially a male and female. Maybe that's why cops argued and joked around so much with each other. Keep it nice and light until you bury somebody with a bullet in their chest. Gee, happy holidays everyone?

Bud said, "I wanna open mine."

"Sure. Go ahead."

The parking lot was pretty much cleared out. Bud opened the bag and pulled out the insulated camouflage shirt and pants I got for him for duck hunting. He grinned and nodded his head. "This's all right, Claire. Thanks. Harve and I've been wantin' to go out to the blind. This is gonna keep me warm as toast."

"Yeah. I figured you guys needed something warm and waterproof. I got him some, too. So you'd match."

"Cool." I could tell he was really pleased. He looked at the package I was holding. "You got me something else, Morgan?"

"Yeah." I felt a little funny about this one. "Here, take it."

Bud tore off the paper and pulled the yellow silk tie out of the box. He looked at me, shocked. "Wow. Totally awesome."

"Remember that time I flew to London with Black? We got that down on the street with all the tailors and clothing shops. You know the one?"

"You mean Savile Row? Are you kidding me? This came outta Savile Row?"

I nodded. "Black said you'd like it. He helped me pick it out, but I paid for it."

"You paid a lot for it, too, I bet."

"Good, you like it."

Bud was caressing the soft silk between his thumb and forefinger. "Wow, Savile Row, I sure wasn't expecting this."

He got a gift bag out of his backseat. It was red and white and covered with Santa Claus faces. It was the one I gave him last year. He was a recycler. "Didn't get this in England, but I know you've been needin' one."

I opened it. A new gun-cleaning kit. I smiled, actually delighted, then picked up two cards stuck in with it. The first one contained a full year's membership in the National Rifle Association. "Man, Bud, thanks. I always forget to renew."

"Yeah. That'll get you the monthly magazine, too."

"Great."

"You probably won't like the other thing much but I figured you might need it now that you're dating the guru."

The second card held a $300 gift certificate to Swank's, a ritzy ladies' fashion shop in downtown Camdenton where even the mannequins looked snooty. I'd never set foot inside, and I probably wouldn't, either.

"How thoughtful, Bud. You trying to tell me you don't like my ripped jeans and ratty sweatshirts?"

"You hate it, right?"

"No, I don't. You're probably right. I might need a dress for something someplace someday. Thanks."

Bud looked sheepish. "C'mon, Claire. You know we're both gonna hafta go to that New Year's Eve gala thing they're havin' out here at the academy, and it's formal. You'd think they'd cancel it, but they say they can't. Anyway, I thought you'd need something to wear if Charlie makes us go."

He was right. I still figured they'd cancel the thing or face lots of criticism. In a way I hoped they wouldn't. It'd be interesting to watch the staff at a social venue. Bud was right about the dress. I didn't have anything remotely suitable for a fancy gala. Imagine that.

"You're right on, Bud. I hadn't thought about it."

Bud smiled, pleased. He blew out a frosty breath and tugged on his gloves. "Sure you don't wanna come over tonight? Say hi to the folks and watch mom try to get us together?"

"Black's supposed to be back tonight, but who knows?

He's a busy guy. I might drop by." I knew I wouldn't, but I didn't want to hurt his feelings.

"Well, if he doesn't show, come on over. Merry Christmas, Claire."

"Merry Christmas. Tell your mom and dad I said hi."

We didn't hug or anything, uh-uh, that was way too sentimental, so I watched him get in to the Bronco and back out of the parking space. He was smiling from ear to ear as he drove off, probably with visions of his new tie from Savile Row dancing in his head. He'd wear it tonight for sure. He had good taste and was immaculately groomed at all times, all right, and I bet if I asked him nice enough he'd go down to that snotty dress shop and pick me out the exact right dress. He'd probably love it. Maybe I'd ask him. Then I wouldn't have to step foot in the place.

Duty on hold for twenty-four hours, and most of my reports done, too, I drove to Harve's house. Traffic was horrendous, everybody in town out buying that last perfect stocking stuffer or picking up the obligatory pumpkin pie from the bakery. I cursed the honking cars and bustling pedestrians but was very glad they didn't know yet about the heinous crimes being committed in their backyards. I checked in and put myself on call, figured that was the least I could do for Marston. Black probably wasn't going to show, anyway. So what? I was preparing myself for that eventuality. He was an important man, busy, busy, the jet-setter of all jet-setters, spending the holidays in Paris and London, for Pete's sake. Why would he rush back to this little hick town? It didn't matter anyway, I told myself. I had crimes to solve and a brand-spanking-new plasma TV to watch.

Most roads were clear or would be until the next load of snow was dumped on them. And that would be tonight, if the forecast could be believed. I almost wished I still lived in L. A., but oh no, bite my tongue. I vowed last summer to never, ever visit that hell on earth again and I meant it.

By the time I pulled up in front of Harve's house, I realized by the other cars parked in his driveway that his relatives were in for Christmas. His brother, Randy, and his family were in from Michigan. Harve never said so, but he'd been looking forward to it. I'd been spending all my spare time with Black, and Harve was lonely. I'd barely knocked on the door when Harve threw it open. The delicious mingled odors of turkey and dressing and baked yams assaulted me like a two-bit crook. My mouth watered, my stomach rumbled. It reminded me of Aunt Helen's house down at Hartville at Christmastime, and it made me miss her and reconsider my decision not to drive down and spend time with her at Ted and Janet Russell's house with their daughters, Paula and Julie. I hadn't made the trip because of Black, but it didn't look like he was showing up. Maybe I would get in my car and go. Why not? Nobody could cook like Janet Russell, except maybe Paula Deen.

"Hey girl, it's about time! You've got to eat with us. Jamie is one hell of a good cook and she's been baking up a storm all mornin' long."

Randy's wife, Jamie, stepped into sight at the kitchen door. She was holding a rolling pin and had flour all over her hands. She waved at me, and Randy came forward and gave me a big bear hug. I'd gotten to know them a lot better last August when Harve and I both were in the hospital for a while.

"How you been, Claire?" Randy grinned. He was a big guy, broad shouldered, friendly, with brown eyes that twinkled with laughter just about all the time. He was a firefighter in Detroit, as much a hero as Harve was. He'd saved a little girl a couple of years ago by hacking his way to her through the roof. He almost died and still bore the scars on his arms. "You look a little better today than you did last time I saw you."

Laughing, I said, "Yep, fifty-some-odd stitches in your shoulder can put you under the weather a bit."

"Seriously, I'm glad you're okay. You and Harve both. That was a helluva ordeal." He glanced in the kitchen then lowered his voice. "Hear you've got another real nasty case. Making progress?"

"Some. It's a little soon."

Jamie yelled for Randy to take her pecan pie out of the oven. He said, "Claire, you stay safe, you hear?"

Harve rolled the wheelchair over to me. "I said you'd stay for dinner. You will, won't you? I'd sure like you to."

"Maybe. If Black doesn't show."

"Don't you worry, he'll show up. The man's crazy in love, I tell you."

It sounded strange to hear somebody say that out loud. Black and I hadn't even said it out loud yet. I wondered if I was in love with him or if I was fooling myself. The idea was scary, sort of brought me to a standstill. Being in love made you more vulnerable than anything else, and in an intimate way I didn't think I was ready for. I'd told Black that from the get-go, and he wanted it to go slow, too. But that didn't mean I didn't want him home for Christmas.

Randy and Jamie's two boys and little girl were watching Dr. Phil on Harve's gigantic television set in the next room. Dr. Phil was telling some guy that he was a big jerk. The kids hooted with laughter.

"I really can't stay, Harve. I just wanted to bring by your Christmas presents."

"Okay, I got you something, too."

He led me to the tree we'd put up last week, which looked really good. There was tinsel now, and more ornaments and icicles. An angel on top.

"Tree looks great."

"Jamie and the kids finished decorating it last night. Here you go, Claire. Merry Christmas. I'm glad we're both here to celebrate it, know what I mean?"

"Oh, yeah." I took a rectangular box wrapped in red foil and a large red bow. It looked like a pair of shoes. Some new Nikes, I hoped. I handed him my gift bag and felt embarrassed. Why was I always so silly about exchanging presents? I guess I hadn't done it enough in my life. The series of foster parents I lived with weren't exactly Kris Kringles. I realized that I was dwelling on my past all of a sudden, due to my sessions with Black, no doubt. Only thing was, I didn't like thinking about it, wasn't used to it, and wasn't going to let it ruin the first Christmas I'd had in a long time with even a shot of having a good time.

Harve, on the other hand, always loved giving presents and was enjoying opening the one I'd given him. He tore into the bag. "Well, now, what'd you know? A boxed set of *The Sopranos*! Awesome."

"I got you all the seasons, too, and there's commentary from the writers and cast members."

Harve found the camouflage clothes in the bottom of the sack. "And insulated camo. All right!"

"I got Bud some, too. Can't have my two best friends freezing out on the lake."

He laughed. "You're coming with us, aren't you?"

"I'm not sitting around in the dead of winter just to kill some poor duck. But Bud said his blind's all built and ready to go."

Harve was beaming. "I cannot wait. When we get back, you and Nick can come over for duck a l'orange."

"Duck a l'orange?"

"Nick said he'd get me the recipe from the Five Cedars' chef. When's he due back?"

"Yesterday, but he didn't make it. Haven't heard from him today. I suspect he got caught up with a patient and delayed his flight. It happens. I'm used to it." But I wasn't used to it. I felt disappointed, and I didn't like the feeling, not one bit.

"Then stay here awhile. No need going down there and sitting around by yourself. At least have something to eat before you go."

"Actually, I stopped and picked up a Kroger's Deluxe, you know, turkey and dressing and all that stuff, just in case Black drags in before midnight."

"Save it for tomorrow."

"Thanks, Harve, really, but I have some gifts to wrap." That was a bald-faced lie. I never wrapped anything, not with those little bags they sold now. Just dump the present inside, and bingo, you were good to go.

"Go ahead. Open yours."

I tore off the wrapper but I already knew I'd like it. The wrapping paper hailed from the Bass Pro Shop in nearby Springfield, Missouri, my favorite store in the whole wide world. They had everything a sportsman/hunter/athlete could ever want, plus a bunch of waterfalls and stuffed bears and foxes to look at.

"Oh my gosh, Harve. What a beauty." I slid the snub-nosed .38 pistol out of the well-oiled, soft brown leather holster.

"After what happened last summer, I thought you might like to carry number two. Got myself one, too. Just in case."

I sat down on the sofa and pulled up my pant leg. I strapped the weapon on just above my ankle. "Man, Harve, it feels good." I strode back and forth a few times, getting used to the weight. "You can't see a bulge, either." I beamed. Now this was a gift worth getting. Harve knew me better than anybody.

"Let's sight it in a couple of days and see how it shoots."

I hugged the guy. He had made my day. "I really appreciate this, Harve."

"Waddaya expect? You're my best friend."

Something in the way he said it got to me, the way his voice cracked slightly. I hugged him. "Okay, I'm gonna get out of here and let you enjoy your family."

"Wish you'd stay."

"I'll be back in a few days to eat the leftovers."

"Sure. Hey Claire, wait, I've got that info you wanted printed out. About that Academy for the Gifted. I also got some hits on fatalities due to spider and snakebites. There's a heck of a lot more than I figured on."

"Yeah, I'll look through that stuff tonight. It'll give me something to do until Black gets here."

I waited while he went into his office and brought out a thick manila file. Dr. Phil was now berating some poor man who liked the Dallas Cowboys more than he liked his wife. I thought for a minute he was going to throttle him. That'd be a headline. DR. PHIL COUNSELS HIMSELF FOR RAGE MANAGEMENT AFTER KILLING GUEST WITH BARE HANDS.

Jamie stepped out of the kitchen holding a pie wrapped in green cellophane and tied with a silver ribbon. "Happy Christmas, Claire. Hope you like homemade pecan pie. We owe a lot to you, you know."

"That's just about my favorite thing in the world."

I left amid a flurry of good-byes and Merry Christmases and after the door shut behind me, I stopped on the back porch and breathed in the bracing, cold air. All around the beautiful, snow-covered cedars and pines brought back other Christmases, when I wasn't so alone. When I had a little boy to buy race cars and fire trucks for and build snowmen with. I remembered how excited Zach had been about Santa Claus coming, and then I saw him lying limply in my arms, big blue eyes staring at me until the light in them died away forever. My mind shut down. Don't. Don't think about him. Don't think about the past. I cannot dwell on him, not now, not ever, it's too painful.

I drove three quarters of a mile to my house, lonely there beside the lake. Even with Black's new addition. I should've put up some Christmas lights that I could click on from my car so it'd look more inviting when I dragged in. There was no sight of Nick, Saint or Black.

My garage door whirred efficiently, and I pulled the Explorer inside and lowered the door behind me. I gathered the boxes of food I purchased for our first Christmas Eve dinner together. If he made it in time. And if he didn't, hell, I had a new .38 now that I could shoot him with. The house was cold and gloomy, so I snapped on the fireplace. That warmed things up considerably. I stared at my little tree standing on the coffee table, looking all naked and forlorn. I'd bought some blinking lights and stuff but thought at the time it'd be fun to wait for Black and decorate it together. You know, start a little mini-Christmas tradition. But maybe it was too early to start up with the sappy traditions. Maybe it was scary, too.

I shoved all the food in the fridge and left the pecan pie on the counter. I sat on a bar stool, looking at it, hungry and bored, and decided a little slice before Black got there wouldn't hurt a thing. It was still warm and tasted great, so I helped myself to a second little sliver. If Black didn't show up soon, I'd eat the whole damn thing just for spite.

The evening progressed, and I tried to get interested in something on the giant television. I found that I didn't like watching television, not even *It's a Wonderful Life*. It wasn't such a wonderful life at the moment, and I couldn't quite relate to Jimmy Stewart's character. More often than not, I'd gotten people killed instead of saving their lives. I found *A Christmas Story* a little more to my liking and ate a third piece of pie.

Black had not called. I finally gave in to the temptation and tried his cell but didn't get an answer. He could be somewhere over the Atlantic Ocean. He could be asleep. He could be having the time of his life at a French and/or English Christmas party. But he better not be. I was just itching to use that new .38.

At one point I was so bored that I actually picked up the freebie copy of Johnstone's book bestowed on us by June Green. I stared at his picture on the front cover and the word jerk kept repeating itself in my mind. Go figure. I thumbed through the pages, examining the old black-and-white pictures. Apparently the academy had been in existence around twenty years, originally built on land donated by some old man named Walter Proctor, who no doubt needed a quick tax break. The academy's stupid name had come from some caves in the surrounding hills, which didn't exactly explain the dome part. Say what you may, it's still an asinine name. Hell, Johnstone probably had to use legal-size paper to accommodate his letterhead alone.

There were lots of grainy pictures of the white clapboard church that now stood in the middle of the academy's quadrangle. Old Proctor had apparently designated that the church not be torn down but kept on campus as a symbol of God's good graces toward the sainted men and women who would give troubled youngsters a new lease on life. Yeah, make me laugh some more. It was a good thing Proctor never met Jesus Johnstone and Company, or he'd be spinning in his grave.

I turned another page and looked at a group congregation picture that resembled the cast of *The Village* having a picnic. I frowned when I saw a photo of a teenager in a white T-shirt and jeans painting church pews. He was waving at the camera with his brush and looked a whole lot like Joe McKay, before he got muscled up and decided he had ESP. There was a smaller boy with him who was looking away from the camera. I was almost positive it was McKay but the caption didn't give names. Another picture looked a lot like Director Jesus as a youth with long hair and cheesy smile, standing beside a minister and holding a Bible, but I couldn't be sure. He wasn't wearing white sandals so it probably wasn't him.

I tossed the book aside and watched Scrooge getting his for a while, then finally clicked off the tube and lay down on the couch and wondered how I'd made it so long without getting killed. So many others had. I thought of Simon Classon. And Christie Foxworthy. I thought of my mother and my aunt and uncle, and all the others who'd died because of me. By that time I was getting very, very depressed. If Black were here, he'd say my survival guilt was kicking in, but, hey, it was all true. He'd say to get up and run a mile or think about work or make love with him, but he wasn't here, so there you go.

I dozed off about eight o'clock and heard in my dreams the roar of Black's boat. I sat up and kicked off the blue quilt. Then I heard the motor whine down and die. It was him. I smiled all over, like a silly goof. But man, was I glad he was back. I went to the door, and there he was climbing out of his boat, carrying a bunch of shopping bags. He looked up at me and waved. He was smiling, looking very happy to be back, and I was so glad to see him that it was downright humiliating. I walked down the steps to meet him and when he was in earshot, I said, "Well, it's about time, Black. I don't like to be kept waiting like this. I could've been at the firing range, practicing my marksmanship."

"I missed you, too."

Then he dropped the sacks and had me in his arms and I felt myself actually clinging to him like some kind of big, needy baby. Our mouths met, hot and breathless, and had a grand old time getting reacquainted. He was holding me off the ground and I clamped my legs around his waist. He broke off the kiss, long enough to mutter, "I'm going to Europe more often if I get a welcome like this."

I smiled and renewed the kissing. He knew how to kiss, he sure did, and I was learning fast under his expert tutelage.

"I missed the hell out of you," he said.

"Me, too," I said.

When he finally put me down, I picked up one of his bags and it yelped. I dropped it and went for my weapon.

"I brought you a puppy. Don't shoot it."

"A what?"

"A puppy. See."

He reached in and brought out a tiny wiggling bundle of white fur. "This, my dear, is a genuine toy French poodle, registered in Paris."

I looked at the little creature. I frowned. "The guys will laugh me out of the department if they see me with a sissy little dog like this."

"He's not a sissy, are you, pup?"

When he shoved the wriggling bundle of fur into my arms, I took it and held it up to the porch light. I couldn't believe it. My heart melted. "It's cute, I have to admit."

"Okay, let's go inside. And don't worry, he's already housebroken."

"What the hell am I going to do with him while I'm at work?"

"He'll be okay inside alone. Or you can keep him in the

garage if you want. It's heated, and I got you everything you'll need to take care of him."

I put the wriggling puppy down and it ran around sniffing everything in sight. It yapped nonstop, high pitched and annoying. "Did you have a good flight?"

He nodded. "I slept most of it. So I'm rested up and ready for you."

"Good. You're going to need your strength."

"That sounds excellent."

We ignored the dog, dropped to the couch, and went into our wrestling maneuvers again, about as breathless and turned on as you can get fully clothed. "Now that's what I missed the most about you," he said at length. "But I can't help but notice there's a new gun strapped to your ankle."

I disentangled, sat up, and pulled up my pant leg. I unbuckled the holster. "Harve's Christmas present. He's always so thoughtful."

He looked it over, handling it expertly, I noticed, then set it aside. He pulled me into his arms. "God, it's good to be back home."

Home, I thought, snuggling into his arms. Me, who rarely had snuggled anywhere for any reason my whole life long. Black was eyeing my tree.

"I see you have a tree. I guess that's a tree, right?"

"I thought you'd help me decorate it."

"Claire, that is undoubtedly the most pathetic excuse for a Christmas tree I've ever seen. It's almost embarrassing to look at it."

"It'll look better when I get the lights on."

"I sincerely hope so."

"Quit being so critical. You hungry?"

"Yes. But I didn't want to stop long enough to pick up anything."

"I have the whole works right over there in my refrigerator."

"Let's eat."

I set out the spread and he pretended like it hadn't come

from Kroger's. We ate together, then decorated the tree, and it did look better once we'd finished. I went up to the bedroom and brought down his gift.

He said, "For me? You shouldn't have. This is for you."

It was a tiny blue velvet box. Oh God, I hope he wasn't going to ruin everything with a engagement ring. "You already gave me my gift, remember? All this." I swept my arm around the room.

"It's not much. Open it."

It wasn't wrapped so I flipped up the lid. Inside lay a silver medallion on a long, slender chain. I was distinctly relieved. I liked him but engagements were against my religion.

"It's a Saint Michael's medal. He's the patron saint of police officers. I figured you could use some protection. I bought it at Notre Dame Cathedral. Actually I got myself one, too. Figured I'd need some help if I kept hanging around with you."

"You're probably right."

He smiled and lifted the chain out of the box and fastened it around my neck. I picked it up and looked at it. It was fairly heavy, bigger than most religious medals, solid silver. "It's beautiful."

"Promise me you won't take it off."

"You're getting superstitious."

"Promise me."

"Okay, I promise."

That satisfied him. He said, "Here's a souvenir from Paris."

I opened the shopping bag and pulled out a black cashmere shawl. It was lined with fine embroidered silk with long silky fringe hanging off the bottom.

"It's Hermès," he said.

I didn't know what the hell Hermès was, but it was pretty and probably expensive. I wondered if I'd ever wear it. Maybe I could use it as a couch cover-up on the rare occasions I got to watch Oprah.

"I brought you some Parisian perfume, too, and a wicker

picnic basket full of French cheese and chocolates and baguettes. Figured Bud and the guys could help you eat them."

"Yeah, good idea. Maybe I'll throw in some BBQ Doritos and keep it in the backseat for Bud to eat from during our next stakeout."

Black laughed.

Sheepish and feeling like a pauper exchanging gifts with a prince, I handed him his pathetic little present. "It's not much. I mean it. I mean, well, you're hard to buy for, Black. What do you give somebody who has everything?"

"I don't have everything, just most things I really, really want." He eyed me in a complimentary fashion.

I laughed as he lifted my pitiful little snowman sack by the handles. He pulled out the book and looked at it. "My God, how in the world did you manage this?"

"I called and hired the best photographer in New Orleans, or at least he said he was. I told him to go out to the bayous and take pictures, then have them bound into a book." I shrugged. "You know, I remembered how you said you thought the bayous were beautiful when we were down there." He was still staring down at the book, slowly turning the pages. "It's not much, though, not like all this stuff you got for me."

Black looked at me, his eyes shining with pleasure. When he smiled, the dimples bracketing his mouth deepened in just the way that turned me on. "I love it. It's one of the best, most thoughtful gifts I've ever been given."

That made me more happy than it even should have.

"There's a picture of your friend, Aldus Hebert, in there, too." I smiled, as he turned the pages one by one.

He said, "I think Lafourche Parish is one of the most beautiful places on earth. It brings back lots of memories of when I was a young boy. Thank you."

He leaned over and kissed me, but I pulled away before we reached the point of no return. "I got you a stocking. Here."

"That's funny, I bought you one, too."

He dug the one he'd bought for me out of a shiny gold shopping bag. It was red velvet with hand-sewn ornaments on it that looked like real diamonds and rubies and came out of a blue Tiffany box. The one I got for him was red and white felt and came out of a blue plastic Wal-Mart bag. Crap. I just could not compete with this guy's buying power. I might as well quit trying.

I discovered that mine held Chanel No. 5 from Coco Chanel's own original boutique and a crystal Christmas ornament in the shape of the Eiffel Tower made by Tiffany.

"Jeez, Black, my gifts look downright silly next to yours."

"I should've gotten you an Uzi."

"Nah, Charlie won't let us use submachine guns. I do like all of this a lot, I really do."

He reached inside his stocking and pulled out the small gold frame that I'd gotten on sale for 60 percent off at Dillard's. But it was pretty expensive originally. It held a picture of the two of us. We were having dinner with some tall candles in front of us. We were smiling at each other. He looked happy. I had my arm in a sling.

He smiled at me. "Bermuda. Last fall."

"Harve took it one night. Remember, the three of us were having dinner outside on the patio. I don't know, there's just something about it that I like. I had one made for me, too." I shrugged, feeling stupid again.

"By God, Morgan, you're sentimental."

I frowned. "No, I'm not."

"Yes, you are. Who would've thought that?"

"I'm not sentimental, damn it, and quit saying I am."

He laughed, then sobered. "I love it, and I love you."

His face was serious now, a lot more serious than I wanted it to be. I didn't want to tell him I loved him. I didn't know if I loved him, maybe, probably, but it was Christmas and I was one happy gal that he was home. He was used to me not wanting to say the words, he was a psychiatrist, he could probably tell me exactly why I wasn't saying it. But he wasn't pushy about me telling him how I felt, thank goodness.

"Really? Then show me how much," I said in challenge, and boy, did he ever.

Dark Angels

Many years passed, and everything went along very well. Uriel became fascinated with American Indians after watching a rented video of Kevin Costner in *Dancing with Wolves*. He loved to run through the woods and pretend to be an Osage Indian, the tribe that Gabriel said inhabited these woods in the old days. They played together out there, wearing breechcloths and moccasins and painting their bodies like the Indians used to.

Gabriel bought two old bows with money he made cleaning up in the operating room, and they practiced on animals they caught and tied to stakes. In one of his books, Gabriel learned about some tiny frogs called poison dart frogs that lived in tropical rainforests in Colombia, down in South America. It said the natives there used the frogs' poison on their arrows and blowgun darts when they hunted prey, so Gabriel ordered some poisonous frogs to breed, and when they had enough to spare, he taught Uriel how to make them secrete their poison.

"Now watch, Uriel. See here, this's how the Indians do it. Remember, never, ever touch these frogs with your hands." He got out a long glass vial with a frog down in the bottom.

"You keep them in here and feed them." He snapped on some rubber gloves and dumped out the red frog that was about three inches long with yellow spots on its back. It had very large black eyes.

"When you want the poison, you take this sharp stick and push it down its throat and out one of its legs. Like this."

Uriel leaned closer and watched.

"See, the pain makes the frog sweat. See that white foamy stuff coming out on its back? That's the most powerful poison."

Gabriel picked up an arrow. "You have to roll the tip of the arrow in this white stuff and the poison'll last a whole year. Can you believe that? Hand me the rest of those arrows. It says one frog'll poison about fifty arrows."

"Man, Gabriel, that's really cool."

For a long time, they tried to figure out how to shoot a human and send him to heaven, but all they could catch in the pits they dug in the woods were small mammals, except for once when a deer fell in and broke its hind leg. They practiced on it, and it died very quickly. And then one day, at last, when they were out playing Indians, they heard a man yelling for help.

Gabriel and Uriel looked at each other and grinned in triumph. They followed the cries to one of their pits. A bow hunter had fallen through the branches and leaves disguising the deep hole in the ground. He was dressed in camouflage clothing, head to toe. When he fell, his bow had caught on a root near the top of the pit. One of the sharp spikes they'd angled up at the bottom of the hole had pierced his thigh. He could not move without excruciating pain.

"Oh, thank God, you found me," he said through clenched teeth.

The pain was going to get a lot worse, Uriel thought, because Gabriel had coated the stakes with frog poison after they'd hammered them into the ground.

"I'm hurt bad. You boys gotta get me an ambulance out here quick!"

Gabriel said, "You shouldn't of been hunting out here on our land, mister. It's posted. You had to've climbed over a barbed wire fence to get in here."

"Yeah. Sorry. I wounded a buck and was following the blood trail. Listen, get to a phone. Call the county and tell them where I am. I'm feeling real sick."

Then Gabriel said, "Hey mister, know what? You're in luck. We're angels come to help you."

The hunter frowned. His gaze moved to the war paint on their faces and bare chests. Then he said, "Please, just call me an ambulance. I've lost a lot of blood."

Uriel laughed. "Hey, we ain't angels of mercy, man, we're angels of death."

The man struggled to pull his leg off the stake but couldn't, and then he shouted angrily, "You little shits, quit playin' around and get me some goddamn help."

Gabriel turned to Uriel and said, "Did you hear that? He took the Lord's name in vain. I think he should be sent on up to heaven, don't you?"

"You bet. He's being rude, and he really shouldn't be cussing at us like that."

"Go ahead, Uriel, it's your turn. You take the first shot."

"What? What are you doing? You gotta help me. . . ."

Uriel carefully notched a poisonous arrow on his drawstring, aimed down at the hunter, pulled back as far as he could, and let the arrow fly. It hit the man's torso, cutting deep into his chest close to the heart. The man screamed and writhed helplessly on the stake.

Gabriel notched his arrow and sent it zinging into the man's right shoulder.

"You're better than me with the bow, Uriel. I need to practice some more."

It was Uriel's turn and he let fly another arrow hard into the man's chest, very close to the first one. It must've collapsed the lungs, because the man's shrieks changed into strange, breathless gurgles. Gabriel prepared his next arrow.

"Please, please, let me go," the hunter sputtered out, crying now, bleeding heavily, his breaths so labored they could barely understand him. He was a big man, over six foot, too meaty for them to propel an arrow with enough force to pierce completely through his body.

They took turns until their quivers were empty, a dozen poison-tipped arrows each, but the trespassing hunter was dead long before they ran out of shafts. Then they looped a rope around his neck, pulled him off the stakes, and hoisted him high up in a tree where the buzzards could pick his bones clean. No one would find him, not out here on Uriel's grandma's land. They could do whatever they wanted there, whenever they wanted, so they built a fire under the corpse and roasted wieners on it for supper.

EIGHTEEN

I awoke in the misty shades of dawn with a warm tongue in my ear. I mumbled, "Black, please, enough already."

When Black whined like a dog, I turned my head and got another wet kiss on the nose. Yes, it was my new Christmas poodle that we'd christened Jules Verne.

"Hey, you, cut that out." The tiny beast climbed onto my chest and stood at attention, wagging its tail to beat the band. Okay, so the dog is cute, maybe even adorable to some women who didn't happen to be homicide detectives, but I'd never used the word adorable in my life, not even about cuddly babies, and I wasn't going to start now.

The clock on the bedside table said six o'clock, that's a.m., mind you. Obviously the dog was still on Paris potty time. He would have to get over jet lag if he wanted to live at my house. Black obviously was still in French time zones, too. Dead to the world pretty much described him. A pillow over his head. Arm holding it in place, warning Jules Verne and me not to lick him awake. Black had had enough Christmas cheer, I suspected. Potty duty was left to me.

Jules Verne made a real theatrical production of pacing

back and forth at the foot of the bed, as if he was working up the nerve to jump into the Grand Canyon. He finally took the leap, landing with a soft thud, then clicking across the hardwood floor to the carpeted steps. He was whining softly. He had to go bad. Then I heard him scampering across the kitchen floor, with lots of clicking nails and whining yips. Jeez, Black had forgotten to get me a doggy door.

Rolling out of the warm bed with enthusiasm that almost came up to zero on my want-to scale, I poked my arms into the sleeves of my red fleece robe and shoved my feet into the huge plush house shoes made like blue dolphins that my Aunt Helen had sent me for Christmas.

Now Jules was sitting in front of the single French door that led out back. He watched me shuffle toward him with a haughty, what-the-hell's-taking-you-so-long-lady look on his little shaved face. So I ask you, who's the trained one, him or me?

"Get ready, dog, you're going to let your hair grow out starting today. No little poufs on the end of the tail of any dog I hang around with. You look ridiculous. And that dumb sequined collar's got to go, too. You need spikes. Look tough, Jules, and Rottweilers will run like hell."

He wagged his pouf, then shot outside the minute the door opened. Then all I could see was his pouf moving slowly above sixteen inches of hitherto undisturbed snow. "Good luck, pup. Welcome to the North Pole."

It was snowing yet again. Lake of the Ozarks was giving new meaning to white Christmas this year. Somebody up there needed to flip the switch and stomp on the brakes.

While Jules Verne did his urgent business—hey, maybe I ought to shorten that to J. V.—I turned and picked up the remote and hit the button for fire logs. Yes, the gas logs were fast becoming my favorite gift from Black. I fired the coffeepot and waited for it to perk and fill my kitchen with that superb, one-of-a-kind, early morning Folgers smell I loved. Outside, Jules was still trying to find a nice bathroom spot that he could climb out of once he did his business. I laughed to myself when he began a sort of hop-for-your-life return to the kitchen door.

The puppy came in, all shivering and shaking with snow crusted on his nearly naked body. Hell, he needed a sweater or something. Didn't it ever snow in France? Maybe he was born on the French Riviera and spent bathroom breaks on the beach. He jumped up and braced his front paws on my legs. He looked up at me like, "please, please, I'm freezing my pouf off." So I picked him up, wrapped him in a kitchen towel, and held him close. He felt like some kind of ice-cold, wiggly rat.

Glancing up at the quiet loft, I found my favorite transatlantic Santa still wasn't stirring. I had a feeling I'd seen the last of him for a while. That's okay. We'd done a pretty good job of getting to know each other again for most of the night, and I needed to do some work, anyway. I'd dreamed I was in that red trunk with Christie Foxworthy and the scorpions, and she'd kept saying over and over, "But what'd I do? What'd I do?"

I shivered, just thinking about it and wondered myself what she did to deserve that terrible fate. I watched the coffee drip. It could've been Rowland. Maybe she wouldn't agree to end the relationship, kept stalking him and his wife. But if that were true, he was one helluva good actor. And why would he flag down that off-duty police officer to check out his house? It could have been a clever ruse to throw us off, but Rowland didn't appear to be made of Einstein material. Not in my book, anyway.

When the coffee was finally ready, I was, too. I poured some into my extra-large white mug, sat down at the table, and picked up the three files full of paperwork I'd gathered on the Classon and Foxworthy murders. I spread them out across the table and hit the light switch on the wall. Black's new black-shaded chandelier flared to life and spotlighted some very grisly autopsy photos. Simon's wounds were a little too graphic this early in the a.m. Never liked oozing pus and putrefying skin with my coffee. Christie's eyes disturbed me even more. Buckeye had determined that she'd been bludgeoned in the head before being stuffed in the trunk and he had figured out the number of bites she suffered, but the one by the Egyptian scorpion was deadly all by itself and was what had killed her.

I started on Harve's reports, and it didn't take long to see the pattern emerging inside his yellow-highlighted timelines. At least a dozen spider bites were reported annually at the lake, about a third serious enough to hospitalize the victims. The serious cases involved brown recluses and black widows, usually encountered where they were hiding in old shoes or stored stuff down in basements. Other victims were usually campers and kids at summer camp.

Harve had circled one newspaper article with red ink. Dated over a decade earlier, about the time Joe McKay got expelled. The headline read THE DOME OF THE CAVE ACADEMY INFESTED WITH BROWN RECLUSE SPIDERS, STUDENTS EVACUATED. I skimmed the two-column report. Exterminators were called in after a kid was bitten, had gotten sick, then was rushed to a hospital. At that point the girl was stable but in serious condition. A follow-up story dated several days later was attached. The photo showed the fourteen-year-old girl sitting in a hospital bed holding her bare arm out toward the camera and showing the deep, purple hole eating away her flesh. It wasn't as deep as Classon's, but just as ugly. Coincidence? I think not. Somebody connected to the academy for years and years was breeding killer spiders for his vengeful urges. We needed to determine who had been there at that time. One thing I did know. Joe McKay had been. According to the article, Director Johnstone had been there, too. Wonder if either one of them had any attachment to this girl. I jotted down her name. Jennifer Blocker. Maybe she was an old girlfriend who'd dumped our psychic master. Or maybe she had preferred ambitious Jesus wannabes.

I flipped through the rest of Harve's research linking the academy to spiders and found nothing significant. I picked up the thick stack of college articles Librarian Man, Morton

DeClive, had printed out for me. Lots of poorly written news releases from the academy itself, effusively touting its innovations and excellence in education. Yeah, right. Lots of pictures of students who'd won this award and that certificate, none wearing red devil masks or sporting oozing wounds. Everyone was posed with the director when he was all decked out in his tropical white suit and a thousand-watt grin. The self-aggrandizing director puttin' it on for the camera.

I paused when Black's picture showed up at some fundraiser, grinning and gripping hands with white-suited Jesus while donating a cool hundred thousand dollars to go toward a new gymnasium for the academy. No wonder everybody around the lake kowtowed to the guy. Surely Black could find a better school to support than one that offered paganism that might or might not include devil worshipping. That creep, Johnstone, probably pocketed most of the donations, anyway. I decided to set Harve loose on a background search of the dear director and see if he could dig up a well-hidden rap sheet. Maybe he should do background on everybody at the academy. They were all freaks out there. I jotted down some names.

My interest perked considerably when I ran across the name Wilma Harte. She was the female custodian who'd disappeared. I stared hard at the woman's picture, wondering about her, wondering if she'd killed herself or if she'd turn up someday. More interesting was why she took off in the first place. My instincts were bristling all over. Something told me that Wilma Harte was connected to Simon Classon, some way, somehow. It sounded like she was his primary butt of cruel jokes. Maybe she hated him enough to kill him. A long shot but it bore checking out. I made a note to put Harve on finding out if she'd surfaced anywhere. I would like to interview that girl, believe you me.

I read over some of the papers I'd printed out about spiders, their habitat and habits. No reported spider-bite homicides. Until now. Then again, that crime would be easy to pass off as an accident. Unless the victim was in a trash bag containing the eight-legged monsters, bound and gagged and hanging from a tree limb. No coincidence, that. But hey, maybe Classon wasn't meant to be found. Ever. Maybe if Stuart Rowland hadn't run off the road and called a wrecker, the killer would have gotten away clean. Maybe the perp planned to cut Classon down and dispose of the body at his convenience.

I got up, dribbled more coffee into my mug. It seemed absurd that this guy was a serial who used arachnids to kill. But now there were two murders with unpleasant little critters sporting lots of little legs and deadly poisons, and a killer who put a lot of thought into how to torture and off people with great gusto but leaving no clues. Maybe he'd had a lot of practice we hadn't found out about yet.

Jules Verne was growling fiercely somewhere. He sounded about ten times bigger than he was. Eager to see how a sissy dog looked when seriously pissed off, I stood up. "Okay, Jules, what's the problem now?"

I couldn't see him but his claws were scratching like crazy on the tiles around the fireplace. He was jumping at something, then running off and circling back. Then he started up with the shrillest yapping in the history of caninekind.

"Shut it, dog. Your buddy Black's trying to get some sleep."

I rounded the couch to pick him up and then I saw what was agitating him. The back of my neck crawled. The biggest spider I'd ever seen was cornered against the fireplace. It was big and black and hairy. A tarantula. Six inches across. Two of its legs were off the floor and waving around like some kind of rearing stallion, ready to fight Jules Verne to the death.

I snatched the puppy up and backed away as if the spider was a crouching tiger. Shudders shook me, and I felt sick for a couple of seconds. Then I took a deep breath and reminded myself that I wasn't afraid of spiders. Hell no, I could step on them, couldn't I? This one might take industrialized slippers, however, so I refrained. Okay. Tarantulas aren't deadly, I think. They just looked like it. Some people kept them as pets and let them crawl up their arms and stuff. They were morons, of course, but there you go.

The hairy monster started tiptoeing its eight legs toward the couch. It couldn't get away or I wouldn't know where it was. And I definitely wanted to know where it was. That got me going. I grabbed my glass cookie jar, dumped out the Oreo crumbs, then edged cautiously around to the other side. Now it was back against the wall, watching me, I feared. Poisonous or not, it was revoltingly ugly. Fighting a serious case of the creeps, I grit my teeth and quickly turned the jar on its side, scooped the spider inside, then set it upright. I left it on the hearth and shivered for about thirty seconds while it tried unsuccessfully to climb up the curved sides of the glass.

It occurred to me then that it might have bitten Jules Verne. I pinned the wriggling pup down on the kitchen counter and checked him out for bites. He licked my hands and kicked against my exploring fingers with all four paws. I didn't see any puncture wounds, and he hadn't yelped in pain so I was fairly confident he was okay.

"What the hell are you doing to that dog?"

Black was looking down over the balcony. He was bare chested and tousled and frowning.

"Looking for a tarantula bite." I put the dog down and watched him scramble helter-skelter up the stairs to Black. "I just trapped the biggest tarantula I've ever seen in my life inside my cookie jar."

"Come again?"

"You heard right."

"Well, I guess I'll pass on Oreos from now on."

"I'm serious."

"Really? A tarantula? Did you smash it?"

"God, no. I want to know what kind it is and if it's poisonous. I have a feeling it's not from around here. Maybe even as far away as Egypt."

"Why Egypt?"

"Because that's where the perp's killer scorpion hailed from."

Black came down the steps a minute later in his black flannel robe and slippers, and Jules Verne cupped in one open palm. The dog's tail looked like a metronome gone berserk.

"Where is it?"

"On the hearth."

"Do you think it's poisonous?"

"I'd rather it wouldn't be."

Black looked somber, which told me that he was thinking the same unsettling thoughts I was. "Do you see a lot of spiders out here?"

"Not giant, icky, woolly tarantulas. Not in the dead of winter. Hey, maybe Santa brought it." I'd tried for humor but neither of us smiled.

I watched him squat down beside the glass jar. "Good God, it's a tarantula, all right. It looks like the kind that's indigenous to the lake. I've seen them on the roads at Cedar Point, especially in the fall. Is this the only one you've ever seen in the house?"

"Yes, thank God." The idea that more of the creepy things might be burrowing through my stuff unsettled me big-time. I got some serious heebie-jeebies and felt like climbing up on a table but resisted the urge. Black would laugh. Tarantulas weren't poisonous. Get a grip, Claire.

"Maybe it was hibernating in the walls the carpenters took down when they remodeled this place," said Black.

"Yeah, maybe a brown recluse or a black widow might, but a giant woods-dwelling tarantula?"

"How else could it have gotten in? There's more than a foot of snow on the ground."

"Maybe somebody brought it in. Maybe to scare me. Maybe to kill me. Maybe it's a poisonous kind that we don't know about." A sobering thought. Maybe the killer had designated me number three.

Black said, "That's unlikely."

I hoped to hell that it was.

"Hey, Black, read through those crime files over there and see if you still say that."

"You're scared?"

"Well, I'm glad I didn't come down here barefoot in the dark and step on the damn thing. The idea of some maniac arachno-murderer infesting my house with hideously hairy spiders doesn't appeal to me, either. You?"

He frowned. "Who's been here lately, other than the carpenters? Anybody? Anything unusual happen?"

"No. But who says I'd know? I don't spend much time here, either. I wouldn't have noticed that thing today if the dog hadn't gone on point."

"Good boy, Jules."

Then it hit me like a laser beam exactly who *had* been in my cabin of late, who had stood only feet from the spot where Jules Verne had cornered the spider, who had knelt down and opened his coat to warm up. "That guy I told you about. The psychic. He was in here, remember, I was on the phone with you."

"Dammit, Claire, I told you not to let him in."

"I'm not saying he brought it in here, but I can't rule it out. He was acting weird, warning me to be on the lookout because I was next, all from his so-called visions." Anger came swiftly. I clamped my jaw. "He's up to his neck in this case, and I've known it from day one. He used a snake once to scare Classon. He could be trying to scare me."

"Are you saying you've been in here for several days with that thing?"

I hadn't thought of that. I frowned but couldn't stop the shudder that shot through me.

Black said, "Okay, let's get some exterminators out here."

"On Christmas morning?"

"That's right. And we'll go to my place until we get a clean sweep."

"No, I'm okay now. Chances are that's the only one. I'm not afraid of spiders, anyway. They're easy to kill. I'll buy a bigger flyswatter."

"Yeah, if you see them first."

"I have a spider guard dog now to alert me."

"Pack a bag, Claire. At least at Cedar Bend we'll know there aren't poisonous spiders in our bed."

"Now, let's not panic. How many spiders could one guy in a four-wheeler set loose in here?"

"Were you in the room with him the whole time?"

"Yeah. I might've glanced away a time or two, but the rest of the time, believe me, my eyes were glued on him. He couldn't have done it, trust me."

"I see one more spider and we're out of here, agreed?"

"You betcha. McKay's not scaring me out of my own house. Animal control will know the score. I'll even donate it to them."

Black looked at the files strewn atop the table. "Is this why you're up so early?"

"Jules needed a potty break. I thought I'd get some work done until you woke up."

"By the way, Merry Christmas."

"Ditto."

He poured himself a cup of coffee. "How about I whip up some waffles and strawberries?"

"As if I keep strawberries in the fridge in December?"

"I'll call the restaurant."

"Not at seven o'clock on Christmas morning, you won't. How about toast and eggs? I'll fix you breakfast."

"Wait, just a second now, I think I just hallucinated."

"I'm good at things you haven't even found out about yet."

"I've found out about a lot of them."

"Ditto."

We grinned a little, remembering, then I left him drinking coffee and watching the giant tarantula trying to get out of the jar while I whipped out a skillet and a package of bacon.

Black moved around the living room, looking under sofas and chairs for more holiday guests. More power to him.

After opening and shutting lots of cabinets and pouring himself a glass of orange juice, he said, "Mind if I take a look?" He pointed at the reports strewn around the table.

"Help yourself, but don't forget, this is highly confidential. Even the people at the academy don't know exactly how Classon died. We don't want the media anywhere near this."

I thought about the storm of reporters and cameramen who'd descended like a biblical plague on us last summer and knew he was thinking the same thing. Neither of us ever wanted to go through that hell again. I cracked half-a-dozen eggs into a bowl. When I looked back, he was sitting at the table intent on the files. Jules Verne was asleep on his lap.

"I think you bought that dog for yourself, not me."

"I like dogs. I haven't had one since I was a kid."

"Want him back?"

"Keep him for pest control until Orkin gets out here. And for God's sake, Claire, use the damn security system I put in."

"This wasn't a break-in. It was Joe McKay and I invited him in." I placed strips of crisp bacon on our plates, beat up the eggs with a fork, then poured them into the hot skillet. The one dish that I liked to cook. Sometimes I even got creative after watching Emeril on the Food Channel. That's when I substitute ham for bacon.

"My God." He looked up at me, horrified. "These people suffered horrible deaths."

"Yeah, I know. Classon for days. The woman went faster."

"This guy is seriously disturbed. And I don't think Classon's his first victim, either. Everything's way too choreographed, too well thought out." He moved to the kitchen counter and sat down on a stool across from me. "He looks like a psychopath, Claire. I think he's more into the torture than the killing. That's probably what he's getting off on."

He stared at me, thinking about it. "You've got to watch your back on this one. I mean it. Don't go off alone and put yourself in a vulnerable position. He's a planner, down to the umpteenth detail. This time he just got unlucky when a car slid in a ditch near the crime scene. Otherwise, Classon's body would never have been found. He'd either have taken him down and disposed of his remains or just left him hanging out there where nobody would ever think to look. He's a sadist and my guess is he probably sat by and watched Classon's terror inside that sleeping bag. With the added horror that Classon was in sight of the school and help that he couldn't get. This perp loves to watch the suffering. Enjoys the victim's fear, probably more than the actual murder. He's going to be hard to catch."

"I'll catch him."

"I'm asking you nicely, Claire. Stay at the lodge with me until you do catch him. He's clever, cunning, and if he did put that tarantula in here, he's interested in you specifically. Has he tried to get to Bud in any way?"

That brought me to a standstill. "I think Bud would've told me if McKay approached him or if he'd found anything in his house. He hates spiders."

"How often do you forget to set the security system?"

"I'm not used to it yet. Give me a break."

"Don't forget again." He tossed a close-up photograph across the counter to me. One of Simon Classon's leg wounds. "Or you'll end up nursing wounds like this one."

"I'm not going to end up like that."

"You're not invincible. You bleed like everybody else."

"I can take care of myself."

"This isn't your run-of-the-mill killer. He doesn't think like normal people, I doubt if he can even act like a normal person. When you find him, he's going to be weird, eccentric, and it'll be hard for him to hide it."

"Like, maybe, pretending to be a psychic? Unfortunately, psycho describes just about everybody at that school. How about working up a psychological profile for me?"

"I'm telling you, right now, without reservation, this guy

is insane. No fancy syndromes, no split personality, no schizophrenia, no disorders. He's a crazy son of a bitch."

"Maybe he's just mean, like a devil worshipper, maybe."

"Devil worshippers are known to mutilate, cut out hearts and other internal organs for sacrificial offerings. But I've never heard of cultists killing victims with poisonous spiders. This is rare, I can tell you that. Rare and deadly."

I stared at him, slightly unnerved by his seriousness. He was spooked. Black didn't spook easily. "Only we would discuss stuff like this first thing Christmas morning, Black."

No smile. No humor. Black was not in a lighthearted mood. "I didn't realize what kind of monster you were up against until I saw these pictures. He'll be hard to figure, hard to track, I think. He'll be somebody who doesn't get along with people, an outsider, a pariah, even. He might have some kind of disfigurement that makes him self-conscious and awkward in social settings. And he'll have access to spiders and a place to keep them, maybe even raise them, like pets."

"We're already on that. Where did he get so many spiders, you think? At this time of year? In the snow?"

"He'll have a secret place, a dark place that he crawls in to play with his little murderous creatures, that's my guess. Maybe a greenhouse out in the middle of nowhere that he keeps warm and humid and dark."

I thought of what Joe McKay had said about me and a similar dark, humid place. I remembered the look on his face when I mentioned the grave. I decided to keep all that to myself. No need to spook Black more than he already was.

"So you think the killer was coming back to get Classon's body after he was dead?"

"Don't you?"

I nodded. "I'm with you on that. I think he wanted Simon to see his colleagues over at the school, moving around while all those spiders ate on him. That makes it ultrapersonal. He knew Simon, and he knows other people at that school. He knew Christie and Rowland and they somehow got on his bad side. He's connected there, big-time. Stuart Rowland himself could be the perp, but my gut tells me otherwise. And you think he's done this kind of thing before?"

"Hell, yes. Plenty of times, maybe not with this kind of torture. He's just hidden the corpses better in the past. You've checked into missing persons, I assume."

"Harve's working on it. He's checking further into this guy, McKay, too. He's involved somehow. I know he is. Don't ask me how. I just do."

"Do me a favor, okay, Claire? Just call it another Christmas present from you to me."

"What?"

"Stay away from McKay. Don't be alone with him, and for God's sake, don't let him in this house again. In fact, don't let anybody in this house again."

I laughed. "That's a little extreme, don't you think?"

"I'm serious."

"You know you don't have to worry on that account. I'm inhospitable by nature."

"Yeah, I'm lucky you let me stay over."

"By the way, Black, you still got that invitation to that big gala deal out at the academy on New Year's Eve?"

"Yeah. Why?"

I divided the scrambled eggs between our plates, rather proud they weren't burnt black. "They're still having it, so I thought we'd go, have some fun, ring in the New Year together."

Black looked skeptical. "You realize, of course, that this is a formal affair."

"That's cool. I can deal with it. I did it once before when I was sixteen. The prom. Worse night of my life. I had to wear panty hose."

Black eyed me suspiciously. "It's black tie, Claire. That means a tuxedo for me and, dare I say it, a dress and high heels for you."

"Just because I don't have any dresses right now, doesn't mean I can't get one."

"You're actually saying that you're going to buy a dress?"

"Luckily Bud gave me a gift certificate at this fancy ladies shop downtown named Swank's. I'll use it to get something suitable."

"Where will you hide your guns?"

"Harve gave me a ankle holster so all I have to do is buy something floor length."

"You're going in disguise to watch your suspects, right?"

I had to laugh. "Hey, don't be rude. You might like me in a dress."

"It'll be interesting to see if you really go through with this. Want me to help you pick it out? There's a perfectly good boutique at Cedar Bend Lodge. Your credit's good there any time."

"Nope. That $300 gift certificate is practically burning a hole in my pocket."

"Okay, you're on. I'm going to New York for a couple of days next week, but I'll make a real effort to be back in time to see you in a dress." He appraised me. "I guess you won't consider staying at my place while I'm gone? There's 24-hour room service."

"Yeah, right, I'll forget all about my investigation and go hide from the bogeyman at your place."

"Here you go, Claire, take another good look at these." This time he handed me Christie Foxworthy's photographs, the one with her wide-open eyes staring up out of the trunk.

"Breakfast is ready," I said with false cheer. "You as hungry as I am?"

NINETEEN

On New Year's Eve morning I found myself loitering on the streets again but this time I was in downtown Camdenton. Luckily, I didn't have to wear fishnets and short shorts to get this job done. Instead, I had on my usual black sweats with the obligatory fluorescent-emblazoned SHERIFF in big yellow letters. Unlike my hooker threads, this outfit kept the johns away in droves.

Truth was I awaited Bud, who was late. The day was overcast and gloomy. Imagine that, right? And fit my mood precisely. Snow-laden clouds lumbered overhead and teased us with a storm. Did I live at the Arctic Circle? Is that it? All I needed was an igloo and a pet penguin. For the past week we'd been doing background checks on the graduates of the academy without a whole lotta luck, and the weather wasn't exactly helping our investigation, either.

Then Bud appeared out of nowhere and strode down the street toward me.

I greeted him politely. "It's about damn time."

"Hey man, I've been checkin' out alibis all mornin' long. You find out yet what kind of spider that was at your house?"

"Animal Control said it was harmless. Lots of them out in

the woods around here, indigenous to the Ozarks. Want me to catch one you can call Fido?"

He shuddered. "Thanks, but no thanks. I've got a goldfish."

"Maybe I'll give it to Shaggy as a late Christmas present. I bet he likes things that are creepy."

Bud glanced around. "Okay, what's up? You get a new lead?"

"Nope. I need a favor."

Bud looked interested. I happened to be a pretty self-sufficient gal. I don't think I ever asked him for a favor before.

"What kind of favor?" Now he sounded suspicious. He looked around some more, perplexed.

"Promise you won't laugh?"

"Yeah."

A couple of teenagers holding hands passed by. I waited a second then lowered my voice. "I need you to help me pick out a dress with that gift certificate you gave me."

Bud laughed. Loudly. With feeling.

I scowled. "Give me a break, Bud. Why'd you give me a gift certificate if you didn't want me to use it?"

He sobered instantly. "Sorry. I went into shock, is all. I always laugh when I'm shocked. Are you really gonna use that gift certificate?"

"Yes."

"For a dress?"

"Yes."

"Wow. I've never seen you look like a real woman before."

"Thanks."

Bud shoved his hands in his pockets. "Hey, I'm honored. Really."

"Well, sometimes you look pretty nice. You know, the kind of clothes you pick out, and stuff." I felt idiotic. "Okay, this thing tonight out at the academy is pretty hoity-toity from what I've heard. I don't know what kind of stuff they wear to things like that so you're going to have to help me out."

He placed his hand over his heart. "I am touched, Claire. I will not let you down."

"You gonna help me pick out a dress, or not?"

"Sure. Swank's is right around the corner. Ever been there?"

"What do you think?"

Bud grinned his cheesiest grin. "Just follow my lead and don't say anything. And don't pull your weapon if they ask you to try it on."

"Shut up, Bud."

We walked into Swank's Couture, as uppity as that sounded, and I stamped snow off my combat boots on their white, velvety-looking rug. A white, three-tier fountain in the foyer made soft gurgles that made me look for the ladies' room. Mannequins that made Boston high-society dames look friendly stood all around in various stages of undress. I immediately hated everything I saw.

Most all the walls were mirrored, with lots of recessed spotlights in alcoves illuminating lots of stuck-up dummies. And I don't mean Bud and me.

A moment later the Ice Queen of Finland walked through some gold velvet tasseled draperies. She had the long shapely legs and proud carriage of Las Vegas showgirls. Bud noticed, stood straighter. His smile deepened; he drooled a little. She looked at us and said, "Hello, my name's Brianna. May I help you find something?"

Her expression, quickly hidden, told me that she thought we desperately needed her help. She pulled herself together, "Oh, I remember you, sir. You came in just before Christmas and bought a gift certificate for some lucky girl." She definitely had an accent, one which called to mind reindeer and Land of the Midnight Sun. What was with all the accents? Was this mid-Missouri or the United Nations?

I said, "Yes, ma'am, Brianna, that lucky girl would be me."

Brianna dragged her eyes off Bud's handsome eagerness and turned her attention on me, as if she hadn't realized until that very moment that I was a girl. Maybe Bud was right getting me a dress. "Oh, hello. Please, what can I do to assist you?"

I presented the gift certificate, glad to get rid of it. "Okay, here's the deal. I need a dress, but I don't want anything with ruffles or lace, and no sequins or gaudy jewelry stuff sewed on it. No embroidery, either, and not sheer, and I don't want any cleavage showing. And it's got to be under three hundred dollars. And it's got to be floor length to hide my ankle holster."

Miss Finland blinked. She looked back at Bud. He shrugged, embarrassed, I guess. "She's a tomboy," he offered.

"Well, we can certainly deal with that," she said, her eyes alight with the challenge of me.

"Uh-uh. No dealing with that, no way. I just need a simple dress to wear to that high-horse ball thing tonight. You know, tuxes and fancy dresses."

Bud said, "Hey, Brianna, you know where they get that phrase 'high horse'?"

Brianna beamed at him. "Actually, yes, I do. I believe 'high horse' comes from the olden days when knights rode big, tall steeds called chargers and everybody else had to ride on donkeys or regular horses. Thus high horse implies something worthy of nobility."

Bud's jaw dropped, then his eyes lit up with astonished admiration. He was in love, I feared. He said, "That's right. How'd you know?"

"I have this wonderful book on the origins of popular sayings. It's really fascinating reading."

Boy, did that ever turn Bud on. I was afraid their hot looks and sappy grins were going to fuse them together for all eternity so I cleared my throat rather loudly. I had a dress to buy and time was a-wasting.

With some difficulty, Brianna broke her steamy, phrase-origins-induced eye lock with Bud. She forced herself to look at me, even though I didn't give a damn about popular sayings. She said, "And this is a black-tie affair?"

"Yeah." I actually knew what black tie meant, and white tie, too, but I let her feel superior. Not that she probably already didn't.

"Please follow me."

As she moved away, Bud leaned close and whispered into my ear. "I'm almost positive she's got the hots for me."

"You'll have to melt her first."

He smiled, pure confidence. "You think I can't? I'm gonna ask her out on a date. She's flirtin' with me, big-time. I know when somebody's interested in me, and she definitely is. And she's read my favorite book. Wow, who would've thought somethin' like this could happen right outta the blue?"

I figured she'd just been checking out his Whopper with Cheese breath.

"Just help me find a dress that doesn't look stupid, okay?"

"Sure."

Fin led us back through the spacious, sparkling shop, past lots more studied spotlights and mirrors and big palm trees and sparkling chandeliers and snurly-lipped mannequins. Some of them had cardigan sweaters tied around their shoulders over matching pullovers. I really hated people who tied sweaters around their shoulders over pullover sweaters. How fake is that? Just stuff the damn thing in a duffel bag or leave it in the car.

"Here we go, miss. Please have a seat in the viewing alcove and let me display some possible choices. Now what size are you? A six, perhaps? Four?"

I shrugged. "I wear a small in bulletproof vests."

Fin laughed, an honest sound, and suddenly I liked her better. "I'll look for something that'll look good with Kevlar."

I watched her move away toward some big mirrors that turned out to be a hidden door. "Hey, Bud, she knows what our vests are made out of. That's a good sign, too. Better grab her up."

We spent the wait quietly comparing notes about the status of our investigation, shoptalk, while she did her thing. When she appeared again, she was pushing a rolling rack lined with glittery floor-length gowns.

"Here we are, Miss Morgan. I've selected several different styles for you to try on."

"How do you know my name?"

"It was written on the gift certificate you gave me. Do you see anything here that suits your fancy?"

Suits my fancy? "I don't really need to try on anything."

"Yes, you do." That was Bud. "Got to, Claire."

"Oh, get real, Bud. I don't have time for this. Just pick one out and let's go. I've got a briefing with Charlie."

"We have a fashion salon in-house with a very talented makeup artist and hairstylist, if you'd be interested," Fin offered hopefully. "You'd be surprised what a difference they can make."

"Can they make me look like those snooty dummies?"

Brianna laughed again. What do you know, she finds me amusing. She glanced around and then lowered her voice. "This place comes off pretty pretentious, doesn't it?"

I was liking her better and better, so I actually considered trying on a dress. Bud was picking through the dresses like Ralph Lauren or somebody, sliding them one by one across the rack. "What color you like, Claire? Here's an aqua one that matches your eyes."

"Nah, too aqua."

"Okay, how about this golden-beige one that matches your hair?"

"Nah, too golden beige."

Brianna took charge. "Miss Morgan, you strike me as a woman who'd go in for simplicity, which is always the best way to go, in my opinion. How about basic black? What about this one?"

She draped it over her arm and held it out for my perusal. I perused it for about ten seconds and said, "Okay, I'll take it if it's under three hundred bucks."

Brianna lifted the price tag and read it aloud. "Well, it's close. It's three fifteen plus tax."

"What else do you have?"

"Claire, for God's sake, it's just an extra twenty bucks." Bud again.

"Okay, okay, wrap it up. I'll pay the extra."

Brianna smiled and took it to the cash register in a different little alcove that looked like a miniature Taj Mahal. It had a chandelier over the cash register so there'd be enough light for rich people to write big checks for little scraps of dresses that cost $315 plus tax.

I dug out the extra cash and handed it to her. She gave me my change and a big white smile. "You'll look beautiful in black with your coloring. Very elegant. The two of you make a handsome couple." She looked at Bud, all disappointed and sad that he was mine and not hers. It wasn't every day you met a good-looking guy that read the same book.

I decided to make her day. "I'm not going with Bud. I have another date. But Bud's single and he thinks you're pretty damn hot."

Bud looked at me as if I'd lost my mind. Brianna perked up. "Really? Is that so?"

"Yeah, I guess I do," Bud drawled out, leaning an elbow on the desk. "How about the two of us meeting for a drink sometime?"

"I'd love to. How about tonight? Six-thirty? You can pick me up here. That's when I get off work."

Bud's mouth actually fell open. Brianna did that jaw-dropping stuff pretty well. But I liked a woman who took control. Brianna was all right. She had obviously fallen hard for Bud's southern accent. Maybe she was from southern Scandinavia.

"Maybe she'll go to the gala with you tonight, Bud. I bet she's got a dress that's suitable. Maybe we can double-date."

"I'd love to," Brianna agreed without hesitation. Bud looked like he'd died and gone to heaven.

Once we were done and outside I shifted the big silver dress box under my arm and fumbled for the keys to my Explorer. "Boy, you got yourself something there, big boy. You got women throwing themselves at your feet."

"How old do you think she is?"

"She looks legal, if that's what you're worried about."

"Man, she's a real looker. Blond, blue eyed, built."

"Thanks for the help."

"Hell, you picked out the first thing she showed you. You should've tried it on, I'm warnin' you. You never know about clothes until you see how it looks in the mirror."

"I never try on anything. It'll fit. Listen, Black'll be back from New York and picking me up around eight. We'll meet you and Brianna out there. I want to snoop around the campus some while Jackass Johnstone is preening in front of the audience."

"See you later." Bud sauntered away, grinning and waving at Brianna, who still stood in the door watching him leave. What was it with him and women? It had to be the sexy drawl. Or the book. I wondered what Brianna would say when she found out his real name was Budweiser.

Later that evening I stood in front of my bathroom mirror, wishing to hell I'd tried on the dress. Or at least turned it over. I shifted slightly and stared at my back. Hell, I was gypped. They forgot to sew on the back half of the dress. The front was all demure and elegant and stuff, long sleeves, soft black velvet with a high turtleneck, but turn around, baby, and I was naked down to my waist. That meant no bra and no shoulder holster. Thank goodness, Harve got me that ankle holster for Christmas. And thank goodness, Black had brought me that fringed shawl from Gay Paree.

I propped a foot on the counter and noticed that the slit in the side of my skirt went way, way up my thigh so I strapped my weapon on the other ankle, just above the black patent stiletto heels, last seen castrating horny guys at a truck stop. But they were the most suitable thing I had to wear with this dress. Combat boots just didn't cut it, nor did black-and-orange high-top Nikes. Besides, I didn't want to embarrass Black.

Peering in the mirror, I fiddled with my hair for a minute then decided to just brush it straight back like Black wore his. Black's hair gel was sitting there so I ran some through my hair. I had a pair of tiny diamond studs that Aunt Helen had given me a couple of years ago so I put those on. I looked down in dread at the Lancôme makeup kit Bud bought me two years ago for my birthday. I'd never opened it. Should I? Like I said, this was a fancy affair and I didn't want to embarrass Black. On the other hand, I didn't want to embarrass myself either, and slathering on a bunch of cosmetics was a good way to do it.

I opened it and picked out a tube of mascara. I coated my lashes, who probably wondered "What the hell?" Then I added some blush to my cheeks and a subdued shade of cinnamony lipstick. Holy crap, I hadn't worn this much makeup since that one prom date I had. I felt dumb, but I know Black would've done the same for me.

When I heard him let himself in downstairs, I picked up the shawl and draped it around my shoulders. I took one last, disgruntled look in the mirror and wondered who the hell that woman was. Black must've wondered the same thing when I started down the steps because he froze where he stood and stared at me.

"Good God, Claire." He had on a tux and looked damn good in it, too. Then he said, "You look beautiful."

"Yeah, right."

I came the rest of the way downstairs and he said, "I hardly recognize you without your weapon."

"Think again." I lifted my skirt and revealed my sweet little gun.

"I should've known."

"How was New York?"

"Okay. Come over here. I'm turned on."

"I don't want you messing up my lipstick."

"I can't promise something like that."

He messed it up all right but that's okay. I had missed him, too. "Okay, Black, that's gonna have to do it for now. We can't be late. Charlie might be there."

"As long as we can finish this up later."

"Oh, one more thing." I twirled around and showed him the purloined part of my gown, not wanting him to have a heart attack at the ball.

"Sweet Mary. Are you really going to wear that out in public?" But he was smiling. "I can't promise to keep my hands off you, not with that much naked skin showing."

"Thus, the cashmere shawl."

Black took it and draped it around my shoulders. I felt like we were in some lame soap opera.

"I think I like you dressed like this. Even better than your prostitute costume."

"Flatterer."

"You smell great, too."

"That's your Irish Spring. I found it in the shower. C'mon, let's go. I hope you left the heater on in your car. They must've made this dress for hot-natured Brazilians."

I picked up my sheriff's parka and draped it over my fancy getup. I wasn't going to freeze my buns off, just to show off my skimpy new dress.

I stepped outside my door and stopped in my tracks.

"Awesome, Black."

"Thought you'd like it."

It was a new Humvee, black and chrome, big and butch. Not the new little ones now sold on car lots, but the huge original one used in Iraq and other battlegrounds. Black didn't do little.

"When did you get it?"

"I ordered it last week. They had to drive it down from South Bend. It'll come in handy in these hills. So you like it?"

"You kidding me?"

"Want to drive?"

"What do you think?"

He opened the driver's door, and I got in. The motor was running. A little screen showed where we were—a frickin' GPS device. It looked like the cockpit of a Boeing 727. I love it. I want one.

"Pretty cool, huh?" Black said, sliding in the opposite side, which was pretty far away from me. The vehicle was big, I tell you.

"Can I have it?"

"Yes."

Unfortunately, I think he was kidding. It drove like a car, a big, wide, macho car, just the kind I liked. I felt invincible. Except for my dress.

Dark Angels

It took the hunter three weeks to rot. They left him in the tree but went back to check on him every day. There was a search party out after him; they'd heard about it on the radio but the police concentrated on the national forest land where he always hunted. Uriel didn't feel bad about him, not even when he saw his wife and three little kids crying on television. The hunter shouldn't ever have broken the law and come onto Uriel's grandma's property, or he'd still be alive.

The older Uriel grew, the better he liked the woods. He and Gabriel had lots of money now, too, and they ordered a couple of Egyptian fat-tailed scorpions to raise and the most wonderful poisonous spiders from Australia that hid in water bubbles on the bottom of swimming pools so when somebody stepped on them, they'd bite and the victims would be dead in ten minutes. It was fun. They'd gotten some pit vipers from Africa and a pair of king cobras from India to breed, and a baby python they put in a pit in the cave to see how big it'd grow. It was wonderful learning about all these exotic creatures and how they killed people.

Gabriel supplied the money. He was dealing drugs now, to other kids and to some adult junkies, too. They never peddled in their own county but drove north or south along the Interstate and sold on playgrounds and alleyways near teenage hangouts. It was easy money, and it just came rolling in. Sometimes Gabriel and Uriel took drugs, too, before they went looking for people they could send to heaven. But they had to be careful and not get caught. As soon as Uriel was of age, they would kill his grandma so he could live in the house alone. It would be better for both of them. What kind of life did she have anyway, always sleeping in her bed? He already stashed some of his spiders in his room there. Even now, when his grandma was awake, she was afraid of Uriel. She'd drink her tea and go to her bedroom and lock her door and not come out. And that's the way Uriel liked it.

One night when they were in the cave together, dissecting the remains of the hunter with newly sharpened scalpels, they heard noises outside in the old hunting lodge above the cave. Terrified the police had found them out, they took their new Remington shotguns and crept through the tunnel to the trapdoor. Outside, they could hear loud heavy-metal music. People were laughing and talking and yelling at each other.

"Ssh, Uriel. You can't make a sound," Gabriel whispered, putting one forefinger to his lips. He climbed the short ladder and slid the inside bolt, then he lifted the trapdoor and peered stealthily into the boiler room. It was empty. The noises were coming from the other end of the lodge. They eased through the trapdoor and tiptoed outside. It was well after midnight but they could see a light flickering inside one room. They inched around to where they could see about half a dozen kids drinking booze and smoking pot.

"We need to kill them, right, Gabriel?" Uriel whispered, his heart beginning to race with excitement.

Gabriel said, "Sure, if you want to."

"Oh, I want to. Let's put 'em in the pit with some timber rattlers."

Gabriel laughed. "You're sure gettin' to be a bloodthirsty little thing, Uriel. Let's go. They got no idea they're gonna die tonight. This's gonna be fun."

A minute later they jumped out together and said, "Boo!"

All the kids stopped what they were doing and stared at them. One girl had already passed out from booze or drugs, or maybe both. She lay on her back in the middle of the floor with her arms flung out.

"You're trespassing on my property," Gabriel yelled. "Get your hands up!"

A tall, skinny boy in a camo jacket stood up. His voice was slurred. "Hey, man, we ain't hurtin' nothing. We just wanted a place to get high and party. We ain't from around here. We got a rock band, man, and we're hitchin' the rails out to L. A. to get discovered. We followed this river from the tracks lookin' for a place to swim and get high. We'll be outta here in the mornin'."

"Don't worry, *man*, we're gettin' ready to have the coolest party you ever been to. Right, Uriel?"

"Right."

"Who're you guys?" That was a girl. She stepped out into the firelight. She was pretty, little bitty with thick, curly dark hair and black eyes. She inhaled deeply on a joint and blew out smoke and said, "We don't want no trouble. C'mon, relax, man, be cool, smoke a little weed. We got plenty."

Gabriel said, "Smoking pot's illegal. You're breakin' the law when you come out here and do this kinda stuff. God's not gonna like it. He's gonna punish you for this."

The boy dressed in camo stepped back. "Hey, man, chill, have some fun."

Gabriel laughed. "You want us to have some fun? Okay, watch this."

He pulled the trigger, and the double barrels blasted the skinny kid in his chest and sent him crashing backward. He slid slowly down the wall to the floor in a lifeless heap, trailing blood smears all the way down. The other kids jumped up and tried to run, screaming and yelling, and Gabriel and Uriel opened fire, shouting scripture and shooting like angels bringing down hell and brimstone, killing in a wild, heady, reckless murder rampage that lasted at least five minutes if you counted the reloading. They were panting afterward, splattered with blood and gore and breathing in the cordite smoke that hovered in clouds around the small room.

Uriel turned to Gabriel. His voice was hoarse. "I thought we were gonna use the rattlers on some of them."

Gabriel threw back his head and laughed. The excited, happy sound rang into the still night and reverberated high in the surrounding trees. "Hell, Uriel, there's plenty more where they came from. All we gotta do is go find them."

Uriel laughed, too, because it was just so true. So very simple. The world was just full of people they could send to heaven. And he and Gabriel were angels, true angels doing God's work. God wouldn't ever let them get caught. He remembered a prayer his mom used to say. "God is great, God is good."

"If any of 'em's still alive, we'll try out some poisons or put 'em in with the snakes, if that's what you want. The dead ones can go in those black trash bags I brought yesterday. We'll hoist them way up in the trees and use 'em for target practice. Nobody's gonna ever think of looking way out here. They're runaways, anyway. Who's gonna give a damn about them?"

"When can we go get some more runaways, Gabriel?"

Gabriel looked at Uriel. "Man alive, kid, you're gettin' to be worse than me, and that's sayin' something. I do believe I've created a monster."

They laughed together as they dragged the bodies outside and stuffed them in trash bags. There was one girl who wasn't quite dead yet. She was shot in the stomach and legs and bleeding all over the place so Uriel pulled her by her feet to the boiler room so he wouldn't get blood on his new Levi's. Excited, he jerked up the trapdoor and shoved her over the edge. She fell to the ground below and thudded like a hundred-pound sack of potatoes.

He and Gabriel jumped down beside her, and the girl groaned when Gabriel grabbed her hair and dragged her down the shaft toward the main cavern. She was half conscious now, and they hauled her to the far side of the spring where they'd dug the rattlesnake pit. The bottom was writhing with dozens of them.

Gabriel said, "Hey! Hey, girl, wake up! We got another big surprise for you. Throw some water on her, Uriel, so she can enjoy this as much as we do." He laughed, his eyes alight with cruel anticipation.

Uriel dipped up a cup of water out of the spring and sloshed it into her face. She sputtered and opened pain-glazed eyes.

"You like snakes, little girl?" Gabriel asked her. "We got some real nice ones for you to play with."

He lifted her head so she could see down into the pit then took his foot and kicked her bodily into the snake pit. Startled by the intrusion, several rattlers began striking at her, over and over, and the girl gave one real terrible scream and tried to crawl away, but then she lay still. The snakes stopped striking after a while, and Gabriel looked at Uriel.

"Oh, well, she didn't last long enough. Next time, though, we won't shoot her first. Then we can figure out how long it takes rattlers to kill a woman."

Uriel looked down at the girl and the way the snakes were crawling all over her and couldn't help wondering who she was and where she was from.

TWENTY

The Dome of the Cave Academy for the Gifted's parking lot was jammed packed with cars, mostly Mercedes, BMWs, and Lexus models. We were the only full-size Humvee. Jesus had provided valet parking, in the person of one Willie Vines. He looked at me like I was an alien but he looked at the Humvee like it was a naked Jessica Simpson. He drove off, grinning big and sitting up straight, probably wishing the kids in the cafeteria could see him now.

Once I stepped inside, I was pretty glad to have on a new dress after I saw the getups some of the ladies had on. It was quite the social affair, it seemed, despite two grisly murders of the staff, or maybe nobody else gave as good a New Year's party as Jesus H. Johnstone. Or maybe they were serving filet mignon and that's why people showed up. I really, really hated the way the stilettos were killing my feet. At least on the stroll, I got to bust people. Black kept a firm grip on my elbow, probably afraid my shawl might slip off.

"Wow." The gymnasium had been transformed into a magical playground for the rich, even better than most senior proms. Dozens of Christmas trees and tiny sparkling lights, with shiny gold and silver and red fabric draped everywhere. Tables with white damask cloths and red candles and white-coated waiters moving efficiently among the elaborately dressed crowd.

"Food smells good," I commented when my stomach growled in an obvious play for attention.

"It is. We catered it."

"No joke. Five Cedars?"

"That's right. Johnstone's buttering me up for another big contribution."

"No wonder. This is the gymnasium that Nicholas Black built, if I recall."

Black handed off his invitation and was immediately identified by the doorkeepers as Mr. Big Donor, scraping and bowing required. It was fun to watch. They led us personally and with lots of smiles to a large round table directly in front of the podium. I looked around for Bud and his new gal pal and found him waving at me from a small table near the bathrooms, one probably reserved for police officers with the audacity to mingle with the elite. No sign of Charlie. I figured he wouldn't show up.

"There's Bud and his date. Okay if they sit with us?"

Black nodded and waved his hand at the nearest kowtower. "I have some friends I'd like to have sit here at my table," he said in his best I'm-the-glory-of-the-universe diction.

"Yes sir, Dr. Black. That will be no problem at all, sir."

I motioned to Bud with an unladylike but detective-like arm jerk. He came rushing over, his new shopgirl in tow. Unfortunately, he also had my psychic nemesis in tow, too. Black stood politely for Miss Finland. Out of curiosity I watched to see if he was looking at her Pamela Anderson display of bare, jiggling cleavage above her dark-blue gown. I noticed Joe the Psychic kept undue attention on my bare back. Black noticed, too, and eyed McKay in unfriendly fashion.

"Maybe you should leave the shawl on," Black whispered in my ear. "Men are starting to drool into their soup."

"Right."

Fin, a.k.a. Brianna, smiled winsomely at me. Oh my gosh, did I just say winsomely? It must be the dress and the mascara. She said, "You look lovely, Ms. Morgan. I knew you would. You made the right choice."

"Yeah, but you should've told me it didn't have a back sewn on it."

She laughed, a tinkling sound that I never could figure out how women made. If I laughed, and usually I didn't, mine just sounded like ha ha ha ha. Not exactly musical. Definitely not tinkling. I wondered if she practiced getting that kind of sound. Laughed scales, or something.

I leaned close and whispered, "Keep your eyes open tonight, Bud. If anyone we've interviewed acts suspicious, let me know. He might pull something here, for the effect."

Beside me, Black said, "I don't believe we've met." He was speaking to Psychic Joe.

When he stretched out his hand to shake, I said, "Watch it, Black, he's a psychic. He might have a vision and tell you you're going to die next Friday, or something."

Black looked at me as if he thought I was being rude. Imagine.

"I'll take my chances. I'm Nick Black."

"Joe McKay." I watched the guy closely to see if he got a shocked or revolted expression on his face when they shook hands. Not that I really believed he could see into the future, but I still felt better when he didn't look horrified or anything. He only smiled and made some inane small talk with Black. At that point I realized he, too, had on a tuxedo, which was a real shockaroo. He was definitely not a Tuxedo Tom type. His long hair was pulled back low on his nape in a blond ponytail that really emphasized his high cheekbones and long-lashed eyes. He looked handsome. But so had Ted Bundy.

Black said, "I understand that Charlie asked you to help Claire with a case."

"That's right. The detective here isn't too thrilled with the idea, though. So now my services are no longer required."

He smiled straight at me, just so everybody knew which detective he meant. Black took my hand and held it. He might as well have stamped his name on my forehead and hung a sign around my neck that said KEEP OFF, PSYCHICS. I reclaimed my hand and independence.

I said, "Sorry. I've just never given much credence to ESP and that clairvoyance mumbo jumbo. I rely on good, thorough police work."

Joe McKay kept smiling. "I agree with you."

So now we were on the same side of the fence, best buddies, huh? "Know what, McKay? Funniest thing. I found a great big hideous tarantula crawling around in my house. Know what else? It showed up not long after you paid me that friendly, warn-off visit."

Everybody at the table stared at me, then turned their eyes in tandem to Joe. He tried to look as surprised as they did. "You found a tarantula in your house?"

"Yep. Sure did. You put it there?"

"No, ma'am. Wouldn't have any reason to do that."

"Not even if it made your visions about my future come true?"

"I don't have to make them come true. In your case, I hope to God they don't."

Black frowned. "What visions?"

"I told her the other night that I saw her in danger. I saw her in the hospital. Pretty bad off, too. That's why I went out to her house. I wanted to tell her she better be very careful."

"And I told him all his visions already happened, last summer."

Bud said, "What kind of danger did you see her in?"

Luckily Jesus chose that moment to step to the podium and adjust the microphone. "Good evening. I want to welcome each and every one of you and wish you a happy New Year. It's wonderful to see such a fantastic turnout. Thank you so much for coming."

His delight and pleasure suddenly metamorphosed into sad and sorrowful. "However, it's a sad occasion for those of us who work here at the academy. As I'm sure you know by now, we've lost two of our staff members recently. Both Simon Classon and Christie Foxworthy were wonderful, wonderful people, great friends to all of us. They will be sorely missed." He paused, for effect, no doubt. "Now I'd like you to stand and join me for a moment of silence to honor their memories and their great contributions to this academy."

Everybody stood and listened to the caterers in the kitchen yell around and clatter dishes. Somebody ought to clue them in on the seriousness of the moment. At least no Classon haters threw ripe tomatoes at his portrait where it was displayed on an easel at the middle of the stage. Christie Foxworthy's picture sat beside it. It looked like her high school senior picture. Huge sprays of white roses sat in front of them. I wondered what the people around me would say if they knew the details of how they'd died. I saw a couple of reporters, whispering together at the edge of the stage. Uh-oh. Questions were not far behind.

The director was back, enough already for the two tortured murder victims that everyone liked so much. "Thank you, and now, everyone, please be seated and enjoy your dinner. We'll have a short program after the dessert course, and then the orchestra will provide music for dancing and the bar is already open. Again, happy New Year!"

So much for Simon and Christie. When Jesus said a minute of silence, he meant exactly sixty seconds. Richard Johnstone sat down and I had to admit he looked better in a tuxedo than his snowy suit. I guess any man does. I had expected him to wear white tails and a matching top hat with his sandals. Across the table, McKay was staring a hole through me.

I said, "May I help you or are you just being your typical rude self?"

He smiled, annoying me more and looking me up and down like I was a Kmart Blue-Light Special. "I was just wondering if Dr. Black would allow me a dance before the night is over."

I said, "I'm sure he'd love to dance with you."

Bud and Fin laughed. So did Black and McKay. I guess I was pretty funny tonight. Black wasn't saying much. I had a feeling he'd lapsed into psychiatrist observation mode. It rather irked me when he said, "Tell me about your activities with police investigations, Mr. McKay. It sounds like fascinating work."

"I don't usually discuss my work."

Black said, "Why not?"

"Because the cops usually ask me not to. In addition to that, I figure it impugns the privacy of the victims and their families."

Wow, the psychic uses big words, and everything.

"I suspect you don't mouth off about your cases, either, Detective," he added, turning to me.

Before I could think up a smart-ass answer, Black changed the subject. "Bud, I compliment your taste on Claire's dress. It's perfect for her."

"Can we please give talking about this dress a rest?" I said. I certainly was in a rude mood. Maybe because I was really, really uncomfortable all dressed up like Gwyneth Paltrow or somebody going to the Oscars. I decided to play nice for a while.

So we all lapsed into some nice, polite, chatty chitchat, and I did have to admit that the food was fantastic. Chateaubriand, no less, and wine and oysters Rockefeller. Just the normal college-dorm fare. The academy had to be paying out the nose for this kind of food, especially if it came from Black's hotel. Apparently, the community backed this place big-time. Nearly everybody in the joint stopped at our table to pass pleasantries with Black, or in other words, suck up. They all stared at me and wished I had on a low-cut gown so they could see the big, ugly meat cleaver scar that got so much publicity last summer. Good thing I didn't get many knives in the back or I'd have to wear a muumuu.

Bud and Fin were getting along great. Psychic Man sat quietly, probably wishing he had a date, too. When he remained pleasant and unobtrusive, pretty much ignoring me, I decided to see if I could probe into his past a bit.

"So, McKay, how long you been back at the lake?"

"About a month."

"And where did you say you lived before that?"

"I didn't."

"Mind if I come out and search your house?"

"Do you have a warrant?"

"Do I need one?"

Black interjected. "Let's dance, Claire."

"I don't know how."

"I'll teach you."

He pulled me up and led me out onto the dance floor with one hand taking liberties down my naked back. "You might want to lay off the guy a little."

"What do you mean?"

"Your hostility to him is palpable. Comes off you in hot waves, like equatorial sand."

"I'm not hostile to him."

He took me in his arms, and I tried to walk around with him in a fairly good pretense of dancing. "Yes, you are. Remember what I always told you when I was your suspect, and you were treating me like crap? You catch more flies, you know."

"He's involved, Black. In fact, I think he probably did it. I just can't prove it yet. There're too many coincidences. He shows up all of a sudden for a home visit, and I find a big hairy tarantula at my house. I take offense to that, big time."

"Then investigate him but don't get emotionally involved."

I looked up at him. I'm tall but he's over six foot. "*You're* telling me that? You tried every trick in the book to hook up with me when you were a suspect."

"Yeah, and thank you, but don't do it again." He was watching the people at our table. "I think I'll get John Booker to dig a little deeper into McKay's past and see what he turns up."

Booker was Black's private detective and old army buddy. Black had paid him to check up on me once upon a time. Because of that, I don't care much for the guy, but he's good at his job, I'd give him that much. And I would love to pry into Mr. Clairvoyance's background. Then I spied Psychic talking to Jesus. When they both threaded their way together toward the kitchen, I said. "Listen, Black, there goes McKay and Johnstone. I'm going to see what they're up to. Cover for me until I get back. Tell everyone that I've gone to the ladies' room."

"Be careful."

"Right."

While Black returned to the table, I wound my way through dancing couples and found the cafeteria door hidden behind a gauzy panel and tiny white lights. I ducked through it and found about twenty people preparing fancy plates with luscious looking chocolate cake dribbled with cherry sauce. I hoped Black remembered to grab me a big piece. There was no sign of my prey. Where'd they disappear to so fast? More important, what were they up to? I took my time snooping around the building without much luck, then walked around the edge of the cooking commotion to the hallway that led to Willie Vines's office. There was something about the kid that made me nervous, something I couldn't quite put my finger on. I found him sitting at his scarred desk reading a book, his valet duties suspended until midnight.

"Hello, Willie."

When he saw me, he jumped to his feet and stared at me like I was an apparition from hell. Maybe he didn't recognize me in half a dress. "Sorry if I'm disturbing you, Willie, but I was pretty bored out there at the big hoopty-doo and I thought I'd come ask you a few more questions while I had the chance. Got a minute?"

He looked around like he wanted to flee down a fire escape. Jittery as hell. Why?

"How'd you like driving Black's Humvee?"

"It's awesome. I never thought I'd get to do somethin' like that. I heard Arnold Schwarzenegger drives one."

"Yeah." I looked at the book he was holding. "What're you reading?"

"Just a book."

"What book?"

I moved closer and picked it up. "The Bible?"

"Yes, ma'am. This here's a fictionalized kind of Bible that tells it like a story instead of all those old-fashioned words."

"You mean like a novel?"

"Yes, ma'am. It's real interesting when you understand it better."

"So you're interested in the Bible?"

"Yes, ma'am."

"Did you take Mr. Classon's course in angelology?"

"Uh-huh. Yes, ma'am."

"How'd you like it?"

"It was good. You know, interestin'. That's how I found out about this book."

"Was Mr. Classon a good teacher?"

"I thought he was mean to people but I liked it when he talked about the angels and all that."

I remembered the medal that Black had given me and wondered if it might get Willie to open up and let down his guard. I pulled it out and cupped it in my palm. "I always wear a Saint Michael's medallion. It's supposed to protect me. He's the patron saint of police officers. He and I are real tight now so nothing bad can ever happen to me. Pretty cool, huh?" I smiled at my little joke.

Willie didn't smile but he looked mightily impressed. "Saint Michael's God's avenger angel. Mr. Classon said he's the first angel God created and is the leader of all the archangels. He's got this big flaming sword that he uses to protect us from Satan. Mr. Classon said he wrestled with Lucifer and cast him down out of heaven."

"Yep, that's him, all right. And he's the one for me. I've been known to wrestle a few guys down from time to time." I smiled some more, the angel-loving detective. But Willie was really warming up to me now. Angelology must've been his favorite class.

He said, "Saint Michael was the one who spoke to Moses on Sinai and taught Adam how to farm and take care of his family, too."

"Wow, he got around pretty good back then, didn't he?"

"Yes, ma'am. And Mr. Classon said he helps people who have real bad nightmares."

"Okay, that clinches it. I'll never take this thing off again."

"Does that mean you have nightmares, Detective Morgan?"

"Sometimes. Do you?"

Willie nodded, and the look on his face told me they must be real doozies, too. "Sometimes I do, and I wake up scared to death."

"Hey, I've been there, Willie. You better get yourself one of these things pronto." I grinned encouragingly as I tucked the medallion back inside my velvet neckline.

Apparently really excited by me now, Willie smiled as if we were true angel cronies. I glanced over at the straight-backed chair in the corner. "Mind if I sit down awhile? I'm not thrilled about being out there with all those phonies. My boss made me come."

That warmed him up some more. "Sure, sit down. I don't like parties much, either."

"How long have you worked here?"

"As long as it's been built."

"No kidding? You must have been three years old when you started."

He grinned a little. "I'm older than I look. I like this job 'cause I don't have to be around people much. I don't like crowds. I like bein' alone, I guess."

I noticed a small frame on his desk and turned it around. It was a head shot of a cute girl with red hair woven into pigtails and lots of freckles. "This's a good picture of Wilma."

Willie began to look uncomfortable. He glanced around, not trying to hide it. "Yeah. She gave me that picture and I put it in a little frame I found in my desk drawer."

"Tell me about her."

He kept his eyes down and squirmed in his chair. "What do you want to know?"

"Was she your girlfriend?"

"No, uh-uh. I don't have no girlfriends."

"Why not? You're a good-looking kid."

Blushing, he still couldn't meet my gaze. "I dunno." He shrugged slightly, then shrugged again. "I just like being by myself."

"So you and Wilma were just friends? Good friends, though?"

"Yeah. She liked to come back here, too, like you did tonight, and just sit and talk some and be away from other people. She didn't like all the mean stuff going on, but she couldn't do nothin' about it."

"I guess it made you mad when Classon picked on her, huh?"

"Yeah. Everybody got mad. She didn't deserve what he said about her, and stuff."

"Did you hear anybody threaten to harm Classon for what he did to her?"

"I heard Mr. Rowland say once that he'd like to flush Mr. Classon down a toilet where he belonged. But everybody was saying stuff like that."

"What about Christie Foxworthy? Did she like Wilma?"

"I guess so. I didn't know her very well. She never paid much attention to me."

I watched him closely. "How did you feel when Wilma

left? Did you want to kill Simon Classon for running her off?"

Willie stared at me, nervously twisting his scraggly mustache. "Yeah, I guess so. I would've liked to throw Mr. Classon in one of those giant trash compactors like they had in that first Star Wars movie and let it crush him up."

Well, alrighty, now. Willie putting his feelings bluntly. Casually, I said, "I guess you didn't kill him, did you, Willie?" I laughed, you know, ha ha ha, you're under arrest.

Willie's eyes widened. He stared straight at me. "Do I need to call a lawyer now?"

Well, that surprised the heck out of me. No more dumb-as-a-stick impersonation. This kid was smarter than he liked people to know.

"Not unless you did it."

"I wouldn't never kill nobody." Li'l Abner was back, blank-eyed stare and all. Under all that, however, Willie Vines watched me like a hawk. Maybe it was time I checked deeper into Willie Vines's past, especially his whereabouts on the days Classon was kidnapped and Christie was stuffed into that trunk. There was more to the boy than met the eye.

"Maybe I do know something, though."

Aha. "Well, maybe you ought to tell it to me, then."

He hesitated, looked toward the door. "What if I'm scared? What if somebody might do something to me if I tell you?"

Now I was definitely hitting pay dirt. "What if you tell me enough to arrest this person so he can't hurt you? What if I promise to protect you?"

More hesitation, real fear in those strange eyes. "I dunno. I'm not sure what to do. . . ."

His gaze suddenly darted past me to the door, and a look of sheer terror overtook his face. I turned around slowly and stared into Joe McKay's face.

"Hello, Detective. I see you've met my old buddy here."

"I didn't know you were friends."

"Yes. He worked here when I attended classes at the academy. He's a real good kid."

"Maybe he could tell me lots of things about you, McKay, stuff you don't want me to know."

"Maybe, but I doubt it. We weren't that close, were we, Willie?"

Willie's face was a peculiar shade of white now. He looked like he was going to throw up. "No, sir. Not really."

"It's almost midnight, Detective, don't you think you should get back to your date?"

"I think you should let me worry about my date, McKay."

Willie got up and came close to wringing his hands. Instead, he wiped damp palms on his uniform pants. Definitely stressed out by the sudden appearance of his old bosom buddy. "I best get the balloons ready for the midnight celebration. The director'll have my hide if I forget."

He scuttled off like a roach avoiding Shaquille O'Neal's great big foot.

"Why don't we get back to the party?" McKay suggested. "By the way, you look hot in that dress."

"Gee, thanks. Now that I know what you think about me, I'll be able to sleep tonight."

He laughed everywhere but inside his eyes. They retained that look of caution they always had. Man, he came off so guilty, I felt like pulling my weapon, arresting him, just to get it over with. We glanced toward the gym as the guests began a loud and raucous countdown to midnight. Time flies when you're not having fun.

"You better get in there, Detective. I bet you turn into a pumpkin at midnight."

I motioned with my arm for him to precede me, not particularly wanting to turn my back on him for fear he stowed feral tarantulas in his cummerbund. He strode off, and I followed on his heels. I made my first New Year's resolution. I was going to nail this guy to the wall so tight he could be his own wanted poster, and now I was pretty sure that Willie Vines might have the hammer I needed to do it with.

TWENTY-ONE

I wended my way back to our table as the New Year's countdown continued. All around me, people were having a great time, donning dumb party hats, blowing on paper noisemakers, tossing glittery confetti everywhere, forgetting all about two stone-cold-dead employees. It made me sick to my stomach. A fountain of bubbly was flowing down a pyramid of stacked champagne glasses. Merrymakers were imbibing like horses at a trough. Dome of the Cave Academy for the Gifted a Baptist college was not. Jesus Johnstone was making beaucoup money tonight for his little neck of the woods Murder U., not to mention his little hippy self. Joe Psychic had disappeared again. I guess I had blinked and missed him.

When I reached the table, Bud looked ready to move in on Fin the minute the crowd yelled happy New Year. Black just looked pissed. On sight of me, he said, "Well, well, look who the cat drug in. Just in time for the end of the party, too."

Sarcasm? Yessiree. I made peace. "Sorry, but you know how it is. Dating a police officer, and all that stuff."

"Tell me about it, darlin'. The story of my life lately."

I smiled, glad about the darlin' part because he only used that in bed, which meant he wasn't too ticked off, or else he'd made romantic plans for later, which, I'm not sure. I hoped, however, for the latter. I decided to exert some wild charm on the guy, something I was relatively new at but willing to give the old college try.

"Hey, I'm back in time to ring in the New Year, right?" See what I mean? Charm just ain't my bag. I leave that to Black. He has enough for both of us.

Everybody was on their feet, laughing, drinking, watching a big digital clock Jesus had hung on the stage. People started yelling out the numbers while I searched the exits for Joe McKay.

"Four . . . Three . . . Two . . ."

When the countdown hit one, Black forgave my unexcused absence and embraced me with some enthusiasm and a bit of subtle groping. Over his shoulder, I watched Joe McKay sidle up across from us. He smirked at me, and it felt like a slap in the face. I knew in my gut that he'd been out somewhere and up to no good.

After a flurry of hugs and kisses and fun stuff, the party broke up with Jesus pontificating on the dais one last time about thanks for coming, drive carefully, and may God be with you, each and every one. Yeah, and don't forget to leave your donation pledges in the basket on the way out.

I bundled up in my parka and stepped outside with Black. Snow was spiraling down until the wind picked up. Then it blew in horizontal gusts straight into our faces. A different kid showed up with the Humvee, all wrapped up in a hooded parka and heavy leather gloves and a big smile. For a second I figured we'd need a crowbar to pry the guy out of the awesome vehicle. But he handed over the keys, and I snatched them. Truth is, I liked the Humvee, and felt like the Terminator in a slinky gown as I slid behind the wheel. Black could be Maria, show a lot of big teeth, and sit in the passenger's seat.

We took off and I felt a little like I was in a 007 plot,

heading across Antarctica with James Bond to fetch back stolen nuclear warheads. I tugged off my gloves and gripped the steering wheel, ready to match wits and endurance with the winter lake gods.

Black adjusted the heater to about, say, 140 degrees and said, "My place is closer. We'll stay there tonight."

I hesitated because it sounded like an order, and I wasn't one of his flunkies. On the other hand, he was right on. Cedar Bend was twenty miles closer than my house and not on a winding, hilly stretch of road. And, we had found that hideously ugly spider there who might have family members who'd moved in, too. I hung a right at the next intersection and headed for his luxury apartments and gigantic steaming hot tub at Cedar Bend Lodge.

Then I suddenly remembered that I now had a dog and thus a responsibility. "What about Jules Verne?"

"I'll send somebody over to get him." Black was holding on to the dash, as if I was driving too fast and sliding around a curve. I righted the skid and regained control. Appeased, Black glanced at me. "So what did you find out when you left me alone at the table for just over two hours?"

"It wasn't just over two hours. Get real. It was an hour and a half. Actually I had a cozy little talk with the janitor slash parking valet slash suspect who knows more than he's telling me. He's hiding something, believe you me."

"What about Joe? He was gone a long time, too. What was he doing?"

"He and the director conveniently disappeared. I went looking for them and found Willie Vines instead. And know what? Joe found me in Willie's office, and Willie was afraid of him. Intimidated. Which is pretty interesting, don't you think? And so is Joe hanging around with the director like they were old buds."

"The director and an former, expelled student having a tête-à-tête smack-dab in the middle of the most important fund-raising gala of the year? Strikes me as a little peculiar, yes. How do you think this baby handles?"

"Good, if you like driving a tank. And I do." I peered into the snow driving into the headlamps. It looked like a psychedelic strobe light. "Everything about that school is peculiar." I glanced at Black, who advised me to watch the road. "What about McKay turning up here all of a sudden, right before Classon was found? Any conclusions you can draw from that, other than he's our perp?"

"Could've been the publicity from last summer drew him back here, especially if he's the killer. I've seen that before, in other cases. McKay reads all these glowing news accounts about you, the brilliant detective, surviving a run-in with a crazy killer. Psychopaths always think they're smarter than everyone else. Maybe he was jealous of the attention and decided he'd match wits with you and see how smart you really are. God, every reporter in the country was down here chasing us around."

I thought of the satellite trucks, the brash, loudmouthed, ego-driven reporters hounding me day and night, microphones shoved into my face. a.k.a. hell on earth. "It's just a matter of time before they get wind of this case."

"Maybe snowstorms'll keep them at bay, but once they sniff out the bizarre details about Classon and that poor girl, they'll swarm in here on snowshoes. And if that happens, you need to stay with me, where they can't harass you."

"Charlie's not releasing facts to anybody. He learned that the hard way. Even the local papers are too busy dealing with this weather to worry about anything else. He said he'd had a few inquiries but he deflected them."

Black said, "So far."

"Right."

His take on the matter wasn't exactly confidence-building. I concentrated on driving, enjoying the feel of the big vehicle. Maybe Black would buy me one, too. Maybe a black one with a personalized license plate that said YOU'RE BUSTED. I tapped the brakes as the snow really got down to business and the tarmac got slicker. The flakes were huge and wet, plopping down so hard and thick that my wipers were yelling

uncle. I sighed with relief when I saw the grand stone entrance and all the Christmas lights turning Cedar Bend Lodge
into a winter wonderland. It was a grand place, all right, with
Black's own unique, I'll-spend-whatever-the-hell-it-takes-to-
be-the-best-and-most-showy concept of life. I heard the faint
strains of the "Mexican Hat Dance" inside my purse and
braked the Humvee to a stop. I flipped the phone open.

"Detective Morgan? This's . . . Willie Vines."

I glanced at Black and said, "Yeah, Willie. You have something to tell me?"

Silence. I listened to the isssh-thump, issh-thump of the
wipers. I was eager now. Maybe we were finally going to get
a break.

"Willie? You still there?"

"Yeah, but . . . I'm real scairt."

"Why?"

"I know stuff that'll get me killed. He'll kill me if I tell."

"Who? Tell me who, Willie."

"What if he finds out?"

"We can protect you. All you have to do is tell the truth.
Where are you now? At the academy?"

"No. I left after I talked to you." More quiet. "I'm pretty
shook up."

"Where are you? We can meet. Talk somewhere private." I
glanced at Black. He looked interested. Or was that annoyed?

"I got a place. Nobody knows about it but me. I stay there
sometimes."

"Is that where you are now?"

"Yeah."

"Tell me how to get there."

"You know Highway 5, out past that old schoolhouse they
made into a museum? It's right past there. The mailbox has a
fish on it, you know the symbol for Jesus Christ."

I frowned. Weird. "Okay, you stay there. Don't talk to anybody. Don't call anybody and don't let anybody come inside."

I shut the phone. "Willie's ready to crack. You want to tag
along?"

"You bet."

I hit speed dial for Bud. It rang twice before he picked up. I said, "Where are you?"

"Brianna invited me in for coffee."

Code for he was spending the night with her. "Willie Vines is ready to talk. Black and I are on our way."

"Shit. Now?" Bud was not thrilled. "Where?"

I told him, took a U-turn on the road, and headed out again.

Black said, "Never a dull moment with you, Detective. Any chance this is a trap?"

"Could be. Willie's pretty tame to take on both of us. He's scared of Joe McKay. You should've seen the look on his face when McKay walked in on us."

"What's the link?"

"That's what I wanna know."

It took almost thirty minutes to find the right mailbox. There was no traffic except a few cars slipping their way home from New Year's Eve parties. The snow did not let up, but the Humvee was like our own personal snowplow.

"There's the mailbox. Looks like he knocked the snow off so we could see it."

"Maybe he called us from out here on his cell."

A single pair of tire tracks led off down a heavily wooded road. Branches rattled against us on both sides.

Black said, "Man, watch it, you're scratching the paint up."

"Sorry."

Half a mile later we saw the house. It was very old, a typical farmhouse sitting in a snowy field. Every light was on. I pulled up out front beside a dark-colored, beat-up old Chevy pickup. I turned off the ignition but left the headlamps on, illuminating the front door. It was standing ajar. My sixth sense quivered alive.

"I don't like this."

"Me, either."

"You gonna wait for Bud?"

"No."

"Maybe you should."

I got out and pulled the .38 out of my ankle holster. My stilettos sank down into the snow and froze my toes. The snow had turned to sleet now, and I could hear it pinging against the Humvee. The motor made cooling sounds. Everything else was silent. Black got out the other side. To my surprise, he pulled out his own .38 from the small of his back.

"You're carrying?"

"I learned the hard way last summer always to be prepared."

I said. "Something's very wrong here."

"Tell me about it."

There were lots of tracks on the path to the front door, going both ways and up the steps. I stood and listened. No sound. No movement. I pulled up the end of my skirt and tucked it inside my parka, just in case I had to kick somebody in the groin. We crept up the steps on either side. It was obvious Black had training somewhere, sometime in police procedure. Probably in his Army Ranger days. I was glad I had him for backup.

I rapped on the door. "Willie? You in there?"

No answer. I pushed the door open with the toe of my stiletto. It swung inward with a long, horror-film creak. Inside, there were signs of a struggle. A massive struggle. Overturned chairs. Broken dishes. Huge pool of blood settling into the shape of California and the Baja peninsula.

Bud's Bronco appeared behind us, the lights flashing across where we stood on the porch. He stopped and got out. Drew his weapon.

"Take the back, Bud. We got blood inside."

He headed around the side, his flashlight beam revealing slanted, shining lines of sleet. Black had his gun barrel up against his right shoulder. I inched inside, back to the door. He followed. Still no sound. Two doors led off the living room. Bloody drag marks provided a red-carpet indicator to one door, probably the bedroom. I tensed as a door was kicked open in the back of the house. Then Bud's shout.

"I'm in. Clear."

Seconds later he appeared at the kitchen door. I gestured to the bloodstained path. We moved together toward it, circumventing furniture and backing along each wall. Black stayed where he was and covered us. The blood trail looked fresh, shiny, and wet on the scarred, dark-green linoleum.

Bud leaned back then darted a quick look inside the room. "Oh God, it's a bloodbath in there."

"Let's go. I'm low."

We moved fast. Bud came behind me. The room was empty. No closets. No hiding places. Just enough blood and gore to take my breath away.

I kept my arms extended with the gun. "Somebody got slaughtered in here."

"Sweet Mary." That was Black, now at the bedroom door.

The twin bed was covered with a chenille bedspread. It was so soaked with blood that at first I didn't realize it was yellow. But that wasn't the worst part. There was a head and torso lying on it, hacked up beyond recognition. And other body parts. More were scattered around on the floor.

A long, sharp machete was lodged in what was left of the chest cavity. The odor of fresh blood, raw and coppery and nauseating, filled the air. My stomach revolted, spewed bile up the back of my throat. I forced it back down but couldn't speak. Nobody said anything, just stared at the carnage. Finally, I said, "Think that's Willie?"

Bud moved closer to the bed, stepping carefully around the mutilated body. He pointed to the torso. "The shirt's got his name embroidered on the pocket."

I looked at a severed foot leaning against the pillows. "Oh God, he had those boots on tonight."

I swallowed hard, not yet wanting to believe it. "This could be a setup, to make it look like him. It's so different from the other scenes. It doesn't add up."

Black said. "Only Willie would have reason to set the vic up to look like himself. And why would he do that?"

Good question. "Who knows? Maybe he's the perp, or maybe somebody else wants us to think so. Buck can tell us that soon enough. Okay, let's step back, take some deep breaths and put on some protective gear before we contaminate the scene."

I phoned Charlie, woke him up, and he was too shocked by the news to even curse me out. He said he'd alert Buckeye and forensics. Yeah, happy New Year, everybody.

I hung up and said, "What's your take, Bud?"

"Looks like it started out in the living room."

"Somebody hacked this guy to bits," Black put in. "This is rage like I've never seen it before. The killer had to be covered with blood. Look at the walls. The ceiling."

"How'd the perp get out without leaving bloody footprints?"

Bud said, "He went out the window. Look."

There were smears on the sill, the lower pane, the window frame. "We're gonna get him this time. He had to have left something behind."

I waited for Bud to stomp outside and bring in paper booties and latex gloves. We all put them on, and I walked to the window, sidestepping pools of gore and torn flesh. I pushed open the window and shined Bud's flashlight on the ground below. The snow was crimson and disturbed. The bastard rolled around and cleaned himself off in the snow. Made a bloody snow angel for us to find. I swept the beam out across the yard. Four-wheeler tracks led off toward the woods.

"He rode a four-wheeler out of here. Just like McKay did at my place. Maybe we can match the treads."

I thought about how scared Willie's voice had been earlier on the phone, how I'd said I'd protect him. My stomach dropped, cold and hard. McKay had to be the perp. My gut was still telling me that, making me sure of it. And I was going to get him for this. Willie Vines was going to be his last victim.

TWENTY-TWO

In the wee hours of New Year's Day Buckeye descended with his team on Willie Vines's place, sweeping the crime scene and pretty much as horrified by the carnage as we were. Dawn came and eventually dazzling blue skies that brought on the mother of all headaches. I swallowed some Excedrin and tried to forget about it, because it would take hours and hours just to clean up the gore and gather body parts. Our interviews had turned up the fact that Willie had no living family. Seemed a little coincidental that all three of our victims were basically alone in the world. Except for Christie, whose relatives hadn't cared enough to show up yet to claim the body.

Black took off around five o'clock to get a few hours' sleep before he checked on his Cedar Bend patients staying at the Lodge over the holidays. It was late morning before Bud dropped me off. I let Jules Verne out to do his business, then crashed for three hours before I was up and dressed and phoning Bud. A call to the director with the sad news about Willie informed us that the director himself could alibi Joe McKay. He'd had drinks after the gala with Joe and two board members and their wives. Apparently the director was considering McKay for an instructor's position at the academy, probably ESP in Ten Easy Lessons. Something told me he'd fit in out there real well. But that wouldn't stop me from leaning on McKay. Willie was terrified of McKay, and now Willie was dead. It was time to pay a little visit to Joe's utopia in the woods and sweat him a little. I picked up Bud in my Explorer.

Bud looked tired but he still had sharp creases in his jeans. Jeez. How'd he do that? His first words were, "Do we have a warrant to search McKay's place?"

"Not yet. Buckeye's gonna call me if they turn up incriminating evidence at Willie's house."

"Where's McKay live?"

"Charlie said he's staying out in the middle of nowhere. His family's old homestead. I'll find it, don't worry."

Out in the middle of nowhere was the understatement of the year. And we thought Willie lived in the sticks. Oh yes, deep, deep in the dark, dark woods well past Willie's house and the academy. Why would a young guy like McKay want to live way out here? Probably because he had lots of skeletons in lots of closets. Closets full of machetes and spiderwebs.

"This is it. Charlie said to look for a rusted mailbox with the name Bulinsky on the side."

I turned onto a snowpacked dirt road. There were no four-wheeler tracks but a car had driven down the road recently.

"Looks like he's home," said Bud.

"Let's just hope he's home with Willie's blood on his clothes."

They drove through naked trees, limbs heavy with snow. The sun was too bright even for my sunglasses, and I felt my headache intensify. We caught sight of a farmhouse a lot like Willie's, but maybe a bit less dilapidated. A brick chimney was billowing black smoke into the crisp morning air. Wood was stacked around as if he'd been remodeling. As we approached, I caught sight of Joe, standing out in the back near a detached garage. He saw us, too, I guess, because he headed at a run for the back door.

I floored the accelerator, and we fishtailed dangerously on a patch of ice and slammed to a stop near the front door. We drew our weapons and jumped out. Bud took the front, easing slowly up the porch steps. I made my way around the side of the house through deep, pristine snowdrifts. At the back I hesitated, aware he could be lying in wait with a sawed-off, double-barreled shotgun or a bloodstained machete, even. Willie's dismembered body came to mind. I swallowed hard, felt a trickle of fear, which I ignored. I darted a look around the corner of the house. Found the backyard was deserted. Lots of trampled snow. A half-built snowman with a carrot nose. Huh? Now that seemed a bit incongruous. Maybe ice-cold killers liked playing in the snow, too. Maybe they packed ice around their hearts to keep them deadly.

Out front Bud beat a fist on the door and yelled "police" and "open up." I kept my gun fixed on the back door, finger on the trigger, fairly certain my friend, Joe, would barrel out any minute, guns a-blazing.

Footprints in the backyard went every which way, obliterating each other and intersecting with motorcycle and four-wheeler trails. A lot of them led into the old garage. The door was up. I sidestepped my way toward it, weapon and eyes trained on the back door. Bud was beating on the front door some more. I took a quick peek inside the garage, leading with my gun, at the ready, oh, yes.

Inside I found McKay's Harley-Davidson, and in the lean-to metal shed attached to the side of the structure, there was lots of junk stacked around: gardening tools, old tires, lawn mowers, empty paint buckets.

I turned and scanned the yard for four-wheeler tracks into the woods. I heard a sound and swiveled my weapon to the house. Joe McKay stood on his porch in a black sweatshirt and denim jeans. "Why hello, Detective Morgan. You looking for something in my garage?"

Mr. Pleasant, all smiley and dimpled up with charm. His breath plumed when he spoke. Mine plumed with molten anger. I called Bud's name, told him to come around while I walked slowly toward Joe, holding the Glock with both hands, pointed straight at McKay and ready to fire.

Joe watched me. I watched his hands. "Beautiful day, isn't it? After all the snow. Weather Channel says more's coming. Sure is different than southern California, believe me, but still a nice change."

I wasn't there to discuss weather patterns and Doppler radar, so I said nothing. But I watched his eyes and detected something different in them. Worry, maybe? Good. I wanted him to be worried. Bud showed up and joined our little meteorological tête-à-tête.

"Well, now, you got Detective Davis with you. And look at those big guns. Hell, if I'd known you two were coming out, I'd've cleaned up some. Would've even shaved for you, Detective Morgan." He rubbed fingertips across his whiskers. His beard stubble was shades darker than his long, sun-bleached hair.

I moved to the foot of the steps and stared up at him. He stared at my weapon. He was nervous; I could sense it. I hadn't seen him nervous before. Maybe butchering some poor kid beyond recognition had stressed him out a little.

"Surely you didn't come out here to shoot me, did you, Detective? Want me to put my hands up and not make any quick moves? Maybe I should lean against the house and spread 'em." Now he was more his smart-ass self and sporting more dimples than a golf ball.

"Know what, McKay, the funniest thing happened last night. Willie Vines got hacked up into a million little pieces."

"Huh?" McKay's deep dimples faded to lines bracketing his mouth.

"Yeah, too bad, right? We were just wondering if you had any blood-soaked clothes lying around your house, maybe with Willie's blood type on them."

McKay frowned. "Know what, Detective? Sounds to me

a lot like you're accusing me of a crime. That so? If you are, you better have something to back it up, or I might just have to cry harassment to my old friend, Charlie, and sue your pretty little ass."

Bud said, "Wow, you're really scarin' us now, McKay. See how we're shiverin' and shakin'? Hey, I know what, how about being nice and inviting us in. You know, let us look around and see for ourselves how innocent you are."

McKay laughed, a regular Jolly Old St. Nick. "Sure thing, Detective. Cough up a warrant signed by a real, live judge and *mi casa es su casa.*"

I said, "You saying we need a warrant to pay you a friendly call?"

"You bet you do, doll. You've zeroed in on me as the perp from day one and I sure as hell won't help you frame me with all the shit going on around here. What's the plan, huh? Planting an eight ball of crack behind my toilet bowl? Not that I don't trust you, but stranger things have happened. Know what I mean? I haven't done jack since I came back here, but you keep coming at me, anyway. Hell, you really think I'd off somebody with you hounding my ass twenty-four/seven?" He kept glancing out over the backyard at the tree line. I followed his gaze and saw nothing but snow and naked trees.

I said, "Where were you last night after the gala?"

"With Director Johnstone at his place. Sort of an informal job interview. Ask him, if you don't believe me. And ask the two advisory board members and their wives who were there, too."

"Don't worry, I plan to." That alibi was a little too convenient for my taste. Maybe we ought to take Director Johnstone in and hammer his story apart for a while.

"You're grabbing at straws, Detective. And if you have a hankering to visit my house, that's fine by me, just show me the warrant. And good luck. No judge is gonna see probable cause to let you rifle through my stuff. You don't have a thing on me, and you never will. Because I didn't do anything. Especially to Willie. I liked that kid."

"Yeah, I can tell you're all broken up."

Bud said, "You're coming off like a lawyer, McKay. Why'd you run when you saw us comin'?"

McKay gestured at a shotgun propped in the corner. "I wasn't expecting company. I'm new in these parts. Couldn't figure anybody I knew would be coming to call on New Year's morning with these kind of road conditions."

"You always give shotgun welcomes?" I said.

Bud said, "You got a real isolated place out here. Wonder why?"

"It's a dangerous world we live in, now you know that, detectives. Man livin' way out here's got to protect himself."

I thought I heard something inside his house. I frowned. "You got somebody in there with you, McKay? Somebody you forgot to mention?"

"Nope. Like I told you before, I'm all alone in the big, cold world. Television's on, though. Rose Bowl parade. Just love those floats made up of flowers. I really got to get back inside or I'll miss seein' the Queen and her Princesses."

I ignored that and glanced around the yard. "What's with the snowman?"

"I guess I'm just a kid at heart, you know? I like snow ice cream, too."

We stared bloody murder at each other for a few beats. This guy was going down.

Bud said, "Yeah, how 'bout those floats? Why don't you let us come in and watch the Rose Bowl game—USC and Texas, right? We're both football fans."

"Yeah. Great idea. Go get your warrant and I'll spring for the pizza and beer."

I said, "You're a real smart-ass, aren't you, McKay?"

He grinned and lapsed into hillbillyese. "Now, you gonna hurt my feelings if you ain't careful there, pretty lady. Hate to be rude but don't want to miss seein' those Rose Princesses."

"Thank you for your cooperation, McKay. I'll see you again real soon, I promise."

McKay walked inside and shut the door. I heard the click

of a lock. Silently, Bud and I trudged back around to the front and climbed into my Explorer. We said nothing, both staring at the house. All the windows were heavily draped. I said, "He's hiding something in that house."

"But he's right about the warrant. We don't have near enough for a judge."

"Maybe we ought to come back when our psychic friend's not home. Get in a little snooping around. You game?"

"You bet."

"Okay, so he's gonna win this round. Let's go see what else we can dig up on this guy. Maybe Black's PI's found something out in California we can pin on him."

I fired the ignition and maneuvered the SUV around. We headed out McKay's road toward the highway. Something about the snowman was bugging me, big, big, time. Adults didn't go out and build snowmen by themselves. Not unless they had a kid. Was that it? He had a kid he didn't want me to know about. Didn't make a lot of sense, but neither did anything else about him.

"He's so dirty, Bud. I can smell him."

"Yeah, ditto. Your instincts screamin' as loud as mine?"

"Louder. I got the feeling McKay was more shaken up than he was letting on. Let's get Charlie to okay a surveillance. Make McKay nervous. Maybe he'll crack and screw up."

I didn't really believe that as I tried to stay in the ruts we'd made on the way in. Bud opened my glove box and started rummaging around. "Got any more Snickers bars in here? I'm starving."

"You're always starving."

"Hell, I was up all night. Didn't have time for breakfast. Give me a break. Just 'cause you never eat, doesn't mean I'm gonna starve."

I grinned. He was right. "Well, then, this's your lucky day. There's a whole basketful of French stuff in the backseat. Black brought it back from Paris and told me to share it with you. Help yourself."

Bud turned and looked around. "What kinda stuff?"

"You know, French stuff—cheese, chocolates, some of that bread they call baguettes, fancy stuff like Black eats. And I stuck in some Doritos, just for you. You think McKay's gonna run the minute we're outta sight? Maybe we should pull over and surveil the road awhile."

"Yeah. It'll be interesting to see where he goes. Don't need a warrant for that."

I searched for a good place we could park out of sight while Bud brought Black's fancy picnic basket onto his lap. "Wow. La-di-da, mam'selle, look at the little buckles holdin' it shut, and everything. Bet they're made outta solid gold. Maybe he left a sappy love letter inside, too. Or gold bullion bars wrapped up in red ribbons."

"Shut up, Bud." I glanced at him. "How about you and Fin? Didn't I see some dirty dancing going on last night? You were still at her house when I called you, too."

"She's cool. I like her. And built, oh my, my, legs a mile long."

A road up ahead looked like a good place to hide and watch, and I accelerated toward it, desperate to come up with a legit reason to persuade a judge to sign a warrant. I hoped Booker was uncovering a bunch of dirt on McKay's background at this very moment. I glanced at Bud when he opened the basket lid, a little hungry myself. I heard an odd clicking sound then stomped the brakes when a snake as big around as my arm lunged out of the picnic basket and straight at Bud.

The SUV went into a hard, sidelong skid across the road while Bud yelled and flailed his arms hysterically, trying to get the snake off him. He knocked the basket and reptile down onto the floorboard and frantically fumbled for the door handle as we skidded off the shoulder and rammed headfirst into a copse of snow-covered cedars.

My head slammed the steering wheel on impact, and there was a burst of white pain, warm blood on my face. It knocked me back against the seat, but I wasn't dazed enough not to get the hell out of the car before the snake got me, too. I jerked the door open and fell out into a deep drift, blood spattering crimson drops across the snow. Groggy with pain, I realized that my air bag hadn't activated. I could see that Bud's had, and I could hear him yelling and fighting to get out the passenger's door.

"It got me, it got me in the neck!"

I pressed my palm against the gash on my forehead and shook my head. I was still dizzy and felt sick to my stomach but I forced myself to crawl around the rear of the Explorer. Bud was on his side, vomiting into the snow. He was holding his jaw with both hands and groaning.

I grabbed the front of his jacket and yelled into his face. "Listen, Bud, listen to me, you gotta lie still. Don't panic, it'll make it worse." I jerked out my cell phone and hit speed dial for dispatch. I grabbed a hunk of snow and slapped it against my forehead to stop the bleeding, then unzipped Bud's coat. I could see the two puncture marks near the base of his neck on his shoulder. I packed some ice on it where it was bleeding from the bite of the fangs.

Dispatch picked up, and I heard myself screaming. "Bud's down, snakebite. Way out on 5, about twenty miles, I think." I forced my voice calmer and searched the road for a distance marker. I found one not far from where we crashed into the trees. "Marker 119. You gotta get an ambulance here fast, you hear me. Hurry, hurry, dammit!"

I looked at Bud, at the wound already swelling, the location of the bite, and I knew I couldn't sit back and wait for the ambulance, not with snake venom entering Bud's bloodstream so close to his heart and brain. I almost panicked then, but knew I couldn't, could not, so I packed more snow on the bite, not knowing if it would help, but not sure what else to do. I knew not to cut the wound and suck out the poison, not if you were close to a hospital and God, what if I hit his jugular? Oh, God, what if the fangs had hit the jugular?

"Bud, c'mon, we gotta get you to the hospital."

We had to get going, meet the ambulance halfway. Every

minute we waited could be deadly. The snake was in the car. I had to get it out. I jerked the Glock out of my shoulder holster and crawled to the passenger door. It was hanging open. I looked inside, and the rattlesnake struck so hard at me that it propelled itself bodily out of the car onto the snowbank. I opened up on it as it tried to coil, deadly rattles clicking, hitting the writhing reptile four times before I could force my finger off the trigger. The sharp blams of my gun retorted and rolled like thunder through the surrounding woods, the smell of cordite pungent in the crisp clean air as the snake continued to jerk and twist in its death throes. I grabbed up a piece of the snake and threw it in the passenger's floorboard for identification, then struggled through blood-soaked snow to Bud. He was writhing in pain, still clutching his throat.

"Bud, you gotta get back in the car. We can't wait for the ambulance. We gotta get you an antidote fast. Hear me, Bud, we don't have time to wait. We gotta go now!"

Bud nodded but he was already violently ill and fast becoming disoriented. I dragged his arm around my shoulders and staggered with him to the backseat. I pushed and struggled until he was sprawled across the seat. The Explorer was headfirst in a drift, and I clawed my way around to the driver's side and started it up, working the steering wheel back and forth until the spinning tires finally gained enough traction. The vehicle shot backward onto the blacktop road. I could hear Bud groaning and vomiting behind me. I wiped the blood out of my eyes and floored the accelerator. I called dispatch again and told them to alert the ambulance that we were on our way to meet them.

Less than ten minutes later flashing blue lights appeared in the distance and I skidded to a stop as the ambulance pulled up abreast of me. Two paramedics jumped out as I scrambled out and jerked open the back door. They got Bud on a gurney, and I grabbed the remnant of the snake and held it up.

"This is the snake, some kind of rattler, but I don't know which kind. Do you have the antidote with you? Give it to him, give it to him!" I was screaming. I could hear my voice shrill, terrified, echoing out through the snowy cedars lining the roadway.

"Yeah, we got it with us. That's a timber rattler. What the hell's it doing outside in the winter? What about you? That head wound looks pretty bad. Did you get bit?"

"No, just Bud. I hit my head on the steering wheel when we crashed."

I helped them get him inside the back, then climbed in with them, leaving my Explorer in the middle of the road. The ambulance lurched forward in a U-turn, siren screaming, and I watched the EMTs work on Bud. I held onto the sides of the rocking vehicle, staring at Bud's disfigured face, already black and blue and grotesquely swollen. And I knew it was happening again. Like it always had. People around me got hurt, got dead, the people I cared about. I thought that was over after what happened last summer, but it wasn't. It was starting up again. Bud could die, and if he did, like always, it should've been me.

Dark Angels

Gabriel and Uriel had a real good time from that day on. Until something terrible happened. Gabriel's daddy suddenly decided that God had called him to go across the ocean to Uganda to preach the Gospel to the unsaved. Gabriel didn't want to go, and Uriel was terrified he was going to lose his only friend.

But it turned out all right because Gabriel talked his daddy into letting him work at this special school way out in the woods. It was called the Dome of the Cave Academy for the Gifted. Gabriel's good grades and good deeds at the hospital made it easy for him to get on there, and after all, it was only until his daddy converted enough Africans so that he could come back home.

Gabriel got Uriel a job at that school, too, to go to after he finished his high school classes each day. About that time, they killed Uriel's grandma with an overdose and then just left her in her bed to decompose. Nobody ever knew because she had become so reclusive that no one came to call on her. It was easy. All their heavenly work was very easy because it was God's will.

Both of them really liked the academy because there were

lots of pretty girls around and Gabriel got his drugs to sell from somebody who worked there. It worked out great for everyone.

Until the day that Uriel found a special girl, his first real girlfriend. She went to the academy, too, and was really, really nice to him. She was pretty in a tomboy sort of way, and she agreed to go to the drive-in with him one summer night. She wore a pink blouse and white denim skirt and white sandals and had pinned pink-and-white-striped ribbons in her blond hair. Uriel thought she looked really pretty. He took her in the van, and after the movie, Uriel took her out to a deserted road in the woods near the old hunting lodge so they could kiss and stuff. He had never kissed a girl, or really even touched one, but she wanted him to touch her and even put her hand up under his shirt and rubbed the hair on his bare chest.

It was the greatest single moment of Uriel's life, even better than killing people. He slid his hand up under her shirt and found out that she didn't have on a bra. They kissed some more and she pulled off her top and pressed herself against his chest, and he almost died from joy and the strange, wonderful feelings rushing through his body.

Then suddenly the door flew open, and Gabriel was there. He laughed at the way they both screamed and scrambled for their clothes, then he grabbed the pretty girl by her hair, yanked her out, and cut her throat in one quick slash of a big butcher knife. The blood shot out like a geyser and sprayed Uriel in the face but he didn't like the taste of blood this time, not hers. The girl crumpled to the ground, dead, without making a peep.

Rage filled Uriel, red and awful, and he screamed and jumped on Gabriel, knocking him backward to the ground. They grappled there, rolling and fighting, slugging each other with their fists, and drenching themselves in the dead girl's blood. They fought until they were exhausted and fell on their backs, panting and coughing. Both had deep cuts in their hands from the sharp knife they fought over.

Gabriel finally got up on his knees and looked down at Uriel, who was crying and sobbing over the girl's lifeless body.

Gabriel said, still breathless, "I don't see why you're so mad. We do this all the time."

"I wanted her. She was nice. She made me feel good."

"Other girls can make you feel good, too. She was trying to take you away from me."

"No, she wasn't. I ought to kill you and send you to heaven for this."

"Or maybe I ought to kill you. Then you can be with her."

"Go ahead. Just try. I'm almost as big as you are now."

Gabriel sat down. "Okay, I'm sorry, all right? I just couldn't help it. I saw you making out with her and I got jealous. I was afraid you'd go off with her or tell her our secrets."

"You've had girls, lots of 'em, and I didn't kill them."

"No, but we made that blood pact, and you know it. We can have sex with any girl we want, but we've got to kill them afterward. I always killed the girls I had sex with, didn't I? Just like we agreed on. And you weren't going to kill her. I could see the way you smiled at her and followed her around out at the school like some kind of lovesick puppy."

"Well, it doesn't make any difference now, does it? She's dead."

"It's against our code and you know it. No women allowed unless you kill them afterward. This is your own fault, Uriel."

Uriel began to cry again and pulled the girl's nearly severed head onto his lap. "She said I was handsome. She meant it, too."

"She left home to get away from her daddy and never went back. Nobody in her family knows where she is. You told me so yourself. All we've got to do is get rid of the body, and everybody'll think she just took off again."

"No! I'm going to keep her and you can't stop me."

"You'll have to keep her in the cave and it won't smell so hot after a while. You ought to know that by now."

"I don't care."

Gabriel sighed and struggled to his feet. "You're actin' like a big baby about this, Uriel. This time is no different than the others. I thought you'd like all the blood. That's why I slit her jugular."

"Just shut up. You make me sick."

"You need to remember who's been your best friend all these years. Me. I taught you everything you know. I was your friend when nobody else wanted you around. Maybe you oughta remember that instead of bawling over some stupid little bitch."

But Uriel wouldn't speak to Gabriel after that, not for almost a month.

TWENTY-THREE

Bud did not die. But he almost did. The EMTs got the antidote in him in time. But that didn't mean he wouldn't. I tried not to think that way. Even if he did live, he was going to be laid up for a long time and the doctor said the pain was bad, real bad. I sat in the hospital corridor outside the CCU, shut my eyes and listened to his agonized groans. The doctors were still with him, anxious but calm, too, well aware his condition could go either way. A bite so close to his heart could've, maybe should've, killed him quickly, and they were taking every precaution.

I rubbed bleary eyes and rested my face in my open palms. I felt dazed, disbelieving, trying to figure when the snake could've been put in that basket. Who? And when? McKay had been in my sight when Bud came around the house. Had he somehow done it the night before? The Explorer was in my garage while Black and I were at the gala but neither one of us had remembered to set the security system when we'd left. But the basket had been in my backseat for several days; anybody could have gotten to it.

The guys in the ER had cleaned and dressed my wound, the same doctor who'd been on duty when they'd cut Simon

Classon out of that sleeping bag full of spiders. Chris Dale, the nurse who was a friend of mine, was on shift, too, and she'd taped a neat square of gauze over the eighteen ugly black stitches it took to bind up the two-inch laceration on my forehead. It throbbed like the devil and I had one hell of a headache that hadn't let up and probably wouldn't, because I refused the painkillers they offered me. I'd lost some blood, too, not too much, but enough to make me feel weak and sick and guilty and angry all wrapped up together which made it even worse.

I heard footsteps coming down the hallway. They stopped in front of me and a hand touched my back and Black's voice said, "You okay? How's Bud?"

I'd called him while they were stitching on me, and I was embarrassingly glad to see his concerned face now. He knelt and held my chin as he peeled back the bandage. He examined my wound critically, as if no other doctor could stitch as neatly as he could. A regular Betsy Ross of the AMA.

"Thought I warned you about ducking and weaving." Our own little personal joke, but his eyes were serious, the vivid blue dark and worried.

"Bud's real bad. They don't know yet if he's gonna make it. They think so but things could change in a hurry."

Black sat down on the bench beside me and drew me close against him. I let him embrace me, the first time I ever had, in public. It felt pretty good to have a friend to turn to. Other than Harve, there hadn't been many true friends in my life, and few lovers, not until Black had come along.

"He'll make it, babe. I called the CCU on the way over, and they told me they got the antidote in him on time, and it's working. It just takes time. People rarely die of rattle-snake bites, not when they're treated quickly and competently. Thanks to you. You got him here in time."

"Oh God." I kept my face hidden in his chest and kept my eyes shut. Maybe if I did, it'd go away. Why isn't life like that, like a videotape, just rewind and start over? Go in a different direction, don't open a basket of French goodies, don't get nailed by a deadly snake.

"Tell me again what happened. You were pretty shaky over the phone."

"Somebody put a rattlesnake in the picnic basket you brought from Paris. I stuck it in the backseat. I was going to give some of the stuff to the guys at work but kept forgetting to take it inside. McKay did this, Black. I just don't know when or how."

"He found a time when you were gone. Probably when the car was in your garage. If he's smart enough to handle poisonous spiders and snakes, he's smart enough to sneak that snake in without anybody knowing about it."

"It's got to be McKay. Everything points to him. I'm going to get him for this, Black, I swear I will."

"Yes, you will. And soon. Booker called me about an hour ago. Guess who's got a warrant out in L.A. on a child abduction case?"

That brought me to attention, along with a wave of pain that knocked around inside my skull like a steel golf ball. I clamped my jaw against it. Black picked up a strand of my hair. "You've got blood in your hair."

I pressed my palm down on top of my head and felt the stiff, caked blood. But I was more interested in what Booker had dug up.

"He snatched a child out in Los Angeles? Now, that fits. There was a snowman in his yard. How old is the missing kid?"

"Eighteen months. A little girl named Elizabeth Duncan. Lived in some big apartment complex in Anaheim. They issued an Amber Alert a couple of months ago, but she just dropped off the face of the earth."

"That would be about the time McKay showed up here. What about a rap sheet? Did Booker find any priors for sex crimes or kiddie porn?"

Black shook his head. "McKay's records are clean. Nothing

like that, nothing that linked him to Classon's murder. No arrest record. No misdemeanor pranks with spiders or snakes or anything else, not since that one time here when he was eighteen. Booker says the guy served in the Marines, got a chest full of medals and an honorable discharge. His superiors commended him highly, used him for lots of special ops when he was in, sometimes even Black Ops, which makes him top of the heap, militarily."

"Yeah, all that may be fine and dandy, but now he's slipped up and we've got him on a California warrant. I thought I heard somebody inside his house. It could've been the little girl. And the snowman means she's probably still alive."

I stood up, blood pumping. I pressed my fingers to my temples and tried to think straight, tried to will the throbbing to stop. "Charlie's in Jeff City but he'll let us serve the warrant when he hears about the missing child."

"C'mon, Claire, you need to go home and get some rest. You've been up all night. Bud's stable at the moment, under sedation. Get some rest. Somebody else can pick up McKary and the little girl."

"I'm going out there now and confront him before he disappears with the kid again."

"How? Your Explorer's still out on the highway."

"Yeah. Buckeye and the guys are out there processing it. Let me take your car. McKay can't disappear if I'm sitting on his doorstep and surveilling him. Charlie's going to give me the go-ahead as soon as I reach him, I'm sure of it."

"McKay's probably already halfway to Mexico by now."

"Look, Black, I'm going out there. You can go, or not. He's not getting away, not after doing this to Bud."

Black did not look pleased, but hell, I wasn't pleased, either. Why did there always have to be an argument? Who'd he think he was? My mother?

"And if Bud crashes?"

A hard hit of hesitation rocked my conscience, and for the first time gave me pause. I had to make sure Bud was okay but Black had hit the nail on the head a few minutes ago. What good was it doing for me to sit here and hold my head in my hands? Bud would want me to get McKay instead of wasting time outside his hospital room. He had a whole staff of doctors and nurses to take care of him.

"They'll call me if . . . anything happens, and I'll head right back here."

Black put his fists on his hips and stared at me with one major displeased expression. One that made his employees jump down, turn around, and pick a bale of cotton. I wasn't much the jumping type. I wasn't the trembling type either. I didn't even say "how high." He was dressed for work, in a custom-tailored navy suit, crisp white shirt, and burgundy-and-gray striped silk tie. His heavy overcoat was black cashmere lined with silk, and expensive. He shook his head. He looked really, really frustrated. He did that a lot when we knocked heads. "Okay, I'll take you out there, but I'm going, too. No argument."

"Sure. Fine. Let's go."

When I finally got Charlie on his cell and informed him of McKay's California warrant, he told me to arrest the bastard and search his house for the kid. By the time we left at the ER entrance, a frigid wind was swirling and twirling snow around our heads. I barely noticed the cold air as I climbed into Black's Humvee.

The late-afternoon sky was iron gray and heavy, the clouds roiling and diminishing light and making everything dark and foreboding, which promised another subzero night. Black's Humvee caused the usual spectacle, with everybody and their dog staring at us. We sure as hell better not rob a bank in the thing. And it wasn't the vehicle I'd choose for undercover surveillance either, but hey, we wanted McKay to see us.

"You sure John Booker didn't turn up criminal convictions in McKay's past? I give you that he's clever, but not that clever."

"The background showed pretty much what Charlie said

it was. Joe McKay has no living family; he's never been married. Been pretty much a loner, even when he was in the military. That's why they gave him dangerous missions that he had a good chance of not coming back from. Records indicate he never showed fear, never seemed to care if he came out dead or alive."

"Maybe that's because he's got ESP and knows when and where he's going to die. That'd take the pressure off. Did Booker find any mention of psychic abilities?"

"No, not a word. Apparently he kept his mouth shut about it. If he has it at all, and I have my doubts."

"Yeah, you and me both. Pretty odd he was so hush-hush until he showed up here. Then all of a sudden, he's John Edward in the flesh and making sure everybody knows it." I rubbed my bandage and closed my eyes against the snow glare. I should've taken a handful of the painkillers they offered me. I reached in my pocket and found one capsule that they gave me but that I didn't take. I popped it in my mouth and swallowed it sans water.

"What was that?"

Sometimes dating a doctor gets on my nerves. "A pain pill they gave me for my head."

"Here, put these on. They'll help." He handed me his sunglasses, which I happened to know came from the ski slopes at Turino, Italy. I put them on and presto, the glare was gone. Wow.

Black said, "What kind of pill was it?"

"I don't remember. Who cares?" I changed the subject. "I know Joe's involved in Classon's murder, Black. The others, too. And if he didn't off them himself, I guarantee he knows who did. And maybe that's just it, maybe he's protecting somebody, somebody close to him."

Black adjusted the defroster as sleet pecked against the wide windshield. "Like who? His family's gone."

"That's what I'm going to find out when I take him in for interrogation." And I was salivating to get my hands on him.

The sleet made the going slow and the day gloomy, as if

things could get any worse. When we reached the spot where
the guys were sweeping my Explorer, we slowed and I asked
Shag if they'd turned up anything. They hadn't. A couple of
fingerprints was about it. We pulled away, and inside I cursed
the snow. Outside, too. Enough already. This was not the
frickin' North Pole.

By the time we reached McKay's road and headed toward
the farmhouse, the ice pellets hitting the car petered off
some and turned into soft, silent flakes.

"He better not be gone."

"He's not. Look."

Lights were on in the farmhouse, yellow squares glowing
in the deepening dusk. We stopped out front, and I'd barely
stepped out of the passenger's side when I heard the buzz of
McKay's four-wheeler firing up behind the house. I drew my
weapon, but before we rounded the corner, McKay was
halfway across the open field that led into heavily wooded
hills.

"Police! Stop!"

I fired a couple of shots in the air, but McKay didn't stop.
Seconds later he'd disappeared into a thicket of cedars at the
far end of his property.

Black said, "C'mon, this Humvee'll go anywhere."

We ran for the vehicle, slipping and sliding, but Black
was grinning as he fired the ignition. "I've been dying to see
what this baby'll do in the woods. Hold on."

Yeah, I admit it, sometimes Black's giant, expensive toys
come in real handy. Like now. Dark was falling over us like
a big, black blanket, making it hard to follow him, but our
headlights reflected off the white snow as we veered and
bounced across the back yard. My adrenaline was pumping
out of control.

"Floor it, Black, don't lose him!"

Even if we did, the four-wheeler would leave a nice wide
track to follow. We hit the tree line, and Black didn't even
slow down. The big tank slammed through the slender cedars,
mowing them down indiscriminately and dumping lots of

snow and slapping evergreen boughs across the windshield. I held on tightly to the dash and tried not to remember how much this rampaging ride was hurting my rampaging headache.

The solitary track was easy to see in the jouncing Humvee's headlamps. We got about thirty yards inside the woods before cedars gave way to ancient oaks with two-foot-diameter trunks that didn't mow quite so easily. Black stopped and idled the Humvee. The windshield wipers swished back and forth with wet, sloppy sounds. "Can't go any farther. The trees are too close together. Either we follow him on foot or get out an APB."

"He's heading for the nearest paved highway. Count on it. The State Patrol'll already be out in force on a night this bad."

I didn't want to give it up, but I wasn't stupid, either. Neither of us was dressed or physically prepared to track a fugitive through the woods at night in a brewing blizzard. McKay had gotten away for now. I stared at the shadowy woods, then went tense when the "Mexican Hat Dance" sang alive inside my leather purse.

Black and I stared at each other, and I let it play. Truth was that I was afraid to answer, afraid it was news about Bud. Bad news.

Black finally fished out the phone. "Nick Black." He listened a few seconds then said, "Okay. I'll tell her."

I couldn't breathe. Couldn't move. Felt sick to my stomach. Then Black smiled, and my entire body went limp with relief. "He's responding better now. They say he's probably going to be okay."

My eyes burned like fire, and I set my jaw, sure as hell not going to cry in front of Black like some kind of little baby. Get a grip. This was good news, not bad. I nodded. "I knew he'd be okay. Great. I knew it all along."

Black squeezed my hand. I took a couple more cleansing breaths, pulling myself together. I didn't like people seeing me all weak and sappy. It didn't happen often but when it did, it had been with Black when he was trying to analyze me.

"Okay, that's good news. Now let's get every damn cop in the state looking for this bastard. I want him behind bars tonight, and then I want him alone in an interrogation room."

Black laughed. "Poor guy. Glad it's not me. I've been there."

I managed a charity smile, but I was not in a joking mood. I was in a bloodletting mood. I stared out through the shifting, drifting snowflakes, where the Humvee's twin beams lasered smoky trails through snow-covered trees. I could see the four-wheeler's tracks and wondered where he was headed now. Maybe he had another lair somewhere. What about the poor little girl he'd snatched? Where was she? Was she in the four-wheeler with him? Or had he killed her, too? I gritted my teeth and made my head pound worse and I wondered what kind of stupid, ineffective painkiller they'd given me until I saw something high up in the trees that looked out of place in the stark black-and-white tableau of tree trunks and falling snow.

"You got a spotlight on this thing, Black?"

"Yeah, a custom job, nice and bright." He flipped on the one outside the driver's window, and I pointed to a giant oak tree about thirty yards off to our left.

"Look up there, real high. See it? The fork of the biggest branch?"

Black moved the bright light slowly across the ground and bushes drifted in deep snow. He steadied the high-powered beam on the target, and said, "Oh my God."

It was a black trash bag hanging from a limb. The wind was buffeting it back and forth but I could see the head clearly visible at the top, just like Classon's had been.

My stomach took a forward roll. "He's a serial. Scan the rest of the trees."

Black maneuvered the brilliant spot from tree to tree and

gradually revealed one swinging black trash bag after another. Deadly cocoons, rocking from snowy limbs like babies in cradles. A macabre dumping ground stretching into the woods as far as the eye could see.

TWENTY-FOUR

Less than two hours after Black and I found the killer's dump site, the woods behind McKay's house were awash with gigantic floodlights. Parka-bundled officers traipsed around in the frigid night, in a gallant but futile effort to preserve a crime scene encompassing several acres of snow-crusted, forested hills. Charlie was back in town, angry as hell, and had the entire department mobilized.

At the moment he stood near the tree where Black and I saw the first body bag. He was beating his gloved hands together for warmth while a consulting captain from the Missouri State Highway Patrol filled him in on their end of the search. So far, there was no trace of Joe McKay, his four-wheeler, or the abducted child. He had not left her behind in the farmhouse, dead or alive, but some of her clothes and a white teddy bear were there. Chances were she was his next, or worse, his latest victim.

Black was gone. Confident, I guess, that I'd be safe enough in the midst of twenty or thirty well-trained officers of the law, all armed and collectively pissed off. He was on his Learjet by now, a late flight concerning some emergency with a high-profile patient at his New York clinic. Obviously he still worried about me but this was something he couldn't ignore, so he'd asked me if I wanted to go, to which I'd replied, "Yeah, right."

Black didn't bat an eye. He knew I took my job seriously. He took his job seriously, too. That's why he left me by my lonesome. He did spend about fifteen minutes insisting that I spend the night at his place while he had my house checked out for creeping or slithering secret-pal gifts. I told him maybe, but truth was, that remained to be seen. If my house was thoroughly fumigated by Orkin, I didn't have to worry, but you can bet the farm I'm shaking out my black-and-orange-hightop Nikes before I step into them.

I tromped through the snow to where Buckeye Boyd was watching a couple of firemen lower a victim into the hands of a waiting forensic team. Buckeye's maroon parka was un-snapped. He had on green lab scrubs underneath. Not ex-actly snow attire. He had on fur-lined camo hunting boots, though. He was hatless, his white hair blowing back and re-vealing a receding hairline that was usually hidden by Captain Kangaroo bangs. His eyes looked spooked. "This vic looks like a youngster, Claire, possibly female, but the body's been out here awhile, I can tell you that. A lot longer than Simon Classon was. After I get her on the table, I'll know more."

"Jeez Louise." That was Shaggy. He came up beside me and stared into the treetops. Glaring lights carved dark planes in his young face and sent our elongated shadows chasing back into the woods where other forensic technicians stared up into other trees with the same horrified expressions. "The lake's getting worse than that town in *Halloween*. What's the name of that guy who killed everybody?"

Buckeye said, "Michael Myers, maybe? Jamie Lee Curtis played the girl."

Shag said, "Yeah. Well, maybe Michael's set up camp here."

I said, "Yeah. Lucky us."

Shag turned to me. "Hey, I heard about Bud getting bit. How's he doing?"

"They think he's gonna be okay."

Shag looked at my bandaged stitches and the ugly bruise on my forehead. "You got knocked a good one. Concussion?"

"A little one, maybe. It still hurts like hell, but I'll live."

"Thank goodness about Bud. This perp's just full of nasty surprises, ain't he?"

"Yeah. Nasty's a good word. Buckeye, did they come up with a final count on victims yet?"

"There's twenty-seven bags on what we think might be McKay's property, which is about two acres, I'd estimate, but there's a couple of other houses nearby which might own some of this land. And there are national forests on two sides that we haven't had time to canvass yet. One good thing, I think some of these trash bags contain animal carcasses. Dogs and cats, maybe, and some other small mammals like squirrels and raccoons."

I stared off into the distance and watched another team working on the ground underneath a tree. Gloved, cameras in hand, they were placing a trash bag on a stretcher. "I can't believe he's gotten away with this for so long. Why hasn't somebody stumbled over these bodies before now?"

"Private property, and so far out in the boondocks you need a map to find it. If he's been gone and the place closed up, there'd be no reason for anyone to come around here. Especially not out back of the house in the woods."

I said, "Wonder if he's been back to town on and off to use this place as his own private hunting and dumping ground."

"Yeah, could be, I guess." Buckeye stomped his booted feet, shivering. He should've dressed warmer. "Did I hear you say Bud was still holdin' up?"

"He's hanging in. There for a while it was hit or miss. I saw the snake strike him. Close to the throat. Right about here." I touched my clavicle and shivered when I remembered how the fang marks had looked.

"You pretty sure McKay's the perp?"

I nodded. "Killing this many victims takes time, unless he got them in groups."

Buckeye grimaced, pulled up his fur-lined hood, jammed his hands into his pockets, and did some more stamping around in the snow.

Shag said, "How're we gonna handle this many freakin' bodies down at the morgue?"

Buckeye said, "Charlie's already requested help from the State Highway Patrol labs. But that's not the worst of it. Most of these bodies are gonna be frozen solid."

I said, "Have you found any viable evidence yet, Buckeye?"

"No, and we probably won't until we get them all downtown. It doesn't appear any of them are in sleeping bags like Classon was, so I doubt if he went to the trouble of torturing them with widows and recluses. I guess that was a special nightmare designed just for Mr. Classon."

Shag said, "Snow's let up some. That'll help get them down and tagged."

I said, "Hate to tell you guys this, but another storm's incoming. Black's pilot had to change flight plans to go around it."

Shaggy squatted down and examined the icy tree trunk with gloved fingers. He turned to me and said, "Hey, Claire, look at this. I think I just figured out how he gets 'em up the trunk and tied off without a line to the ground."

"How?"

"You know my bud, Steve Granger? How he's always on me to go out deer huntin' and stuff?"

"Yeah, so?"

"Well, I finally went with him the other day so he'd get off my back about it, and he's got this cool deer stand thing he bought down in Springfield at the Bass Pro Shop. He says it's a climbing deer stand, or something like that. And guess what? It makes these same kind of notches." He aimed his flashlight on some small chunks cut into the bark. They were identical to the ones at the Classon crime scene.

"What'd you mean, climbing deer stand?"

"It's pretty awesome really. You carry it in the woods on your back, you know, folded up like a regular backpack, and then you unfold it and stand up inside it and make it walk up the trunk with a strap you put around the tree trunk. You know, sorta like those lumberjacks you see having races up to the top of those big redwoods out in Oregon."

Buckeye reached down and touched the scarred bark. "I've used those things. It'd work just like Shag said. But the perp'd have to put the body inside, between him and the tree, or he could carry it on his back, I guess. Then he'd only need a rope to tie the victim onto the limb then climb the whole rig back down. He's strong as hell to do something like that."

I gauged the distance up to where the body had been hanging. "Unless he hoisted the body up first, then climbed up and tied it off up high. Maybe we oughta get your friend out here and see if he could do that with a hundred-pound sandbag."

Shag said, "Cool. I'll give him a call."

I said, "I guess you're going to open the bags down at the morgue."

"None of these vics are going to wake up like Classon did. They've been out here a very long time, years, maybe. I bet he quit for a while, gave up the killing spree for some reason, then gave in to temptation again when he came back home. That's my best guess."

"Right. Or there could be a fresh killing field just like this one somewhere in California. God only knows how many he's done."

That thought was chilling. I gazed around, thinking the scene looked like something out of Dante's *Inferno*, with all the smoky lights and silhouetted men and women bending over corpses and lowering them with ropes and shadows passing in and out of the trees and over the bright snow cover. A scene from hell, all right. And the devil made his escape in a four-wheeler.

By dawn my Explorer was released back to me, swept

clean, and sans any other rattlesnakes. I drove straight to the hospital and checked on Bud. He was sleeping, still in CCU, still doped up, but they took mercy on me and let me go in. I hardly recognized him. His face looked purple and black and grotesquely swollen. His lips were dark, too, and about three times their normal size. He opened his eyes, and I tried to keep it light.

"You look like crap, Davis."

"Thanks." He mumbled something else through those horrible, thick, engorged lips, and I finally realized he'd said, "You should see the snake." He attempted a grotesque grin, and so did I. Neither of us quite made it work.

"I shot the hell out of that frickin' snake. It didn't know who it was messing with. All this medicine and stuff making you feel any better?"

"Just peachy," he rasped out. "And just when I was makin' time with Fin."

I did smile then. "Nurse said she's been down here to see you five times already. You were just too out of it to know."

He shut his eyes as if too tired to hold them open. I said, "It was McKay, Bud. We found more victims in the woods behind his house. Everybody's out there tonight processing the scene. Buckeye's bound to find enough evidence to nail him."

Bud peered at me. His right eye was blood red. "You get him?"

"Not yet, but we will, sooner or later. Everybody in the state's in on the hunt."

Bud's eyes drifted closed, and he didn't move again. I sat beside the bed and watched him sleep, then I listened to the steady beep and watched the lights on the monitors, just to make sure he was still breathing. Then, when I couldn't hold my head up any longer, I lay my cheek against the mattress beside his hand and slept hard until a nurse woke me and told me I had to leave.

I drove straight home but stopped at Harve's first to tell him what had gone down and make sure he was all right. He was fine and invited me to stay with him until the evil spider meister was behind bars. The offer was tempting, especially with Black gone. I told him maybe, then got in the car and headed to my cabin, not as thrilled to be going home as I'd been just after Black had remodeled the place. Deadly critters had that effect on me, just took the sweet out of home sweet home.

I ignored the garage and pulled up out front. I sat looking at my house. It looked the same, not at all as if a psychopath with a pouch of spiders and a basket of rattlers was on the loose. I was loath to go inside, which means I was scared as hell of what I'd find now, even after exterminators had treated the place. McKay's surprises were getting deadlier.

There were no motorcycle or four-wheeler tracks, no footprints. I took time to walk around outside the house but saw nothing in the snow under my windows and doors but an undisturbed, beautiful carpet of white. No crawling spider tracks, no curvy snake trails, which was a good thing. The front walk was cleared, so I climbed onto the front porch and peered into the window. Everything appeared normal. I looked for Jules Verne but didn't see him. I didn't hear him either, which was not normal. The ramification of his silence sent a massive shudder undulating up my spine. Spooked, I turned the key and pushed open the door.

Everything seemed fine, normal, warm and cozy, the light I left on glowing in the early-morning gloom, except for one thing. My feisty little puppy dog was nowhere to be seen, no excited yapping, no little white face watching for me out the front window or barreling down the stairs to greet me. Don't panic. Maybe Black dropped by and took him to Cedar Bend so the exterminators could sweep the house. Somehow I didn't believe that.

I swallowed hard and knew what McKay had done before I saw one of my white kitchen wastebasket bags laying on the kitchen floor. A thick lump rose and clogged the back of my throat.

I pulled the Glock out of my shoulder holster and stood

very still. Not a sound, but my sixth sense was screaming like a banshee. Filled with utter dread, I went down on one knee beside the bag. I pulled open the yellow ties affixed in a bow. When I saw a little body covered with arachnid silk , I backed away against the kitchen counter, shut my eyes, and tasted bile, caustic and terrible.

"Damn you, McKay."

Sidestepping the bag, I didn't touch it again, couldn't bear to look at poor little Jules Verne. Black should've left him in Paris; even animals aren't safe around me. Then, like a lightbulb going off, it dawned on me that even a hundred spiders couldn't have killed and cocooned a pup that fast. I had been here yesterday. Black had been here later that afternoon and so had the Orkin men. I moved back to the bag and dumped the rotting carcass out on the floor. Most of the spiders were dead but I had to smash two or three under my boot before I examined the body. It was a squirrel. I could see the bushy tail.

Breathing easier, hopeful now, I searched the house, looking for the dog, cautiously, back to the wall, finger near the trigger, careful not to open any baskets. I found myself shivering with revulsion, and, yes, fear. Never in my life had I been afraid of spiders and bugs, that was Bud, poor disfigured Bud, but the horror of how McKay's victims had died was having a strong, negative effect on me now, and the arachnophobia had kicked in and was growing stronger by the minute. Lots of other phobias, too.

The ground floor was untouched as far as I could tell so I looked up the steps that led to my bedroom loft. Then I moved up one step at a time, leading with my gun. I hoped McKay was hiding up there, I hoped he'd try to get the jump on me so I could open up on him.

At the top of the stairs I could see into the bedroom. Jules Verne lay on the bed, a strip of silver duct tape wrapped around his snout. More tape held his back and front legs together. He was on top of the comforter, shivering all over, and his muffled whimpers became frantic when I moved toward him. I checked out the bathroom and spotted twenty or so brown recluse spiders crawling around in the bottom of my bathtub.

I slammed the bathroom door, shuddering uncontrollably, checked out my closet for assailants, then picked up the poodle and headed for my car. Forget clothes, forget toothbrush, forget everything, I wanted the hell out of there.

Outside, I took time to check out the Explorer again, totally paranoid now. It was clean so I climbed inside, locked the doors, then took out my pocketknife and cut the tape off Jules Verne. The poor puppy whined inconsolably, dug at a spot in my lap where he tried to burrow bodily into my open coat. Like I said, even my pets learn real quick about the existence of monsters. Maybe that's why I'd never had any dogs or cats. Maybe Jules would want Black to book him a return flight to Paris ASAP.

I backed out in a hurry and, as a result, slid off in a snowbank. I braked and looked down at the snow lining the lake's shore. The water was mostly frozen, my dock locked in ice, so Black wouldn't be coming to call for a while in his Cobalt 360. Then I saw the four-wheeler track running parallel along the bank at the edge of the water until it cut out in to the woods north of my house.

Anger surged, swift and awful and helpless, and I hugged Jules Verne against my chest as I stared at evidence that fully incriminated McKay once and for all. I wondered when the hell McKay had come to my house with his evil cargo of deadly creatures. I shook with rage for a few minutes, then I got hold of myself, calmed down, and vowed again to get him. He was toying with me, toying with what was mine. Nobody did that and got away with it.

I sucked a couple of deep breaths like my yoga tape told me to do when spitting mad and ready to murder. I drove up the road and stopped beside Harve's mailbox. I sat there with the motor idling, the heater blowing lukewarm in my face, and my dog zipped up inside my parka. Involving Harve in this would be stupid. Harve had gotten involved last summer with my case and had almost died as a result. That wasn't going to happen again. Not with McKay loose and growing more lethal. He'd gotten to Bud and Jules Verne. Tried to get me and Black. Harve wasn't going to be next.

I drove on. I'd take Black's advice and stay at Cedar Bend where security was tight and lots of people were around, where even a black widow spider couldn't squeeze through the security screen Black had set up after the murder there last summer. And I wasn't worried about Black. He'd pretty much proved to me that he knew how to take care of himself. The thought of being driven out of my house was like a thorn under my toenail, but at the moment a smarter move was to stay with Black until I got my hands on McKay. And at this point, I was ready to move heaven and earth to get him.

Dark Angels

Uriel was in love. He'd found the perfect girl for him, a girl at the school where he worked. He thought about her all the time, longed to be with her all the time. Now Gabriel was so jealous that he was being mean and trying to hurt her. Uriel was frightened. He was afraid Gabriel would get so angry that he'd kill her the way he'd killed Uriel's other girl-friend.

Then on a weekend when Gabriel went to an educational conference held in the nearby city of Columbia, Uriel felt safe enough to bring his girl down into the cave and show her all his reptiles and arachnids. She was afraid at first and held back, but after he had explained everything and told her how beautiful and special his creatures were, she had loved it, too, and said she didn't care and wanted him to teach her how to raise spiders and snakes. She said she loved him and would do anything in the world for him, and they'd made love there in the cave, the very first time for both of them.

Uriel had never been so happy. But now Gabriel had returned, and Uriel was late meeting him at the cave. So he was in a hurry when he got to the boiler room and unlatched the water heater. He jumped down into the tunnel, terrified

Gabriel would get angry and lose his temper, but Uriel had been at his girl's house and hadn't wanted to leave her. That's why he was late, but Gabriel could never, ever find out about it.

Uriel followed the shaft into the domed cavern but didn't see Gabriel anywhere. He stood very still and listened. Something about the place seemed spooky tonight, not like it had felt earlier when he'd been there with his love. It was completely quiet, except for faint scratches of the scorpions and the rustle of snakes in the leaves on the bottom of their cages.

Then out of nowhere, Uriel was tackled from behind and knocked to the ground. It was Gabriel, and Uriel tried as hard as he could to fight him off, but Gabriel was violently angry and fought like a maniac. They rolled on the ground until Gabriel had him pinned underneath him. He doubled his fist and hit Uriel in the head, stunning him for a moment. Uriel stared up at his friend, his benefactor, shocked and horrified at the black rage he saw in Gabriel's eyes. Gabriel sat on his chest and grabbed him by the throat with both hands. His face was red, his words harsh and low and furious.

"You brought that little bitch down here, you bastard. To our private place, to our secret lair. I thought I could trust you, but now everything's ruined. You stupid little fool, don't you see? She'll get pissed off at you someday and tell the police what we've done. We'll end up in prison, both of us, and it'll all be your fault. How could you do this to me, how could you? I trusted you!"

"No, I didn't, I didn't bring her here. I swear."

"Liar! I saw you. I knew you were sneaking around with her and lying to me about it. There wasn't any conference in Columbia. I stayed here. I watched you bring her down to our secret place. I saw you screwing her. And now she's got to die."

Uriel lay still and stared up at Gabriel's demented face. "No. No way. I love her, Gabriel. And there's nothing wrong with that. There's no need for you to be jealous. I love you, too. You're my blood brother, you'll always be the most important person in my life." Uriel felt the tears well up and begin to burn. "Please, just let me have her. I'll do anything you say, anything, if you'll let me have her."

"No, no, no! We made a pact that we wouldn't have women. And if we did, then we'd kill them afterward. I've always kept up my end of the bargain. Now it's your turn. You shouldn't have brought her down here. Now she's gotta die, and you gotta do it."

Uriel fought Gabriel's grip on his neck, unable to stop weeping. "No, no, please, Gabriel . . ."

"Shut up your sniveling, Uriel, you hear me? Shut your damn mouth and listen good. You go get her right now and bring her to my house. Tell her I want to meet her tonight, tell her I've given the two of you my blessing, tell her whatever the hell you want. Just get her there, and then you're going to kill her while I watch. You got that? You can do it any way you want, but she's gonna die tonight. Do you understand me? Do you? This is your punishment for breaking our code."

Defeated, Uriel nodded but couldn't stop sobbing.

"If you don't do it, Uriel, I will. You understand that? I'm gonna do her, then I'm going to put her in a sleeping bag with some widows and watch her die a long, slow, horrible death."

Gabriel climbed off Uriel, then jerked him to his feet by the front of his shirt. He shoved him toward the tunnel. "Now go get her and meet me at my house and don't make it too late. I've got to go to work tomorrow. This is your fault, Uriel! How could you have been so stupid?"

Uriel obeyed, but as he drove to his love's house he could barely see the road ahead for his tears. He could not kill her. He loved her too much. But how could he lose Gabriel? Gabriel was everything to him, had always been everything to him. And Gabriel would kill her if he didn't.

Outside his love's house, he sat in the car and wiped his

tears on his shirt sleeve. Then after a long time, he got out of the car, walked up the sidewalk, and knocked on her door. His heart ached, and he hated himself for what he was about to do.

It was much later that night when Uriel held onto his love's arm and guided her up the front steps to Gabriel's front door. He felt sick to his stomach, really sick inside his heart. She was so young, so happy and smiling, so eager to do whatever Uriel asked of her. She loved him. He felt afraid now that the time was at hand to do what had to be done. She wanted to lift the door knocker and he let her. It fell with a clang against the brass plate. They waited, and she smiled up at him the whole time, her eyes glowing with love.

It didn't take long for Gabriel to open the door and admit them. He grinned at Uriel, and Uriel could tell Gabriel was pleased that Uriel was willing to sacrifice his true love for their secrets. He invited them inside, and Gabriel took the girl's hand and kissed the back of it, as if he was very glad to see her. He asked her how she liked her job at the school and told her how pleased he was to finally meet the girl that Uriel loved so much. He turned her away from Uriel and pointed out some of his artwork so that Uriel could strike her from behind when she wasn't expecting it, just like they'd planned.

Uriel clamped his jaw. He knew what he had to do, but he didn't want to. He wasn't sure he could. Oh lord, how could he? He looked around for something heavy to wield. He picked up the heaviest object he could find and crept up behind Gabriel and the girl. He raised it high in the air and brought it down as hard as he could. Then he fell to his knees and wept with horror and remorse at what he had been forced to do.

TWENTY-FIVE

By the time I reached Cedar Bend with Jules Verne, my headache had worked itself into a frenzy of sharp, shooting pains and throbbing temples. I felt exhausted. Hell, I was exhausted. I wished that Black was home but he was in New York, for at least three days, more if he got snowed in. I guess the guy's become a habit, after all.

His personal security guard, a six-foot-six giant of a man by the name of Jerry Presson, saluted me as if I had on Queen Elizabeth's fancy jeweled crown, so I wished him a subdued happy New Year and cuddled poor, shivering Jules Verne on the elevator's quiet swoop up to Black's palatial crib.

The place was pretty much pitch black and silent so I snapped on this fancy chrome-and-glass lamp in the hallway near the elevator. I hadn't been here often without Black, and the sprawling penthouse seemed lonely and strange in all its black-and-tan glory; even the whisper-footed staff had faded into the woodwork. Or maybe Black had given them New Year's Day off. He was pretty good about stuff like that.

More important, the penthouse was spider/rattler free, and that was a mighty big plus in my book. Nonetheless I checked the shiny cherrywood floors and listened for the skitter and rattle of scorpions, and whatnot.

I was too sleep deprived to worry long, but I checked out every nook and cranny in Black's huge, ultramasculine bedroom, threw off the sheets and shook them like I was trying to kill them, and armed myself with a small can of Raid I found under the kitchen sink. Finally, Jules Verne and I slipped between varmint-free smooth black satin sheets together and gave it up.

The nightmares began at once, an extension of my life, I guess. I dreamed that Black was a huge, hairy brown recluse with his handsome face smiling and winking at me, and Bud was a snake with six arms that had rattles for fingers that kept grabbing at me. I was a field mouse trying to get away from them but instead ran straight into a huge, sticky white web that Joe McKay had spun high in the trees behind his farmhouse. He was sitting in his four-wheeler in the middle of that gigantic web, grinning and dimpled up, with a little kid wrapped in silk wiggling in the web beside him. A midnight snack, no doubt.

I awoke with a start and found myself drenched in sweat. I was more frightened by McKay's deadly methods than I'd realized, which really ticked me off. I was pretty shook up and couldn't get a hold on it. Everything was so damn awful, so insane, downright scary even. That's right, I am scared, and I don't like it. So is Jules Verne. He is whimpering and burrowing deep under the covers. Must have had the same dream as me. After all Jules had been through, Black was going to have to invest in a canine shrink.

I raised up on one elbow, snatched my cell phone off the bedside table and punched in the hospital's number. Bud's nurse said he was doing better but had a long way to go. Then I called the department and found no one had picked up McKay during the night. The autopsies on the new victims wouldn't start until mid-afternoon so I got out of bed, showered, dressed, and strapped on all my guns and wished I had more than just two. I stuck some extra ammo clips in my pockets in case I got to unload on McKay, slipped into my parka and shoved my trusty can of Raid in my other pocket, just in case. Suddenly that miniature aerosol can was my bestest, most trusted friend. The "Mexican Hat Dance" erupted in the quiet room, and I grabbed my cell phone.

Black said, "Where are you?"

"At your place. I found a couple of unwelcome home presents at my house."

"Oh my God. What?"

"Just a cobweb-coated squirrel in a plastic bag so I'd think it was Jules Verne. It scared the hell out of me, let me tell you, but don't worry, Jules's fine."

"Goddamn him."

"We can only hope. Oh, yes. McKay taped up Jules but didn't sic any spiders on him, so I guess down deep he's an animal lover. Too bad Simon Classon wasn't a Pekingese. Oh, yeah, I forgot, he put a bunch of brown recluses in my tub, too, so I decided to skip my bubble bath today." My attempt at glib was definitely not coming off. Actually, it sounded more like I was trying to break all my teeth off at the gums. I wouldn't have laughed at me, either. I sounded creeped out, because I was creeped out. Soon it appeared that Black was creeped out, too.

"Don't go back there, Claire. I mean it. Don't do it. And that's it, I'm out of here, to hell with this consultation. They'll have to handle it without me. He's getting too close, and his warnings more deadly. I don't understand why he's continuing with it. He's got to know you're not scaring off. And it doesn't seem like he's really trying to hurt you, just trying to warn you off." He finished his comments with a couple of rather creative obscenities, some of which I'd never heard him utter aloud but that I'd been thinking lately, too, then he asked, "How's Bud?"

"Better, but not good. No sign of Joe McKay yet but we've got every officer in the state looking for him."

Another rather unique curse, one with French Cajun overtones from his Louisiana youth, I suppose. "Yeah, and I better warn you, Claire, the media's picked up on Classon's murder. They're calling the guy Spiderman."

"Oh, crap." I hadn't even thought about the media jackals, figured they were too busy with blizzard updates and keeping their heads warm without messing up their hair. I walked to the windows in search of satellite trucks. None had mushroomed up during the night. Not yet.

Black was still asking me questions. "What about the victims in the woods? Any IDs?"

"Buck thinks one is a young girl, teenager, maybe. The body's too decomposed to be a recent kill."

"Claire, this is not good. This is too morbid. This guy's been killing for years and getting away with it."

"Don't worry, I'll get him."

"Don't you mean *we*? As in the rest of the department?"

"Sure. That's what I meant."

"Don't go after him alone, Claire. Promise me."

"I can't go after him. I don't know where he is."

"If the weather holds, I can be back by tonight. Tomorrow morning at the latest."

"Great. And, Black, you better call that exterminator again. He might want to give my bathtub another spritz or two."

"Just stay away from your place. No use taking chances."

I was only too pleased to agree. Not that I thought McKay would show up there again. He was hiding out in some dark hole, waiting, biding his time, like one of his goddamned spiders.

"Listen to me, Claire, you've got to be more careful. Don't do anything reckless."

"Who, me?"

Dead silence. I could almost see his teeth clamping. "This guy's dangerous as hell, and he's got it out for you."

"Yeah, I noticed. Somebody targeting me and my friends. Imagine." I shut my eyes and remembered last summer and last year and all the years of my past when the people around me died because somebody hated me.

"This time's different. He's not targeting your friends. He's targeting you. They're just getting in the way."

"Now that makes me feel better."

"None of this is your fault. Remember how we talked this out. It's him doing this, and him alone."

"I thought it was over."

"This is different than before. This guy's after you because you're on to him." I said nothing so he said, "How does this make you feel?"

There you go, psychiatrist mode kicking in. But he'd helped me before so I played along. "How do you think I feel?"

"I think you'll blame yourself and pull away from people who care about you."

"Right, and funniest thing, that saves the lives of people around me."

"Remember our sessions. This is not your fault. You've got a dangerous job, and sometimes bad things happen to people in law enforcement."

"Right."

"I don't like the way you said that."

"Right."

"For God's sake, Claire, listen to what I'm saying! Don't go off and try to prove something."

"Right."

Black fell silent, except for a highly exasperated sigh. He usually didn't react when I badgered him. Guess I need to be civil. And he was right, of course, and I knew it.

"I'm not going to do anything stupid. I'm heading out to the crime scene now. About fifty officers are out there sweeping the woods, who can babysit me. Anyway, I've got my Glock and new .38 snub-nosed, all snug in their beds and ready to blow away anything that moves."

"Just so you don't play Rambo."

"You're no fun anymore, Black."

"You're getting on my nerves."

"Well, everybody's got to have a hobby."

He laughed but he definitely was not amused. "I shouldn't have left."

"Get off it, Black, I'm a big girl, remember? A real, live, experienced police officer, trained and everything. I've even slapped a few criminals behind bars. Give me a break with the gloom and doom."

"Right."

I smiled. "See you when I see you. Stop worrying and take care of your patients. No sense rushing back here, just because I'm in deadly danger from a deranged arachnicidal maniac."

"Be careful. Duck and weave, et cetera, you know the drill."

"Right. Ditto."

"Are you wearing your Saint Michael's medallion?"

"I never take it off."

"Well, don't. I'm superstitious."

We hung up, and for some reason all his dire warnings made me feel better. Loved, even, maybe. I zipped up my parka and left Jules Verne nervous as hell and tiptoeing around and avoiding highly dimpled men toting black trash bags. I checked out my Explorer inch by inch, then sprayed Raid under the seats, much to the naive amusement of Mike, the burly security guard. Obviously, he had never seen a Egyptian fat-tailed scorpion.

Outside, it was sunny, bright, and a little warmer, which had probably been met with cheers and whoops of joy at the crime scene. When I got back to McKay's little farm of horrors, four SUVs and the county crime scene van were still there. I checked out the house, where Buck's team was dusting for fingerprints and looking for blood spatter, without much luck. Shag was squirting around with a spray bottle of Luminol to see if McKay had washed up any gore nice and tidy-like.

I got back in my Explorer and jounced my way across the back field. I could still see the wide tracks Black and I had made in the Humvee. I could also see that all the bodies were now down and had been transported to the medical examiner's office for autopsy. Buckeye Boyd was still on scene, still shaking his head, still chain-smoking. I wondered how many packs of Marlboros he'd gone through. I wondered if I should start smoking. Maybe it'd calm my nerves.

"Hey, Buck. You been here all night?"

He nodded and flicked the butt to the ground. It hissed when it hit the snow. "Yeah, I supervised retrieval. But I'm done. I'm going home, get some shut-eye, then I'll start the autopsies."

"Any kind of IDs on the bodies?"

"Nope. Most of them were nude, nothing we could trace."

"Think one might be that lady janitor that took off without telling anybody?"

Buckeye shrugged. "Looks like the perp had a field day, really ran the gamut, Claire, I mean, men, women, children. It's sickening, surreal. Like, I mean, where's David Duchovny and Gillian Anderson? I keep expecting them to show up any minute, coats open and flapping."

Buckeye was a big fan of *X-Files* reruns.

The wind shivered through the tree branches. A branch cracked and fell in a shower of snow. I pulled up my hood and stared at the frayed ropes still dangling where the killer tied the victims off under the arms. They swirled in the wind like hair on a corpse.

"I think I'll take a look around, Buck. How about letting me use that four-wheeler over there?" I pointed at the small off-road vehicle parked about twenty feet away.

"Sure. The state guys used it to search the perimeter. When you get done, leave it where you found it. They're picking it up later."

I climbed on, got the thing going and roared along the tree line just outside the yellow crime-scene tape. I slowed and surveyed the tree trunks marked with the yellow tape, the ones in which the bodies had been hoisted.

When I reached the back of the kill site, I shut down the four-wheeler. Silence dropped like a heavy shroud, and then

I heard the distant voices of the criminalists wrapping up their work at the scene. The scent of pine surrounded me, mixed in with gasoline fumes emitted by the four-wheeler. I searched the ground. Lots of footprints everywhere, and I mean lots. Teams of investigators had tramped around throughout the night, trying to find something. It looked like smaller groups, two and threes, spread out through the woods, searching, searching.

I was looking for McKay's four-wheeler tracks, and when I found them, the disruption of the snow looked like my colleagues had already checked it out. I climbed on the four-wheeler and followed McKay's trail about a mile due north to a steep rock outcropping. The tread marks led into a small stream that was frozen along both banks. Water trickled down the middle of the bed, plenty wide enough for McKay to ride through in a four-wheeler.

I hunkered down at the edge of the stream and then walked the bank about thirty yards in each direction. There were lots of bushes and trees growing along the opposite shore at the base of the cliff, all mounded with snow but with no exit point that I could see where McKay could have left the stream. There were no tire tracks on the sandy bottom that I could detect. My gut told me the rippling water had already erased them.

Trampling footprints led me up a high hill behind the stream. I drove my four-wheeler to the top of the ridge and stopped. I could see a ramshackle building down below. It looked like an old motel. Out here in the middle of nowhere? An old hunting lodge, maybe. I followed the swath of disrupted snow down the hill atop knee-deep drifts. I managed to keep the four-wheeler upright and approached the dilapidated building, which was inundated with footprints of investigating officers. I shut off the ignition and dismounted at one end of the structure. I could hear the stream, wider and faster here, splashing over rocks in its rush to the lake.

Snow looked like surging ocean waves against the north side of the lodge, but the sun had melted a lot of it off the south side. I spent some time searching for tire tracks in the icy mud in case McKay had left the streambed in this vicinity. It looked like the other investigators had, too. McKay could not disappear off the face of the earth. If he'd left a track, I was going to find it.

I stomped packed snow off my boot treads and turned my attention to the lodge itself. One end had been burned to the ground, maybe two or three rooms deep. The remaining rooms were practically destroyed by wind and weather. I found roof cave-ins, broken-out windows, and missing doors. Empty beer bottles and soda cans and dead leaves everywhere. One room had discarded drug syringes and graffiti scribbled on the walls. It looked like someone had riddled the walls with bullet holes, and there was a scorched place on the floor. The place had been used by junkies, all right. An excellent place to shoot up. An even better hunting ground for a psycho after human prey. I wondered if the kids who drank and partied and drowsed in heroin dreams and who left broken bottles and cups littering the ground were in the trash bags we'd found swinging in the trees just over the hill.

I walked from room to room looking for names scrawled on the walls. Maybe it would help us identify victims. And I found plenty, calling cards of human quarry, kids that were young, reckless, experimenting with drugs and alcohol while their parents worried at home.

Brandi luvs Tommy. Bobcats Rock. Tell mom I'm sorry. Heather and Jimmy. Friends 4 Ever. LYLAS, Kimberly S.

LYLAS meant Love you like a sister. I'd seen other girls write the same thing in their junior high notebooks. I was never in one school long enough for anyone to write that about me. Once I even made up some names of friends in case anybody looked at my notebook, which is pretty damn pathetic but it seemed a good idea at the time. I jotted down the names in my notepad to match up with missing persons. Maybe I'd get lucky.

The room on the end looked like a boiler room. Trash

everywhere, sodden cardboard boxes, beer cans, plastic grocery sacks, rotted leaves and branches. It was filthy, but the roof was completely intact, making it darker inside than the other rooms. There was no writing on the walls. No charred traces of bonfires on the floor.

Suddenly claustrophobic, I walked outside and inhaled deeply, letting the fresh air cleanse my mind of the young people who'd frequented this hidden place in the woods and were now probably dead. Somehow I knew they had become McKay's victims, too, just like Classon and Christie and Willie Vines. The sky was overcast again, gloomy, foreboding. I wondered when the weather gods were going to give us a break and move on to Alaska. Lake of the Ozarks had never seen a winter so severe. I wondered if Black's pilot could make it in before another storm hit.

Unfortunately, I missed him. I'd gotten used to him saying that the bad things weren't my fault, that Bud wasn't in intensive care because of me, that McKay hadn't gotten away as slick as a whistle. Sometimes I even believed him. Not at the moment. He'd better get home soon, or I was going to be less than cheerful.

I poked around the place and found nothing suspicious and no indication that McKay had been there. But it was one helluva good place to hide. Probably nobody but a few hardcore drug addicts lucky enough to survive McKay's web knew the place existed. I decided to put in for the county fire department to burn it down for an exercise drill.

I walked around behind the boiler room and looked out over the river to where another high hill rose above the opposite bank. The water gurgled and splashed, oh so happy, and the snow began to drift down as a cardinal took flight in a flash of bright red from an oak branch overhanging the stream. Hey, I was standing in a Christmas card. Hell was just over the hill.

No footprints headed up the rise so the snow cover was Robert Frost pristine and looked like a white Caribbean Sea. I decided to check out the next hollow and see if I could find where McKay drove out of the water. Hey, maybe his four-wheeler could fly, like the bicycles in *ET*.

My four-wheeler couldn't fly, in fact, couldn't even glide, and it wasn't going to make it up the deep, heavy drifts, so I climbed the hill on foot. I slipped and fell a couple of times but used the slender saplings on the slope to pull myself the rest of the way up. Panting with exertion, I stared out over tree-spiked, white-caped hills stretching into the distance. Another beautiful scene but no tracks leading me straight to McKay and an easy bust. No footprints. No nothing. An untouched wilderness where no one had set foot since the last snowfall.

So I stood at the top of the world and rested with my back against a tree. Then in the deep, deep quiet of snow-crusted woods, a faint sound filtered to me, one that definitely did not belong in this isolated wilderness. A child was crying. Nearby. Very faint, the sounds blown to and fro by the rising wind. The anguished wails rippled cold chills up my spine that had nothing to do with icy temperatures.

TWENTY-SIX

I stood up, muscles tight, a sudden dread consuming me. The cries weren't coming from the old lodge. They were ahead, somewhere out in the woods in front of me. I waded through deep snow, fighting my way toward the sound. The farther I moved away from the lodge, the louder and more plaintive the cries became. Had McKay abandoned the abducted kid, Elizabeth, out here? To die alone in the snow? Then I remembered Simon Classon's torturous end and what McKay was capable of. I pushed harder, trudging my way along, my boots and pants crusted hard with snow.

About fifty feet off the crest, moving parallel to the lodge, I saw a tiny wisp of steam drifting out of the ground. It looked like it was coming from some kind of fissure in the rocks, from an underground cavern, maybe. Networks of caves pockmarked this part of Missouri, especially in the hills around the lake, and I struggled toward the opening, pulling out my cell phone and punching in dispatch. I was almost to the hole, still trudging through the drifts, when Jacqee picked up.

"Jacqee, it's Claire. Listen to me carefully, this is serious. I need backup out here at the McKay crime scene ASAP. There's an old building just over the hill from the kill site, and I'm pretty sure Joe McKay might be hiding with the kid in a cave somewhere underground—"

Without a hint of warning my feet suddenly plummeted out from beneath me as I stepped off into a sinkhole hidden by drifting snow. I dropped the phone, desperately grabbing at the ground for anything to hold on to but I shot down through the icy crust and hit the ground hard about twenty feet below. My left ankle turned hard and I felt something give with a blinding burst of pain. I groaned and grabbed my foot, as the collapse triggered an avalanche from the hill above and buried me in a cold, dark grave.

I couldn't breathe. Pure, mindless panic hit me, and I clawed frantically in the snow, digging with both hands until I finally broke through to fresh air. I gulped it in great heaving breaths, my heart hammering. I had burrowed out into pitch blackness, and I used my hands to feel around. Rocks covered the ground, and struggling to pull my legs from the heavy snow, I elbowed my way out in to the darkness and collapsed weakly on my back. I was pretty freaked out, panting hard. I knew I had to get hold of myself and quick. I could not panic.

Okay, think straight, clear your head. Both my ankle and forehead hurt like hell, but I wasn't gonna think about that. I had a cell phone that probably had caved in along with me. Maybe I could dig back into the drifts and find it. I felt for the Maglite clipped to my belt and breathed easier when my hand closed around it. I clicked it on and shined it around me.

I was in a cave, all right. The ceiling was low, about three feet above my head. It was too low for me to stand so I pushed myself to sitting and groaned when I jarred my injured foot. I untied my boot laces and shined the beam on it. It felt like I might have cracked a bone in my foot, twisted my ankle at the very least. I packed some snow around, knowing I needed to bind it up somehow, but there was nothing I could use for a splint, so I'd just have to keep my weight off it as best I could.

I lay down again, feeling a little nauseous and light-headed and shaky from pain. Then I heard the child start up again, her screams echoing from somewhere in the distance. She sounded terrified, and she was underground, too, probably in a connecting cavern. I grit my teeth and sat up and shined the light around. Craggy rock walls loomed dark and shadowy and cobwebby, eerie in the flashlight's beam. Lots of jagged stones were piled around on the ground, and I moved the Maglite slowly over them and around the interior until I found a low opening against the floor that stretched off into darkness. I crawled over to it on my hands and knees and listened to the child's wails reverberate up from somewhere down its length.

It had to be Elizabeth, the missing child, and she was definitely at the other end of the shaft. And that meant McKay was down there with her. But he didn't know I was on to him, not unless he heard the cave-in, which was unlikely. I clamped my jaw against the pain and shined my flashlight down the passage. It was so thick with spiderwebs that I could barely see farther than a couple of feet, but I could still hear the little girl. Chances were the webs were chock-full of poisonous spiders, brown recluses or widows or God knew what, but it looked like I was going to have to go through them to get to the child.

I remembered the can of Raid I'd stowed in my jacket. I took it out and took a few minutes to saturate my jacket and pants. I pulled up my hood, covered my face with one arm and sprayed it all over my head. Oh boy, did I ever *not* want to do this. Okay, deep breath, the spiders won't like the Raid, will probably scamper away and hide and think you're their worst enemy. They're more afraid of you than you are of them. Right.

I focused the bright beam inside the passage. It was a tight squeeze, just big enough for me to squirm through. What if I got stuck inside? What if it was a dead end and I was trapped where I couldn't move? That thought sent a barrage of goose bumps rippling my flesh but I could still hear the child's frenzied screams echoing up to me. On top of that I didn't have any other choice except to sit in this cold black hole and hope my fellow officers arrived at the scene, decided to follow my snow trail up the hill to the fissure and dig me out of the avalanche with their bare hands. And if I did wait to be rescued, McKay might decide in the meantime to kill the little girl with his widows and recluses, while I sat and listened to it go down at the other end of this nice, long, spider-infested tunnel. He might be doing that right now. That might be the reason she was crying so hard. So there you go. Decision made.

"Man, does this ever suck," I muttered under my breath then added a couple of obscenities I rarely ever used but that this occasion definitely called for. I took the can of Raid and sprayed it over the thick mass of webs hanging at the mouth of the tunnel, big-time encouraged when a rather large black widow ran like hell across her fancy web and out of sight. Good sign. Encouraging, but not enough to stop the great big shudder convulsing my body. I knocked down as many sticky webs as I could with my flashlight and started a slow combat crawl through the tight opening. I could hear my own breathing, and it sounded like a marathon runner having an asthma attack. It sounded scared as hell, too.

Webs were massed around everywhere, hanging down, the sticky strands adhering to my face and hood and flashlight as I forced myself through them. The spiders kept skittering away from me and my light, thank God, probably wishing I was more like Little Miss Muffet. It occurred to me that this tunnel could be McKay's incubator for future arachnid assassins in training. His own private spider-breeding farm. I wondered what else he was breeding and thought of Egyptian fat-tailed scorpions. The shudders commenced again until I shoved that ghastly picture out of my mind, moving slowly and spraying the webs in front of me, my eyes burning as I pulled my shirt up over my nose and mouth and tried not to choke on the caustic fumes.

After about ten feet of hell on earth, I could see a dim

light ahead of me. The spiders were still fleeing the Raid so I increased my pace, knocking the webs away, killing as many of them as I could with the flashlight, getting panicky again. The narrow tunnel felt like it was closing in on me, and I had to get out! I couldn't stand it!

I crawled faster and finally wriggled bodily out of the passage into a small cavern. I went up on my knees, shivering and shaking and beating sticky webs out of my hair and off my clothes and hoping to God I hadn't gotten bitten. I hadn't felt anything, but my research had told me that victims rarely felt the bite of a recluse. I forced myself to sit still and conquer my revulsion and fear. Okay, you're out, you did it, nothing ahead of you could be worse than crawling through that horrible place. I hoped.

The ceiling was high enough for me to walk, bent over. My flashlight beam illuminated another passage that descended deeper underground. I braced one hand on the wall, unzipped my parka, and pulled the Glock out of my shoulder holster. I disengaged the safety and limped down the tunnel, gun and flashlight trained toward the child's voice.

The deeper I went, the warmer the temperature became. The air felt close and damp and fetid, earthy like that in a reptile house, and smelled of sulfur and rotting flesh. There was a corpse somewhere nearby; I'd worked enough homicides to recognize the sickening-sweet odor of decomposition.

I swung my light around in the darkness in front of me. The odor became stronger the closer I got to the body. I stopped when I finally found it. It was a woman. She was dressed in a pink shirt and white denim skirt. She was lying on top of a military sleeping bag, one exactly like the one we found Simon Classon inside of. The body had been decomposing for quite a while, but I saw the woman's blond ponytail tied up with pink-and-white-striped ribbons. There were spiderwebs in her hair and on her clothes.

I moved closer to the victim, holding on to the wall for support. She held flowers in her hands. Fresh flowers. White lilies. Somebody had been visiting her recently. There were glass votives sitting around the body, the candles inside half burned down. Framed pictures of angels similar to the ones I'd seen over Simon Classon's staircase were propped against the walls near her. I moved my light beam along the walls and found candle holders and kerosene lamps hung above the body. I backed away from it and stumbled across something and almost fell. I caught myself on the wall and put my light on another decaying body, this one more recently dead and half covered with dirt. I put my parka up over my nose and mouth and moved past the two corpses and farther down the passage, holding on to the wall for support.

The stone wall was cold and jagged where I braced my palm but I hardly felt the pain in my foot anymore. Instead I concentrated on all the danger signals going off in my mind as I approached a large round hole opening out into yet another cavern. I was very close to the little girl now.

I crept the rest of the way, careful not to kick the rocks. I sure didn't want anybody arranging a welcoming party for me. At the opening I stopped and searched the interior. It was a huge cavern, and high above in the domed ceiling sunlight slanted down from a narrow fissure in the rock, illuminating everything in a smoky, surreal dusk. I stowed my Maglite in the pocket of my parka and steadied the Glock with both hands.

I could see a hot spring bubbling up out in the middle. Plumes of warm mist rose over the surface and made the air hot and humid. Glass tanks and old fish aquariums sat around everywhere, crammed full of snakes and spiders and other horrible things. A nearby case was long and rectangular, and held what looked like human remains partially covered in arachnid silk. I could see the spiders creeping around inside. My skin crawled. I swallowed down intense aversion. What kind of monster's den was this? What heinous acts had been perpetrated in this hidden, subterranean hell? I was shaken to the core and fighting hard to get over it.

I peered through the gloom. Nothing moved but spiders

and scorpions and snakes trapped inside their cages. I could hear muted rustles and scratching, like the sounds I'd heard coming from inside Christie Foxworthy's trunk. The child was quiet now, and I wondered why. I hesitated, searching the murky interior of the cave for a way outside. There were maybe half a dozen intersecting tunnels leading off the main dome, all dark and deserted and draped with webs. All I had to do was figure out which one was the right one.

I took a cautious step between the nearest cages and almost jumped out of my skin when a huge rattlesnake struck at me, its fangs hitting the side of its tank and sending rivulets of venom sheeting down the glass. I stumbled back, weapon trained on it and backed into another aquarium containing a huge black widow. It seemed to watch me malevolently as it swayed back and forth in its tangled web.

"Hey! Who's there? Help me, help!"

It was a man's voice, loud and scared, apparently alerted by the noise I'd just made. It came from the other end of the cavern, and I quickly pivoted my weapon in that direction. The voice was familiar, but I couldn't place it. It wasn't McKay. I limped slowly through dozens of ugly, nasty glass tanks full of ugly, nasty creatures. Leading with my gun, I hoped to hell Jacqee had alerted back up and they were outside searching for me.

I could hear the child again. Whimpering now as the man continued to yell for help. Then everything went silent again. No sound. As if all the spiders and snakes were poised and holding their breaths, just waiting for a chance to jump out and get me. Every nerve and fiber in my body was screaming *turn, run, get out, flee*, but I forced myself to move deeper into McKay's little cave of horrors. As I left the rows of tanks and reached a wide empty area beside the spring, I saw the little girl. She was standing up in a heavy packing crate that sat on the ground near the water. She was holding on to the top of the crate and resting her forehead on her hands. She was sobbing.

I remained where I was and searched the cave again for

McKay. He could be hiding anywhere among the shadowy tables crowding the walls. I was expecting him to show up any minute. He'd been in the Marines; he was trained in combat, Special Ops, no less. I couldn't let him get the jump on me. I kept my gun out in front, my finger on the trigger. I could feel my heart thudding hard against my breastbone.

Slowly, cautiously, still swiveling my weapon from side to side, I made my way to the little girl. She had on pink fleece pajamas that zipped up the front, the kind with feet in them. She didn't see me until I knelt beside her. Then she raised her face and let out a short, shrill shriek, lurched backward away from me, and sat down hard. There was a fresh bruise on her cheek.

"It's okay, baby. It's okay. I'm here now," I whispered, my eyes still searching my surroundings. It shocked me when she suddenly flew at me, grabbed hold, and clenched her arms around my neck. I lifted her out of the box, and she clung trembling to me as if she'd never let go. She felt little and frail and solid and smelled of milk, and for one shining moment she became Zach, in my arms again, his small arms holding on to me so tightly, calling me Mommy. I'd not been around any small children since Zach died, and I felt a singular kind of joy, a fading memory that disappeared abruptly when the man screamed again from somewhere off to my right.

"Help me! Help me! I know somebody's out there! Hurry, hurry, you gotta cut me loose!"

The child would not let go and clutched me in a near stranglehold. I murmured soothing words and shifted the baby onto my left hip as I focused my aim toward the man's voice. It had sounded like Willie Vines. Alive. Panic-stricken. But Willie was dead. Or was he?

I searched the darkness hugging the walls and edged slowly toward the place where the voice was still calling for help, keeping my back against the wall. I needed to put down the baby but I couldn't bring myself to do it. She was terrified, shaking all over. I'd have to pry her out of my arms.

Then I saw him, and was shocked to the core that it really was Willie. His wrists were bound together and tied up over his head to an iron hook hammered into the wall. He was bleeding from the scalp. Blood ran down his face and into the neck of his white T-shirt.

"Oh, thank God, thank God you came!" Willie cried. He burst into tears, his sobs echoing around the domed cavern.

I was more interested in the other person bound to the wall a few feet away from him. A woman. She stared wide-eyed at me as I moved closer but she didn't move, didn't say a word. Her eyes looked glazed, as if she were in shock. I recognized her at once by the red pigtails. Wilma Harte, the girl who had disappeared from the academy. Again I felt threatened, deep in danger, like I was standing in the jaws of a bear trap. I stopped and listened. I heard nothing. No sign of McKay.

Willie started to twist against the ropes, still blubbering. "Please, please. Cut us down. McKay's gonna come back and kill us."

My intuition was screaming so loud now that I shivered with dread. At the sound of Willie's voice, the little girl began to whimper. Nothing looked right about this. Something was very wrong. "Where's McKay?"

Willie became agitated again and twisted frantically against the ropes. "I don't know! He took off but he said he's gonna kill us. We gotta get outta here before he comes back."

I kept my weapon trained dead center on Willie's chest. This man was supposed to be dead. And if he wasn't, who the hell's body had been butchered beyond recognition inside his house on New Year's Eve? I wasn't about to cut him down, not yet. "That's Wilma Harte, right?"

"Yes, yes, McKay's had her down here all along. He's done awful things to her. She hasn't said a word but just stares with that awful expression. Please, you gotta help us!"

The sulphuric fumes from the hot spring were making me sweat, making me feel a little sick to my stomach, but I had bigger problems to worry about. "Did McKay hit the baby?"

"Oh God, yes, it was awful. He slapped her when she wouldn't stop crying. He's crazy, I tell you. He bragged about killing Simon and Christie and lots of other people!"

"We found a mutilated body in your house last night. Dressed in your clothes. Who was it, Willie? Why would McKay want us to think you were dead?"

"I don't know. There was a girl who watched the kid. Maybe he killed her, too. He likes killing, I tell you. He knew I was gonna tell you the truth and he followed me home. Hit me over the head and when I woke up, I was down here with Wilma. This is where he tortures people and he's coming back! Cut us down, cut us down!"

I wasn't sure what to believe. I held on to the baby and moved slowly to my right, still searching for McKay. I knew he was here, somewhere. Plastic trays, maybe four feet by five, were full of spiders and sitting around on the ground, lots of them. It looked like the spiders had been killing and eating each other. Dead ones littered the bottom. When I was sure McKay wasn't hiding in close range, I found the rope securing Wilma's arms and set her free. She dropped like a sack of sand to the ground and curled up in a fetal position.

I moved around to Willie. He was getting close to hysteria now. I didn't trust him one bit. I didn't believe a word he said. I put the child on the ground and pulled out my handcuffs. Elizabeth grabbed hold of my leg and wouldn't let go. She was whimpering and hiding her face against my knee. I released Willie's arms but kept the gun trained on his chest as he fell to his knees. He massaged his bruised wrists and stared up at me. "You gotta believe me, he's sick in the head. He'll kill you. He'll kill all of us, including that poor little baby."

"Hold it right there, Claire. Don't move a muscle."

McKay's voice, behind me. I whirled around, not sure where he'd come from. He was standing about six feet away. He had a brick of C-4 explosives in one hand. He held what looked like a TV remote control in his other hand, but I knew what it was. A remote detonator. He was going to blow up the cave. I took a step backward where I could keep my eyes on both men. I held my weapon on McKay. My voice sounded calmer than I felt.

"Get down on your knees, McKay. Right now."

He shook his head. "You're making a big mistake, Claire. They're the ones you're after, I swear to God. Willie's been killing people for years and hanging them out there in the trees, and now she's helping him. I'm trying to stop it. That's why they're tied up. I'm going to blow up this hellhole and everything in it."

I backed off a couple more steps, where I could hold all of three of them in my gun sights, pivoting my weapon from McKay to Willie to Wilma, not sure now who to believe. Wilma was cowering against the wall, covering her head with both arms.

Willie took a step toward me, his voice pleading. "He's lying. I haven't done nothin' like that. I was gonna tell you about him that night after the gala when I called you. I was gonna tell you how he'd come back here after he got out of the Marines and started killing people again. You heard him. He's gonna leave me and Wilma down here and then blow the place up!"

Then McKay moved closer, still holding the detonator. He was a big guy, trained to kill. I kept my weapon pointed at him. "Don't come any closer, McKay. I'll shoot you if you give me a reason. Put the explosives down. Now."

Very slowly McKay placed both the explosive and detonator on the ground. His eyes never left mine. His voice was as soothing as Willie's was frantic. "Listen to me, Detective. You cannot let Willie go. He's the killer you're looking for. You gotta believe me."

"Yeah, right. And I guess he stole this little girl from your neighbor out in California, too. I know all about the Amber Alert that went out on her. Get your hands behind your back. You've got a child abduction warrant out on you, and I'm taking you in."

"You got it all wrong, Claire. Elizabeth's my daughter. I

didn't know about her until I opted out of the Corps. Her mother and I were together for a while but she got into drugs after I left on my last tour. Now she's a crackhead and lets her new boyfriend abuse my kid. That's why I took her. And I won't let her go back to that kind of life." He stopped speaking and glanced at Willie. So did I. Willie had not moved. Then McKay said, "Claire, if you let Willie go, he'll kill us both in the worst way imaginable. He'll kill Elizabeth, too. Let me tie him up again, then you can decide which of us is telling the truth."

"No way. I'm taking both of you in and we'll figure out later who did what. For all I know you're in on this together. Now get down on your belly, both of you, and spread 'em! Now! Do it!" Both of them looked guilty to me, and I'd feel a helluva lot better once I got them cuffed and on the ground. I glanced at the woman. She hadn't moved. She was making muffled moans.

I cuffed McKay first, hands behind his back, and he turned his face toward me as he lay on his stomach. "You're making a big mistake, Claire. You're gonna get us both killed."

"Please, don't believe him. I've been afraid of him since I was a kid," Willie cried. "He's evil, sick in the head. I thought he was gone for good when he joined the Marines, but then he came back and started following me everywhere and pretending to be my friend. He wants to kill me, you heard him."

Now that McKay was cuffed, I felt more in control. He was too strong, too dangerous to take any chances with. I could handle somebody of Willie's size better. I said, "Get on your knees, Willie, and put your arms behind your back."

Willie dived to his left so quickly I couldn't get a shot off. He darted in behind a glass tank teeming with small black scorpions.

"Stop, Willie, or I'll shoot!" But I couldn't shoot him without shattering the tanks of snakes sitting all over the place. I could hear him moving behind the tables and limped after him. Elizabeth let go of my leg and ran and threw herself down on McKay. I followed Willie's movements with my weapon.

McKay had scrabbled up on his knees now, Elizabeth clinging to his neck. "Uncuff me, uncuff me, goddamn it! You don't have any idea what he's capable of!"

Willie's voice called out from behind a glass case writhing with copperheads. "Better not shoot down here, Claire. A ricochet'll dump out all kind of trouble."

"Guess again, Vines. I'd rather take my chances with snakes than with you. Step out here where I can see you."

"Behind you, Claire," McKay yelled.

I whirled around just in time to see Wilma Harte about ten feet away. She was holding some kind of blowgun to her lips. Something stung my thigh, and I pulled the trigger, then jerked the small dart out of my leg. My bullet shattered a case of rattlesnakes, and the reptiles hit the floor in a slithering, clicking mass. I backed away from the snakes. Elizabeth started screaming and pressed herself against McKay.

I edged left toward McKay, fumbling for the key to the cuffs, searching for movement among the tables. Both Wilma and Vines had disappeared into the shadows, and I was already feeling the effect of whatever drug had tipped the dart. I stumbled toward McKay with the key, fighting the dizziness assailing me. I couldn't see straight, couldn't maintain balance. I fell to my knees and tried to toss the key toward McKay. It hit the floor near his feet, then I went down onto my side, the Glock slipping from numb fingers. The last thing I heard was Wilma's voice, echoing strangely and hauntingly in my ears.

"Uriel, we got them now, both of them! I get to kill her! You can have McKay. . . ."

Dark Angels

Uriel trained Claire Morgan's gun on McKay while Wilma bound his feet tightly together. McKay deserved to die, but Uriel didn't know what to do about the detective. He looked at her, where she lay immobilized by his tranquilizer dart. He was scared of her. He had feared her ever since she had told him that the Archangel Michael protected her. He had seen the special silver medal hanging around her neck. What if Michael came to avenge what they'd done to her and brought down God's wrath? And he and Wilma had killed Gabriel, too. He shut his eyes, stifling a sob in the back of his throat. Gabriel had died the most horrible death, and Uriel had done it to him, his own blood brother. What if the Archangel Gabriel joined up with the Archangel Michael to punish him?

Oh God, he felt sick inside, desperate and afraid. He had let Wilma talk him into killing Gabriel. It was all Wilma's fault, and now he was so sorry, so very sorry he'd done it. Gabriel would've still been alive if it weren't for Wilma. She'd messed up everything. She had convinced him to clobber Gabriel in the head and stuff him into that sleeping bag with all those recluses, then hang him in a tree where he could see the academy. And Uriel had done it, all of it. For her. Because she'd told him that she loved him better than Gabriel ever could. And because Gabriel was going to kill her, and Uriel couldn't bear that either.

God help him, he missed Gabriel so much he could barely stand it. And now Wilma was always playing loud heavy-metal music in the cave and talking about the devil and painting pentagrams on the floor so she could try to conjure evil spirits. The archangels were probably furious with him. Even his namesake, Uriel. He watched Wilma grab Claire Morgan's coat and drag her toward a spider tank. Wilma wasn't trembling and faking fear anymore. Now she was laughing out loud, all excited. But she didn't know the power of the archangels and what Michael might do if they harmed the detective.

"Stop, Wilma, let go of her. How many times I gotta tell you that we can't hurt her? The Archangel Michael protects her. She told me so herself. She showed me her medallion."

Wilma dropped the detective to the ground. "Oh, Willie, don't be so stupid. She doesn't have angels protecting her or she wouldn't be lying here helpless. You've got to quit with all this angel mumbo jumbo. We gotta kill them, and you know it. All of them, just like Simon. You told me if I joined up with you I could send people to heaven, too."

"I told you not to call him Simon any more. Call him Gabriel like I do. That's his name, and call me Uriel."

Wilma sighed. "Oh, whatever. I know what, you can call me Lucifer. Lucy for short." She laughed.

"Lucifer's a fallen angel. You shouldn't compare yourself to him. That's sacrilegious and you'll be punished."

"Well, it was your precious Gabriel who taught me all about the fallen angels in his stupid angelology class."

Her retort infuriated Uriel. He loved Wilma, he loved her, loved having sex with her. She'd helped him when Joe McKay came back and was following them everywhere they went and telling them he knew Gabriel and Uriel had killed his little brother, Freddy. And it had been Wilma who'd bludgeoned Christie over the head at Stuart Rowland's house. They had been lying in wait for Stuart. Stuart had been the one who had pointed the detectives in Uriel's direction and accused him of dealing drugs. Stuart was supposed to die in that trunk with the scorpions, not Christie. But then Christie showed up unexpectedly to get back the devil mask she'd given to Stuart, and Wilma had knocked her on the head before Uriel could stop her. She said she hated Christie and accused her of flirting with Uriel, but that wasn't true.

It seemed that once Uriel had introduced Wilma to killing, she had wanted to kill everybody, had liked it a lot, even more than he did. She acted crazy and said she was sending people to hell instead of heaven. She talked about the devil all the time and stole people's pets and sacrificed them. She'd wanted to sacrifice the detective's little white dog but Uriel wouldn't let her. Truthfully, she had begun to frighten Uriel. He feared she might be in league with Satan and that the Archangel Michael would smite him down for being with her.

Joe McKay was yelling at him now from where he lay bound on his side. "Willie, Willie, listen to me, you've got to think this through. Claire's too good a cop to come in here alone without calling for backup. And if she did, the cops'll know where you are and they're gonna swarm all over this place. If you and Wilma kill a police officer, every cop in the state's gonna hunt you down. Let us go, and you and Wilma can take off now while you still can."

Uriel considered what McKay had said. He had always been scared of McKay, too, from the very beginning, back when he was a little orphan boy, right after his family had been killed in the car crash. Then McKay had come back and watched their every move. Soon McKay got involved with the detectives, helping them find Gabriel's murderer, leading them closer and closer to Willie. That's when they had to kill his babysitter and steal his kid so he'd back off. But McKay was smart enough to follow them to the cave and watch how they got inside. Nobody had ever done that before. That's how he got the jump on them and tied them up. If Claire Morgan hadn't shown up, he and Wilma both'd probably have been blown to smithereens by now. They owed the detective for that much.

Uriel said, "They ain't gonna find us down here, no way, McKay. The detective didn't come in through the boiler room or I would've seen her. She came down one of the tunnels. Gabriel and me hid out down here for going on twenty years, and nobody's ever found the way down until you followed me."

"Yeah? But you and Simon never offed a cop, either, did you, Willie? The whole force is probably outside right now, searching for her. Don't kid yourself. They won't stop until they find her."

Wilma jumped up angrily and walked over to McKay. "Shut up, McKay. You don't know shit about what we've done. If you hadn't come back here and stuck your nose in our business, nobody ever would've found out about us." She turned back to Uriel. "Hey, Uriel, maybe we oughta just kill her now and throw her body outside where they can find her. Then they'll think we're long gone."

McKay struggled to his knees, his little girl clinging to his neck. "You're a damn fool if you listen to her, Willie. She's the one who got you to kill Simon, isn't she? He'd still be alive if it wasn't for her. You miss him, don't you? You've been best friends ever since you moved here, and now he's dead. I bet it was her idea to put him in that sleeping bag, too, right? Bet you wouldn't have tortured him like that."

Uriel felt tears welling up again, hot, burning. It was true. Everything he'd said was true. Wilma saw that he was getting all broken up about Gabriel, and she came over and pressed her body up against him and rubbed around on his loins. She always did that when he began to miss Gabriel and then they'd make love and he'd feel better. She rubbed her hand over his chest and spoke to McKay, "Guess what, McKay? None of this would've ever happened if it weren't for your stupid little brother, Freddy. He was the first one

Gabriel and Uriel killed together. And you know what else? It was an accident, they really didn't even mean to. But afterward, Uriel says they were glad they did, because he was a little jerk. He pushed Uriel into his mother's grave, so he deserved to die."

Uriel shut his eyes, remembering how he'd felt that day so long ago when he was down in his mother's grave and Freddy was shoveling dirt in on him. Gabriel had saved him that day, loved him like a brother, taken care of him.

McKay fought his bonds, his face twisted with rage. "Willie, you bastard. I always knew you and Simon Classon did it. Even back then, right after it happened, when the two of you were always hanging around and whispering together in church. I just couldn't prove it. And I saw that old lodge in my dreams, night after night, and I knew it had something to do with Freddy's death. That's why I tried to burn it down."

"Yeah, we knew you suspected us. But you fucked up when you put that snake in Gabriel's grade book. And you fucked up now, too. You shouldn't never have come back here again after all this time. Now you're a dead man, and so's that little girl over there you stole from her mother. And so is the detective. We're gonna get outta here and leave you down here to rot, the lot of you. Nobody's ever gonna find you."

Wilma was looking at Uriel now, her face disappointed. "Oh, c'mon, Uriel, let's put them in with the spiders before we leave. They deserve it. And if they get loose, they'll be witnesses against us and we'll have to go to jail. Then we can't be together any more. That's why we killed Simon, remember? To be together forever."

Uriel remembered and it cut him straight through his heart. "We never, ever should've done that. I miss him too much. He taught me everything I know. You shouldn't have made me do it. He didn't deserve to suffer like that. I don't know why I let you talk me into it."

"Because he was going to murder me, that's why. He told you to kill me or he was going to, just like he did that other girlfriend that you keep in that tunnel over there. He was jealous because you loved me better'n him. But we showed him, didn't we, we really turned the tables that night when you took me to his house. He never saw it coming, never knew you were going to kill him instead of me."

Uriel said nothing. Everything she'd said was true. But he still missed Gabriel. He watched Wilma go over and jerk the child away from McKay.

Now McKay's voice sounded desperate. "Willie, don't let Wilma hurt Elizabeth. She's just a baby. She can't identify you. Please, I'm begging you, drop her off somewhere safe, at a hospital, anywhere, just don't hurt her."

Uriel smiled. "So now it's you doin' the begging, McKay? You were going to kill us. Were you gonna show us any mercy? Uh-uh. So why should we care about savin' your kid?"

"The angels won't like it if you kill an innocent baby. You think they'll go easy on you if you hurt her?"

That gave Uriel pause. He hesitated, not sure how he could get himself out of such a big mess. Wilma grabbed his arm.

"Hey, Uriel, we don't have to kill the kid. Maybe we'll just take her along with us and make her our new little protégé. That's what you said I was, right? How would you like that, McKay? Us teaching little Elizabeth there all about spiders and snakes. She'll grow up thinking we're her mommy and daddy. She'll want to be just like us. Wouldn't that be cool?"

Uriel looked at the child. He liked that idea a lot. He'd always wanted to have a family. They could get married, and nobody'd ever know Elizabeth wasn't their own child. He smiled. Maybe Wilma was right, after all.

TWENTY-SEVEN

I could hear their voices. I was vaguely aware of what was going on around me but my vision was blurry. I lay on the ground but couldn't move my arms and legs. I felt numb all over. It sounded like Wilma and Willie were arguing, and the child, Elizabeth, was screaming, a shrill, terrible sound. I fought to open my eyes and finally was able to focus on the scene before me. Willie was standing very close. Wilma was shaking the little girl, yelling at her to stop crying, and McKay was up on his knees on the ground, handcuffed, his feet bound, trying to make Wilma stop.

Then in the distance, faint and faraway, a gun was fired. Everybody froze. I shut my eyes. My backup was outside, looking for me. It was a matter of time before they found us.

"Wilma, you stay here and keep an eye on them. I'm gonna make sure they haven't found their way in. And don't hurt them, you hear me, don't hurt them, especially the detective!"

Willie ran past me toward one of the tunnels, and then suddenly Wilma was directly over me, grinning down into my face.

"Know what, Detective, I don't believe you've got any

archangels protecting you, not for one single second. But we'll soon see, won't we? Maybe I can prove to Willie once and for all that you're not invincible."

She grabbed the hood of my parka and drug me toward the tanks. I still couldn't move my muscles, had little feeling in my arms and legs. She stopped beside a big tank sitting on its side, and I heard a latch click. Then she rolled me over into the tank on my side and closed the side panel. I could see McKay through the dirty glass. He was on his back, trying to get the handcuff keys while Wilma was busy with me.

I tried to shake myself awake and make sense of what was going on. The drug was wearing off, and my mind was clearing. I could move a little now. I shifted my head and realized the side of my face was resting against a soft padding of cobwebs. Oh God, I was in a spiders' nest.

I struggled to move arms that felt like lead weights. Above me in the glass lid were holes about the size of quarters. I couldn't see any spiders or scorpions, but I knew something was already in there with me.

Then Wilma loomed over me. I could see her innocent-looking face staring down at me. "Willie likes you, Detective, thinks you're special because of that stupid medallion you wear. He thinks you're pretty and smart, but guess what? I don't like you, and I don't like the way Willie treats you. I gave up everything for him. So I've got to get rid of you or you'll end up arresting us. So, darlin', if you've got a special lifeline up to the clouds and the Archangel Michael, you better use it now."

I tried to speak but nothing came out.

"That's right. You ain't gonna be able to talk for a while, you know. Willie tipped these darts with just the right amount of poison. He and Simon practiced shooting darts and arrows on lots of people to get just the right dose. They're all dead now, 'cause Willie says if you get too much it stops the heart, but you only got enough to paralyze you. It'll wear off but you'll probably wish it didn't."

My arms and legs were tingling. Maybe I'd diminished

the effect of the drug when I jerked the dart out so fast. I shut my eyes. Just hang on for Charlie and the guys. They'll be here, all I had to do was hang on.

I tried to remain calm. I was in a bad spot, all right, but I was okay, just temporarily immobilized. There was a chance McKay would get the cuffs off, and if there were spiders in with me, already biting, I couldn't feel them. I still had the Raid sprayed on my clothes. I thought about Simon Classon, and other victims hung up in black plastic bags, and wondered if they'd started out in this same glass tank.

I watched Wilma move away and pick up a big rock. McKay was back up on his knees, working to unlock the cuffs behind his back. He was watching her, too. Willie was nowhere to be seen. Wilma moved up behind McKay, and when she raised the rock over his head, he tried to evade her but couldn't get away. He took the blow in the back of his head and went over on his face like a downed tree. He didn't move again. Elizabeth started screaming and clung to his lifeless body, and I knew he was out for the count. If either of us was to get out of this place alive, it was now up to me.

I still had the .38 snub-nosed strapped on my ankle. I could feel the weight of it. I just had to figure out how to contort my body enough to reach it. Wilma's face appeared directly above me. Her freckled face and red pigtails made her look young and harmless. Pippi Longstocking from hell. She spoke conversationally, as if I'd come to visit and we were having a real good time. "Simon, I mean, Gabriel, you know, I just can't get used to calling him Gabriel. Anyways, he was inside this very same tank. We knocked him out at his house and brought him down here. He lasted almost an hour without getting bit but then he went all hysterical and started slapping at the recluses, even though he raised them and knew all about them and what made them bite."

Wilma glanced toward the tunnel where Willie had disappeared. "Willie hit him first but he couldn't bear to hurt him anymore, so I had to do it. Simon deserved it. He treated me like dirt for months out at the academy, tried to get me fired, and then told Willie to kill me. But I got the last laugh, didn't I? Wanna see the games I played with him?"

I twitched my fingers slightly to see if they worked. They did but without much sensation. Wilma loomed over me again.

"Look up here, Detective. This here is a great big black widow spider." She held it up for me to see. It was in a small glass test tube. "We gotta get this done pretty quick if you got backup comin' down here, but I'm not gonna kill you right out. I'm gonna give you a fighting chance to get found before you die because I liked the way you and that other guy, Bud, bought Willie that cheeseburger and let him eat with the other kids in the cafeteria. Willie felt real bad about how Bud got bit by that rattler I put in your picnic basket. Yeah, that was too bad. Willie said Bud's a good guy. And he wasn't putting pressure on Willie and me the way you was. You just had to keep coming around and asking Willie nosy questions."

Wilma looked around. "I sure hate to leave this cave. We've had lots of fun down here. Now when I drop this little lady down in there with you, don't you move a muscle. Got that? Maybe you'll live long enough for the other officers to get here, if you do what I say."

I took a deep breath and waited. As if one spider was going to make me faint. Hell, I just crawled through a tunnel full of spiders. No way one bite was going to kill me. They'd done worse stuff than this on *Fear Factor*. I kept my eyes on McKay where he lay on the ground. He had not moved; blood was pooling on the ground underneath his head. Elizabeth was squatted down beside him, no longer crying, her wide blue eyes watching silently, as if she knew something horrible was going to happen.

Okay, okay. It's just a little black widow spider. But it wasn't little. It was over an inch long, shiny and black and deadly. I tried to remember what I'd found out about them on the Internet. They weren't as deadly as brown recluses, but they were dangerous. I think it said a person could die without proper medical treatment. But I'd get that, as soon as I shot my way out of this glass box and put a couple of slugs between Wilma Harte's eyes.

"Oooookay, Detective Morgan, here we go. Let's see if you got more guts than that awful Simon did. He begged and begged at the end after we got him down here. But I showed him not to mess with me."

Wilma chose a hole right above my stomach, upended the vial and dumped the huge spider on me. I watched it bounce off my parka, and every fiber, every muscle of my body screamed to shrink away, to brush it off, stomp on it, get it off me. I didn't. I shut my eyes. If I can't see it, it's not there. Let the Raid handle it. Remember yoga, I'm someplace else, someplace faraway and nice and safe, one with the universe, one with the spider.

"I wonder if you'll lie so still if I put in another one? What do you think? Wanna make a bet?" Wilma the Witch, at her most charming.

Wilma rushed off, then she was back. Holding up another glass test tube. "This here one's a brown recluse. I think they're the prettiest things. So did Gabriel before we killed him. Uriel said they used them on lots of people when they were kids. Wonder how Willie's pretty detective's gonna do now? This one's a bit cantankerous. He bites sometimes even when you don't move. And you won't even feel it. It can bite you a hundred times, and you won't know where until it starts hurtin' and rottin' out the skin. Pretty awesome, huh?"

She chose a hole just above my chest and dropped a spider the size of a silver dollar onto my breast. God, surely I wasn't going to die like Simon Classon did, here in this hidden cave with a couple of homicidal maniacs, my body paralyzed, spiders crawling all over me. Somehow, some way, I remained calm, trying to force my muscles to move while I kept my eyes on the big brown recluse. It stood where it landed for a few seconds, as if undecided where to go. Then it got a whiff of the Raid and couldn't get off me fast enough. Hell, I was going to write a thank-you note to the Raid company when I got out of there.

I heard gunshots, closer now, and I knew this wouldn't go on much longer. I just had to stay alive until they forced their way in. Then Willie was back. He was furious, his face was flushed red. "I told you not to hurt her, damn it. I told you! She's protected. We can't fight against the Archangel Michael. He's stronger than Uriel and Gabriel and all the rest of the archangels put together. Gabriel told me so."

"It don't look like he's doin' much to help her at the moment." Wilma laughed. "To hell with the archangels. They can't do anything—"

It happened so fast I could barely believe it. Willie had my service weapon in his hand and pressed up against Wilma's temple. "That's blasphemy. And you're a blasphemer. You're not what I thought you were. You made me kill Gabriel, and he loved me."

Wilma's eyes were scared now, her voice shaking. "I'm so sorry, baby. I'll get her out of there, if you want. C'mon, let's go. We'll take the baby, and get clean away. I'll do whatever you say."

Willie took the gun down from her temple but he was sobbing and pointing the gun at Wilma's chest. Oh, God, he's wigging out. He's going to kill her then he'll panic and shoot all of us. I wrenched my body as hard as I could down toward my feet, nearly pulling my arm out of its socket as I struggled to reach my ankle holster. Elizabeth was screaming for her daddy, and Willie was screaming for her to shut up. He turned the gun on her, and I strained until my forefinger finally hooked the handle of the .38. I jerked it out, got my finger on the trigger, and held it down. The slugs shattered the case into a million pieces of glass, and I rolled out, barely feeling the jagged shards tearing my clothes and slicing my skin. Willie fired at me but the shots went over my head. He grabbed Elizabeth and headed for the tunnel with her. Wilma snatched up McKay's detonator and took off after him. I stood and fired a quick round at her but the bullet hit the wall and ricocheted off the rocks and shattered a couple of glass tanks. I knelt beside McKay and unlocked his cuffs. He was conscious but groggy and moving slow. I desperately worked to loosen the rope binding his feet.

"McKay! McKay, get up! They've got Elizabeth. We gotta stop them!"

I knew I didn't have time to wait on him so I left him there, struggling unsteadily to his feet while I took off into the dark tunnel after Willie and Wilma. Inside the passage, I kept low, weapon ready to fire. Elizabeth was screaming somewhere up ahead, giving me a way to follow. I stopped for a second and leaned against the wall. I only had a couple of bullets left in my gun, and I dug desperately through my pockets, wanting to reload before I faced them. I found only the 9-mm clips. No .38 caliber shells. I grabbed my flashlight and hurried after them but soon heard the echo of running feet in the passage. I couldn't tell what direction the footsteps were coming from. I pressed myself against the wall and almost blew McKay away when he lunged into sight.

"Where's Elizabeth? Who's got her?"

"Willie's got her up ahead. And Wilma's got the detonator."

He took off ahead of me and I shined the light ahead of us as the shaft twisted and turned its way upward in a gradual ascent. We followed the sounds of Elizabeth's screams and minutes later we caught sight of them. I took aim when my flashlight illuminated Willie but he turned around, holding the struggling, screaming baby in front of him.

"Go ahead, shoot, but you'll hit the kid!" he screamed.

Then he darted left into the darkness and Wilma went right. She had the detonator in her hand. We ran to where they parted company.

"I'm going after Elizabeth," McKay shouted. "You get the detonator before Wilma blows the place."

He took off, and I ran into the darkness after the girl. I could hear her ahead of me, running on the loose rocks. She knew the tunnels better than I did but I couldn't let her get outside first. She was crazy; she'd blow the place with all of us inside. The ground began to descend again, and I realized she was leading me back down toward the domed cavern.

I finally took a turn into a larger tunnel that was partially lighted from cracks up above and saw Wilma just ahead at the base of a ladder. She swung herself up the rungs and disappeared from sight. I hit the ladder right behind her and pulled myself out into the boiler room of the old lodge. I stopped in the doorway as she ran toward the woods, slipping and sliding on the icy snow. I braced my weapon with both hands.

"Stop right there, Wilma, or I'll shoot."

I fired a warning round over her head, and she spun toward me, holding the detonator out in front of her. "You do, and I'll press the button. I will."

"You'll blow up Willie if you do. You don't want to do that. Put it down on the ground, Wilma. You and Willie can survive this. I'll help you get a lawyer." I started moving toward her.

"No, no, Willie knows the quick way out. McKay's the one who's gonna die." She laughed and pressed the button. My slug hit her at midchest and sent her crashing backward into deep snow. I heard a terrible roar behind me and took off running but the concussion of the explosion slammed me from behind and tossed me forward into the air. I hit hard against a snowdrift and covered my head as the burning timber and debris from the lodge rained down all around me and made hissing sounds in the wet snow.

My ears rang from the blast but eventually I heard shouts from the hill past the stream and knew it was Charlie and the guys. I felt the heat on the back of my parka and rolled in the snow to put out the flames then started a fast crawl away from the burning structure. More of McKay's explosives went off underground in muffled blasts about five seconds apart, caving half the hillside in on the caves below.

I looked back at what was left of the burning building and hoped to God that McKay had gotten Elizabeth out in time. Then I lay my head back in the cold snow and waited for somebody to find me.

EPILOGUE

The hospital stay wasn't so bad, considering. I got a cubicle in critical care next to Bud's, which was pretty nice because of that buddy thing we've got going on. Black showed up quick enough to bawl me out for getting myself in trouble some more. I couldn't mind too much; after all, I was alive. Black was at the foot of my bed, arrogantly scanning my chart, ready to critique my doc's prognosis and order the nurses around. Right now a couple of the nurses were eyeing him appreciatively and whispering and smiling. He had that effect on women, especially nurses.

He said, "You're lucky you got out of that hellhole alive. And it looks like only one recluse bite is showing necrosis. That'll mean less scarring at the wound. And the broken bone in your ankle will heal fine now that it's set, if you stay off it. And trust me, you will."

He meant business and for once I was ready and willing to listen to his medical decree. I had been worried about spider bites, and a vision of Simon Classon's corpse rose in my mind, the horrible, deep holes eaten into his flesh. "Am I going to have a big ugly hole in my leg?"

"No, they cleaned out the necrosis pretty well. It's going

to hurt like hell for a while but you won't need a skin graft. It'll probably just leave a shallow scar."

"I can handle scars."

"Yeah, you've had way too many." His expression was generally pissed off. "We've got to talk about this penchant you have for putting yourself in the hospital. You know that, right?"

"Yeah, sure. Anytime."

Next door, I heard Bud's side rail rattle, then a groan.

"Hey, Bud, you okay?"

"Hell, no. I got bit by a goddamn timber rattler. How'd you think I feel?"

Good, he was better. He was cussing.

"Well, I'm banged up, too. No snakebites, though."

His next words cinched that he was on the road to recovery. "Hey, Claire, you know why cobras sway to flutes?"

"No, why?"

"It's not the music. It's the movements of the flute."

"I guess you got that outta that book I bought you, huh?"

"Nope, I saw it on the Discovery Channel last night while you were in surgery gettin' your ankle set."

Black and I smiled at each other. When Joe McKay walked in, a big bandage wrapped around his head, Black stood. "Hell, it looks like an Iraq triage unit around here."

"Tell me about it," Joe said. He looked down at me. "I hear you're gonna make it."

"Yeah. I'm okay. How's Elizabeth?"

"Some bumps and scratches but, thank God, that's all. It could've been real bad."

"Yeah. I thought you both were dead."

Black said, "You think Willie got out?"

"I knocked him down and took off with Elizabeth. I doubt very much if he made it out before the blasts started going off."

I said, "He's sick in the head. So was Wilma."

McKay said, "Yeah, I knew he and Simon were dangerous but I didn't realize how bad they really were. All I wanted was to prove they killed my little brother for pushing Willie into a grave when he was little. Simon got him out and that's why Willie was so blindly loyal to him. We went to the same church they did. Did you know about any of this?"

I shook my head. I didn't know much about Willie Vines except that he was a dead psychopathic, angel-loving serial killer.

"Were you really going to blow up Wilma and Willie with the cave?"

"I was going to blow them both to hell."

I didn't blame him for that but I didn't want to say so, either, not exactly a police-officer kind of remark. Instead, I said, "Where's Elizabeth now?"

McKay lowered his voice. "She's at Charlie's house. Jacqee's watching her." He glanced at Black then back to me. "Could I have a private word with you? Won't take long."

I knew then why he'd come. And again, I couldn't blame him for what he was about to do. "Mind giving us a minute, Black?"

Black minded, all right, but he's a stand-up guy, so he said, "How about a Pepsi? Bud, you want me to get you anything?"

"Yeah, two Big Macs and fries, super size it."

Black kissed me on the cheek; his alpha-male way of staking his claim, I suppose. Surprisingly, I didn't mind. Joe McKay sat down and pulled the chair close to my bed. He kept his voice low.

"Charlie's gonna work with me on the California warrant. He got me bail until the hearing and said he's willing to back me up and help me get Elizabeth back. So I got to ask you. You gonna help me out, too? Talk to the judge?"

There it was, *the* question. "What about Elizabeth's mother? She has legal custody, right?"

For once McKay wasn't putting on the charm. His blue eyes were serious, pleading, even. "Delia's a hard-core addict. Got into all kinds of illegal drugs after I left for the Persian Gulf. I didn't even know Elizabeth existed until I got back to the States and looked Delia up. She's in jail now for possession. Her loser boyfriend had Elizabeth. I've got a DNA analysis in the works to prove she's mine. You vouch for me along with Charlie, and I'm pretty sure everything will work out. My clean military record's gonna help. And the fact that I tried to help you solve Classon's murder."

I thought of my baby. The pain I felt when I lost Zach. The hole in my heart that never heals over. "Does Delia love Elizabeth?"

"She's too strung out now to love anything but the drugs. Her boyfriend was slapping both of them around, but she stayed with him for the hits he gave her. She had Elizabeth living in a crack house, for Christ's sake."

"You should've gone through the courts with this, McKay. Grabbing her like that was stupid."

"I didn't have much choice. Social services gave her back to Delia twice. I had no legal claim then, but I will as soon as I prove paternity."

I stared at him, not liking the position he was putting me in. It went against my grain to buck the system but this time there were plenty of good reasons. "I'll talk to Charlie and see what we can do. I can't promise you anything, and I won't do anything illegal. But I'll vouch for you."

McKay looked mightily relieved. He smiled. "I'm thinking about settling down around here and raising her. Maybe you could be her godmother or her favorite Aunt Claire, something like that."

Again, I thought of my own little Zachary, how he'd felt the last time I held him, when blood was leaking out of his chest. I looked away. "I'm not so good with kids."

McKay said, "I owe you big-time for this, Claire. I mean it. Anything you ever need, ever, just let me know."

"Tell me the truth then. You really a psychic?"

McKay grinned. He picked up my hand and held it flat between both of his. "I'll tell you this much. I've seen the two of us getting pretty hot and heavy together in the future.

Which sounds damn good in my book. So you tell me, Claire. Is that gonna happen?"

Now I was really embarrassed but not as embarrassed as when he pressed his lips to the back of my hand about the time Black walked in with my Pepsi. I jerked my hand away, and McKay's dimples went wild. "Keep in touch, Claire. I plan to."

"Right."

McKay nodded to Black, who stared him out of the room. Black walked to the bed and popped the tab on a can of Pepsi and poured it into a cup of crushed ice. I didn't say anything.

"Want to tell me what that was all about?"

"Sure. He asked me to marry him and move to Rome, the one in Italy, actually, so we could be private investigators together and help Interpol solve cases. You know, I catch 'em. He blows 'em up."

He cocked an eyebrow and handed me the cup. I took a sip.

"And?" he said.

"And, I told him that I liked you better so I was going to stick around here and let you buy me some more expensive gifts. Like my own personal Humvee."

He smiled and adjusted my straw. "Good answer."

From the next cubicle, Bud said, "I was serious about those Big Macs, Doc. And get me a couple of fried apple pies, too. They're two for a dollar now."

Black and I laughed, then I laid my head on the pillow, shut my eyes, and hoped to God that Willie Vines had died in that explosion.